MASTERS OF ROME

Robert Fabbri read Drama and Theatre at London University and worked in film and TV for 25 years. He was an assistant director and worked on productions such as *Hornblower, Hellraiser, Patriot Games* and *Billy Elliot*. His life-long passion for ancient history inspired him to write the Vespasian series. He lives in London and Berlin.

MASTERS OF ROME

ROBERT
FABBRI

CORVUS

First published in hardback in Great Britain in 2014 by Corvus,
an imprint of Atlantic Books Ltd.
This paperback edition published in Great Britain in 2015 by Corvus,
an imprint of Atlantic Books Ltd.

10 9 8 7 6 5 4 3 2 1

A CIP catalogue record for this book is available from the British Library.

Paperback ISBN: 978 0 85789 965 1
E-book ISBN: 978 0 85789 964 4

Printed in Great Britain by CPI Group (UK) Ltd, Croydon, CR0 4YY

Corvus
An imprint of Atlantic Books Ltd
Ormond House
26–27 Boswell Street
London WC1N 3JZ

www.corvus-books.co.uk

For my friends through life:
Jon Watson-Miller, Matthew Pinhey, Rupert White
and Cris Grundy; thank you, chaps.

And in memory of Steve Le Butt 1961–2013
who sailed west before us.

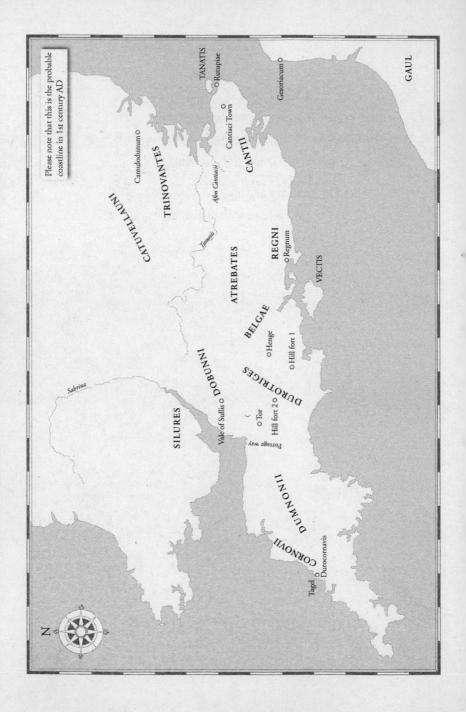

Please note that this is the probable coastline in 1st century AD

N

GAUL

Gesoriacum

TANATIS
Rutupiae
Cantiaci Town
CANTII
Afon Cantiaci

Camulodunum
TRINOVANTES
CATUVELLAUNI

Tamesis

REGNI
Regnum
ATREBATES
VECTIS

BELGAE
Henge
Hill fort 1
DUROTRIGES

Sabrina

SILURES

Vale of Sullis
DOBUNNI
Tor
Hill fort 2
Portage way

DUMNONII
CORNOVII
Tagel
Durocornavis

PROLOGUE

❧ ❧

BRITANNIA, MARCH AD 45

THE FOG THICKENED, forcing the *turma* of thirty-two legionary cavalry to slow their mounts to a walk. The snorts of the horses and jangle of harnesses were deadened, swallowed up by the thick atmosphere enshrouding the small detachment.

Titus Flavius Sabinus pulled his damp cloak tighter around his shoulders, inwardly cursing the foul northern climate and his direct superior, General Aulus Plautius, commander of the Roman invasion force in Britannia, for summoning him to a briefing in such conditions.

Sabinus had been surprised by the summons. When the messenger, a tribune on Plautius' staff, arrived with a native guide the previous evening at the XIIII Gemina's winter camp on the middle reaches of the Tamesis River, Sabinus had expected him to be bringing his final orders for the coming season's campaign. Why Plautius should order him to travel almost eighty miles south to meet him at the winter quarters of the II Augusta, his brother Vespasian's legion, seemed strange just a month after the legates of all four legions in the new province had met with their general at his headquarters at Camulodunum.

Unsurprisingly, the tribune, a young man in his late teens whom Sabinus had known by sight for the last two years since the invasion, had been unable to enlighten him as to the reason for this unexpected extra meeting. Sabinus remembered that during his four years serving in the same rank, in Pannonia and Africa, he was very rarely favoured with any detail by his commanding officers; a thin-stripe military tribune from the equestrian class was the lowest of the officer ranks, there to learn and obey without question. However, the scroll the young man bore was sealed with Plautius' personal seal, giving Sabinus no choice but to curse and comply; Plautius was not a man to tolerate insubordination or tardiness.

Reluctantly leaving his newly arrived senior tribune, Gaius Petronius Arbiter, in command of the XIIII Gemina, Sabinus had ridden south that morning with an escort, the tribune and his guide, into a clear dawn that promised a chill but bright day. It had not been until they had started to climb, in the early afternoon, up onto the plain that they were now traversing that the fog had started to descend.

Sabinus glanced at the native guide, a middle-aged, ruddy-faced man riding to his right on a stocky pony; he seemed unperturbed by the conditions. 'Can you still find your way in this?'

The guide nodded; his long, drooping moustache swayed beneath his chin. 'This is Dobunni land, my tribe; I've hunted up here since I could first ride. The plain is reasonably flat and featureless; we only have to keep our course just west of south and we will come down into the Durotriges' territory, behind the Roman line of advance. Then tomorrow we have a half-day's ride to the legion's camp on the coast.'

Ignoring the fact that the man had not addressed him as 'sir' or indeed shown any respect for his rank whatsoever, Sabinus turned to the young tribune riding on his left. 'Do you trust his ability, Alienus?'

Alienus' youthful face creased into a frown of respect. 'Absolutely, sir; he got me to your camp without once changing direction. I don't know how he does it.'

Sabinus stared at the young man for a few moments and decided that his opinion was worthless. 'We'll camp here for the night.'

The guide turned towards Sabinus in alarm. 'We mustn't sleep out on the plain at night.'

'Why not? One damp hollow is as good as another.'

'Not here; there're spirits of the Lost Dead roaming the plain throughout the night, searching for a body to bring them back to this world.'

'Bollocks!' Sabinus' bravado was tinged slightly by his realisation that he had neglected to make the appropriate sacrifice to his guardian god, Mithras, upon departure that morning, owing to the lack of a suitable bull in the XIIII Gemina's camp; he had substituted a ram but had ridden through the gates feeling less than happy with his offering.

The guide pressed his point. 'We can be off the plain in an hour or two and then we'll cross a river. The dead won't follow us after that – they can't cross water.'

'Besides, General Plautius was adamant that we should be with him soon after midday tomorrow,' Alienus reminded him. 'We need to carry on for as long as we can, sir.'

'You don't like the sound of the Lost Dead, tribune?'

Alienus hung his head. 'Not overmuch, sir.'

'Perhaps an encounter with them would toughen you up.'

Alienus made no reply.

Sabinus glanced over his shoulder; he could, again, just see the end of their short column, as the fog seemed to be thinning somewhat. 'Very well, we'll press on, but not because of any fear of the dead but rather so as not to be late for the general.' The truth was that the superstitious part of Sabinus' mind feared the supernatural as much as the practical part feared the wrath of Plautius should he be kept waiting too long, so he was relieved that he had been able to retract his order in a face-saving manner. It would not do to have people think that he gave any credence to the many stories of the spirits and ghosts that were said to inhabit this strange island; but he did not like the sound of the Lost Dead and, even less, the thought of spending the night in their dominion. During his time on this northern isle he had heard many such stories, enough to believe there to be a grain of truth in at least some of them.

Since the fall of Camulodunum and the surrender of the tribes in the southeast of Britannia, eighteen months previously, Sabinus had led the XIIII Gemina and its auxiliary cohorts steadily east and north. Plautius had ordered him to secure the central lowlands of the island whilst the VIIII Hispana headed up the east coast and Vespasian's II Augusta fought its way west between the Tamesis and the sea. The XX Legion had been kept in reserve to consolidate the ground already won and ready to support any legion that found itself in trouble.

It had been slow work as the tribes had learnt from the mistakes of Caratacus and his brother, Togodumnus, who had tried to take the legions head-on, soon after the initial invasion, and throw them back using their superior numbers; this tactic had failed disastrously. In two days, as they tried to halt the Roman advance at a river, the Afon Cantiacii, they had lost over forty thousand warriors including Togodumnus. This had crushed the Britons' resolve in the southeastern corner of the island and most had capitulated soon after. Caratacus, however, had not. He had fled west with over twenty thousand warriors and had become a rallying point for all those who refused to accept Roman domination.

A light breeze picked up, gusting east to west across their line of travel, swirling the mist and clearing a swathe off to Sabinus' right. He pulled himself up in his saddle, feeling a relief that visibility had cleared, if only by a few score paces in one direction. He began to mutter a prayer to Mithras to shine his light through the gloom of this fog-bound island and help him to ... he caught a fleeting glimpse out of the corner of his eye, he turned to look but it was gone, the wind sucked the mist back in and doubt clouded his mind as to whether it was a movement he had seen or it was just his imagination feeding off the tales of horror that were hard to banish from his head. The stories could never be unheard.

During the two months that Plautius had been forced, for political reasons, to pause north of the Tamesis, waiting for the Emperor Claudius to arrive and take the credit and glory for the fall of Camulodunum, the XIIII Gemina had probed west along the river. It was at this time that Sabinus first began to hear reports from his officers of strange apparitions and unnatural occurrences: a legionary had been found, barely alive, flayed and yet still in uniform; his dying words had been of daemons that sucked the flesh from his limbs. Another had been found dead, drained of blood, and yet with no wound on his body or trace of the life-giving fluid seeping into the ground close by. Spectral figures in long, luminous robes that glowed with an unnatural fluorescence were sighted regularly, especially near to the mounds covering the tombs of the ancients and the many henges of both stone and wood that seemed to be, along with the sacred groves, centres for the Britons' barbarous religion.

At first Sabinus had put this down to the overactive imaginations of superstitious soldiers but, after Claudius' departure, he led his legion further inland for the final month of the campaigning season and had felt something that he had never been aware of anywhere else. He could only describe it as an ancient presence. That – and the disembodied howls and cries that plagued their nights – had convinced him that there was a power here that he did not understand; a power that was linked to the land where, no matter how strongly he was protected by the light of his lord Mithras, he was an interloper.

The following year they had carried on moving slowly inland, investing hill-forts one by one and fighting off raids on their supply lines and ambushes on their columns by Caratacus' warriors. The further they went the greater grew his feeling of unease and it was almost with relief that he withdrew his legion back south to their winter quarters on the Tamesis at the end of that season. He had brought up the subject with Vespasian last month, when the legates had met with Plautius at Camulodunum to discuss the next season's campaign, but his brother had dismissed his fears as soldiers' yarns; and yet there had been a look in his eyes that had led Sabinus to believe that he too felt a similar unease.

Sabinus tried to put his worries to one side as the column rode on slowly across the plain studded with tufts of rough grass. The breeze strengthened, shifting the fog, tugging it this way and that in wispy tendrils so that occasionally visibility improved enough to see the way ahead until, a few moments later, another gust would cause their view to be clouded again.

To force his mind away from the superstitious depths that the eerie conditions had taken it to, Sabinus glanced sidelong at Alienus and studied him. He noticed a ruddiness to his cheeks and a certain stubbiness to his nose and, although his face was quite slender, he thought that his family must have some Celtic blood. That would explain his cognomen, Alienus: foreigner. But then, he reflected, what family from northern or, for that matter, central Italia did not? His own roundish face and bulbous nose could hardly be described as classically Latin. 'Are your people from the north of Italia, Alienus?'

'Hmm?' The young tribune blinked his eyes as if emerging from a private reverie. 'I'm sorry, sir, what did you say?'

Sabinus repeated the question.

'No, sir; I'm from the south coast of Britannia. I'm the grandson of Verica, King of the confederated tribes of the Atrebates and the Regni. My Britannic name is also Verica after my grandfather.'

Sabinus was surprised. 'Your Latin is excellent.'

'Thank you, sir. My grandfather fled to Rome five years ago, after Caratacus had dispossessed him of his kingdom, and he took me with him. Like all Britannic princes in the south, I'd already had a good education in Latin and so I soon became fluent.'

'And Claudius granted you citizenship?'

'Yes, and equestrian rank. I took the name Tiberius Claudius and then added the cognomen Alienus because it amused me and so I became Roman as my grandfather wanted. General Plautius took me onto his staff as a favour to him so that I could begin to make my way up the various offices and perhaps even become a senator. I'd be the first Briton to do so.'

Sabinus nodded his approval at this thoroughly Roman ambition. 'I was sorry to hear of Verica's death. Just last month, wasn't it?'

'He was old and expected to die; he had no regrets. He'd reclaimed his kingdom, been made a formal client-king of Rome and had ensured a strong heir in his nephew, Cogidubnus.'

'Why not his grandson?'

Alienus smiled. 'He said I was too young, the people wouldn't accept me and I understand that: how could a nineteen-year-old who hasn't been seen by his people in five years rule? Cogidubnus is also seen as a man who stood up to Rome before he was subdued by her; I on the other hand am seen as a man who voluntarily joined Rome's legions.'

'So you'll go to Rome after you've ...' A freshening gust cleared the fog around them, momentarily unveiling a burial mound not ten paces away to the left; the words died in Sabinus' throat as the breeze blew the vapour back, shrouding the tomb once again but leaving its image burnt in his mind.

Dark murmurs and muttering came from the column behind – clearly he had not been the only one to witness the ill-omened sight. When he glanced back he saw more than a few of the troopers had their thumbs clutched in their right hands and were spitting on the ground to avert the evil-eye. A barked order from decurion Atilius brought his men back to order but the damage to their already fragile morale was done and they cast nervous looks to either side as the thinning fog billowed around them, fearful as to what it might reveal next. Amongst the Romans only Alienus seemed unruffled by travelling so close to the mound, which struck Sabinus as odd seeing as he had shown a natural disinclination to remain too long in the vicinity of the Lost Dead.

Another swirl in the fog, up ahead, drove that thought from Sabinus' mind; his heart skipped a beat. A giant's leg, solid and broad, appeared in their path as if the monster had taken a great step towards them and planted it there that instant – yet there had been no trembling of the earth and no booming report of the footstep. Then the second leg materialised through the miasma, equally silent. Shocked troopers hauled on their mounts' reins, causing many to rear and whinny, shattering the silence. Sabinus looked up in alarm; the lower torso was becoming visible but above the waist was still lost in the fog. Another leg on either side emerged; there were at least three of the monstrosities lined against them.

Sabinus drew his sword and glanced over his shoulder. 'Atilius, form two lines. Stay together!' he bellowed at his escort as panic mounted. Turning back to face the threat, he gasped; the breeze stiffened; more legs appeared to either side and they were all connected by one long lower abdomen that was not flesh and bone but stone – cut and shaped stone slabs of great magnitude. Sabinus realised that he was gazing at a henge, a stone henge; the biggest that he had seen.

Calming his horse he turned to the guide to find him missing. 'Shit! Alienus?' He could see no sign of the young tribune either. Behind him the decurion was managing to restore some order amongst the troopers. Then, to his left, Sabinus glimpsed two horses galloping away through the mist; as they disappeared, spectral figures materialised, moving towards them, now visible, now not. He felt cold dread rise in his belly; that glimpse of movement had not been a figment of a wild imagination. He looked the other way; scores more of the ethereal shapes, indistinct in the eddying mist, seeming to glide over the veiled ground, were heading their way.

They were surrounded.

When the first slingshots cracked into the turma from both sides, Sabinus felt an illogical relief: it was not the Lost Dead that faced them but men, live men who could be fought and killed.

The screaming started; but it was bestial, not human. The slingers were aiming low, at the horses' legs; they had not come to deal out death, Sabinus realised, but to take captives.

'Atilius!' Sabinus roared, pointing his sword north, back the way they came. 'Our only chance is to ride through them together.'

Atilius yelled at his men to turn; the turma struggled to form line in the hail of shot thwacking in from both sides. Five horses were already down, writhing in shattered-bone agony, their dismounted riders, screaming, struggling to clamber up behind one of their comrades. Two more horses fell thrashing to the ground, hurling one trooper clear but crushing the other; he lay still, his head at an unnatural angle. The unseated man rose shakily to his feet to be punched back, with a sharp howl, arms flailing, body arced over buckled knees, crashing to the ground with a pulped hole where his nose had been.

Sabinus urged his mount forward. 'With me!' Risking the uneven ground he drove his horse into a canter; the surviving troopers followed, unsheathing their cavalry *spathae* ready to cleave their way through their tormentors, who were now less than fifty paces away.

Another hail of slingshot scythed through their ranks, bringing down six horses, head first, their muzzles ploughing into the grass as their splintered forelegs collapsed beneath them; the riders cried to their comrades not to leave them behind. But their pleas were in vain.

A shot fizzed past Sabinus' knee; the slingers were still aiming low. He kicked his heels and slapped the flat of his blade hard on his mount's rump; the beast burst into a gallop. The slingers turned and fled. Sabinus' heart raced, stimulated by hope. But in the instant that he thought they would run their attackers down a new terror sprang from the ground: a double line of spearmen, concealed until now, raised themselves up to kneel on one leg; each supported a long, ash-shafted boar-hunting spear, their butts wedged in the turf and the leaf-shaped, iron heads aimed at the horses' chests.

With no time to react, the turma ploughed into the bristling hedge of honed iron. The blades sliced into taut equine muscle, crunched through bone to burst into the cavity housing vital organs beyond. Blood, pressurised by huge hearts working to the limit, exploded from the ghastly rents in the beasts' chests as they impaled themselves, their momentum forcing in the spearheads until they came to a juddering, haft-bending halt on the iron crosspieces at their base.

Sabinus was flung forward onto his mount's neck, his red-plumed helmet spinning away over the enemy line. An instant later he was hurled back as the stricken animal reared, shrieking in agony, yanking the embedded spear from the grip of its blood-spattered wielder and cracking the skull of the man next to him as the beast twisted in its torment.

Landing with a lung-emptying crunch on his back, Sabinus just had the presence of mind to roll to one side as the dying horse crumpled onto its rump and then tumbled backwards, its legs scrabbling weakly in the air as if it were trying to canter its last.

Sabinus pulled himself to his knees, gasping for breath, and felt his head crack; a white light streaked across his vision. As he faded into unconsciousness he realised the bitter irony of being led into a trap by a spy passing himself off as a Roman called 'Alienus'.

It was a scream that brought Sabinus back to consciousness: a scream of fear, not of pain. He opened his eyes but could see only thick stems of rough grass; he was on his belly, his hands fastened behind his back. His head throbbed. The scream stopped and he could hear a low chanting.

Trying to ease himself over, he felt his stomach churn and then convulse. A gush of thin vomit sprayed onto the grass; its sour taste lingered on his tongue and its reek, as it dribbled out of his nostrils, turned his insides again, forcing him to heave once more.

Breathing fast and shallow he forced himself onto his back, spitting out the residue of the noisome fluid. The fog had lifted and the sun was setting. He raised his head; he was within the henge. Blurred figures were moving around. The scream resumed, drowning the chant. One of the figures raised an arm, paused, and then brought it crashing down; the scream was abruptly curtailed, replaced by a long croaking gurgle and then silence.

He felt the temperature suddenly drop. Now his eyes had begun to focus he could make out the figures. They were filthy. Their hair, dishevelled and matted into clumps, fell halfway down their backs; their beards, twisted into strands, were equally long. They each wore a single, long-sleeved garment, belted at the waist and reaching their ankles, that may have at one time been white but now looked as if patches of mould and mildew had been allowed to fester on them for years.

Sabinus shivered and let his head slump back onto the grass with a groan; if there was one thing that he feared more than the spirits of this land, it was their servants: the druids.

'You're awake then, legate,' a voice said with remarkable cheerfulness.

Sabinus turned to see Alienus walking towards him. 'You treacherous little cunt!'

'Hardly; to be treacherous you have to betray your own people. You can't accuse me of that; I'm a prince of the Atrebates.' Alienus squatted down next to him. 'Not all of us have bowed the knee to Rome like my cowardly grandfather or my vainglorious cousin who has stolen my birthright and now rules in my place; they've brought shame to my people. Caradoc, or Caratacus as you call him, may have been my people's enemy but he at least stands up to the invaders. He's of our blood and would preserve our ways and our gods, and for that he deserves our support to throw you back into the sea.'

'So that you can carry on your petty squabbles living on the fringes of the world?'

'It may be the fringes of *your* world, but this island is our whole world and before you came we were free to organise our lives according to our own laws and customs. Can you blame us for wanting to keep it that way?'

'No, but you're being impractical.' Sabinus shivered again, his toes were frozen. 'Rome has come to stay and you'll cause the death of many of your people realising that.'

'Not now that we have you.'

'What do you mean?'

'Today is the spring equinox; the few survivors from your escort have wetted the altars of our gods with their blood in honour of the day – but not you. You're the one we came for. We knew that to get you, it had to be before you went out on campaign. You wouldn't have believed a summons from Plautius after.'

Sabinus' teeth started to chatter as a deep chill crept up his legs. 'How did you forge his seal?'

'If you have access to documents with his seal intact on it then it's not that difficult; you've got three months to work it out.'

'What for? Why not just kill me now?'

'Oh, you're too precious for that. It would be a waste. The druids have decided that the most potent sacrifice to offer the gods on behalf of Caratacus – to strengthen him in his struggle – is a Roman legate.' Alienus raised his eyebrows and pointed at Sabinus with a half-smile. 'That would be you.' He indicated with his head towards the druids who were standing in the golden rays of the setting sun that flooded through two of the arches in the henge to exactly illuminate the altar stone. 'And Myrddin, the head of their order, who knows about these things, has decided that the most auspicious day and location for that sacrifice will be the summer solstice in the grove of the sacred springs.'

Sabinus looked over to the druids as they continued their chant and realised that no heat was coming off the sun's rays but, rather, a cold power, filled with malice, emanated from the group, chilling its way up him like a series of freezing breaths; and yet Alienus seemed unaffected. Sabinus' mind started to slow, rendering it incapable of questioning. His eyes began to frost over; with a final effort he spat a weak globule of vomit-tainted saliva into the spy's face. 'I'll be gone by then. My brother will come for me.'

Alienus wiped his cheek with the back of his hand, smiling without humour. 'Don't worry, Myrddin wants me to ensure that he does come and that he brings his doomed legion with him. I think you'll agree that two legates would be much more powerful than one; and a brace of brothers would be the most potent sacrifice to win the gods' favour for the army that Caratacus is now assembling. And Myrddin always gets what he wants.'

Sabinus' vision went white as the coldness settled on his heart; he felt a malevolent presence draw him away from consciousness and he screamed until he was deafened. But no sound emerged from his frozen lips.

PART I

❦ ❦

BRITANNIA, SPRING AD 45

CHAPTER I

VESPASIAN SECURED THE leather thongs of his chinstrap with a tight knot, pulling the articulated cheek-guards close about his face. He shook his head; the helmet stayed firm. Satisfied, he nodded at the slave waiting upon him; the man – in his early twenties – stepped forward and draped a deep red, heavy woollen cloak about his shoulders, fastening it with a bronze brooch in the shape of a Capricorn, the emblem of the II Augusta. Despite the two mobile braziers in the tent, there was a morning chill and Vespasian was pleased with the garment's extra warmth. He grasped the hilt of his sword, tugged it, checking the weapon was loose in its scabbard, and then glanced at the slave as he stepped back, his task complete. 'You may go, Hormus.'

With a short bow, Hormus turned and disappeared through dividing curtains into the sleeping area at the rear of the *praetorium* tent – the headquarters of the legion and living area of its legate at the heart of the II Augusta's camp.

Picking up a cup of warmed wine from a low table, Vespasian strode over to his desk, covered in neat piles of waxed wooden tablets and bundles of scrolls; he sat down and opened the despatch that had caused him a sleepless night. Sipping his morning drink, he reread it a couple of times, his full face drawn into a strained expression, and then clacked the tablet down. 'Hormus!'

'Yes, master?' the slave answered, scurrying back through the curtains.

'Take this down and then have a messenger set out with it immediately.'

Hormus sat at his smaller, secretary's desk, took up a stylus, poised it over a clean sheet of wax and nodded his readiness to his owner.

'To Gaius Petronius Arbiter, senior tribune of the Fourteenth Gemina, from Titus Flavius Vespasianus, legate of the Second Augusta, greetings.

'My brother, Titus Flavius Sabinus, did not arrive at the Second Augusta's camp around the time of the spring equinox; nor was there any meeting scheduled here between General Plautius, myself and my brother. I know of Tribune Alienus; he is the grandson of the late Verica of the Atrebates. I vaguely recall coming into contact with him a few times whilst he has been serving on Plautius' staff during the last two years and I have no reason to doubt his integrity; but neither do I have any reason to believe that his loyalties may not still lie with the rebels. What was he doing leading my brother to a meeting that did not exist? If you are positive that it was to here that they set out fifteen days ago then I can only assume that Alienus was, after all, never truly one of us but, rather, a Britannic spy. Therefore, my brother is either a prisoner or, the gods forbid ...' Vespasian paused, not wanting to say the word that had tormented him all night as he contemplated Sabinus' possible fate.

Although Sabinus – almost five years Vespasian's senior – had terrorised him as a child and treated him with scorn as a young man, their relationship had gradually changed over the last dozen years or so and matured into one of mutual respect. It had been Vespasian's part in helping his brother recover the lost Eagle of the XVII Legion that had brought the two siblings close enough to communicate without constant bickering. Sabinus had been under threat of death from the Emperor Claudius' powerful freedman, Narcissus, for his part in the assassination of Caligula; his fellow conspirators had all been executed. However, owing to the intervention of the brothers' old acquaintance, Pallas, fellow freedman to Narcissus, Sabinus' role had been covered up and his life spared on condition that the siblings retrieved the final Eagle still missing after the German rebel, Arminius, destroyed three legions in the Teutoburg Forest in the year of Vespasian's birth, thirty-six years previously.

Although the Eagle's return to Rome did not go exactly as planned, it was recovered and the brothers found themselves back in favour with the real power in Rome: not the Emperor but his freedmen. Their success had forced Sabinus to admit that he owed his brother his life and it was with a heavy heart that Vespasian completed his sentence: '... dead.'

Vespasian waved a hand, dismissing his slave, and downed the rest of his wine, praying to Mars, his guardian god, that somehow Sabinus was still alive; although why the Britons would spare any captives he did not know as they were well aware that Plautius refused to bargain with their lives. To be sold into slavery to the tribes in the north or the west was the best that any man could hope for and that was a living death. But, if that was the case, at least there would be a chance of finding him.

The two guards outside the tent crashing to attention and the sound of someone entering brought him out of his reverie. The prefect of the camp, Maximus, the third most senior officer in the legion, marched briskly in and snapped an immaculate salute honed by almost thirty years of service.

Vespasian stood out of respect for his junior in rank but senior in experience. 'Yes, Maximus?'

'The legion is deployed, sir! We're awaiting your orders should the parley prove to be unsuccessful.'

'Is Cogidubnus talking with them?'

'They wouldn't allow him and his two bodyguards to enter the fort so he had to negotiate from outside the gate; he's still up there.'

'Very well; I'm on my way.'

Vespasian walked out through the gates of the II Augusta's camp, built on a low flat-topped hill that ran gently down to a stream at its base. The guards on the gate, staring rigidly ahead, presented arms with overemphasised stamps as he passed.

His primus pilus, Tatius, the most senior centurion of the legion, and his thick-stripe tribune, Valens, were waiting outside along with the thin-stripe tribunes: five of them, teenagers or in their early twenties, and here to learn. A quarter of a mile ahead of them stood another hill, round like a giant molehill, three hundred feet high and half a mile across at its base, which stood apart from the surrounding undulations for no apparent reason other than to provide a formidable fortified refuge; and fortified and formidable it was. Three-quarters of the way up its summit, two great ditches, each ten feet deep, had been carved out of its circumference and filled with fire-hardened, pointed stakes. The slope before them was steep and had been cleared of all trees and bushes, except, as Vespasian had noted on his circuit of the fort upon arrival, the western slope on the far side; that was too steep for an assault and bushes had been allowed to flourish on it. Behind the inner ditch, the excavated earth had been piled up and packed down to make a steep mound on top of which a palisade of thick logs, twice the height of a man, had been constructed. Hundreds of warriors lined its length and behind them, amongst the scores of round huts that covered the summit, waited many more along with their women and children, plenty of whom, Vespasian had learnt from bitter experience, were capable of using a sling or hurling a javelin to deadly effect.

On the downwards slope between Vespasian and the hill-fort stood the II Augusta in two lines of five cohorts each; rank upon rank of iron-clad heavy infantry, their burnished helmets glowing golden in the newly risen sun as they stood, motionless, beneath their standards fluttering in a chill breeze. Vespasian had ordered this display not because he intended to send the full might of his legion against the enemy; the ditches would make that impracticable and a waste of legionary life. No, the non-citizens of the more expendable Gallic auxiliary cohorts would make the first assault. The parade was purely to intimidate the defenders and aid Cogidubnus, the new King of Rome's allies, the confederation of the Atrebates and the Regni, in his negotiations with the chieftain of this sub-tribe of the Durotriges who had been trapped in their hilltop redoubt by Vespasian's lightning move inland, to the northwest, in the first days of the new campaigning season.

The thrust had been initiated by the report from a Britannic spy, in Cogidubnus' pay, of the muster of a large war band at the fort, perhaps under the command of Caratacus himself, in preparation to strike eastwards, behind the line of the II Augusta's advance, to harry their supply lines in order to force the legion to turn and deal with them, thus delaying considerably their spring campaign.

The legion's arrival and surrounding of the fort the previous evening had been so swift that none of the Britons had managed to escape; those who had made it over the palisade had been quickly cut down or picked up by the legion's Batavian auxiliary cavalry, which had skirted around the fort specifically to prevent anyone escaping and calling for aid. The spy's estimate that there were upwards of four thousand men of fighting age within had been confirmed by prisoners less willing to endure the knives of their inquisitors. However, they had all denied Caratacus' presence to the point of death.

Caratacus' plan will not work now, Vespasian thought with a self-congratulatory half-smile, putting his anxiety for his brother to one side and concentrating on the matter in hand. The scene before him would have impressed him four years ago when he had first taken command of the II Augusta, but now, after two seasons' campaigning in Britannia, it was a common sight for him; he counted them in his head and reckoned that this was his ninth siege.

Although the defences were almost a mile in circumference, there was but one entrance and that was facing Vespasian; but it was not a straight route up the hill to get there. The crossing points in each ditch were at different points, forcing an attacker to zigzag during the ascent, exposing their flanks to constant missile fire from the men on the walls. Many auxiliaries would die in a frontal assault just to reach the gates and then many more would perish as they tried to batter them down with the ram that stood ready, encased in a wooden housing covered with dampened leather to protect it from the fire-pots that would surely be hurled down from above.

But Vespasian was hoping that it would not come to that as he watched three mounted men, Britons, turn their horses and ride away from the gates. As they did there was a commotion on the palisade next to them; a figure jumped down, rolling as he landed, before fluidly regaining his feet and pelting towards the three riders. One slowed, braving the few javelins hurled down at the fugitive, and leant back, his arm outstretched towards the fleeing man who leapt, grabbing the proffered hand, and using his momentum swung himself up behind the rider. The horse reared in fright, almost unseating the men, before its rider brought it back down with a brutal tug of the reins and kicked it forward to thunder down the hill in the wake of his two comrades, now passing through the gap in the outermost ditch.

Vespasian waited with his officers in silence as they galloped down the hill, each man knowing that the news they brought would decide the fate of them all that day, one way or another.

There was a stirring amongst the legionaries as the horsemen passed through their formation; centurions and optiones bellowed at their men for silence.

'I think the lads can tell by the expression on Cogidubnus' face that the news is not good,' Maximus muttered as order returned to the legion.

Vespasian grunted. 'Of course it's not good; who would try to escape from a fort that was going to surrender?' The strained expression returned to his face as the riders drew near and their demeanour confirmed Maximus' conjecture; but he also knew that their unwillingness to surrender may mean that there was an even greater prize at stake.

'Their chieftain, Drustan, has sworn that they will fight to the death of the last child,' Cogidubnus confirmed as he brought his horse to a halt. The fugitive, a young man with long matted hair, wispy stubble and a slim face smeared with dirt, slipped from behind one of the accompanying horsemen to the ground. 'I offered them their lives and the status of allies of Rome with the right to bear arms.'

Vespasian tensed. 'He's in there, isn't he?'

Cogidubnus spoke to the rescued man in his own tongue; he nodded his head as he replied. 'Yes, legate, he's in there; my agent here says he arrived two days ago.'

Vespasian glanced at the spy, astounded that such excellent information could have emanated from so unlikely a source. The man kept his head bowed; with his ragged clothes he looked more like a slave than a warrior. 'And now he hopes to slip away whilst a whole sub-tribe sacrifices themselves for him.'

'It would seem that way.'

Vespasian turned to his officers. 'Gentlemen, I want this place completely surrounded before the assault starts; nobody must be allowed to pass through our lines. I've a feeling that by our swift action we may have cornered Caratacus.'

It had taken less than half an hour for the II Augusta to redeploy; each cohort had formed up in four ranks of one hundred and twenty men, standing in silence, encircling the hill, sealing it so that none might escape. Vespasian looked up the slope ahead of him, over the heads of the first cohort, to where three Gallic auxiliary cohorts, of eight hundred men each, were formed up, shields raised against the long-range slingshot raining down from the warriors on the wall, just over a hundred paces away. At the head of the central cohort stood the dark form of the ram's housing surrounded by the century that had received the much-prized honour of leading the assault. In front of them to the left stood the eight hundred eastern archers of the Hamian auxiliary cohort and to their right were the legion's sixty *ballistae*, bolt-shooters.

Vespasian steadied his horse and brought his right arm sweeping down; the *cornicen* next to him blew one low, rumbling note on his G-shaped horn. Simultaneously a crewman from each bolt-shooter thrust a flaming torch at the oil-drenched wadding wound around the tips of their three-foot-long wooden missiles and the Hamians ignited their arrows in small fires set along their line. With the massed thrumming of bows and the staccato thwacking of high-torsion engines releasing, hundreds of burning projectiles soared through the air leaving trails of black smoke in their wake, like plough-furrows in the sky.

The assault had begun.

The first volley tore over the palisade to punch into the wattle and daub walls and thatched roofs of the many round huts behind it; shrieks of the wounded indicated that it was not just the buildings that suffered. As the Hamians released a second volley from their powerful re-curved composite bows of wood and horn, Vespasian saw, with satisfaction, the first few thin tendrils of white smoke rise from within the fort. The Hamians managed six more volleys before the bolt-shooters released again; above, the smoke trails had smudged together into a thin grey pall that arced over the field to merge with the thickening fumes emitting from the fires feeding on thatch. Flames now licked up, under-lighting the denser clouds of smoke with a deep orange hue as the conflagration grew; here and there billows of steam added to the thickening atmosphere attesting to the fire-fighting efforts of those trapped within the fort. Their disembodied shouts floated down over the II Augusta as the hail of slingshot from the warriors on the wall, as yet untroubled by the arrows passing over their heads, continued to beat into the shields of the Gallic cohorts – with little effect.

A young tribune galloped down the slope towards him.

'Are the Gauls ready, Vibius?' Vespasian asked as the lad pulled up his mount and saluted.

'Yes, sir. The two support cohorts have been issued with scaling ladders as you ordered.'

'And Valens' diversionary attacks?'

'Yes, sir; he has enough planking to span the first ditch.'

'Ride back down to him and tell him not to wait for the Gallic auxiliaries to make it to the gate. I want him to go immediately to keep as many Britons as possible occupied away from fighting the fires. Is that clear?'

'Yes, sir!' With a perfunctory salute Vibius turned his horse and galloped away under another flaming volley.

Vespasian glanced at Maximus, seated on a horse next to him, and allowed himself a grin of enjoyment. 'Time to clear the walls for our gallant Gauls.' He nodded at the cornicen. 'Second target.'

This time the man blew two shorter notes; the effect was immediate: the Hamians lowered their trajectory, sending shaft after shaft at the warriors manning the palisade whilst the ballista crews adjusted their sights to the same effect. By the time the first bolts pounded into the smoke-wreathed palisade it was clear of the enemy, who had hunkered down, unwilling to risk their lives until the situation made it necessary; they were all well aware that that moment would come soon.

The clearing of the wall was the signal that had been pre-arranged with the prefects of the Gallic auxiliary cohorts and for the first time that day a shout erupted from the Roman lines. The lead cohort moved forward up the steep hill towards the gap in the foremost ditch, its first century pushing and pulling the ram in its midst; the lucky few toiling safely within the structure and the rest hauling on the two ropes to the front or the bars ranged down the side or pushing from behind. The second century led the way to provide some cover to the front whilst other auxil-iaries crowded around their comrades heaving at the great engine of war, sheltering them with their shields to the sides; but no shots came from above as the Hamians continued their strafing of the wall. The two support cohorts raced ahead from either side, quickly passing over the crossing points in the nearer ditch and then fanning out along the rim between it and the last ditch, left and right to either side of the gate. Crouching down under their shields, scaling ladders laid on the ground before them, they waited for their comrades with the ram to arrive. On up the hill the ram ground, gradually gaining momentum, the solid wooden wheels, turning on goose-fatted axles, rumbled over the earth, closing in on the first obstacle.

It was for this moment that the Britons were waiting; the gap in the ditch, only forty paces from the palisade, was angled to the left and narrow, no more than six feet wide so that a wagon could just pass safely through. The ram's housing had been especially adapted overnight so that its wheels just fitted, leaving no room for the men heaving on the side-bars and, more crucially, no room for the protective shield-bearers to either side. The leading second century passed through first and formed up in two ranks, one kneeling, one standing, making a wall of shields facing the enemy. As the engine followed, the men to either side were forced to fall back and wait; the ram lost momentum and the auxiliaries manhandling it lost their shelter. As one, hundreds of heads appeared over the palisade, arms twirling leather slings above them; many fell back, pierced by feathered shafts, into the fires beyond, but the majority managed three swift revolutions before releasing and then ducking back down to reload. A hail of shot sped unseen down onto the auxiliaries; much clattered off the protective wall of the second century's shields but enough pounded in on the first century, felling men with shattered limbs and pulped faces as their comrades strove on, knowing that to flee with the whole legion watching would bring a shame upon them too heavy to bear. A few men from the second century ran back to haul the dead and wounded out of the way of the heavy wheels and to take over the empty places on the ropes; auxiliaries behind added their weight to the effort and the ram again picked up speed.

Another volley of ballista bolts hissed over the toiling centuries' heads, punching warriors bodily back, skewered and arcing blood, as they reappeared on the wall, slings reloaded. Yet, braving the Hamians' constant rain of arrows and indistinct in the thickening smoke, those still standing again whirled their slings about their heads, quickly achieving the velocity for another deadly salvo that pummelled into the target, dropping men with shrill shrieks or in deathly silence. Once again the ram's progress was slowed, but not before the back wheels cleared the gap and the protective shield-bearers could again stream through.

A huge cheer rose from every man witnessing the feat and Vespasian found himself gulping in air; he had not taken a breath for some time. Glancing left to the south side of the hill he saw that Vibius had delivered his message. Valens was on the move with the legion's second, third and fourth cohorts, now formed into columns, eight men abreast. In front of each formation, long planks had been thrown across the first ditch and pioneers had climbed carefully down their sheer sides and were now working between the stakes, raising upright supports for the temporary bridges.

Satisfied that his second in command was progressing with all due haste, Vespasian turned his attention back to the hill, now swathed in roiling smoke. The ram was just visible being manoeuvred right to negotiate the gap in the second ditch, twenty paces from the gate. The second century had already crossed and had formed up as before to shield their comrades from as much missile hail, both slingshot and now javelin, as possible – although the more acute angle so close to the palisade made their efforts of little account and, as he watched, two men on the ropes fell. But the ram kept on moving, its front wheels now halfway across the gap. The Hamians and bolt-shooters continued their volleys, although it was largely by guesswork as the figures on the palisade were only visible intermittently. The two supporting Gallic cohorts remained shielded and ready on either side of the gate, ladders now projecting skywards from their midst.

Vespasian looked down at the cornicen. 'The first cohort to advance!'

An ascending series of three notes rumbled from the bronze instrument. Vespasian saw the standards of the five double-strength centuries of the legion's élite cohort dip and then, to the bellows of their centurions and optiones, one by one they marched forward towards the gap in the first ditch. Now it was all about breaking down the gate to let those seasoned killers in.

But disaster had struck.

Through the eddying smoke the ram was just discernible; it was listing to the right. Vespasian tensed, straining his eyes; a gust cleared his view for a few moments, enough time to watch the earth crumble beneath the rear, right-hand wheel and see it slip over the edge. The housing crashed down onto its back axle, the angle causing the suspended ram to swing to the right, stunning many of the auxiliaries labouring within the structure and skewing it even more with its momentum. For two or three quickening heartbeats the engine teetered on the brink as men rushed to its left side to cling to it, hoping that their weight would somehow avert the inevitable.

But the inevitable, as ever, happened.

Beginning with a slow lean that quickly accelerated, the housing crashed, with a splintering and cracking of wood that could be just heard even over the din of the assault, to its ruin onto the stakes in the ditch below, taking the men inside down with it onto the fire-hardened points. For a moment its front end stood perpendicular before it toppled back, lengthways along the ditch, disappearing from view.

Vespasian kicked his horse forward. 'Maximus! Stay here and give the orders; keep the momentum up and tell the Hamians and the artillery to aim for the wall above the ram.'

Confident that he had left the overall command of the assault in the hands of the most experienced man in the Roman ranks, Vespasian urged his horse into a gallop up the hill; the turma of legionary cavalry, acting as his bodyguard, followed in his wake. He sped past the legion's first cohort, overtaking them halfway up, and then dismounted and ran on, with his escort following, through wispy smoke. Keeping his shield high, he passed the eight remaining centuries of the Gallic cohort who had stopped, unsure of how to proceed now that the means to open the gate had been taken out of commission, and arrived at the second ditch in the shadow of the gate. 'Where's your prefect?' Vespasian demanded of the auxiliary centurion of the third century as he too crouched with his men, shielded against the hail of shot.

The man indicated with his head towards the ditch. 'Down there, sir, trying to sort out the mess.'

'Bring your century and follow me; I want you to form up in testudo on the gap facing the ditch and be prepared to haul the ram up.'

'Sir!' The centurion's battle-hardened face set firm with resolve, evidently pleased to have a direct order in the chaos.

Vespasian ran forward at the crouch, his shield taking hit after hit; his red cloak and tall horsehair plume making him highly conspicuous. Behind him he heard the bellowed orders of the centurion getting his men on the move. Reaching the ditch he looked down; the housing lay on its back, mangled. Stakes jutted out along its twenty-foot length; a few were slimed with gore, protruding from impaled bodies and, in one case, the back of a broken skull. In amongst the wreckage the surviving men of the first century worked furiously trying to clear a way to the ram and tending to the wounded whilst the second century did their best to shield their comrades, although the archery and artillery concentrated on the wall above them meant that very few

Britons risked exposing themselves to try a shot. Nevertheless, three men from his escort stood over Vespasian, protecting him with their shields.

'Prefect!' Vespasian shouted, spotting the cohort commander amid the carnage. 'Cut the ram free and pass it up to those men in the gap.' He pointed to the third century now forming a testudo, holding their oval auxiliary shields over their heads and to their front and sides creating a reasonably safe leather and wood box around themselves. 'Forget about the wounded for the moment; we need to open that gate before the assault falters.'

The prefect acknowledged the order and bellowed at his men to start cutting the ropes that suspended the ram from its housing.

Vespasian turned to two of his escort crouched behind him. 'Run to the support cohorts on either side of the wall and tell them to start scaling the palisade as soon as they see the ram lifted out of the ditch.'

With a salute to their commander and a nervous glance between them the two men scampered off. Down in the ditch much of the protective leather had been stripped away from the wooden frame and the ram was clearly visible; the last few ropes were being cut and the prefect had gathered all his able-bodied men along its length ready to lift the great trunk – almost two feet in diameter – either by the hooks to which the ropes had been fastened or by cradling it underneath. The final rope was left attached to the ram but unknotted from the housing; an auxiliary hurled the loose end of it up to the centurion of the third century, who fed it into his men's formation.

'Lift, you whoresons!' the prefect roared at his men.

Vespasian made a mental note to mention the prefect in his report to Plautius.

The ram rose from the ground. Javelins hurtled down from above in increasing numbers as the defenders realised what was being attempted; the second century's shields vibrated with their impacts.

The ram was brought up to shoulder level and the slack was taken out of the rope as the men within the midst of the testudo lowered their shields and made ready to take the strain.

Vespasian glanced around his shield, up at the top of the palisade; men were still braving the Hamian and artillery volleys in order to disrupt the operation that, if it was successful, would spell their deaths as surely as an arrow in the eye. As he looked, two Britons were punched back by feathered shafts; two more immediately took their places, such was the defenders' desperation to halt the progress of the ram.

The auxiliaries raised the ram above their heads and began to feed it, foot by foot, up into the heart of the testudo as the javelin storm increased, felling three of the work-party; the prefect rushed to add his support to the weight, bellowing at his men to go faster. Vespasian held his breath, knowing that he was powerless to speed things up; the men were working as fast as possible and his shouting at them as well would make no difference. He steeled himself for what he knew he must do as soon as the ram was back up, knowing that the chances of success would be greatly increased if he fought in the front rank, sharing the danger with his men. How he wished that his old friend, Magnus, always so useful in a fight, was with him to guard his right shoulder and not a thousand miles away in Rome.

The ram juddered and a shriek pierced through the tumult.

'Get that fucking thing out of his hand!' the prefect roared.

Without any ceremony the javelin skewering an auxiliary's hand to the ram was yanked out; the man fell to his knees nursing the bloody wound as his comrades toiled on, heaving the ram the last few feet up out of the ditch and into the testudo. The Britons now concentrated their efforts on the partially shielded formation as the ram was passed through its middle.

Vespasian ran to the front of the century and took up position next to the centurion at the head of the ram, grasping a hook whilst keeping his shield above his head. 'Get them turned to face the gate!'

The centurion screamed the order; the century rotated ninety degrees as javelins pounded its wooden roof. Glancing left and then right, Vespasian could see the two supporting cohorts making their way down into the second ditch with their tall scaling ladders, drawing a little of the defenders' attentions away from the ram. He shared a grim but determined look with the centurion and gave a brief nod.

'Forward at the double!' the centurion cried.

Hefting the ram in their midst, the auxiliaries broke into a jog, behind them the remainder of the cohort followed up. Within a few pounding heartbeats they covered the last twenty uphill paces to the gates; without stopping, they crashed the ram into them with a heavy report, shaking the structure but doing no discernible damage.

'Swing it back on my mark!' Vespasian cried. 'And now!'

As one the men carrying the ram withdrew it and then swung it forward with all possible momentum, cracking it into the gates whilst their comrades did their best to shield them from the constant rain of missiles. Again the gates shook and again the auxiliaries swung.

But then came what Vespasian had been dreading but somehow had to be endured. Clay pots filled with red-hot charcoal crashed down onto the upturned shields, fragmenting into sharp shards and releasing their scorching contents onto the men underneath. Vespasian stifled an agonised scream as a glowing coal fell onto the back of his hand; it was all he could do not to relinquish his grip on the ram's hook as the burning lump rolled off leaving seared skin and the stench of scorched flesh. Cries from all around attested to the effectiveness of the stratagem but somehow the ram was swung again and then again.

Now there was a crack of light between the gates and Vespasian's hopes soared. 'Keep at it, lads!'

With another resonating blow the gates shifted back a bit more, widening the gap; figures could be seen through it rushing to lend their weight to the defences. Javelins now flicked overhead as the remainder of the cohort's centuries loosed their primary weapons at the defenders, punching many of them back, arms flailing, eyes rolling, shrieking into the fires beyond. Yet still the fire-pots fell onto their upturned shields; as Vespasian turned to encourage the men one screamed in agony as his woollen tunic suddenly ignited and Vespasian felt a sticky liquid slop through a gap in the shield-roof.

'That's oil, sir!' the centurion yelled, his voice taut with dread as flames burgeoned on their makeshift cover.

The ram again thundered forward; the auxiliaries, faces racked with fear, heaved at it with the extra strength afforded by desperation as oil, ignited by the glowing charcoal scorching their upturned shields, dripped down into their formation. The gates shuddered as the bar across them cracked; the ram returned with brutal force, splintering the bar and driving the gates ever back. A spear punched through the gap, cleaving the centurion's mouth, shattering teeth, and slicing through soft tissue and bone to burst out of the back of his neck in an explosive spray. Vespasian lowered his burning shield to face the threat as all around him the men of the century dropped the ram and slammed their shoulders into the two gates, edging them back. More spears thrust through the gap, cracking into Vespasian's shield and those of the auxiliaries who now stood to either side of him. They stood firm as the men on the gates strained with the defenders in a contest of strength and will; gradually but inexorably the gates ground backwards as men from the next century rushed to aid their comrades. The gap widened even more and the shield-wall extended; javelins now hissed towards them, thumping into their shields that dripped flaming oil. To his rear, Vespasian could hear the other centuries' officers bellowing orders at their men to storm the breached defence; he sensed bodies forming up behind him and felt relief at the arrival of support – even if it was not Magnus.

The gates shifted another couple of feet and in the swirling smoke beyond, back-lit by flaming huts, stood a mass of warriors. With a volley of sleek-pointed javelins announcing their intent, they charged.

Holding his smoking shield tight before him, Vespasian led the auxiliaries' response, breaking into a jog for the few closing paces before the two sides collided just inside the gates. The moment before contact, in an action instilled by years of repetitive training, the auxiliaries punched their shields forward and up as they stamped their left legs down, planting them squarely on the ground whilst thrusting their swords, underarm, between the gaps at their adversaries' groins. The shock of impact crunched through Vespasian's frame as he strained his left arm to hold back the weight of the charge, hunkering down behind his shield to avoid the wild slashes of long swords and the overarm thrusting of spears. The auxiliary next to him, blood already splattered on his chain mail, screamed in an unintelligible tongue; Gallic, Vespasian assumed as he furiously worked his sword arm forward to feel it jar against wood. The weight of the file behind him pushed into his back and a shield was thrust over his head, protecting him from projectiles hurled from the wall to either side. Javelins from the rear ranks hurtled overhead, slamming into the packed mass of defenders compacted by warriors at the rear surging forward against a Roman line that held solid. Another punch with the tip of his weapon brought a lingering scream from ahead as he felt it tear through yielding tissue; warm fluid slopped onto his sandalled feet as he twisted his blade, rolling his wrist left then right, before abruptly yanking it out. He felt a body slither down his shield and jabbed his sword down at it as he stepped over his fallen foe, praying that the man behind him knew his business and would ensure that the warrior was despatched.

Another warrior stood in his path, snarling under a drooping moustache, his naked torso smeared with blue-green vitrum swirls, brandishing a slashing-sword above his head. With lightning speed, the weapon flashed towards him, left to right; Vespasian ducked under the swipe at the same moment as the Gallic auxiliary to his left raised himself to stab overarm at the throat of his own opponent. With a wet crunch the blade seared through the Gaul's neck, cutting off his stream of obscenities, severing his head and sending it spinning, spiralling blood, away into the fray. Vespasian sliced his weapon down, taking the Briton's arm off at the elbow while the headless corpse sank to the ground disgorging its contents in a crimson fountain as the heart pumped on for a few beats; the freshly carved stump added to the gore spraying about and the warrior screamed, looking incredulously at his shortened arm. It was the last thing he saw; Vespasian's sword punched back up into his throat as an auxiliary from the second rank stepped into his decapitated comrade's place.

Vespasian took another step forward; gradually the auxiliaries were pushing their way into the hill-fort. How the support cohorts were doing in their attempts to scale the palisade to either side of the gate, Vespasian had no idea; he did not even know if they had made it across the final obstacle with their twenty-five-foot ladders that would just reach the top of the palisade from the bottom of the ditch. He pushed on, punching with his shield boss, stabbing with his sword and stamping with his feet, working his body to its limits as the cacophony of battle swirled around him along with the smoke from burning thatch, cocooning him in a world of brutal images and ever-present danger.

How long he struggled for he could not tell but profound weariness was beginning to envelop him. He forced his aching muscles on, waiting for an opportunity to relieve the front rank with fresh troops; but the press of battle prevented this. His breathing had become ragged and he could feel his reactions slowing; he knew that he would not survive long if he stayed to the fore of the fight. Yet how could he, the legate, retire from the combat by himself? Straddling another body as the man behind him stabbed the tip of his weapon into the stricken man's throat, Vespasian felt a ripple flow through the tightly bunched defenders, from south to north; suddenly the timbre of the Britons' yells changed from defiance to surprise. As he worked his blade he saw from the corner of his eye a couple of Britons further back look nervously over their shoulders. They had been hit in the flank; somewhere along its length the Romans had succeeded in scaling the palisade. Now he knew that they were in and all he had to do was survive for a few racing heartbeats more.

Sensing that victory was imminent, the auxiliaries pushed forward into the wavering Britons, stabbing and hacking with blood-slick blades, each step forward easier than the last as the enemy lost cohesion and resolve in equal measure. Through a break in the smoke, Vespasian glimpsed Roman helmets away to the left: legionary helmets, not auxiliary. Valens had made it over the palisade with his three cohorts, fifteen hundred men. Now they just had to clear the way for Tatius' first cohort to enter the hill-fort. They, along with the three auxiliary cohorts already joined in the assault, would be enough to prevail, whilst the rest of the legion and Gallic cohorts and Cogidubnus' recently raised Britannic cohort would prevent any escape. Caratacus would be at least killed, if not captured alive.

Caught between the two-pronged attack and the fires to their rear and suffering casualties at a steadily increasing rate, the Britons broke, fleeing into the smoke.

Glancing up, left then right, Vespasian saw the defenders leaping from the palisade anxious not to be caught between the auxiliaries coming through the gates and those of the two cohorts now streaming over the walls, the Hamians and artillery having ceased their volleys. However, he was under no illusion that it was over. 'Halt!' he shouted to the century that had led the charge. 'Move aside.'

The century's survivors – Vespasian estimated that they were down to half their number – gladly complied and stepped out of the way in an unmilitary fashion, too exhausted to care about drill, as the rest of the cohort streamed into the fort, their prefect at their head.

'They'll regroup beyond the flames, prefect,' Vespasian called. 'Keep your lads tight together.'

With a half-made salute the prefect led his men on into the smoke as the legion's first cohort doubled through the gate. Vespasian did not bother to give Primus Pilus Tatius any orders; four years working closely with the veteran centurion had taught him that the man knew his business.

It was with relief that he saw his cavalry escort, now remounted, following the first cohort into the fort. He took his horse from the decurion and hauled himself wearily into the saddle. 'Thank you, decurion, I don't think I could walk another pace.'

'Then you ain't exercising enough,' a voice from behind him commented.

Vespasian spun round, his eyes murderous.

'Perhaps you should do more riding of a different sort, if you take my meaning?'

Vespasian's face broke into a broad grin. 'Magnus! What in the name of all the gods are you doing here?'

Magnus rode up to Vespasian and proffered his arm. 'Let's just say that Rome's a bit unwelcoming for me at the moment, but I think that can probably wait until later, sir, seeing as you seem to be in the middle of storming a hill-fort.'

Vespasian grasped his friend's muscular forearm. 'I'm intrigued, but you're right, it can wait until I've caught Caratacus.'

Vespasian rode past the last of the smouldering huts. All around lay the bodies of the dead – women and children as well as warriors – sprawled, bloodied and broken. Ahead of him, lined across the hill-fort, from the southern wall to the northern, stood the II Augusta's first and second cohorts, supported by the third and fourth. Beyond them was a mass of warriors and their families.

'Looks like they're going to surrender,' Magnus observed, scratching his grey hair. 'They must have decided that a life of slavery is preferable to an honourable death. I'll never understand these savages.'

'That suits me; it'll save a lot of Roman lives and I'll get a healthy cut of the profit from their sale. But if they are surrendering it must mean that Caratacus is dead.'

'Or he's escaped.'

'Impossible, the fort is surrounded.'

Magnus grunted, his scarred ex-boxer's face betraying his scepticism at that assertion, as they dismounted.

Cogidubnus was waiting for Vespasian next to Tatius. 'They are willing to surrender; Drustan and Caratacus are dead.'

'Where are their bodies?'

'Drustan's is with them but they claim that Caratacus' corpse was completely burnt in the fire.'

'Bollocks!'

'That's what I thought; but if they're willing to surrender they must be confident that Caratacus is safely away.'

Vespasian scowled. 'Take their surrender; he can't have got out of here.' He turned to Tatius. 'Have every hut searched for trapdoors and other hiding places and whilst the lads do that have the prisoners pass through the gates one by one so that Cogidubnus can examine each of them.' He turned back to the Briton. 'Even the women; you never know what he could be disguised as.'

Cogidubnus nodded and walked away with Tatius to organise the surrender and search of the hill-fort.

Vespasian turned to Magnus. 'Something is not quite right here. Come on.'

He kicked his horse towards the south wall and, dismounting, climbed one of the many ladders leading up to the walkway that ran around the palisade's entire length. Magnus followed him up.

Looking out around the hill's circumference Vespasian saw what he expected: it was surrounded by cohort after cohort with never more than a fifty-pace gap between each one. 'Surely no one could get through that.' They walked around to the western and then northern sections; every angle was covered.

'Perhaps he was burnt after all,' Magnus suggested.

'No, if he died they would have saved the body to prove it.'

'Then he must be hiding.'

'Sir!' Tatius called from under the west-facing wall. 'We've got something.'

Vespasian and Magnus ran back and climbed down to the primus pilus; in his hands he held some wooden boards.

Vespasian looked at the ground at his feet; it was a tunnel entrance, just wide enough to admit a man. 'Shit!' He pulled up the remaining boards and saw a ladder within; he climbed in.

He headed down into darkness with Magnus following. After descending ten feet or so he came to a level tunnel; light could be seen at its far end. He speeded up, anxious to get out of the close confinement. A few moments later his head popped out into the open; in front of him were stakes: he was in the ditch below the palisade. Opposite was another tunnel leading to the second ditch; he made his way through the stakes and climbed in. Pulling himself along with his arms for a dozen or so paces of gradual descent he emerged at the other end into the second ditch. He dusted himself off and looked around. On the far side was the only growth of bush that had been allowed to cultivate around the defences on the steep west slope; foot-holes led up the ditch's side beneath it.

Magnus joined him. 'So this is how he got out.'

Vespasian pointed to the foot-holes. 'Yes, and that's how he got away.' He climbed up the vertical bank and peered into the bush; there was a narrow path cut through it that went on for thirty paces down the hill. He crawled down its length and came out into a dell in the hillside, deep enough to obscure him from both the walls above and the auxiliary cohort on station at the base of the hill.

'He could have got to here unseen,' Magnus said, peering over the edge and down to the troops at the bottom, 'but the rest of the way down is open ground; our lads are bound to have seen anyone coming out of here.'

'Let's go and ask them.'

Vespasian and Magnus jogged over to the auxiliaries; their prefect strode forward to meet them. 'The fort is ours, legate?'

'It is, but we're missing one vital component, Galeo. Did anyone come out?'

The prefect looked confused. 'Just the man you sent an optio to bring out: the spy.'

'What spy? What optio?'

'The young lad seemed too young to be an optio but it was hard to tell under all the grime on his face.' He pulled a scroll from his belt and proffered it to Vespasian. 'But he had written orders with Plautius' seal on, giving him permission to get our agent out of the place before it fell, so he wouldn't get killed in the chaos of the assault.'

Vespasian glanced at the scroll, knowing immediately that it was a forgery. 'When was this?'

'Just after the attack started.'

'Where did they go?'

'They rode off, around the fort heading for our camp.'

'Are you sure that they didn't turn away and ride off?'

'I don't know; I didn't pay them any attention once they'd gone.'

Vespasian's fists clenched. He felt like pummelling the man although he knew that it was not his fault; he had been duped. 'This optio, did he give his name?'

'Yes, sir; Alienus.'

Vespasian raised his eyes to the sky. 'I might have guessed.'

'So he was from you?'

'No, prefect, he was not.'

CHAPTER II

'WE PICKED UP their trail, sir; they doubled back and headed west.' Lucius Junius Caesennius Paetus, the young prefect of the Batavian auxiliary cavalry ala, reported in clipped patrician tones, standing to attention on the opposite side of the desk to Vespasian in the praetorium tent. 'Judging by the tracks, they were a good two hours ahead of us. After five miles or so they met up with a group of at least thirty horsemen and changed direction to just north of west. By that time the light was fading and we had to turn back.'

'Thank you, prefect. Maximus, have you had the legion's casualty list?'

'I'm just waiting for the second, third and fourth cohorts' reports; they suffered the most scaling the walls. I'll bring it to you when it's complete.'

'Has there been a report of an optio going missing just before the attack?'

Maximus looked surprised. 'How did you know, sir?'

'A guess. Well?'

'The optio from the sixth century, ninth cohort went missing just before the assault started as the cohort moved into position.'

'Thank you, Maximus.' Vespasian looked over to Cogidubnus, seated to the right of him next to Valens. 'How long is it since you've seen your cousin Alienus?'

'Verica's grandson? Why?'

'Because I believe that he was the man masquerading as the optio who got Caratacus through our lines.'

The Britannic King thought for a few moments. 'Not since he was a boy, well before he went to Rome, say six or seven years. Why?'

'Could you identify him?'

'I doubt it after all this time; he'd be a man now and I only saw him a few times as a lad.'

'A pity.' Vespasian looked at the crude map rolled out before him; there was not much detail on it south or west of where they were, just the coastline of the peninsula that narrowed as it ran southwest into the ocean and marked with a couple of rivers. 'Where do you think they're headed?'

The Briton got up and peered at the map in the lamplight. 'My western scouts who came back in this afternoon reported another hill-fort about here.' He pointed a dirty-nailed finger at the map slightly north of west of their present position, almost halfway to the sea on the north coast of the peninsula.

Vespasian noted its whereabouts on the map; most of the markings were in his hand, the cartographic record of the island being sparse to say the least. 'How large is it?'

'Larger than this one; it's got three ditches and four ramparts.'

'Is it occupied?'

'According to my men there is a small force holding it but not more than a few hundred; it would seem that most of the warriors were called to muster here.'

'Question the prisoners and find out all that you can about the place.'

Cogidubnus nodded.

Vespasian considered the facts for a few moments, running a hand through his thinning hair. 'We'll need to take it anyway as we move west, although I can't imagine that Caratacus will let himself be caught in a siege again. What's between here and there?'

'Hills and some flat land; there are a few settlements but none are fortified so they'll probably be abandoned as we approach them.'

'What news from the scouts in the north?'

'They're not back but if any hostile body was close enough to threaten us they would have sent a message.'

'Have that agent of yours report to me, he may know something about the place.'

'I will, as soon as I can find him.'

'What happened to him?'

'I don't know; he disappeared soon after we brought him down.'

Vespasian paused, frowning. 'How long has this agent been working for you?'

'He appeared before me about four months ago, just as you were settling into your winter camp, saying that he was an Atrebas who'd been captured by the Durotriges as a child and had spent ten years as a slave on a farm. He'd managed to escape and came to me to offer his services in return for some land of his own to farm; he said that it would be easy for him to pass unnoticed in and out of any Durotrigan hill-fort as he had no status. I could see the logic of that so I accepted; and, having so nearly caught Caratacus today, I think that I was right to do so.'

Vespasian nodded before studying the map again. After a few moments he pointed to a small peninsula attached to the southern coast by a thin strip of land, about thirty miles directly south of the hill-fort. 'This looks like a good sheltered anchorage for the fleet; have your scouts had a look at it?'

Cogidubnus squinted at where he was pointing. 'They're not good judges of nautical affairs, but they said that there are a couple of fishing settlements on the eastern side of the promontory, but there is another well-fortified settlement about six or seven miles inland from it.'

'Then we'll take that on our way down to the coast having dealt with this next problem.' Vespasian turned to Valens. 'Get a message to the fleet and have them rendezvous with us there in ten days' time with next month's supplies.'

'He'll leave at first light.'

'Good. Maximus, we'll leave the Gallic cohort that led the assault here to garrison the fort; I expect they could do with the time to lick their wounds. Have another cohort escort the prisoners back to our winter camp; the slave-traders can assess their value there. The legion will strike camp before dawn tomorrow and force-march towards this hill-fort; there is a chance that we can get there by dusk. Paetus, you will take your Batavians and ride at the speed of Mercury and get to the western side of that fort without being seen; take one of Cogidubnus' scouts as a guide. I want you to intercept anyone who tries to leave the place; and I mean anyone, even the ugliest old crone.' Vespasian stood, leaning on the desk with his hands; his officers also got to their feet. 'Gentlemen, once again speed is essential. The chances are Caratacus will leave that fort in the morning and head on west; but if he doesn't, I want him caught like we had him today, although this time we do not allow him to escape. We'll take these two forts, resupply with the fleet and then continue west along the coast to this estuary here that marks the border between the Durotriges' and the Dumnoni's lands.' He pointed to a large river mouth twenty or so miles from the rendezvous point. 'This is our objective this season and then we'll strike north across the peninsula to the northern coast next year to link up with our allies the Dobunni's land. Any questions?'

There was a general shaking of heads and positive mumbling.

'Gentlemen, you have your orders; dismiss.'

The officers saluted and they and Cogidubnus turned and left.

'You didn't ask them the obvious question,' Magnus said, sitting in the shadows in the far corner of the tent.

'How do they think that Caratacus and Alienus communicated to effect the rescue?'

'Precisely.'

Vespasian smiled, raising his eyebrows. 'That's because I've just worked that out. They didn't need to; Alienus was in the fort already.'

'What do you mean?'

'Hormus!'

The slave appeared from the private quarters. 'Yes, master.'

'Fetch us some wine.'

With a bow, Hormus disappeared.

Vespasian sat opposite Magnus and told him of Sabinus' disappearance whilst being led to a fictitious meeting by Alienus and then of Cogidubnus' agent escaping from the fort just before the attack.

'You're saying that these two people were the same man?' Magnus said after digesting the information.

'Yes.'

'They can't be; Cogidubnus' agent had long hair and the tribune Alienus must have had short hair.'

'It's a wig.'

'Ah, yes; I suppose it could be.'

'Of course it is and that and the dirt smeared over his face prevented me from recognising him. Which means that he's a double agent. Cogidubnus doesn't recognise him either because it's been so long since he saw him and he thinks that he's his man; he wasn't surprised when Alienus made a break for it and then personally vouched for him. He doesn't even know that the treacherous little shit speaks Latin; they spoke together in their own language. No one was suspicious that he managed to escape from a fort filled with armed warriors only a few of whom bothered to try to bring him down with javelins and they all missed, even at such close range, because he then confirmed that Caratacus was inside.'

'But he was the one who told you that Caratacus might be there in the first place.'

'I know, which means that Caratacus wanted us here; he used himself as bait to draw us in.'

'Why? What's he achieved by having four thousand of his warriors either killed or enslaved?'

'I don't know but there must be a bigger picture in which that sacrifice is justified. A means to an end.'

Hormus returned with a tray and placed it on the table between them.

Vespasian waved him away. 'We'll serve ourselves; leave us. So once he'd got us here he had to remain, otherwise the tribe would have surrendered in the face of such odds; only his presence would've induced them into that sacrifice. But then he had to escape. He knew that there was no way he could get through our lines unless he pretended to be a Roman agent being smuggled out of the camp; to do that he had to get a man to pose as a Roman. Alienus was ideal: he speaks fluent Latin. It was set up and Alienus played the part perfectly: having seemingly made a daring escape, the double agent disappears at the same time as an optio goes missing and then within an hour an optio calling himself Alienus appears with forged orders to escort a spy out of the camp by a secret tunnel that no one in this army knew about.'

Magnus picked up a clay pitcher and poured them both a cup of wine. 'But why did he give that name? He could have used any name he liked.'

'That troubles me too; someone that devious wouldn't have made such an elementary mistake.' Vespasian took a sip of wine and ruminated as he savoured its taste. 'He must have wanted me to know that it was him; but why? I shall have to think about that, but in the meantime I'll keep after him because at the moment he's my only chance of finding out what happened to Sabinus.'

Magnus took a healthy gulp of wine. 'I have to say, it don't look good for him.'

Vespasian rubbed his forehead, feeling the exertion of the day catching up with him. 'Yes, well, I'm not going to believe the worst until it's proven to me.' He took another sip and looked across the table at his friend of almost twenty years. 'But tell me, why are you here?'

'Ah, well. There was a bit of a misunderstanding about the ownership of a burning tenement block on our area; I've been moving the Brotherhood's finances into property. Anyway, once it was resolved, a couple of people ended up not too well, if you take my meaning?'

'Dead, you mean?'

'In a manner of speaking, yes. So I thought it best to remove myself from Rome while it was all sorted out.'

'You mean my uncle Gaius is covering your tracks for you?'

'I'll admit that Senator Pollo is using his influence on my behalf.'

Vespasian smiled, shaking his head; having witnessed a few times the criminal activity undertaken by the South Quirinal Crossroads Brotherhood, of which Magnus was the *patronus*, the leader, he decided not to enquire further into the subject. The shady underbelly of Rome was, thankfully, a long way away. 'So, other than clearing up your mess, my uncle's well?'

'Ah! He does have a few difficulties of his own, not least his trying to remain publicly uncommitted but privately supporting both sides in the ongoing feud between the Empress Messalina and Claudius' freedmen.'

'Narcissus, Pallas and Callistus are still trying to remove her?'

'Yes, but Claudius won't believe a word against her. Despite the fact she's fucked everyone in Rome with a working penis under the age of seventy they can't convince the Emperor of her infidelity. Last winter she had a competition with Scylla – know her? The most artful and expensive whore in the city – as to who could satisfy the most men in one whole day and night; and by satisfy they didn't just mean a quick coupling up against the wall. No, this had to be to the highest standards of the profession and witnessed by crowds of people; every sort of technique had to be employed so that the men were physically – and quite literally – drained. *That's* what they meant by satisfied. It was the talk of Rome for months; everybody heard about it but, according to your uncle, when Pallas and Narcissus – but oddly enough, not Callistus, actually – both separately told Claudius about it he dismissed the story as the lascivious imaginings of jealous minds and reminded them that she was the mother of his two children and therefore it was impossible that she would act in such a grossly improper manner. Some people prefer not to see the truth.'

'In Claudius' case I think it's more because he's got such an overinflated opinion of his own abilities that he can't believe anyone would prefer someone else to him, even though he's a fool that drools.'

Magnus considered this for a few moments. 'I suppose he reckons his saliva-dripping ruttings to be the height of prowess.'

'Yes, and I expect Messalina is intelligent enough not to disabuse him of that notion. Who won, by the way?'

'What? Oh, Messalina by one, with a score of twenty-five in twenty-four hours, each one completely exhausted.'

'Well, I suppose it keeps her occupied and her thoughts away from Flavia and the children.'

Vespasian had been living in constant fear for his wife and two children, Titus and Domitilla, since Claudius had requested that they live in the palace, ostensibly so that Titus could be educated alongside his own son, Britannicus. However, Vespasian knew it was not the real reason – that was far more sinister. The Emperor had been manoeuvred into making the offer by Messalina's brother, Corvinus. Having made an enemy of Corvinus almost ten years previously, before his sister had become the Empress, Vespasian and Sabinus had then helped Narcissus, Claudius' most influential freedman, foil Corvinus' attempt to hijack the invasion of Britannia for his and his sister's personal gain. Claudius had not believed Corvinus had been plotting against him and had pardoned him, leaving Vespasian exposed to his continued hatred. In revenge and to demonstrate the power that he held over Vespasian, Corvinus had persuaded Claudius to invite Vespasian's family to the palace: at any time they chose, Corvinus and Messalina could dispose of Flavia and the children. Claudius had been only too pleased to make the offer, thinking that he was conferring an honour on one of his victorious legates rather than putting him at the mercy of the ambitious and unscrupulous Corvinus and his depraved, power-mad sister.

'I've got letters for you, including one from Flavia,' Magnus said.

Vespasian grimaced. 'The only time she writes nowadays is when she needs more money.'

'I did warn you about marrying a woman with expensive tastes. Anyway you must be doing well out of the invasion; that was a lot of captives you got today.'

'Yes, but the slave-traders are constantly lowering the price they pay for them claiming that we're flooding the market.' Vespasian raised his eyebrows incredulously.

'Whereas you think that they're lying and just taking a bigger percentage for themselves?'

'Wouldn't you?'

'Of course I would.'

'And they're probably paying Plautius a cut to make sure that he doesn't look too closely into their dealings.'

'If they're sensible; and if he's sensible he's taking it. What are you going to do about it?'

'I'm not sure yet; it's very difficult to put any pressure on them as they stay so far behind the lines, nice and safe and surrounded by bodyguards.'

'Then draw them out; don't send the captives back to them, make them come to you to assess them.'

'I thought about that but they'll just offer less per slave because they'll claim, with some justification, that their overheads are higher as they have further to transport their stock.'

Magnus scratched the rough grey stubble on his chin, sucking air through his teeth. 'I see your point; it would seem you're stuck with the situation.'

'Oh, I'll have them – somehow; don't worry about that.'

Magnus' scarred and battered face creased into a grin in the dim lamplight. 'I'm sure you will; I know it pains you being cheated out of money almost as much as it pains you to spend it. You must've been in agony when you bought Hormus.'

'Very funny.'

'I thought so. But back to my news: Caenis told me to tell you that she's got a very comfortable apartment in the palace next to Flavia and she and Pallas are keeping a close eye on Flavia's safety. She says that she sees her and the children daily.'

'That's good to hear; but what a bizarre situation ...'

Vespasian still found it hard to comprehend how Caenis, his lover for almost twenty years, and Flavia, his wife, seemed to have become friends in the four years that he had been away from Rome. Caenis had been the slave of his patron, Antonia; she had freed her in her will. However, as it was illegal for senators to marry freedwomen, Vespasian had been forced to look elsewhere for a mother for his children; Flavia had married him knowing that his mistress was no threat to her position as wife. The rapprochement between the two women had begun in the aftermath of Caligula's assassination when both their houses had been searched by Narcissus' agents looking for Sabinus; they had joined forces in a bond of mutual outrage at Vespasian when he had brought his wounded brother home without explanation. It was Caenis who had pieced together what had happened: that Sabinus had secretly taken part in the assassination in vengeance for Caligula's brutal rape of his wife, Clementina. Both women had realised the imperative of ensuring that the fact never became public knowledge. The secret shared had created a mutual respect that now seemed to have turned into friendship.

'... I dread to think what they talk about.'

'Yeah, I know, it don't bear contemplation; but the main thing is that she and Pallas are keeping her safe. Flavia still has no idea that both Messalina and Corvinus are a threat to her or the children's safety and Pallas reckons it's best to keep it that way.'

Vespasian looked dubious. 'I suppose he's right.'

'Course he is, sir. He knows the workings of Claudius' court as well as anyone; he's convinced that if Flavia was to live in fear then she could well do something stupid and offend someone important. As it is she sometimes dines with Messalina because Titus and Britannicus have become such good friends.'

'Yes, she mentioned that in her last letter – she was full of it. I wrote back trying to explain that it's not such a good thing for our son to be too friendly with someone who could become emperor, even though he's only six. A lot of future emperors never fulfil their promise and their friends can suffer too.'

'Well, there ain't anything that you can do about that at the moment; worry about it when you get back to Rome.'

'That could be another two years at this rate.'

'Two more years to get rich in.' Magnus drained his cup and then rummaged in his bag; he brought out five scrolls and placed them on the table. 'I'm off to find a spare tent; I'll leave you with these. There's one from Flavia, Caenis, your uncle, your mother and Pallas.'

'Pallas! What does he want?'

'How would I know? The letter's addressed to you.'

Vespasian lay on his camp-bed, perusing the last of his letters in the flickering light of the single oil lamp on a low table next to him. The first four had been much as expected: words of love and reassurance from Caenis; news of dinner parties and a request for more money from Flavia; complaints about Flavia's attitude to parenthood from his mother, Vespasia; and advice from his uncle as to which political factions to pretend publicly to support and which to really support privately upon his return to Rome. It was the fifth letter, which he was now rereading, that had caused him some surprise.

It had seemed odd that Pallas had chosen to send his letter via Magnus rather than use the official couriers that daily set out from Rome on the long journey to the new province; but when he had seen the content of the letter he realised that Claudius' powerful freedman had been frightened that the missive would be intercepted. As a veteran of imperial politics, Pallas was forever embroiled in intrigue and as Vespasian finished the letter for the second time he shook his head, chewing on his lower lip, his expression strained; even here on the fringes of the Empire he was not beyond the reach of the schemes and plots of his masters back in Rome.

Hormus slipped through the entrance to Vespasian's sleeping quarters with his breastplate, helmet and greaves all freshly polished and hung them on his armour-stand. 'Will there be anything else, master?'

Vespasian glanced at the letter again. 'Yes, Hormus; ask Paetus to report to me an hour before dawn. Wake me by then.'

The slave bowed and went about his errand. Vespasian rolled up Pallas' letter, placed it with the others on the table, and then blew out the lamp. In the dark of the tent he closed his eyes to the sound of almost ten thousand men settling down for the night and the scent of the smoke spiralling up from the smouldering wick.

The lamp was burning when Vespasian opened his eyes; he shivered despite being well wrapped in woollen blankets. Feeling more tired than when he went to bed, he sat up; the flap to his sleeping quarters was swinging as if someone had just passed through. 'Hormus!' He waited a few moments, yawning deeply; there was no reply. 'Hormus?' Untangling himself from the blankets he sat on the edge of the bed, stretching.

'Yes, master,' his slave said, walking in, wiping the sleep from his eyes.

'Bring me some bread and warmed wine.'

'Yes, master.'

'Is Paetus here yet?'

'I'm sorry, master?'

'You heard me.'

The slave shook his head looking nonplussed. 'No, master, he's not; I only got back a couple of hours ago. It's at least five hours until dawn.'

'Then why did you wake me?'

'What do you mean, master?'

'The flap was swinging when I woke up – you'd just gone through it.'

Hormus was looking increasingly confused. 'I was asleep in my bedding-roll just the other side of the entrance.'

'Then who came in?'

'No one; they would have had to step over me; I would have woken.'

'Are you sure?'

'Yes, master, no one came in.'

'Then who lit the lamp?'

Hormus looked at the spluttering flame and shook his head mutely, his eyes wide.

Vespasian felt another chill. The hairs on the back of his neck and on his arms bristled.

'The wick must have just reignited,' Magnus asserted, looking down at the offending item four hours later.

Vespasian shook his head, his expression again strained. 'Impossible, it was completely out; I remember smelling the smoke from it.'

'Perhaps Hormus is lying; perhaps he did light it and then pretended he didn't to scare you.'

'Why would he want to do that?'

Magnus hunched his shoulders, spreading his hands. 'I don't know; perhaps he just doesn't like you. Or perhaps he's been planted by the enemy to distract you, take your mind off the campaign.'

'Don't be ridiculous. He wouldn't need to do that; he could kill me in my bed any night.'

'How long have you had him?'

'I bought him soon after you left for Rome, so May last year. I've had him nearly a year; he's placid, meticulous, unobtrusive and, I believe, honest, as nothing has ever gone missing.'

'What is he?'

'He's a slave.'

'Yes, I know that; I mean what was he?'

'He was born a slave, that's why I chose him; he's never known anything else so I wouldn't have to tame him. I think he said that his mother was originally from somewhere around Armenia; he doesn't know who his father was but I suspect that he was his mother's owner. She never told him and died when he was ten. That's all I know about him.'

'So you're sure he wasn't lying?'

'Yes. So if he didn't do it, who did?'

'Well, I don't know, sir; does it really matter?'

'Yes, it does; it matters greatly.'

'Why?'

'Because last night someone got past the guards at the front, past Hormus sleeping outside my door, into my room and then for some strange reason lit my oil lamp and then walked back out.'

'Or some*thing* did.'

'Now you're being ridiculous again.'

'Am I? You know what this island's like; you heard the stories: the strange spirits, wraiths, old gods that have been here for centuries, from even before the Britons arrived. Things that we don't understand. Ancient things.'

'I'll admit that this is a strange place. Sabinus talked to me about it when I saw him at Plautius' briefing this winter; he told me about a legionary who had been found dead, with no visible wound and yet there wasn't a drop of blood in him. Another had been flayed alive and yet was still wearing his uniform; apparently before he died he rambled on about spirits that sucked the skin from his limbs. I pretended to Sabinus that I didn't believe it, that I thought they were just exaggerated legionary stories designed to frighten the new recruits.'

'But you did believe them?'

'I don't know; I suppose there has to be some truth in them somewhere.'

'The island is haunted, there's no doubt. I never like being on my own, especially outside the camp at night. I always get the feeling that I'm being watched and it don't feel like human eyes on me, if you take my meaning?'

Vespasian did but did not like to admit it.

'Do you remember the power of the Germanic gods we felt in the forests of Germania Magna? It felt like our gods were weak there compared to them because we were so far away from their home. Here we're even further away and, what's more, we're across the sea. What chance do our deities have to protect us here in a country full of strange gods and daemons and the druids who seem to feed off their power? I spent my time constantly clutching my thumb and spitting to avert the evil-eye while I was last here and I'm sure that I'll be doing the same thing this time.'

'I'm sure you will. But whatever power there is in this land and however the druids harness it and whatever sacrifices they make to their gods to try to ensure that they keep them safe there's one thing that *I'm* sure of: no god or daemon or spirit, wraith, ghost or whatever is going to waste its time coming into my sleeping quarters and lighting one little oil lamp.'

Magnus slumped down on the bed and heaved a sigh. 'Then as I said: either it reignited because you hadn't extinguished it properly or Hormus is lying to you.'

'Master,' Hormus said, standing in the entrance, 'Paetus is here.'

'Back to Rome immediately?' Paetus looked confused as he stood in front of Vespasian's desk an hour before dawn. 'There's nothing that I'd like more; but my replacement hasn't arrived yet.'

'As the senior decurion, Ansigar is more than capable of looking after the ala until he does.'

'I suppose so; but why now, all of a sudden?'

'Politics, prefect,' Vespasian replied, aware as ever of the difference between the young man's patrician accent and his Sabine country burr; he had always tried to lessen it when talking with Paetus' father, his long-dead friend, but now he no longer felt the need to obfuscate his background.

'But I'm not eligible to take my seat in the Senate until next year at the earliest; I'm not involved in politics yet.'

Vespasian turned Pallas' letter over in his hands. 'Every Roman of your class is involved in politics sooner or later, Paetus, and I'm afraid your turn has arrived now whether you like it or not. Sit down and I'll explain.'

Paetus took a seat opposite Vespasian.

Vespasian unfurled Pallas' letter and scanned it again before raising his eyes to his young subordinate. 'This letter is from one of the most powerful men in Rome, one whom I am lucky enough to call a friend but upon whose friendship I cannot presume. So, when I get a request from him, I know better than to refuse it because, however it's been worded, I'm well aware that it's an order.'

'Who's it from?'

'It's from Marcus Antonius Pallas, freedman of the late Lady Antonia. Upon her suicide he, quite naturally, transferred his allegiance to her only surviving son, the Emperor Claudius.

'Now, I don't need to tell you what the Emperor is like; you have seen him for yourself and have no doubt formed your own opinion. I will not say anything treasonous about him to you nor will I get you to compromise yourself in that way by asking you to express your true opinion of the man. Do I make myself clear?'

Paetus nodded slowly. 'As clear as you can, sir; I believe from the phrasing of that sentence that our opinions are broadly similar.'

Vespasian allowed himself a half-smile as he inclined his head in acknowledgement. 'We understand each other; good. So therefore it won't surprise you to learn that Claudius is not much more than a figurehead emperor who is subject, in the main, to the will of four, normally conflicting, forces.'

'I had heard that that was how the government worked at the moment although I don't know the details – I haven't been in Rome since before Caligula's death and it's not something to discuss in letters nor speak loosely about in the officers' mess.'

'A very wise precaution and one which we shall now ignore in the privacy of this tent. Three of these four forces are Claudius' freedmen: Pallas, the secretary to the Treasury; Callistus, whose sphere of influence is justice and the law courts; and then there's his chief freedman, Narcissus, who's been with him the longest and was responsible for keeping him safe during the reigns of Caligula and Tiberius – he's the imperial secretary, in charge of Claudius' correspondence and diary. That means he has complete control over all foreign and domestic policy as well as access to the Emperor; no one can get to Claudius except by going through him. No one, that is, except for the Empress, Messalina. Neither Narcissus nor Messalina are happy with this arrangement – both feel that the other exerts too much influence on their malleable Emperor; Callistus and Pallas meanwhile both squabble for second place behind Narcissus whilst supporting him in his feud for the mastery of Rome with the Empress. Now, whatever you might think of this and however outraged you may be that the Senate has no influence in the matter, it is best to be pragmatic and accept the situation because there is nothing that you or I can do to change it. Would you agree?'

'It would seem that we have little choice.'

'Very little indeed. The only choice most of us have is which one of these four people to support in order to gain advancement; but I'm afraid that in your case you've had that decision made for you.'

Paetus frowned. 'By whom?'

'By me, and I apologise for that, Paetus. I promised your father, who was my good friend, that I would look out for you. It was a promise that I did not keep that well and I've compounded that fault by getting you involved in the feuding of those in power.'

'When?'

'When you reported to me, two years ago, that your scouts had told you that Corvinus had not stopped his Ninth Hispana on the northern bank of the Tamesis River as ordered, but had carried on. I told you not to tell anyone and that I would inform Plautius when I felt the time was right; in doing so I made you complicit in a plot against Messalina and her brother, Corvinus, which had been set in motion by Narcissus. They are no doubt aware of your part and so that makes you their enemy. Pallas is also aware of it and wants to use the fact to help bolster his position. If you don't co-operate he will halt your career and that gives you no alternative other than to go to Rome and do his bidding.'

Around the camp *bucinae* sounded the general reveille, announcing yet another day under the Eagle of the II Augusta.

Paetus paused for a few moments' reflection before acknowledging with a small hand gesture the veracity of his commander's words. 'What does he want me to do?'

'He wants you to do what any man of your age and class would do: he wants you to go back and get elected as one of the quaestors. He will see to it that you don't get posted to a province but, rather, serve as an Urban Quaestor, as your father did, so that you can take your seat in the Senate immediately.'

'That's what I was planning to do as soon as my replacement arrives; why the rush?'

'Because Pallas wants you to be back in time for this year's elections; he wants you to be in place in the Senate by next year, not the year after.'

Paetus leant forward in his chair. 'In place to do what?'

'In place to be prepared to act as a witness at a treason trial.'

'Who's to be prosecuted?'

'Corvinus, of course, and you're to be the star witness, a senator from the Junii, one of the oldest and most renowned families in Rome, who can swear that the Ninth Hispana carried on across the Tamesis without provocation and their legate thereby committed an act of treason.'

'I could swear to that.'

'I know and so does Callistus, which is why Pallas thinks that it will never come to trial, it'll never get anywhere near a court.'

'But Callistus is the secretary in charge of justice.'

'Yes, and as you know from when he tried to have Sabinus, you and me killed four years ago he's ...'

'And me,' Magnus' voice came from the shadows.

'Yes, and you ... he's the most duplicitous, slimy piece of treacherous filth that ever walked the corridors of the Palatine Hill and that is saying something indeed.'

Paetus grimaced at the memory of Callistus' treachery when he, Paetus, had helped Vespasian and Sabinus in the search for the lost Eagle of the XVII Legion.

From outside the murmur of thousands of waking voices gradually grew into a constant hubbub, punctuated by bellowing centurions encouraging the less keen from their blankets.

Paetus' face brightened. 'If it means that I'm going to get a measure of revenge on him, then I'm willing to do whatever Pallas wants.'

'It will. Callistus has made it a habit to change his allegiances at what he considers to be the right time. He used to be Caligula's freedman but when it looked for certain that it was only a matter of time before Caligula fell to an assassin's blade he decided to hasten that moment and join in the conspiracy against him by allying himself with Narcissus and Pallas.' Vespasian glanced at the letter again. 'Now, according to Pallas, it seems that he might be thinking about changing sides again and throwing his lot in with Messalina or, at the very least, backing both sides.

'But apart from Callistus failing to report an outrageous infidelity of Messalina's to the Emperor, Pallas hasn't any positive proof of this matter. However ...' Vespasian paused to see whether the young man had the political acumen to finish the sentence; he was not disappointed.

'... however, if a prosecution were to be brought against the Empress's brother which would carry the death penalty if it were proven, then Callistus would be obliged to delay it or dismiss it out of hand if he was secretly supporting Messalina, thereby exposing himself.'

'Exactly. But it gets better than that; it's all about timing. Pallas is convinced that Narcissus will soon be in a position to bring down Messalina so the prosecution would be brought just before he presents the damning evidence to the Emperor and Callistus will go down with the Empress.'

'That'll suit me perfectly.'

'Indeed, as it suits me.'

'And me,' Magnus put in.

'Yes, and you. But more to the point it suits Pallas because he'll secure his place as the second most powerful man in the Empire.'

Paetus raised his eyebrows. 'Just one more step to negotiate, eh?'

Vespasian contemplated the implication of that remark for a moment, enjoying the mingled smell of woodsmoke and cooking, seeping into the tent. 'I don't know about that but he's certainly thought this step through.'

'So who will bring the prosecution?'

'Ah! That's the problem for you. Obviously it can't be Pallas, as Callistus would see through the ploy straight away, so he's chosen someone to act as his proxy. Someone whose career has been halted since his half-sister was assassinated along with her husband, Caligula.'

'Corbulo?'

'Yes. He's desperate to be given a province; he's had no advancement since he was consul six years ago.'

'But he's a jumped-up snob from a family that can't even boast one consul before him.'

'Prefect! I would remind you that I come from an even newer family. Do not let the fact that the Junii can trace their family back to before the Republic prevent you from working with men who have slightly less lineage but pretend to more.'

'I apologise, legate. My personal views on *Gnaeus Domitius Corbulo* will not be an issue.'

Paetus' emphasis on Corbulo's full name implied he was not being exactly truthful, but Vespasian decided against pursuing the point. 'Good, let's hope that his less than favourable opinion of you is likewise put to one side.'

'I've got one question.'

'Go on.'

'Apart from the chance of revenge on Callistus, what's in this for me?'

'In the long term you might be thrown a scrap or two but the real reward is short term: as I said, you'll get the chance to further your career; but that's mainly because you'll get to keep your life.'

CHAPTER III

THE SUN GLOWED deep golden as it dropped beneath the covering cloudbank's western extreme, out towards the horizon. Warm evening light brushed the undulating belly of the low, grey blanket with colour as it dispensed a gentle drizzle; the drops were back-lit by the dying orange rays in a way that Vespasian had never seen before. The weather on this island continually surprised him.

But the quirks of the weather were not what interested him as he sat on his horse surveying the silhouetted hill-fort that the day's march had brought them to, just a quarter of a mile distant, somewhat detached from a line of hills running to the southwest. 'We'll lose a lot of men trying to take that. Any news from your scouts, Cogidubnus?'

The Britannic King shook his head. 'I'm beginning to think that they won't be coming back; they would have arrived here about two hours before us. It's starting to look like they've been taken prisoner or killed.'

'What about the scouts in the north; have you heard from them yet?'

'No, a message should have arrived today. I admit I'm worried.'

Vespasian contemplated that news for a few moments. In the two years since Cogidubnus had surrendered to Rome he had proved his loyalty and Vespasian had come to trust him; if he was concerned about something it was as well to take notice. 'Have you sent more out?'

'Yes, with orders to report back at first light.'

Vespasian nodded his approval and looked again at the three great ditches that encircled the hill's irregular, triangular summit separated by four concentric earthen ramparts, each the height of a man, the innermost being topped with a stout palisade; a few heads could be seen peering towards the Romans. 'We'll never get men across all those obstacles and up to the wall with scaling ladders.' He examined the main gate in the northeast corner and then looked at the lesser one in the southwest. 'It'll have to be co-ordinated assaults on the two gates if they don't see sense and surrender.'

'I ain't never known a savage see sense,' Magnus muttered, not altogether to himself. 'Present company excepted, obviously,' he added quickly as Cogidubnus shot him a dark look. 'Not that I think you're ...' He trailed off before getting himself embroiled in a matter of honour.

Vespasian glared at his friend.

Cogidubnus snorted and turned his attention back to the fort. 'Even then it would be a bloody day; a force of a few hundred could easily hold both gates if there're no diversionary attacks on the ramparts.'

Vespasian assessed the problem ahead and saw that the Briton was right. 'Then we go in at night.'

'If Caratacus is in there then he will have a very good opportunity to escape in the confusion of the attack under the cover of dark.'

'Do you think he's still there?'

'I doubt it; he would have left at first light, knowing that we would be following him here.'

'I think so too; so therefore balancing the slight risk of Caratacus slipping through our fingers against the amount of Roman lives that we'll save by going in at night, it's worth the risk. That way we've a chance of surprising them and also getting a cohort or two to the walls if we can find a weaker spot in the defences.'

As they scanned the earthworks for such a place the gates opened; three men were led out by half a dozen warriors. They were thrown to their knees, shouting at the tops of their voices in words unintelligible at that distance. Three simultaneous flashes in the evening sun silenced them and their bodies slumped forward as their heads rolled away down the hill.

Cogidubnus turned to Vespasian, anger burning in his eyes. 'We have our answer. They were good men.'

Vespasian pulled on his mount's reins, turning back towards the labouring legionaries of the II Augusta who were now constructing a new camp having force-marched all day. 'A night assault it is then.'

'The lads have been told to get some sleep now, it'll be a short night,' Maximus reported to Vespasian in the crowded interior of the lamp-washed praetorium tent.

Vespasian glanced around the shadowed faces of his officers. 'If you're all happy with the plan and your orders, then I suggest that you do the same, gentlemen. There'll be a silent reveille at the sixth hour of the night; any man making unnecessary noise will be dealt with severely. Primus pilus, make sure that your centurions understand that; I know it goes against their nature to give orders in anything quieter than a bellow but tonight they're going to have to try.'

'They've all been told, legate, and are all prepared to bring down righteous retribution on malingerers with no more than a purr.'

'Good. So to recap, the four cohorts taking part in the initial phase of the assault, as well as the Hamians, will muster in the Via Principalis immediately after the reveille. The rest of the legion and the auxiliaries will stand-to in the camp ready to march out and form up in front of it in support once the assault has begun and noise won't be an issue. The gates will be opened at the seventh hour, after the moon has set, and all five cohorts will be in position an hour after that, giving us four hours until dawn to take the fort. Goodnight, gentlemen.'

With a chorus of crashed salutes the officers turned and made their way from the tent. Vespasian slumped down onto his chair and rubbed his eyes, dismissing any thought of writing his report to Plautius about yesterday's storming of the hill-fort.

'I've warmed you some wine, master,' Hormus said, stepping out from the private quarters.

'What? Oh, put it on the desk.' Vespasian watched his slave approach; his eyes were lowered and everything about his demeanour spoke of subservience. 'Do you think that I believe you lied to me about the lamp?'

'It doesn't matter what I think, master; it won't alter anything.'

'But surely you don't want me to think that you are untrustworthy?'

Hormus placed the cup before his master. 'No, but if you believe me to be so then how can I change that?'

'By telling me the truth now.'

'Master, before you bought me I had three owners in my life; my first master, in Lugdunum, in Gaul, used to bugger me brutally from almost before I can remember—'

'But he was probably your natural father!' Vespasian cut in aghast.

Hormus raised his eyes slightly so that he almost met Vespasian's. 'Whatever I was to him in blood had no bearing upon how he treated me or my sister.'

'You have a sister?'

'I did; whether I still have, I don't know.'

Vespasian picked up the cup and blew on its hot contents. 'Tell me.'

'After my mother died our master lost interest in us as he always used to abuse us in front of her; it made it more enjoyable for him. With her gone we were nothing more than two extra mouths to feed, so he sold us. Where my sister ended up I don't know; she was a couple of years older than me so old enough for the brothels.'

'What happened to you?'

'I was sold to an elderly man who not only buggered me but forced me to do the same to him and whipped me if I was unable to. He died two years ago and his sons sold off his slaves as a job lot to the slave-trader, Theron. He locked me and twenty others in an airless wagon and transported us to Britannia to sell at a premium to officers in the invasion force who would rather not have freshly enslaved locals near them, for obvious reasons.'

'And it was quite a premium that he did charge, the rogue. But what has all this to do with telling me the truth about the lamp?'

Hormus met Vespasian's eyes for the first time in their relationship. 'Because, master, in the months since you bought me I
have never been happier in my whole life.' His gaze dropped back
down to the floor. 'You don't abuse me or beat me; you don't
starve me nor do you give me a cold stone floor to sleep on, and
my duties are not arduous. Why would I risk that happiness by
lying to you about anything, let alone something as trivial as
whether or not I lit a lamp?'

Vespasian looked at his slave, realising that he had never
before really noted the young man's features. He would be able
to describe him, yes, but only in broad terms; the fact that his
thin nose was slightly upturned, his eyes hazel, his chin weak and
slightly undershot beneath a patchy, black beard trimmed
without any special attention to regularity had not previously
pierced his consciousness. It was an unremarkable face, the face
of a man of no consequence, the face of a man whose definition
of happiness was made up entirely of negatives. 'I believe you,
Hormus.'

Hormus looked up again; his eyes were moist and a faint smile
quivered on his lips. 'Thank you, master.'

Vespasian waved the gratitude away and instantly regretted
the gesture as the smile faded and Hormus' chest heaved with a
suppressed sob. 'I'm sorry, Hormus; I understand why you feel
thankful. Now, enough of this; if you didn't light the lamp and if
you are sure that no one came into my room then how do you
explain it?'

'I can't, master. All I can say is that my mother told me that
when something strange happens it is a god trying to warn us
about something and that you should pay special attention to
anything that seems not quite right.'

Vespasian thought about this for a few moments, sipping his
drink. 'I suppose that could make some sort of sense,' he mused
eventually. 'A god, one of my gods, perhaps my guardian god,
Mars, would have the power to do that; it's well known that the
gods can manifest themselves. It's a lot of trouble to go to just to
frighten me, but to warn me, now that's a different matter. What
sort of signs have you had?'

Hormus looked momentarily confused. 'Me, master? What god is going to bother with the likes of me; what god even knows I exist? But a man like you, a powerful man, would easily come to their attention and if you have made a big mistake or overlooked something then it would make sense that they should try to warn you. My mother knew this because she was the daughter of a great man – but he was also a foolish man; she told me that twice he had received a warning from the gods, both times after he'd had a conversation with his younger brother. One time it was a cup that shattered just as he picked it up and the other time it was a torch lighting itself, just as your lamp did. His wife, my grandmother, told him that it was a god trying to warn him that he was making a mistake in trusting his brother and that he should kill him or, at the very least, exile him. He took no notice of her or the god and laughed the whole thing off. The next time the brother came, he came with many men and killed him and his wife and sold all his children into slavery.'

'So you're the grandson of a chieftain?'

'No, master, I'm the son of a slave woman.'

'Have it your own way.' Vespasian downed the rest of his wine and stood. 'I'm going to bed now, wake me in three hours.'

'Yes, master.'

'And thank you, Hormus; I shall think about what happened yesterday and see if there is anything that a god might take the time to warn me about.'

Vespasian shivered; his breath steamed in the cold night air as he stood, watching rank upon rank of shadowy figures emerging from the camp's gates. Even though the men had been given orders to muffle their equipment, tying rags around their scabbards and hobnailed sandals, there was still the occasional metallic clank or jangle that made Vespasian look nervously towards the dark shadow that was the fortified hill. The many fires within the settlement had all died down, leaving just a few trails of smoke rising as darker smudges in a sky that was almost completely devoid of light.

'It's a nice night for it,' a voice whispered behind him.

Vespasian turned to see the dim outline of his friend. 'What are you doing here, Magnus?'

'I haven't had a decent fight for a couple of years so I thought that I'd come and join in this one.'

'Then you're mad, risking your life when you could be in bed.'

'Not as mad as them in the fort; if there are really as few as we think then it's only a matter of time before we get in and they get dead. I don't understand them; they actually goaded us into attacking them by killing the scouts in front of us.'

'Yes, they know that they can expect no quarter now.'

'So why do it, then? They could have just held out for a few days and then negotiated their surrender once honour had been satisfied. It's almost as if they want us to kill them.'

'There is something strange about their behaviour; I can't quite put my finger on it.' He told Magnus of Hormus' theory about the lamp lighting itself.

'A warning, eh? Well, I suppose it's possible. The question is: what's the mistake that you're making? Is it about attacking this place in general? Or about attacking it at night? Or is it something completely different, like something to do with Sabinus, for example?'

'I don't know; but something is nagging me.'

The uneasy feeling continued to gnaw at Vespasian as he advanced with the first cohort to the base of the hill below the northeastern gate a hundred uphill paces away. He waited in the dark, running through the events of the last couple of days in his mind, as the other cohorts moved silently into position: Valens with the second away to his left below the southwestern gate, and Maximus with two Gallic auxiliary cohorts and the Hamians filling the ground between them. From the fort there came no sound; but the relief that Vespasian felt at still being in the position to surprise the defenders was tempered by his inability to exactly place his cause for concern. Unable to discuss the matter further with Magnus, standing next to him, owing to his order of complete silence, he was obliged to wait in fretful contemplation of the puzzle until he heard Valens' signal telling him that the furthest cohort was in place.

A thrice-repeated series of owl hoots echoed through the night; it was the sign that Vespasian had been waiting for. He nodded to Tatius who raised his arm and slowly brought it down; the signal was repeated by his brother centurions and the first cohort, with scaling ladders at the ready, moved off at the double up the slope.

The assault had begun.

Struggling to keep their footing in the near-total darkness, the men of the legion's élite cohort increased their speed as they passed through the gap in the outermost ditch; it was now imperative to get their ladders up and men onto the palisade before too many of the defenders were roused from their slumber. Vespasian kept pace with them, with Magnus wheezing at his side, as they ascended in virtual silence; he kept his eyes fixed on the dim outline of the defences but no movement was evident nor were any cries of alarm raised. He pressed on, his heart pounding, as the cohort filed through the gaps in the next couple of ditches, and still the alarm had not been raised within the fort. Then he remembered the urgency with which the three prisoners had been shouting before their execution.

Shit.

He swerved away from the cohort and stopped dead.

'What is it?' Magnus puffed, pulling up next to him.

'There's no one in there! That's what Cogidubnus' men were trying to warn us about before they were executed; they weren't pleading for their lives, they were shouting at us.'

'What about the men who killed them?'

'They are the only ones inside; enough men to light all those fires to make it look as if there's a whole war band in there. They've sacrificed themselves to draw us into the trap; the threat's from the north. I've got to get back. Find Tatius, and tell him to form the cohort up on the slope facing north as soon as he can.'

'Will he take an order from me?'

'He'd better or we could all end up dead.' Vespasian pushed his way back against the oncoming surge of legionaries until he reached the optio of the sixth century of the first cohort in his position at the rear of his men. 'Optio, get a message to Valens to

72

forget the assault and to have the second cohort take up position outside the southern gate, facing west; he'll get reinforcements and fresh orders soon.'

The man stared at him in incomprehension for a moment.

'Now!'

The optio saluted and raced off as the cohort came to a halt and ladders were thrown up the wall.

As the first men began the ascent of the palisade to either side of the gate a long booming note rumbled from a *cornu*; its call was taken up by the cornua of other cohorts. To his right, Vespasian saw the glow of the Hamians' oil-soaked portable braziers igniting; within a few moments hundreds of fire-arrows were streaking through the dark leaving trails of sparks in their wake as they disappeared over the walls into the hill-fort. No screams came from within as the Romans raised their voices into a battle roar.

Cursing the fact that he had, for silence's sake, left his legionary cavalry in the camp, Vespasian ran as he had never run before.

Almost tripping over his own feet, he hurtled back down the hill, grateful for the faint light provided by the Hamians' repeated, but wasted, volleys. After a lung-tearing final burst across the flat ground from the base of the hill, he came to the camp as the third cohort was marching out at the head of the rest of the legion.

Spotting their primus pilus, Vespasian slowed and turned, falling in next to him, catching his breath. 'Take your men at the double and form up facing north at the base of the slope. The first cohort will arrive on your left flank and the rest of the legion will form up on you; we will be taking a defensive position, understand?'

'What's happening, sir?'

Vespasian glanced to his right; and then he saw them coming out of the north. 'That's what's happening. Now go!'

In the distance a dozen or so faintly luminescent, tiny figures were seemingly gliding slowly towards them; behind them was a shadow, darker even than the night. The primus pilus took one look, bellowed an order, a cornu boomed twice and the cohort sped off with a jangling of gear and regular pounding footsteps across the dark ground. The rest of the legion streamed along behind them, orange flickers from the fires now burning up in the fort playing on their burnished iron armour and helmets.

Vespasian ran on to where the legion's cavalry detachment and his five thin-stripe tribunes were mounting, having walked their horses out of the camp. He pushed the youngest one out of the way. 'I need this, Marcius.' Leaping into the saddle he shot a glance at the most senior of the young tribunes. 'Blassius, now get this right: ride to Maximus and tell him to bring the Hamians and one of the Gallic cohorts to the bottom of the hill and then you take the other Gallic cohort round to the southern gate and link up with Valens and the second cohort; if he's not there get him out of the fort. Tell him that we're under attack from the north and he's to prevent any attempt to outflank us. Understood?'

'Yes, sir.'

'If they don't try and take our flank, he's to work his way around the fort and come at the bastards from the west; I'll send the Batavians to him. Report to me when you've done that. Now ride!'

With the briefest of salutes Blassius spun his horse on its hind legs and took off.

Vespasian glanced north over the heads of the legionaries still spilling out of the camp; he shivered. The spectral forms were less than two hundred paces off, their arms raised and waving. Behind them, now dully illuminated by the blazing fires on top of the hill, ran thousands of darkling figures, stretched out to either side and fading into the night.

Vespasian turned back to his tribunes. 'Caepio, find the other two Gallic cohorts and tell them to prevent any of the bastards coming around behind the camp, and tell Cogidubnus to bring his Britannic auxiliaries to me as soon as he can.' Without waiting for an acknowledgement he looked down at the young man he had unhorsed. 'Find the Batavian Cavalry, Marcius, and send them after Blassius and then get yourself a horse and bring the

Gallic auxiliary cavalry to the bottom of the hill. Sergius and Vibius, you follow me.' Cruelly kicking his mount into action, he sped away with the remaining tribunes and legionary cavalry following as a howl of hatred issued from the night-shrouded host bearing down on them.

The pace of the II Augusta's deployment was now frantic as the threat closed but Vespasian sensed that it was not fast enough as he raced along the column of doubling cohorts. Reaching the front he glanced to his right: the Britons were less than a hundred paces out and their pace seemed to have increased. Ahead he could see the first cohort forming up on the slope but to the left the Hamians and the Gauls were still a quarter of a mile away. 'Turn and face!' he bellowed at the third cohort's primus pilus.

The centurion shouted the order, raising his arm in the air, a cornu rumbled and the cohort's standard rocked from side to side; the third cohort came to a standstill a hundred paces short of the first's right flank.

There was no time to fill the gap.

Along the column the deep call of the cornu was echoed and the remaining cohorts halted and turned to face the enemy as the first long-range javelins struck. The luminescent figures could now clearly be made out as matted-haired, long-robed druids whose filthy garments glowed dimly in patches with an uncanny light; in their hands they brandished writhing snakes. Next to the central druid ran a huge man in a winged helmet shouting his triumph at having caught the legion deploying: Caratacus. Caratacus, the Britannic chieftain whom no Roman had seen since his defeat at the battle of the Afon Cantiacii two years previously; since then he had struck terror into every legionary in the new province for his ruthless irregular resistance to Rome's conquest. With ambushes, lethal harrying of supply columns, patrols and outposts and pitiless usage of prisoners and collaborators, Caratacus had more Roman blood on his hands than any other Briton on this island; and now he was about to cover himself in more. Vespasian realised that Caratacus had played him all along.

Vespasian led on the one hundred and twenty men of the legion's cavalry detachment to cover the gap as the javelin shower intensified, drumming down with a rapid staccato beat onto the upturned shields of the II Augusta.

With the Britons now no more than thirty paces from contact, Vespasian reached the right flank of the first cohort who had just completed a scrambled deployment four ranks deep. He slowed his mount. 'Turn right and form line!' The *lituus* blared and the troopers reined their horses in and around, turning from a column two abreast into a line two deep. Without waiting for the decurions to dress the line, Vespasian drew his sword, raised his arm and roared, 'Charge!'

As one, the legion's cavalry surged forward, taking their wild-eyed, frothing mounts directly into a canter and then quickly accelerating them into a gallop, swiftly closing the distance between them and the warriors heading for the gap in the Roman line and the chance to cut it in two with fatal consequence. Missiles rained down on them, felling a dozen horses as if an invisible tripwire had been placed in their path.

'Release!' Vespasian yelled, his voice raised an octave by the tension in his chest and belly. At a low trajectory, more than one hundred sleek javelins hissed towards the oncoming front rank of Britons, thumping into them, punching many back with arms flailing and mouths gaping with sudden agony. To either side hundreds of *pila* hurtled from the Roman ranks. The druids flung their squirming serpents with shrill curses at the legionaries as they drew their swords; they then stopped still, letting the warriors behind, led by a baying Caratacus, engulf them and take the full force of the barbed-pointed, lead-weighted weapons flitting across the gap between the two forces. Back and down many went, but the survivors dashed on for the final twenty paces, following with glee their leader who had worked the first chance in two years of annihilating one of Rome's killing machines.

Vespasian bellowed incoherently, urging his horse on as troopers drew their spathae and tensed their thighs around their mounts, bracing for impact. The joy of the warriors charging for the gap vanished and they cried in terror as the dim shapes of horsemen thundered towards them, threatening the horrific death of infantry caught in the open by cavalry. The men in the front ranks wavered and slowed, but the weight of numbers behind them pressed them ever forward; an instant later they collided in a maelstrom of human and bestial limbs. Vespasian swept his sword horizontally, cleaving heads and raised arms as if scything ripe barley as his mount ploughed on, head raised in fright, neighing shrilly, trampling every man in its path, leaving them broken and twisted. As the cavalry crunched into the fracturing Britannic line their momentum decreased violently; the horses shied from desperately wielded spears and swords and the troopers found themselves fighting in pockets, having failed to keep formation in the desperation of their disaster-averting charge. Vespasian reared his mount, using its flailing forelegs as weapons as he punched and cut with his short infantry *gladius* at the howling warriors around him, slicing open chests and splitting faces as the troopers to either side slashed their longer cavalry spathae to greater effect; but now, with the initial drive of the charge soaked up, the infantry began to regain the advantage of numbers. Without the benefit of a shield-wall the cavalry were in danger of being overwhelmed; many were ripped from their mounts.

Then a massive communal grunt of exertion rose from the left as the first cohort made contact and the brutal, mechanical sword work of the Roman war machine began to the accompaniment of the shrieks of eviscerated men. A similar sound followed from the right, but much amplified, as the rest of the legion slammed into the tribesmen who had so suddenly appeared out of the night.

Now the killing began in earnest.

Vespasian parried a wild cut from a long slashing-sword, its inferior quality iron buckling in the spark strewn impact; kicking his right leg forward, he slammed his hobnailed sole into the wielder's face, crushing the nose and punching the warrior back into the men behind, knocking them off balance. Taking advantage of the momentary lack of adversaries, he pulled his horse back and signalled for the second-rank trooper to take his place. Looking around he saw that the Hamians and Gauls behind them were now close enough to relieve them. Just to his right he glimpsed Sergius, one of the two tribunes whom he had brought with him, dragged screaming from his horse. Now was the time to withdraw his cavalry before too many more succumbed in what was, essentially, an infantry fight. They had served their purpose; the young man had not died in vain.

'Disengage!' he called to the *liticen*.

The shrill call of the lituus rose above the surrounding clamour; Vespasian urged his horse back towards the Hamians as the surviving troopers pulled away from the surging Britons, if they could. The warriors began to follow the retreating cavalry, mercilessly cutting down those still trapped in their midst, as they saw once again the gap open in the Roman line.

But the prefect of the Hamian archers knew what was required of him as he saw Vespasian galloping towards him yelling and pointing at the obvious danger. He immediately halted his command thirty paces from the gap; as the retreating troopers swerved left and right out of the Hamians' line of sight the eastern archers let fly a volley of shocking, close-range intensity. The front two ranks shot directly at the Britons racing through the rend in the Roman formation, drilling their shafts deep into the lead warriors, twisting them to the ground, long hair wrapping around agonised faces, whilst the rear two ranks aimed high; the second low-trajectory volley from the front ranks hit as their arrows poured down from above to bring the surge to an abrupt halt as if it had slammed into an unseen wall. A third and fourth volley, each with fewer than five heartbeats between them, beat the Britons back as if the wall itself was shunting forward, leaving only the dead behind it. Suffering grievous losses both from the head-on barrage and the metal-tipped hail pelting from the sky the warriors turned to flee, leaving the ground carpeted with their dead.

But their retreat exposed a new threat, a threat that made the blood run cold in all who beheld it. A dozen druids were revealed as the last of the warriors escaped to the safety of their shield-wall; they stood motionless, chanting, unheard above the ringing resonance of battle. But it was not their presence that chilled the heart, nor was it the fact that despite the continued volleys of the Hamians not one fletched missile touched the softly glowing figures; it was another presence, a presence unseen but not unfelt, a presence that surrounded them, protected them and exuded an air of malevolence that caused despair to well up within all who suffered it.

Vespasian gasped as if the air was in short supply as he gazed upon what he could not comprehend. Verica's words telling him of the druids while sailing back from the Isle of Vectis almost two years previously came back to him:

'When my people came to this island – the bards deem it to be about twenty-five generations ago – the people we supplanted worshipped different gods; they had built great henges in their honour, ancient beyond reckoning. The druids dedicated these places to our gods but still the presence and power of some of the island's gods persisted and they demanded worship. The druids took on that responsibility and uncovered their dark secrets and rituals; they keep the knowledge to themselves and they're welcome to it; but what I know of it fills me with dread.'

Was this then that power that the old King had spoken of? That 'cold power that cannot be used for good'?

For a few moments there was an audible lull in the fighting as the malice emanating from the eerie company pierced the consciousness of both Roman and Briton. The Hamians' archery tailed off; the druids began to move forward.

Vespasian roused himself from the dread-induced paralysis. If the power that the druids wielded was allowed to carry all before them then the line would be split asunder and the II Augusta would soon cease to exist. He kicked his reluctant horse onward, heading directly for the luminous group of priests as they slowly moved forward protected by an invisible aura; behind them the Britons had started to advance again.

Suppressing the horror welling up inside him, Vespasian screamed incoherently, brandishing his sword as he closed on the druids; such was their concentration on their incantation that they took no notice of the oncoming threat. He urged on his increasingly unwilling mount, ready to swipe the head from the lead druid's shoulders, but when he pulled his arm back for the killing blow he felt himself suddenly rise as if he had been hauled out of the saddle by an unseen hand from above. His horse reared, screeching; it toppled backwards as if violently shoved and Vespasian flew from its back. He landed with spine-jarring force amongst the dead; the air was pushed from his lungs and his eyes lost focus. As his vision cleared he saw the druids coming on in the glow of their own luminescence and the flicker of the conflagration now raging in the hill-fort: old and young, dark-haired or grey, all wore a symbol of the sun around their necks and had an image of the crescent moon hanging from their belts. All chanted in unison and all stared at him with cold satisfaction as he lay catching his breath on the ground, and Vespasian knew, with profound certainty, that they had come for him; they had drawn him towards them in a reckless charge.

Vespasian felt a chill grasp at his feet as the druids approached and the malevolent atmosphere enshrouding them began to slip over him; he stared in terror, unable to move, although he instinctively knew that not to do so would mean yielding to the power that was gradually creeping up his body. He screamed 'No!' repeatedly, deafening himself, and yet no sound came from his lips. He could see nothing else but the hunger of the druids for him alone; he could hear no sound from the battle that he knew was still raging. The chill had become so intense that his teeth were now chattering and his heartbeat, which should have pounded with fear, decreased. A flash crossed his vision from the right and he felt a jolt in the power, now slithering up his thighs, freezing his bones to the marrow. His muscles spasmed in shock and his chattering teeth clenched in sudden pain; his head jerked back and his jaw relaxed. The chill abruptly disappeared. He could hear again, he realised, and the sound was the cries of men dying in torment, men dying very close by; and mingled with their cries was a word, shouted repeatedly: 'Taranis!'

Pulling his arm from over his eyes he saw, as if Time's chariot had slowed, a sword rising through the air, flashing reflected fire-light, trailing dark gobbets of blood, as it left a head spinning in its wake above the robed body to which it had once belonged, standing as rigid as a statue. Mesmerised, he followed the sword's arc as it carved through the air to slice into the cheek of another druid, exploding his teeth from his mouth as his jaw slumped open to hang by a few gory sinews that vibrated with the inarticulate, bestial roar that issued from the gaping throat. Cogidubnus kicked the stricken man aside and slammed his weapon, point first, into the chest of the next druid; the rest turned and ran. Vespasian came back to his full senses; he grasped his sword lying next to him and jumped to his feet as the Britannic King despatched the rearmost druid with a savage, double-handed cut across the small of his back, severing the spine and slicing the kidneys in two.

Vespasian looked past the fleeing druids; the Britons were wavering, unwilling to advance into the gap now that the spell their priests had woven was broken; to either side the fighting had resumed with renewed intensity, the cold malice now replaced by hot blood-lust. 'Cogidubnus! With me!' Vespasian grabbed his horse's reins, leapt into the saddle and urged the beast away over the carpet of dead, out of the line of the Hamians' aim as they, as if coming out of a trance, prepared to release another volley.

The King chased after him as the shafts began to fly, picking off the remaining druids and felling many of the warriors who had moved closer.

'Thank you, my friend,' Vespasian croaked, once they were clear. 'I'll wait till later for an explanation.'

Cogidubnus grimaced. 'It will be hard for a Roman to understand.'

'Try me.' Vespasian pointed to the Britannic auxiliaries formed up behind the second cohort, along with the Gallic cavalry with Marcius at their head; behind them the last three cohorts of the II Augusta had deployed in a second line as a reserve. 'But in the meantime have your men ready, I'll need them soon.' With a nod, Vespasian kicked his horse and drove it towards the Hamians who were keeping up a relentless barrage of missiles at the shield-wall across the gap. But Vespasian knew that arrows would not hold the Britons back forever; arrows would eventually run out.

'Open your ranks to let the Gauls through,' he called to the Hamian prefect as he sped past, 'and then get your men onto the fort's palisade.' He just caught the man's hurried salute as he pushed on towards the Gallic infantry, directly behind. A series of cornua rumbles told him that his order had been promptly obeyed as he came to a skidding halt next to the cohort's command post.

Identifying the prefect as the same man who had let Caratacus through the line just two days previously, he resolved to forgive him if he played his part well. 'Prefect Galeo, take your men through the Hamians and link up with the first and second cohorts.'

'Yes, sir! Do you want—'

'Don't talk about it, do it!'

The prefect swallowed and crashed a salute. He bellowed the order to advance and the eight hundred Gauls moved forward at the double. Within a few moments they were filtering through the Hamians' formation; the archers ceased their volleys as they passed and then turned towards the fort once they were clear.

As the Gauls reached the open ground they broke into a charge, preventing the Britons from encroaching too far forward now that the arrows had stopped flying. Roaring the battle cry of their forefathers they threw themselves at the Britons' shield-wall with a mighty clash of iron.

The gap had been plugged but as Vespasian looked along the Roman line he saw that, in the centre, it had started to buckle and the reserve cohorts were retreating.

Once again digging his heels into the bruised flanks of his mount, Vespasian forced the tiring beast into action; speeding past the depleted legionary cavalry now rallying next to their Gallic comrades he caught sight of his prefect of the camp. 'Maximus! With me!'

The veteran spun his horse and accelerated it after his commander.

Within a hundred pounding heartbeats, Vespasian reached the first reserve legionary cohort as the bulge in the line deepened and the clamour from the Britannic host intensified. 'What the fuck are you doing marching away?' he roared at the primus pilus. 'Get your cohort in to support the centre with its weight.'

'But you just sent a legionary cavalry messenger with orders for us to fall back, sir.'

'Fall back? With the line threatening to break? I gave no such order; now, get forward before we're all dead.'

The centurion saluted and bellowed the order to turn and advance. Vespasian rode on up the reserve line of a further retreating two cohorts, halting them. 'You stay here with these cohorts, Maximus. We're holding a defensive position. Hold the line at all costs, understand?'

Maximus nodded and grinned. 'How long do you expect us to hold?'

Vespasian offered a quick prayer to Mars to guide him in the art of war as he turned his horse. 'Until I hear from Valens and can contrive a counter-attack that will break the Britons' will.'

CHAPTER IIII

VESPASIAN BROUGHT HIS mount to a violent halt next to Cogidubnus, who was waiting with the young tribunes, Marcius and Vibius; behind them stood the Britannic auxiliaries with the Gallic cavalry and the now rallied remnants of the legionary cavalry, fewer than eighty troopers in total. Blassius arrived moments later.

'I left the other Gallic auxiliaries with Valens and the second cohort as you ordered, sir,' the tribune reported, shouting against the din of combat along the third of a mile front. 'The Batavians were just arriving with him as I left. He said that there was no one in the fort.'

'I know there was no one in the fort,' Vespasian replied, trying to keep his voice level but failing. 'What about a flank attack? Were the Britons trying to force a way around behind the fort?'

'No, sir, not by the time I left. Valens had begun to move around the hill; he reckoned that, provided he doesn't encounter opposition, it would take a quarter of an hour before he would be in position for a flank attack.'

Vespasian ran a hand through his hair, his face taut. 'Yes, that's what I thought.' He glanced up the Roman line; the reinforced centre had pushed back but the Britons' assault showed no signs of abating. 'We need to break them before they wear us down. Are your men ready to be blooded, Cogidubnus?'

The King held his look. 'They will prove their loyalty to Rome and reap their revenge on Caratacus for his years of subjugation of the Atrebates and the Regni.'

'I'm sure they will. Have some men collect the ladders left up by the gate and then take your lads down into the outermost ditch. I'll meet you there; we can use it to work our way behind the Britons' line.'

'The rebel tribes' line,' Cogidubnus corrected.

'Indeed, the rebels' line.' Vespasian turned back to Blassius. 'Go up to the Hamians …' Vespasian faltered, looking over the tribune's shoulder; there were no archers lining the fort's palisade silhouetted by the fires within. 'The Hamians! Where in Hades are they?'

Cogidubnus pointed south; the rear of the eastern archers' column could just be seen, a few hundred paces away, disappearing into the night. 'They turned around and marched off south soon after you left.'

'I gave no such order.'

'I saw a legionary cavalry messenger ride up to them and then they turned and left. I assumed that he must have come from you.'

'That's the second false message.' He paused, suddenly realising what was happening. 'Alienus! It must be him. Which way did he go?'

'I didn't notice.'

Blassius frowned with recollection. 'One passed me just now heading around the fort towards Valens' position.'

'Gods below! Blassius, take a half turma of the Gauls and get after him; capture him before he stops Valens with another false message. I want him alive.'

Blassius saluted and hurried off, and Vespasian turned his attention to Marcius and Vibius. 'Marcius, take another half turma of the Gauls and get those Hamians back to the fort as fast as they can run; and I mean run. I want them on the palisade shooting down into the flank of that hairy horde now! Vibius, we're going to force a gap between the ditch and the left flank of the line; when we do, take the rest of the cavalry through and take the long-hairs in the rear.'

The young man saluted, determination written on his face but with anxiety in his eyes. Vespasian prayed that the former would overcome the latter as he turned back to Cogidubnus. 'Let's get this done; we don't have much time.'

'It looks like we'll have to get out of that ditch without archer support,' Cogidubnus observed.

'I'm afraid so, my friend.'

'Then it's just as well that a quarter of my lads have slings.'

'What are you doing here?' Vespasian asked, seeing Magnus walking down from the fort's gates; behind him a party of Britannic auxiliaries collected up the discarded ladders used in the abortive assault while the rest of the cohort clambered down into the outermost defensive ditch just behind the first cohort's line.

'Ah! Watching the shambles I think is the nicest way I can put it. What the fuck's going on?'

'Alienus has been riding around the field posing as my messenger, giving false orders; but despite that, we've just managed to hold off a surprise night attack for the last quarter of an hour in what I would describe as a desperate scramble to stay alive, not a shambles. Now if you've got nothing better to do than criticise then I would suggest that you piss off back to bed and wait to see whether you wake up in the morning with a Briton's spear up your arse or not.'

Magnus looked out over the battle raging below. 'No, I'll stay. What made you guess they were coming?'

Vespasian turned towards the ditch. 'There's no time for that now.'

'Where're you going?'

'Down into that ditch with a whole load of Britons who promise me that they would rather kill other Britons than Romans.'

'Then I'd better come along and make sure that they keep that promise.'

The cacophony of ringing metallic clashes and human cries of pain, encouragement, fear and despair grew deafening as Vespasian weaved his way through the sharpened stakes embedded in the bottom of the ditch; the Britannic auxiliaries followed behind. They were level with the line of combat but the rampart on the front lip of the ditch hid them from the combatants' sight.

Vespasian raised an arm, halting the auxiliaries. He looked up to his left; the silhouetted palisade was still devoid of archers. 'Shit!' he hissed under his breath, turning to Cogidubnus next to him. 'We can't afford to wait. We'll have to do this with your slingers; how many have you got?'

'The front rank of each century, so two hundred.'

'They'll be spread out along the column; how do we sort them out to send them forward first?'

'I've already done it; they're all at the front. I'll take them forward with five of the ladders to about fifty paces behind the rebels' line and get them into position. As soon as we're there I'll give a signal of a repeated short note on the cornu and we'll start shooting into their rear.'

Vespasian waited until the slingers were clear before ordering the cohort's primus pilus to lean the remaining ten ladders at intervals along the side of the ditch with the remains of the centuries, each headed by its centurion, waiting in readiness at the bottom. He took his place at the foot of the first.

As he watched the cohort get into position in the gloom of the ditch, Vespasian caught his breath and tried to steady himself after the frenetic race to save the legion. It had been less than half an hour since he had stepped out of the first cohort's formation realising that there was an unseen danger approaching from the north; his pulse quickened again as he contemplated what would have happened had he not made the connection in time. He looked at Magnus next to him. 'If it hadn't been for Hormus we could well be dead by now.'

'So even the humblest of slaves can save a legion.'

'Indirectly, yes. I realised what I had overlooked: the significance of Cogidubnus' scouts in the north not sending any message: they were all dead. Then I put together two things that we'd talked about the other night and realised that we had been drawn into a trap. Caratacus put himself up as bait and sacrificed those people in the last hill-fort to draw me here; he'd arranged to meet up with all those horsemen after he'd escaped to make his tracks obvious. He wanted me to know where he was going. But to make absolutely sure I followed, Alienus gave his name to the auxiliary prefect knowing that I would have found out by now that it was he who had betrayed Sabinus – and to find Sabinus I need Alienus; so I had to come.'

'I suppose when you look at it that way it was all too neat.'

'Exactly; and then when there was no alarm raised in the fort and I remembered those condemned men shouting so urgently I knew that there was no one in there; it was a trap and we'd been goaded into a night attack.'

'And the savages were just waiting out there to the north and they very nearly got us.'

'They still might.'

Magnus felt the weight of his gladius, contemplating the honed blade. 'Not if I have any say in the matter.'

Vespasian looked along the ditch; the centuries were in position. 'Come on, Cogidubnus, what's keeping you?'

After a few more thumped heartbeats that added to the tension racking his body, Vespasian heard the low call of a cornu from behind the Britons' line. With a nod to the primus pilus he pushed the ladder upright so that its head appeared over the top of the rampart and scaled its twenty-foot height with a speed that reflected the desperation of the situation. Propelling himself onto the top of the rampart he found himself level with the third rank of the Roman defence, who were struggling to keep their footing on the steep slope, hunched down behind their shields as they pushed them into the backs of the men in front in a desperate attempt to hold back the horde that had pressed them for so long. Unlike the Romans, the Britons were not tightly packed but rather in loose formation to best utilise their long slashing-swords; they flowed back and forth hacking and cutting at the rectangular semi-cylindrical shields and iron helmets of the rigid front rank of the II Augusta's élite cohort, braving the blood-dripping blades that punched out from between the gaps in the shields.

With a quick glance to his right to assure himself that Vibius had brought the cavalry into position, Vespasian swept his sword from its scabbard and pelted along the crown of the earthwork, Magnus and the primus pilus following, as slingshots cannoned into the exposed backs of the rearmost Britannic warriors, felling many and causing consternation to spread through their haphazard, loose ranks. Taken by surprise, the Britons looked up to see Roman soldiers, with long hair flowing from beneath their helms and drooping moustaches framing their bellowing mouths, appearing above them; for many the lapse in concentration meant that it was the last thing they saw.

'Second Augusta! Second Augusta!' Vespasian roared in warning to the legionaries below, hurling himself into the midst of their foes, punching his shield boss into the upturned face of a startled warrior and taking him crashing to the ground underneath him as all around the unblooded auxiliaries of Cogidubnus' cohort leapt down onto their fellow countrymen in the name of Rome.

Raising himself to his knees, Vespasian jabbed his sword tip under the ribs of the concussed man beneath him whilst raising his shield over his head, deflecting a downward cut from his left. Bellowing obscenities, Magnus barrelled past, body-checking the perpetrator as behind them more and more auxiliaries piled down from the earthworks, crashing into the Britons' flank, using their downhill momentum to great advantage. Without order in their attack they had no formation but careered on regardless of lack of support to either side, creating a melee of individual combats as they inveigled their way deep into the Britons' fracturing flank. The aim of the slingers adjusted with the auxiliaries' progress, thinning out the rearmost warriors so that the push through them was becoming oblique. But then came the sound that Vespasian had been hoping for: the wet hollow thuds of arrows thumping into chests close by.

Punching his sword into the temple of a kneeling wounded warrior, Vespasian pulled back from the front rank of the advance and shouted at the auxiliary primus pilus, 'Get some order into your lads, close them up!' The officer acknowledged and drove forward roaring at his men to form up on him. Vespasian stood, breathing deeply, allowing the rest of the cohort to stream past, their rate of progress gradually increasing in line with the panic spreading along the Britons' line.

But Vespasian knew that it was far from over. Looking behind him he saw that they had cleared about twenty paces of the first cohorts' frontage; it was enough. 'Pull your men back from the rampart, Livianus!' he ordered, picking out the centurion from amongst the bloodied, exhausted front-rank legionaries by the transverse horsehair plume on his helmet. 'Make a gap for the cavalry.'

Livianus nodded his understanding and immediately began shouting at his battle-weary men as Vespasian ran back to the rampart and scrambled up it. Looking down along the battle's front from his high position on the hill his heart faltered: it was concave and the two cohorts that he had left in reserve with Maximus had been deployed; there were no reinforcements left. But worse still: there was now fire in the II Augusta's camp; he could do nothing but pray that Caepio, with the last two Gallic cohorts, could deal with the incursion. 'Valens, where are you?' he muttered to himself as the gap between the first cohort and the ramparts finally opened. Vibius' arrival at the head of the cavalry was as prompt as Vespasian could have wished for. The young tribune stopped by Vespasian to return his horse; Vespasian mounted and spoke to Vibius privately. 'Our centre could break very soon if it's not supported. Cause as much carnage to them there as you can, buy us time with your lives or we're all dead; understand?'

Vibius swallowed hard and sucked in a lungful of air through his nose as he realised what was being asked of him and his men. 'Yes, legate, I understand; trust me to do my duty.'

Vespasian reached over and grasped the young man's shoulder. 'Thank you. Now go.'

Vibius kicked his mount forward, looking dead ahead with blank eyes; the Gallic and legionary cavalry streamed through the gap behind him unaware of what their legate was expecting of them.

'You look like you've just been told of a death in the family,' Magnus said, walking over to Vespasian as the last of the cavalry sped out into the open; his forearms, chest and face were smeared with blood.

'Not me,' Vespasian replied, his face grim as he watched the troopers ride down the hill into the distance. 'But I've just demanded that perhaps five hundred other families will get that news.'

'Well, sir, it's a lot better than eight thousand families.'

'I know that, so I had no choice.' Vespasian shook himself. He felt sick to his very core but he knew that there had been no alternative if he was to preserve the main body of his command, and also his career, intact. He forced himself to watch as Vibius and his cavalry thundered into the Britons' centre, just grey silhouettes at that distance but each silhouette was a man whom, in all likelihood, he had sent to die.

Where was Valens?

Cogidubnus' auxiliaries had cleared the Britons from the hill; the first cohort was now unopposed and the Hamians up on the palisade were too distant to be able to shoot with any effectiveness into the enemy. Still with no sign of Valens' flanking move, Aulus Plautius' advice came to Vespasian's mind: *In war you should never wish for what you don't have, it takes your mind from using what you do have to its best effect.* 'Magnus, run up to the fort and tell Marcius to bring the Hamians down here. I want them to follow up the advance, just behind Cogidubnus' left flank to ensure that none of the hairy bastards slip round.'

'Oh, so I'm a messenger-boy still, am I?'

Vespasian looked over his shoulder as he urged his horse away down the slope. 'Just do it!' Galloping along the body-strewn frontage of the first cohort he came to Tatius' position on its extreme right abutting the Gallic auxiliaries whose timely charge had plugged the gap in the Roman line, less than half an hour before. 'I'm glad to see you still with us, primus pilus.'

'A good few of my lads aren't.' Tatius looked down at the tangled corpses, both Briton and Roman, and spat a blood-tinged gobbet of saliva into the face of a gutted warrior at his feet; a slight twitch indicated that there was still life within. 'They were fucking relentless; we only managed to rotate the ranks once.' Tatius slammed his foot onto the man's throat, crushing his windpipe.

'Take your cohort and double round to the centre. Maximus is in command there and he needs help.'

Despite his exhaustion, Tatius gave a sharp, veteran's salute. 'We'll be there.'

Fighting off the fatigue he shared with Tatius, Vespasian moved on to find the prefect of the Gallic cohort, now half clear of the fighting as Cogidubnus' auxiliaries, finally in proper military formation, shoulder to shoulder, swept their countrymen before them; on their flank the slingers maintained a continuous barrage to ease their path through the dead.

Although the screams of battle rose up to the heavens in a multi-octave dissonance and the pounding of metal and leather-clad wood pulsated in manic accompaniment, Vespasian was now inured to all sound; all except one: the sound that he had prayed for. It came from over his left shoulder, faint but to Vespasian plainly audible: the shrill blare of a lituus. He turned in his saddle; the Batavians appeared from behind the hill, flecked with firelight from the inferno above them. Behind them doubled two cohorts, one legionary and one auxiliary; Valens had arrived. Now was the time to take the initiative.

'Prefect!' Vespasian called, finally spotting the Gallic cohort's commander. 'Pull your men in behind Cogidubnus' lads; I'll order him to move aside so that you can take his place and create a broader front. One more effort from you and we'll be safe.'

The prefect nodded grimly and turned to his primus pilus to sort out the details of the manoeuvre as Vespasian kicked on towards Cogidubnus, his heart feeling lighter than at any time since he had woken to find his lamp mysteriously burning, two nights ago. With the first cohort to reinforce it, the centre could withstand for a while yet and now that Valens had arrived he could take the fight to the Britons rather than just scrambling a defence. They would win through.

As his horse pounded past manoeuvring auxiliaries, Vespasian felt, for the first time in his life, a real closeness to his guardian god, Mars, who had warned him of his oversight. Mars, the god to whom his father had dedicated him at his naming ceremony, nine days after his birth, at which the portents, Vespasian knew from an overheard conversation of his parents, had predicted a destiny, preordained. Yet what that destiny was, he did not know; his mother had sworn all those present to secrecy and no one had ever spoken of it to him. However, now he had witnessed the power of the god, he could believe that, whatever his destiny, Mars truly held his hands over him and would guide him to it.

The lituus blared again as Vespasian drew up next to Cogidubnus and quickly gave him his orders. He looked up; the Batavians had galloped ahead of Valens' main force; now, perhaps, he could relieve Vibius – if the young lad still lived. With a nod to Cogidubnus, he set out to intercept the Batavians, just two hundred paces away; Ansigar rode at their head with Blassius next to him. Vespasian cursed under his breath: Alienus must have avoided capture.

The gap quickly closed between Vespasian and the oncoming cavalry; to his left the Hamians could be seen jogging down the hill. He swerved his mount around and joined the head of the column next to Blassius. 'Alienus?'

Blassius shook his head. 'He just disappeared; we caught sight of him as we went around the hill but he saw us. When we reached Valens there was no sign of him and no one could remember seeing him.'

'Shit! Well, I'll worry about him later; get back to Valens and tell him that as soon as he is level with Cogidubnus they're to swing round and crush the Britons against the legion; Cogidubnus is ready for it but Valens must hurry before the Britons see the trap coming.'

Blassius pulled his horse away and galloped back to the oncoming infantry. Vespasian felt his heart quicken but this time it was not with fear or anxiety, but the scent of victory: victory that just under an hour ago had seemed an impossibility in the face of the horror that had sprung out of the night. Smiling to himself, thinking of how Magnus would have spat and held his thumb to avert the evil-eye if he had shared such premature thoughts with him, he turned to Ansigar, the bearded, senior decurion of the Germanic Batavian cavalry. 'We head over there.' He pointed to where Vibius' depleted command could be seen rallying, making ready for another charge at the deeply packed Britannic centre that had now been forced to fight both to the front and rear.

'And after they break?'

'Ride down as many as you can; I want them to remember the Second Augusta.'

'What about her Batavian auxiliaries?'

'I want the Britons who come into contact with you to remember nothing – ever again.'

Ansigar grinned beneath his full, blond beard. 'I pray that your wish will be granted.' He shouted in his guttural language to the liticen behind him as he swung to the right aiming for the centre of the battle. With a blare of the instrument, his finely trained troopers started to fan out and without losing pace the column began to manoeuvre into a line, four deep.

But then shouts from within the ala disrupted the move. Vespasian turned to his left to see a lone trooper veering away to the north; in the dim light he could see that he was not wearing trousers like the rest of the Batavians, but was dressed in the uniform of the legionary cavalry. 'Alienus!' Vespasian pulled his horse left, pointing at a couple of troopers in the front rank. 'You two with me! Ansigar, you ride on.' He sped after the fleeing spy, the two Batavians following him, out into the darkness beyond the reach of the twin fires now blazing on the hill and in the camp. He trusted the animal sense of his horse not to stumble but kept as close to Alienus' track as possible; he would be able to risk more speed than Alienus who would be riding blind. He could just see him and judged that he was about fifty paces ahead. Glancing at his two companions, he counted at least half a dozen javelins in their holsters. 'We've got to bring him down, understand?'

The Batavians growled their affirmation, reaching back for a javelin each whilst controlling the mounts with prodigious skill as they thundered over the ever-darkening ground.

'Pass me one,' Vespasian shouted, stretching out his hand whilst keeping his eyes fixed upon his quarry; he sensed that they were gaining. He felt a javelin pressed into his palm; he fiddled with it, getting his forefinger through the looped thong midway down its shaft. They rode on, the barrel chests of their mounts heaving. Despite the darkness, Alienus was becoming clearer; they were gaining.

'We'll try a shot!' Vespasian called, clenching his calves tight around his horse's sweating flanks to gain purchase. The Batavians did the same, throwing back their right arms. With colossal effort all three raised themselves from their saddles as they thrust their arms forward, hurling the missiles away into the darkness. Alienus remained mounted but suddenly skewed to the left and then just as quickly veered back again to the right.

Vespasian thrust out his hand again. 'Another!' A javelin was quickly passed over as Alienus continued to swerve, shortening the distance between them. Again Vespasian braced himself against his mount, judging the diminished distance and the rate of Alienus' deviations. With another huge effort he and his companions hurled their sleek weapons, but this time at a lower trajectory. Alienus' mount again changed direction abruptly and then veered back with equal force but not smoothly; it let out a shrill neigh that rose in pitch, bucking to try and remove the javelin embedded deep in its rump. Vespasian slowed his horse as the stricken animal kicked out again with its back legs, this time with such violence that it dislodged its rider. Jumping from his saddle, Vespasian sprinted forward, whipping his sword from its scabbard as the unhorsed man crunched down onto his back. He rolled over and got to his knees as Vespasian brought the flat of his sword slamming round onto the side of his head, sending him rolling to the ground, unconscious. Vespasian kicked the body over and looked down at the man who had betrayed Sabinus, his brother.

CHAPTER V

V ESPASIAN AND MAGNUS picked their way through the piles of
bodies that marked the line of combat like driftwood delin-
eating the extent of high tide. Dawn had broken in the east, red as
blood as if in mimicry of the slaughter that had preceded it. The
dead lay on the field in their hundreds, twisted, broken, dismem-
bered and slimed with offal, blood and faeces. Here and there a
groan indicated that life still lingered in some pain-racked body.

As the sun rose the scale of the killing became clear. Valens'
cohorts had joined up with Cogidubnus' auxiliaries and the
Gauls and together they had swung round onto the rear of the
Britons, trapping many and consigning them to an inevitable
death; no quarter had been offered or expected. Caratacus,
however, had seen the danger that had appeared out of the west
and, realising that his chance to annihilate one of Rome's
dreaded war machines had passed, had fled back into the night
with the majority of his warriors. The Batavians and the surviving
Gallic and legionary cavalry had pursued them, harrying the
broken Britons and preventing any attempts to rally. They had
still not returned but their passage north was littered with
corpses that were now being picked out by the rising sun.

'There must be ten of their dead for every one of our lads,'
Magnus observed as they came across a knot of legionary casualties that were being untangled by one of the many burial parties
searching the field for Roman dead and wounded.

'The first reports indicate that we lost over three hundred
with double that wounded,' Vespasian replied looking into the
lifeless eyes of a young legionary and bending down to close
them before walking on. 'Most of our dead or wounded were
either from the cavalry or the fourth cohort at the centre of the

line, but every unit suffered to some degree. Some will need a couple of days to lick their wounds.'

'What about the others?'

'I'll use them to probe north and make sure that the enemy aren't regrouping, and whilst that's happening I'm going to use the time to find Sabinus.'

'Has Alienus said anything?'

'Not yet, he's still groggy but he will; every man has his limit and I intend to find Alienus'.' Vespasian stopped next to a dead auxiliary. 'He's from the cohort that plugged the gap, so they should be around here somewhere.'

After a short while searching amongst the dead they found what they were looking for: the corpses of the druids. Vespasian knelt down next to an older man whose long, grey beard and hair were matted into clumps and festooned with what looked to be the bones of birds. Looking at the dead man's dirty robe, Vespasian ran his hand over it and realised that the staining was not just the result of years of continuous usage without thought of hygiene; some of it had been put there deliberately. As he pulled his hand away he found it covered with fine off-white threads. On closer examination of the robe he saw that it was coated with these fibres; each area of staining was in fact a colony of thousands of threads interwoven with each other and sewn onto the garment. 'They look like the roots of some sort of fungus,' he observed, pulling off a chunk and sniffing it.

Magnus picked off another bit and placing it in the palm of one hand he cupped the other over it and put his eye to the small hole left at the join; after a few moments he looked back at Vespasian, proffering his hands. 'Have a look.'

As Vespasian's eye adjusted to the dark he became aware of a faint luminescence within. 'So that's how they make their robes glow in the dark. It's not magic after all, it's just luminous fungus roots, thousands of them.'

'You'd better make that known around the legion; the lads will feel much better if they understand that the glowing robes are just a trick and not the result of some spell or influence from one of their accursed gods.'

'I'll get the robes stripped off them and display them in front of the praetorium. It'll help morale.' Vespasian got to his feet and hailed one of the burial parties; having given instructions to the optio commanding them, Vespasian and Magnus headed back towards the still smouldering camp past where the body of young Vibius had been found. 'I'll write to his parents. They should be told that he did his duty despite knowing that my orders would mean his death.'

'You shouldn't blame yourself for it, sir, he's not the first man you've sent to his death and nor will he be the last.'

'Yes, I know, but he was the first man I did so knowingly – and he knew it too. I could see in his eyes that he understood in that instant that there would be no career in Rome's service to bring credit to him and his family, and yet he went.'

'He certainly wouldn't have had a future if he hadn't gone.'

'He couldn't have been more than twenty. I keep on wondering what I would have done at that age in his position.'

'Exactly the same. When Fortuna grabs you by the foreskin and leads you to an early death there's fuck all that you can do about it. It's just the way the dice roll and it don't do to brood on it. Give him a decent funeral, praise his name to the lads and then forget about him because one thing's for sure and that is he ain't coming back from across the Styx; but what he did last night prevented Charon from being very busy today ferrying the entire legion over to the far bank.'

Vespasian nodded. His face tensed as he contemplated what might have happened.

'And stop looking so strained; it's not good for the legate to appear as if he's struggling with a solid stool.'

'I nearly lost the legion last night because I marched into a trap! I'm not surprised that I look shaken; even had I survived, it would have been the end of my career, and everything that I've worked for would have disappeared.'

'But you didn't lose it, did you? You saw the trap just before it was sprung and it was your actions that turned what would have been a crushing defeat into some sort of victory. Now whether you want my advice or not, you're going to have it. Put last night behind you, stop feeling sorry for yourself because a few people died and look instead at what you gained: another hill-fort garrisoned, a demoralising and humiliating repulse of Caratacus' best move so far that may well make a few more chieftains question his leadership, and, above all, on a personal level, you can claim the glory of another victory, not to mention the fact that you have Alienus who may well hold the information that will help you find Sabinus.'

Vespasian put his arm around his friend's shoulders. 'You're right of course; it's just that the shock hasn't quite worn off yet. I need to concentrate on what's important now: I'll send for Cogidubnus; I need to talk with him before we question his cousin.'

Alienus suppressed a scream and shook his head repeatedly, sending sweat arcing left and right in the brazier's glow; the stench of his scorched flesh filled the dim interior of the tent whose only piece of furniture was the wooden chair to which the naked spy was strapped.

'I'll ask you again before the iron goes further up your thigh: who has my brother and where are they keeping him?'

'I've told you, he's dead!'

'Then tell me where his body is.'

'I don't know!'

Vespasian nodded at the optio standing next to the brazier; with his hand protected by a thick leather glove the man pulled the iron from the fire, its tip glowing red. 'Near the top of his thigh so that his cock and balls feel the heat; but don't touch them – yet.'

This time Alienus could not stifle the scream that pulsed through his whole body together with the searing agony of the burn; his wrists and ankles strained against the straps that bound them as his cry of torment wafted the smoke rising from the blackened flesh.

Both Magnus and Cogidubnus winced at the suffering but Vespasian remained resolute. 'The next one will roast your genitals and you'll be pissing like a woman for the rest of your days.'

Alienus hyperventilated for a few moments after the iron was withdrawn and replaced in the brazier; blood had started to flow from beneath his bindings. 'You're going to kill me anyway so that's no threat.'

'Who said anything about killing you? How can I expect you to tell me the truth if you've nothing to gain by doing so? I'm going to let you live; Cogidubnus has agreed to vouch for you and keep you under house arrest in his kingdom. It's just up to you to decide in what condition you take up his generous offer: whole or with crucial bits missing?'

Alienus lifted his head; his mouth was set rigid with pain but his eyes narrowed in hatred as he regarded his cousin. 'Live at the whim of that piece of filth? The man who, along with my grandfather, betrayed our people and sold our freedom to Rome.'

With one fluid motion, Cogidubnus stepped forward and slapped the flat of his palm across Alienus' face, jerking his head right in a spray of sweat and blood. 'Now you listen to me and try to do so without your callow mind being clouded by the confused thinking of youth. For the last two years you have aided Caratacus, the man who supplanted your grandfather from his throne and forced your people, the confederation of the Atrebates and the Regni, to pay tribute and provide men to fight for him. Your grandfather freed them from that shame and I preserve that freedom, whereas you would hand us back into the thrall of Caratacus.'

'I would free us from Rome! We pay tribute to the Emperor and our men fight in his auxiliary cohorts; what's the difference?'

Cogidubnus sneered, shaking his head, before carrying on slowly as if talking to a bright but misguided child. 'The difference is that we get something for our money when we send it to Rome: we get peace and the chance to live on our own land under our own laws with our own king.'

'You!'

'Yes, me. But what did we get when we paid tribute to Caratacus? Poorer, whilst his tribe, the Catuvellauni, got richer. We had a king who did not live amongst us or even speak our dialect yet expected our men to fight and die for him in his endless petty wars away to the north and west, waged solely for his own glory. Did our men get paid for fighting for him? No, yet they were forced to; however, Rome gives them silver and will give them citizenship when they finish their service and they fight as volunteers, not conscripts.'

'But they fight their own countrymen.'

'Countrymen who two years ago looked down on them as the spawn of a defeated kingdom and treated them little better than slaves.'

Vespasian stepped back into the light of the brazier. 'Rome is here to stay, Alienus, and it makes no difference to us how harsh the terms of surrender are for each tribe or each individual; that's something that your cousin here has realised. Help me get my brother back and you can live under the supervision of Cogidubnus with the chance of reconciliation with Rome. Thwart me and I shall burn you bit by bit not for your submission but for the pleasure of doing it. You have my word on both of those assertions.'

Alienus glanced at Cogidubnus and then back at Vespasian. 'Why should I trust you?'

'Because I want Sabinus back more than I want you dead, and if giving you your life is the price that I have to pay then so be it. I won't go back on the bargain, as Mars is my witness, because to do so would put Sabinus' life in jeopardy.' Again he nodded at the optio who once more took up the glowing iron. 'So, I'll ask you one final time as an intact man, who has my brother and where are they holding him?'

Alienus' eyes flashed around the room, looking at each man in turn; indecision played in them.

'Take the hair,' Vespasian whispered to the optio, who smiled.

With a quick jab, the iron was thrust into the thick growth of pubic hair; with a flash it ignited, encircling Alienus' genitals with a brief ring of fire. The young man yelped, looking down at his burning crotch. 'The druids! The druids have him!'

'That's better. Where?'

'I don't know!'

'Of course you do. Optio.'

Alienus watched the iron being withdrawn from within the brightly burning charcoal and brought slowly towards his singed groin. He looked in terror at Vespasian who raised his eyebrows questioningly.

Alienus broke. 'I left him with the druids at the Great Henge of Stone, up on the plain, east of here. They're keeping him for sacrifice at the summer solstice. I was meant to lure you after him to this place where we were going to crush your legion and capture you so that it could be a double sacrifice.'

'Which druids did you give him to?' Cogidubnus demanded, stepping forward.

'Druids from the sacred springs.'

'Does that mean anything to you?' Vespasian asked Cogidubnus.

He nodded slowly. 'Yes, they maintain the rituals of an ancient goddess, one our forefathers found already here when we arrived. She lives in a valley about thirty miles to the north and never leaves it; she constantly has to tend to her five hot springs and her sacred groves. She commands great power – she can heat water so that it's too hot to touch. Her name is Sullis.'

'We could be there and back in two days; three at the most,' Vespasian said, holding his arms out for Hormus to untie the straps securing his back- and breastplates.

'Assuming we don't run into the remnants of that army that fled in the same direction,' Magnus pointed out, slumping down on a couch.

Cogidubnus looked dubious. 'It's one thing travelling to and fro; it's quite another snatching your brother, if he *is* there, from Sullis' valley. Who knows what powers protect it; you felt the malevolence that surrounded those druids last night.'

Vespasian rubbed his sore shoulders as Hormus bent to remove his greaves. 'But you managed to break through whatever was shielding them.'

Cogidubnus pulled a pendant from under his tunic. 'This is the Wheel of Taranis, god of thunder.' He held out a golden, four-spoked wheel, the size of his palm, which Vespasian recognised as having belonged to Verica. 'Taranis is a true god of the

Celts; he rules the heavens and spins his celestial wheel to produce thunder and lightning. He has great power and my people have worshipped him since we came out of the east, long before we crossed the straits from Gaul to Britannia. My uncle gave me this on his deathbed; every king of the Atrebates and Regni who wears it can expect Taranis' protection, even against the dark gods that the druids awoke on this isle. So wearing this I had no fear when I attacked those druids; the power they wield is only effective if men are frozen by its malice and fear to oppose it.'

'Frozen? That's exactly how it felt; it was a deep chill in the very marrow of my bones, creeping up me so that all I could think of was the horror of being engulfed by it. I was helpless. But tell me, is it a trick like their luminous robes or is it real?'

'It's real, I can promise you that, but what dark gods they conjure to create it, I don't know; the druids keep the secrets of their lore buried deep.'

'Next time I shall sacrifice to my guardian god before facing them.'

'That might help against the power we experienced last night but against Sullis in her own valley? I don't know.'

Vespasian sat as Hormus took his armour away for cleaning. 'What do you suggest then, Cogidubnus? I have no choice but to go; it's my brother.'

'Firstly, if we go we can't take a large force; if they suspect we're trying to rescue Sabinus, they'll kill him. Ten men at the most; I'll pick the best of my auxiliaries and get some clothes stripped off the dead for us all. Secondly, we need to protect ourselves somehow. There is a man that I've heard about but never met; he came here from one of the eastern provinces of the Empire about eight years ago. I've been told that he has an understanding with the druids; for some reason they fear him. Perhaps he could help us.'

'How?'

'He preaches a new religion and is said to have great power; not the cold power of the dark gods of this land but power of a different sort, a power that helps him withstand malevolence.'

'Is he a Jew?' Magnus asked.

'A Jew? I don't know what that is but if it's someone who believes in just one god then he could be, for that's what I've heard about his beliefs. He prays to one god and believes that a crucified kinsman of his was that god's prophet.'

Vespasian looked at Magnus, understanding dawning on his face. 'You don't think that it's him, do you?'

'I certainly hope it is because he owes you a massive favour for freeing him from those slavers in Cyrenaica.'

'And he owes my brother for releasing the body of his crucified kinsman to him and not the Temple Guards when Sabinus was a quaestor in Judaea. He's honour-bound to help us if he can. Where is he, Cogidubnus?'

'I'm told that he was given land on a large tor by Budoc, King of the Dobunni, between here and Sullis' valley, about fifteen miles away. If we leave at midday, after a couple of hours' sleep, we could be there before dusk.'

'Do you know this man's name?'

'It was a name like I'd never heard before.'

'Is it Yosef?'

The King thought for a few moments. 'Yes, that sounds right, Yosef.'

Vespasian walked into his sleeping quarters to find Hormus still wiping the congealed blood from his armour with a damp cloth. 'Leave it, I won't be needing it during the next couple of days; you can do it while I'm away.'

The slave rose, keeping his eyes to the ground. 'Yes, master. Shall I prepare something to eat?'

'Let me sleep for two hours first.'

With a deferential bow of the head, Hormus turned to leave.

'Hormus,' Vespasian said softly, stopping his slave. 'What's the greatest achievement in your life?'

'I'm sorry, master, I don't understand the question.'

'Yes you do; tell me what it is.'

'I have never achieved anything other than to stay alive.'

Vespasian sat down on the low bed, undoing his belt. 'And in achieving that today you've also achieved much more, Hormus; it was your warning to me last night that saved almost five thousand legionaries and nearly the same number of auxiliaries. Although they don't know it, every man in this camp owes you his life. What do you think of that?'

Hormus looked baffled. 'If what you say is true, then I don't know what to think.'

Vespasian smiled as he lay down and closed his eyes. 'You've got a couple of days to think about it. Send a message for Maximus and Valens to report to me when I wake.'

Vespasian rubbed his temples, trying to alleviate the headache that had assailed him since waking as Maximus and Valens marched smartly up to his desk and saluted. 'Sit down, gentlemen; some wine?' He indicated that they should help themselves from the earthenware jug on the desk. 'What's our situation, Maximus?'

'All but the fourth cohort from the legion could be considered combat ready,' the veteran replied, pouring a cup. 'However, the auxiliaries are a different matter: the two Gallic cohorts you left with Caepio to guard the camp took a battering as they prevented a flanking move and then had a hard time of it removing a band of long-hairs that had broken into the camp. The damage wasn't as bad as it looked, it was mainly the palisade that was burning; the Gauls kicked them out before they got to the tents.'

'I'm pleased to hear it; I shall personally commend Caepio and the two prefects.'

'They'll be busy for the next day; between them they lost nearly a third of their centurions and nearly as many optios and standard-bearers. They could fight if pressed but the chain of command is fractured. Of the other two Gallic cohorts only the one that was with Valens here is fit for immediate action – the other one lost nearly fifty dead and almost two hundred wounded plugging that gap.'

Vespasian grimaced even though he had known that the toll would have been high. 'What about Cogidubnus' Britannic auxiliaries?'

'Minimal casualties; and I think they proved their willingness to fight for Rome.'

'They certainly did; they have no love for Caratacus. And the Hamians?'

'They're fine, better than the cavalry; the Gauls need a hundred and forty remounts to bring them up to just over half strength and the legionary cavalry are down to an effective force of two turmae.'

'Just sixty-four left?'

'I'm afraid so; only the Batavians came out of it relatively unscathed. They came back in about half an hour ago reporting the enemy scattered over a large area; most seem to be heading northwest. And there's no sign of Caratacus.'

Vespasian digested the information for a few moments. 'Well, it's not as bad as it could have been, gentlemen. Tomorrow morning we'll probe northwest to make sure they don't regroup and double back. Then we'll head back down to the sea and rendezvous with the fleet to resupply before moving west along the coast to this season's objective. I'll leave Blassius here to garrison the fort with the badly mauled cohorts. Valens, you take five legionary cohorts, the Britons and Batavians and head northwest for a couple of days; I want every male of fighting age you come across in chains. Maximus, you take the other four fit legionary cohorts and the Hamians and the Gallic infantry and push north. There's a valley thirty miles in that direction – Cogidubnus will lend you some scouts to help find it. All being well I'll rendezvous with you there at dawn the day after tomorrow.'

'May I ask where you're going, sir?'

'I'm going to get my brother out of that valley and when I have done that we're going to destroy everything in it.'

'That must be it,' Cogidubnus said as a high tor, devoid of trees, about three miles distant and standing apart from other hilly features, came into view as they crested a hill. 'If we hurry we should be there well before sunset.'

'Provided we don't run into any remnants of that army,' Magnus grumbled, adjusting his sore behind in the saddle of the stocky native pony that had borne him, stoically, the last ten miles.

'We're safe enough with the scouts ranging around us!' Vespasian snapped, fed up with Magnus' complaining, which had been going on ever since he had donned the chafing trousers four hours earlier.

During the course of the short journey they had seen a few groups of straggling warriors from the defeated army but had paid little heed to them other than to avoid them; dressed in their Britannic disguises, they passed as just another unremarkable band of fugitives heading home.

Having dismissed his officers that morning, Vespasian had prepared for the journey and the coming encounter with the druids with a carefully observed sacrifice to Mars of a young ram. The animal had willingly come to the altar and had not struggled unduly under the threat of the blade; its liver had been in perfect condition and there had been no tumours or unsightly blemishes on any of the other internal organs. It had been a perfect sacrifice and yet his unease at facing the strange power of the druids again had not abated; indeed it had grown with every mile they had travelled from the camp, hence his short temper. He looked sidelong at Magnus who sat hunched in his saddle scowling, refusing to meet his eyes, and he berated himself for taking out his nervousness on his friend. It was in sullen silence that the small column made the last part of the journey.

They ascended the tor from the less steep western side, passing through ancient abandoned earthworks, on up towards a rectangular wooden building perched right on the very summit; smoke spiralled up through a hole in the centre of its thatched roof. Whilst still fifty paces away from their destination the door opened and a middle-aged man with a greying beard and a black headdress stepped out; he wore a long white robe and had a black and white patterned mantle over his shoulders. In his left hand he bore a staff which he held up as a greeting. 'Welcome, Legate Vespasian, I've been expecting you for some time now, but when I saw the fugitives from Caratacus' beaten army this morning I felt sure that you would be here by nightfall.'

Vespasian looked into Yosef's kindly dark eyes, dumb-founded; he had only been told of the man's presence in Britannia a few hours ago and yet he had been expected.

Yosef turned to Cogidubnus. 'And welcome to you, King of the Atrebates and Regni; I am told that of all the kings on this isle you are the one that has your people's interests paramount in your heart. I pray to God that it is true because the Britons will have need of strong leaders if they are to submit to Rome and not be trodden under.'

'You do me honour.'

'No more than a man who stood up to Rome before bowing to her irresistible strength deserves.' Yosef held out his right hand to help Vespasian from his pony as he dismounted. 'You look surprised that I knew you were coming; you shouldn't be. I've known that you and Sabinus were here in Britannia since the day you both landed at Rhudd yr epis, or Rutupiae as you Romans call it. I've watched your progress west with interest.'

'Then you've heard about Sabinus?'

'Yes, I have and I know that's why you are here and what you require of me. And although I am well aware of how much I stand to lose, I will help you and honour the debts that I owe you both.' Yosef smiled at Vespasian and put his arm around his shoulder, as if he was an old friend, and led him to the door. 'Righteous men like you and your brother can always expect help in the dark.'

Vespasian's eyes took a short while to get used to the gloom of the interior, which was lit solely by a fire burning in a hearth at its centre and a single oil lamp on a table next to it that was prepared for four people. The rest of the room was sparsely furnished: a couple of benches laid out opposite what looked to be an altar at one end and a curtained-off sleeping area at the other.

Yosef indicated the chairs around the table as Magnus and Cogidubnus followed them in. 'Please sit, my friends.' As his guests took up his invitation, Yosef walked up to the altar and retrieved two jugs, a loaf of bread and a shallow earthenware cup. 'If you would humour me, I'd like to offer a prayer for the safe return of Sabinus.' Yosef placed the items on the table and then poured wine into the cup and mixed it, Roman style, with water from the second jug. He then picked up the loaf of bread and said a prayer over it in the language of the Jews before breaking it into four pieces and handing one each to his guests; he placed a morsel of his portion in his mouth. 'Eat.'

Vespasian tore off a hunk and chewed on it as Yosef picked up the cup and raised it to eye-level whilst reciting another prayer; having finished he placed the cup to his lips and drank. 'Share this with me,' he said, proffering the cup to Cogidubnus; the King took a sip and then gave it to Vespasian.

Vespasian took it; it felt rough to his touch and it had a dent in the rim as if the potter had mistakenly put too much pressure on it with his thumb as he placed it in the kiln. Vespasian drank and then passed the cup to a puzzled-looking Magnus who drained it in two mighty gulps; its residue dribbled down his chin, which he wiped with the back of his hand while handing the empty vessel back to Yosef.

Apparently satisfied with the ritual, Yosef sat down and poured wine into the cups placed in front of each of his guests while they ate their remaining bread. 'We will sacrifice a lamb before we leave tomorrow at dawn. Yeshua has gone to fetch one.'

Vespasian recognised the name. 'Yeshua? Wasn't he your kinsman who was crucified?'

'Yes, you have a good memory, that was his name, but it's his son that I was speaking of. He and his mother and sister have been living with me here in Britannia for the past couple of years.'

Vespasian remembered the woman, Miriam, kneeling before him in gratitude after he had saved her and her children from the ravaging mob of Jews in Cyrene who had howled for their blood, urged on by the agitator, Paulus. 'I thought she said that she was heading for southern Gaul?'

'She did but even there it became too dangerous for her. You remember that Paulus of Tarsus was sent by the High Priest in Jerusalem to kill them in order to wipe out all trace of Yeshua's bloodline.'

'Yeah, that was some riot the bow-legged little arsehole caused,' Magnus put in from behind his cup.

'But we saw him four years later in Alexandria,' Vespasian said, 'and he had become a follower of Yeshua's; he was preaching something about eating his body and drinking his blood to gain redemption and the kingdom of heaven through him. It seemed to be complete nonsense.'

'It's not nonsense, he was talking figuratively; but as I told you back in Cyrenaica, Yeshua's message was for the Jews alone. He preached that to be seen as righteous in God's eyes a Jew should treat others as he would be treated himself. But Paulus has now corrupted that message; he claims that Yeshua was God's son and died on the cross to cleanse the world of sin for both Gentile and Jew alike, whether they follow the Torah and accept circumcision or not. Anyone who knew Yeshua would know that he was just a man, a good man, a prophet even, but nothing more; if he had been the Messiah he would have fulfilled his role. Obviously it's a blasphemy but it's a very powerful one. The idea that your sins are forgiven provided you follow Paulus' version of Yeshua and through him you will be allowed into God's presence in an afterlife that Paulus has invoked from nowhere is a message that sits well, with the poor especially. Those who have nothing in this world would dearly love to believe that they will have everything in another.'

Vespasian thought back to Hormus telling him that no god would even have noticed his existence. 'Yes, I can see that being very attractive, especially to slaves.'

'Quite so. And to make it more appealing and easier to understand for the better-off, Paulus has added facets of Mithraism. He is very well acquainted with it, having been brought up in Tarsus, one of the biggest Mithraic cities in the Empire. He has created a virgin birth for Yeshua, which would make his mother laugh if she still lived, and, like Mithras, has it witnessed by shepherds. He's also encouraging the Mithraic hierarchy of priests even though Yeshua rejected priests and temples, arguing that no man should have dominion over another when it came to understanding and worshipping God. But Paulus calculates that the educated classes will be attracted to the power that priesthoods would give them. Paulus knows that a new movement consisting only of the meek will get nowhere; he needs the wealthy and the powerful. But the worst thing that he has done is to create the idea that Yeshua was pure, almost as if sex was a sin, and should only be performed for procreation. So now, instead of wanting to kill Miriam and her children in order to wipe out Yeshua's blood-line, he now wants to kill them because they are proof that his version of Yeshua is nothing like the real man. His lies would be undone and this new religion that he is trying to create would fall apart if his followers knew of Miriam's existence.'

'But surely all those who knew him in Judaea knew that he was married and had children?'

'Oh, yes, but it is not them that Paulus is preaching to. Yeshua's other disciples preach his real words to the Jews in order to make them better Jews; but Paulus travels all over the East preaching his lies to people who never knew Yeshua and therefore can be made to believe anything about him. Paulus is afraid of Miriam and calls her a whore; he sent men to Gaul to murder her, young Yeshua and young Miriam. They nearly succeeded but she managed to escape and fled to take refuge with me here, out of the Empire.'

'But now the Empire has come to find you?'

'Exactly. Where can she and the children be safe now? But that's a problem I'll address after I've helped you retrieve Sabinus.'

'Cogidubnus tells me that the druids fear you.'

Yosef chuckled softly into his beard, lines creased around his eyes. 'I wouldn't put it that strongly but, yes, they are certainly wary of me. The powers of their supposed gods cannot affect me because I know them for what they really are: lesser daemons; angels that fell from God's grace with their master, Heylel, the Son of the Morning. These daemons who masquerade as gods are pale shadows of their master; what power they do have is in their malice, but that is also their weakness because they cannot use it to do Good. The power to do Good is the greatest force in this world; it is a God-given power. Yeshua had it and through his teachings I have learnt how to use it.'

Magnus looked unimpressed. 'What are you going to do then, walk into their valley, do them a couple of favours and say nice things to them?'

Vespasian shot his friend a venomous glance. 'That's not helpful.' However, he could not help but sympathise with Magnus' cynicism. 'But I have to admit, Yosef, that I don't understand what you're talking about.'

Yosef put up a conciliatory hand. 'That's all right; I can see how strange it must sound to someone who does not believe in the one true God. I cannot explain it to you; you'll just have to trust me and see for yourselves. The daemon that they will conjure is known as Sullis. She is full of wrath and her anger heats the springs. Heylel, her master, dragged her down with him against her will when God expelled him from His presence. He keeps her locked in that valley and she cannot escape, however much she would like to. That will be the key to it; I know, I have been there. We will rest tonight and then travel to the valley tomorrow. To have our best chance of success we must go in at the dead of night, once the moon has set but before the morning star rises, which is, as his name suggests, the embodiment of Heylel or, as you could say in Latin, Lucifer.'

Vespasian stared at Yosef, trying to decide if the man was in earnest. As when he had first met him all those years ago, he could find no guile in his eyes; he quite evidently believed what he had said. It now came down to whether Vespasian felt that he could put his faith in this strange mystic. He turned to Cogidubnus. 'What do you think? Can we really defeat the power of Sullis as Yosef says?'

Cogidubnus pulled on his moustache for a few moments, observing Yosef, who returned his look with a serene smile. He reached into his tunic and pulled out the Wheel of Taranis. 'If faith in this sign can work for the Kings of the Atrebates then I see no reason why this man cannot do as he claims if he has equal faith in his god.'

Yosef nodded. 'You are right, my lord.' He pulled on a leather thong about his neck and brought out a pendant.

Vespasian saw with surprise that it was the same as Cogidubnus', a four-spoked wheel; but then he noticed the downward spoke had been extended so that it looked like a cross with a circle around its top.

Yosef held it up to Cogidubnus. 'You may be surprised that I too have my own version of the Wheel of Taranis. I have adapted it to symbolise my faith and yet keep it recognisable to the people of this land whom I hope to convert to Yeshua's teachings of Judaism and bring them close to the love of the one true God.'

Magnus grunted. 'I can't imagine that anyone here is going to be too keen to have their foreskin cut off.'

'It's a small price to pay to come closer to God.'

'You can keep your god and I'll keep my foreskin.'

Magnus' theological musings were brought to a close by the opening of the door; a handsome woman in her mid-thirties walked in accompanied by two children, a boy in his early teens, holding a lamb, and a girl a year or two younger. It was more than ten years since Vespasian had seen Yeshua's woman, Miriam; he had not thought about her once and could only vaguely recall what she looked like.

Miriam, however, recognised him instantly. She walked quickly across the room, knelt at Vespasian's feet and clasped his knees. 'Legate Vespasian, every day when I look at my children I think of your mercy and how you saved their lives; every day I say a prayer for you.' Behind her the two children looked at Vespasian in awe.

Vespasian placed his hand under her chin and lifted her face. 'Thank you for your prayers but I can assure you that they're not necessary; please stand.'

Miriam got to her feet. 'I will always pray for you, legate, as I shall always pray for your brother who gave me my husband's body back. I have seen him, you know?'

Vespasian grabbed Miriam's hand. 'When and where?'

'A few days ago. Yosef sent me to the valley of Sullis once he was sure that you would be arriving soon. The druids allow people to take the hot water from the springs for medicine. They have Sabinus there in a wooden cage hanging from an oak tree in one of their sacred groves by the hottest of Sullis' five springs; he's naked and filthy but he's not without hope. I made sure that he saw me and he recognised me; he knows that someone is coming for him.'

'He's always known that someone would come for him; that *I* would come for him.'

Magnus frowned, chewing on the last of his bread. 'Let's hope that it's just Sabinus who knows that someone's coming and not everyone else in that valley.'

Yosef stood and walked over to Yeshua. 'I'm afraid that is a vain hope; the druids will be expecting us. The very fact that they've made no attempt to hide Sabinus means that they want you to come.' He took the lamb from Yeshua and cradled it in his arms. 'Tomorrow at dawn I shall offer this lamb and ask that God blinds them to our arrival and confounds their plan to capture you, Vespasian, and make a double sacrifice of two brothers, both legates. They think that will be very powerful; so you see, they've always wanted you to come.'

CHAPTER VI

VESPASIAN LOOKED DOWN into the valley of Sullis from high on a hill to its southern edge. Thickly wooded with a river meandering through it, the vale's only sign of human habitation was a small pier on the north bank at the apex of a large dog-leg in the river's course.

'The river is known as the Afon Sullis,' Yosef informed Vespasian, Magnus and Cogidubnus. 'The ferry that operates from that pier is the only way across without getting wet.'

'So we'll be getting wet then,' Vespasian observed, watching a small round boat being paddled away from the pier.

'Yes, the river curves around behind this hill; we can swim the horses across to the northern bank out of sight of unfriendly eyes.'

'Apart from the ferryman and his passenger I can't see any eyes, either friendly or unfriendly,' Magnus said, scanning the thick green canopy that covered the valley's floor.

'There're plenty under there, you can count on it; and all very unfriendly. They'll be mainly around the five sacred groves that surround each of the springs. They're all within the curve of the river.'

Cogidubnus shielded his eyes from the low, late-afternoon sun. 'Which one will we make for?'

'If they still have Sabinus above the hottest one then it's about four hundred paces from the ferry and almost exactly in the middle of the curve.'

'I'll have a couple of my men go and take a look once it gets dark.' Cogidubnus turned and addressed his ten followers in their own tongue, pointing to the area of wood indicated by Yosef.

'We should aim to be there by the eighth hour of the night.' Yosef turned his horse and kicked it away down the hill.

Vespasian took one last look at the valley before following; it looked so peaceful and yet it was home to unspeakable horrors. And he would soon have to face them again.

'My men should be back very soon,' Cogidubnus said, observing the progress of the moon across the night sky.

Vespasian shivered and wrapped his cloak tighter about his shoulders; the temperature had dropped with the sun and they had not dared to risk a fire despite still being damp from crossing the river. 'Do you think that your god has blinded the druids to our coming, Yosef?'

'The sacrifice was accepted this morning and we had no trouble on the journey here; Miriam and the children are praying for us and that will help me raise the power that I'll need. But only with a lot of luck will we escape detection altogether.'

'Oh, so we do have to rely on luck, do we?' Magnus muttered, less than impressed. 'I thought that all this religious stuff that you've been going on about, the one true god and all that, meant that we had a guarantee of divine protection.'

Yosef smiled benignly in the dim moonlight. 'God cannot always do everything that is asked of Him.'

'Then he's no different to any other god, is he? They seem to spend their time turning up with a little help whenever they fancy rather than when you ask them to. And if this god that you seem to be so keen on really was the only god then I'm not surprised to find him unreliable because he must be very busy.'

'He is everywhere,' Yosef agreed as the soft rustling of leaves heralded the arrival of Cogidubnus' two scouts.

Cogidubnus spoke to them briefly and then dismissed them to wait with his other followers.

'Well?' Vespasian asked.

'It seems that Sullis is a powerful goddess; my men said that the closer they got to her springs the more they felt her presence.'

'But what about Sabinus, is he still there?'

'They could see a cage suspended from a tree but they could not get close enough to see whether there was anyone in it. There were druids close by.'

'How many?'

'More than a dozen.'

'Any warriors?' Magnus asked, gripping the hilt of his sword.

'None that could be seen; but that doesn't mean there aren't any. If there are, though, there won't be many as this is a religious place, not a settlement. They're not our concern; my men will deal with them. It's the druids and the goddess that we have to worry about.'

'You look to the druids and leave Sullis to me,' Yosef said, tapping the leather bag slung over his shoulder, 'and remember, she's not a goddess, she's just a daemon.'

'As far as I'm concerned there ain't any difference,' Magnus stated. 'She's a supernatural being who demands worship. Men worship her, therefore she's a goddess. Granted, she may not be as powerful as Jupiter Optimus Maximus, Donar or Taranis but that makes sense because there is a hierarchy to the gods, just like with men. Men can't be all equal and nor can gods. Which leaves us with the nice irony of you, Yosef, using the power of what you profess to be the one true god against a lesser goddess. I'd say your god's claim to be the only god is a little tenuous, wouldn't you?'

Yosef repeated his benign smile. 'Perhaps you Gentiles attribute the word "god" too easily to forces that you don't understand. There are supernatural beings other than Yahweh; I would not call them gods but you would. Heylel or Lucifer, for example: he has power but less power than Yahweh; you would call him a god, a lesser god like Saturn compared to Jupiter, but Lucifer is just an angel who has fallen from grace. Then there are Gabriel and Michael, they are archangels who live with Yahweh; again you would call them gods, because they're supernatural beings.'

'Do you worship them?'

'No, but we honour them.'

'Ah!' Magnus pointed his finger at Yosef. 'What's the difference?'

'When Yahweh revealed himself to the Jews he told us that we should not worship other gods, only him, because he would not give his glory to another.'

'And yet you "honour" these archangels. You see, if he told you not to worship other gods, that implies that there are other gods, so I think you've got your argument the wrong way round: you Jews don't attribute the word "god" enough. You've got all these gods that you just pretend are something else to keep this Yahweh happy. Whereas if you just accepted that Lucifer, Gabriel and all the rest were gods then your religion wouldn't be much different from everybody else's and perhaps you'd find yourselves fitting in a bit more because you wouldn't consider yourselves so special.'

Again Yosef chuckled into his beard. 'Magnus, my friend, I can't argue with your logic except to say that there is no other God.'

'And yet we're just about to go and deal with one!'

Vespasian got to his feet. 'I've had enough of this. Whether Sullis is a goddess or a daemon or an angel – whatever that is – makes no difference; we're going to have to defeat the druids that use her power in order to rescue Sabinus and I've asked for the protection of my guardian god, Mars, just as Cogidubnus is protected by Taranis and Yosef has his Yahweh. Whether they're all different or all the same but with different names is completely irrelevant to me so long as I feel the hands of a god being held over me – because having faced these druids once I know that's what I need.'

Cogidubnus heaved himself off the ground. 'The moon will set in an hour; we should get ourselves into position.'

Magnus held his hand out to help Yosef up. 'Whoever's right and whoever's wrong there is one certainty and that is we all need gods. I'm looking forward to seeing how yours proves himself to be the one true god.'

'You'll never get proof, Magnus; you just have to have faith.'

Vespasian stayed close to Cogidubnus, only just visible a pace in front of him, as the two scouts led them towards the springs of

Sullis. The forest thickened as they probed deeper and soon the canopy was so dense that the stars were totally obscured and the gloom was complete. The air had become thick and heavy to breathe and had an acidic tang to it that grated in his throat. Sweat had begun to trickle down his forehead and he sensed the temperature rising steadily as they closed on Sullis' realm. A low-hanging branch brushed against his ear, startling him; he reached out to push it aside and felt it dripping with moisture.

'I'll take the forests of Germania any day,' Magnus muttered from behind him. 'At least they didn't make you feel like you were going into the *caldarium* with your clothes on. Wearing fucking trousers in the hot bath, who'd have thought it?'

'I thought you were going to say: "it ain't natural".'

'Well, it ain't natural; but you're mocking me now, I can tell.'

'Sorry, it's just to ease my nerves. I think that at the moment I'd rather be anywhere but here.'

'Yeah, well, I reckon that's something that we can all agree on, even Yosef; and I expect that Sabinus is thinking exactly the same thing.'

'I hope that he *is* thinking.'

'We'll find that out soon enough.'

Vespasian collided with Cogidubnus who had stopped suddenly. Just beyond him the two scouts had gone down onto their knees.

'What is it?' Vespasian whispered.

One of the scouts spoke softly to the King and indicated ahead.

'He says that we're close; he can tell by the air, it's dense with Sullis' power.' Cogidubnus whispered something in his own tongue to the rest of his men behind Yosef. With remarkable stealth they fanned out in the dark with hardly a twig disturbed. 'Now we shall have need of our gods,' the King muttered, pulling out his Wheel of Taranis from beneath his tunic.

Before Cogidubnus had completed the motion a shrill shriek off to their right pierced the heavy atmosphere, chilling their hearts despite the humidity. A score of torches suddenly ignited thirty paces away, their flames leaping up, bathing the underside of the canopy with a flickering glow and revealing a cage dangling from a high branch. Vespasian turned towards the light, his hands clammy and his hair lank with sweat, and was shocked to see his breath steaming out before him as if he was in a snow-covered land.

And then he saw them.

Out from behind each column of flame appeared a long-robed figure; the druids walked a couple of steps forward and stopped at the edge of a steaming pool that bubbled at its centre. Again the shriek was repeated and Vespasian saw that a young girl, naked and no more than ten years old, was in their midst; the two druids to either side of her held her firmly by her long, golden hair. Tears streamed down her face and she screamed again in abject terror; urine squirted from between her legs. A vicious curved knife was put to her throat to force her head back and a ball of some sort of food was forced into her mouth. A hand clamped her lips tightly shut so that she could not spit and fingers pinched her nostrils together. Unable to breathe she swallowed and, an instant later, convulsed. Her mouth and nose were released and immediately emitted thick streams of blood; blood seeped from her eyes and ears and flowed free from between her legs. She tried to cry to the heavens but her voice was drowned by blood flooding in her gorge and she sprayed a thick mist of crimson into the air. Her knees buckled but she remained upright, supported by her killers. The druids chanted a short prayer and Vespasian recognised the word 'Sullis' as they threw the still-twitching small body into the pool whose steaming waters turned red with the innocent blood.

It seemed to Vespasian, watching in horror, that the sacrifice had lasted an age but in reality it had been the work of fifty or so heartbeats. Glancing up at the cage he could make out a figure slumped within, motionless, taking no notice of what passed beneath. He drew his sword and heard the rasp of metal as his companions followed his lead; he started to edge forward with dread gripping his bowels but with his desire to rescue his brother overriding everything.

'Stay back!' Yosef shouted, raising his staff in the air with one hand whilst rummaging in his bag with the other.

The bubbling in the pool increased, buffeting the girl's body, which was floating face-down and still emitting streams of blood; her hair, now stained crimson, spread out from her head like some ghastly bloom.

Yosef pulled the cup with which he had shared wine with Vespasian from his bag and walked steadily towards the pool's edge, holding his staff horizontally before him, as if warding off the druids on the far side. They began a deep chanting and the turbulence in the water increased; the body undulated on the raging surface and then, as Yosef knelt by the water's edge, it was forcibly sucked under. The turbulence ceased and the waters calmed; Yosef dipped his cup in the steaming pool and filled it. The druidical chanting continued and Vespasian felt all their eyes burning into him. Yosef rose to his feet and planted his staff in the soft ground at the pool's edge; he held the full cup towards the druids, bringing out his personalised Wheel of Taranis. He intoned a prayer loudly in his own tongue, his words rising over the druids' chant; they increased their volume and Yosef did likewise.

An explosion of water erupted from the centre of the pool; drops from the spray splashed onto Vespasian's face. They were hot and he closed his eyes and wiped them away. When he opened them again he choked on a stifled scream: the girl stood upright in the middle of the pool, her feet just below the surface, and her eyes, which should have stared lifelessly, rolled in their sockets. Words came out of her mouth; deep guttural words unintelligible to Vespasian, but he did not need to understand them to comprehend that this was the voice of a malevolent goddess. His knees weakened and sweat streamed down his face; his breath steamed from his mouth in short puffs and he felt a fear that he knew he would not be able to control. He wanted to turn and run but the sheer horror of the sight transfixed him as the small child's body, now the manifestation of Sullis, glided through the steam towards Yosef, issuing dark sounds full of malice. And yet, the visible proof of the existence of the goddess fed his faith in all gods and with chattering teeth he whispered a prayer to Mars, knowing that he would be heard, imploring him to aid Yosef in his struggle with the monstrosity.

Yosef kept up his prayer as the ghoulish entity neared him; the druids' chanting intensified as if it had become a battle of wills.

Yosef released his Wheel of Taranis and pulled his staff out of the ground; Sullis was now no more than three paces from him. Her mouth twitched unnaturally as she uttered her filth, blood seeping from her, her eyes turning uncontrollably; her arms remained at her side, limp and swaying. Yosef pointed his staff at her so that the tip touched her blood-streaked chest; she stopped.

Vespasian shook with fear and cold in spite of the heat emanating from the goddess's spring; he was vaguely aware of Magnus next to him muttering prayers to every god that he could think of, even Yosef's. Cogidubnus had raised his Wheel of Taranis and was beseeching the god to strike down this apparition with cleansing lightning.

Sullis pushed against the staff; Yosef's arm was rigid but the pressure of the goddess made it shake. Slowly and inexorably it was forced back and Sullis closed on him. He kept up his prayer, almost shouting, his voice insistent, whilst holding his brimming cup before him, its water now cooled and no longer steaming. His gaze was fixed on those unnatural eyes that only a short while before had stared in terror at the world for what should have been the last time.

Yosef's arm continued to be driven back by a force incommensurate with the size of the body applying it; and yet he did not flinch. He continued shouting into the ghastly face. Vespasian felt that he was ordering her to leave; the same words were being constantly repeated whilst the goddess rumbled her refusal. Behind her the druids chanted on, their eyes all fixed on Vespasian and with cold realisation he understood that they were willing Sullis on towards him; only Yosef stood in her way and he seemed to be weakening.

Yosef took a step back and Sullis followed; she was now no more than a foot from the edge of the pool. Taking another step back, Yosef raised his cup. Sullis moved forward, still straining against the staff; her feet left the pool. The moment that Sullis glided onto the damp ground surrounding the pool Yosef dropped his staff. The hideous goddess flew at him, her voice changing to a note of triumph. Yosef flicked his cup, splashing the water into Sullis' face; the goddess stopped as if it had not been liquid but, rather, solid rock that had hit her. The druids faltered; one or two of them wailed in despair. The possessed corpse convulsed and Yosef grabbed its shoulders, shaking it. Vespasian sensed that it was trying to retreat, to get back to the safety of the pool from which it had arisen so abominably.

'Now for the druids!' Yosef shouted between exhortations in his own language for the goddess to depart.

As if a spell had been broken, Cogidubnus rushed forward, his men flowing after him around the pool. Vespasian remained rooted, unwilling to move whilst Sullis remained manifest.

Yosef still had the goddess by the shoulders but her struggles were weakening. Suddenly her head fell back and her mouth opened and from it issued a wind that was more than a deep exhalation; it reminded Vespasian of the beating wings of the Phoenix as he stood beneath it over ten years before. It was a warm wind, not chill and malevolent as he would have expected to issue from Sullis, but, rather, peaceful and contented.

'Return to God!' Yosef cried in Greek as the wind rose up through the canopy. 'You are free from Heylel; return to God and rest in His bosom until the End of Days.'

The limp body of the sacrificed girl fell to the muddy ground; it was completely pale and devoid of all blood. Yosef looked at it with sorrow as he placed his cup back in the bag.

Vespasian glanced at Magnus; incredulity filled their eyes; their breath no longer steamed. 'I believe, however long I live, that that will be the most dread . . .' He trailed off, unable to articulate his terror.

Magnus nodded, vacantly. 'That really weren't natural.'

Cries from across the pool drew Vespasian's attention as Cogidubnus and his men scythed into the druids who, instead of fleeing, stood wailing in despair at the loss of their goddess and accepted death; they were soon obliged and lay pierced and bloodied on the ground beneath the gently swaying cage. Vespasian shook his head, bringing his mind back to the matter in hand. 'Help me to get Sabinus down, Magnus.'

Running around the pool, Vespasian kept well clear of its water, fearful of what other abominations it might hold. When he arrived underneath the cage Cogidubnus was already staring up at it, blood-slick sword in hand.

'There seems to be a pulley system,' the King informed him. 'I'll send up one of my men to lower it.'

It was the work of a few moments to get a man up into the tree; he soon reached the branch around which the rope was tied off. Untying the knot he began to feed the rope out.

Vespasian held his breath, watching intently the figure slumped on the floor of the descending cage. As the cage reached his eye-level the figure suddenly rolled over. Sabinus' emaciated, bearded face peered at Vespasian in the flickering torchlight. 'You took your time getting here, you little shit.'

It did not take Magnus long to force the lock and Vespasian helped his weakened brother out and to his feet. He was smeared in his own filth and his bones jutted through his tight, thin skin; yet despite that he managed to stand upright. He shook off Vespasian's arms and staggered towards the water.

'What are you doing?' Vespasian asked as Sabinus fended off his attempts to help him.

'I'm going to wash my arse in that pool now that it's been cleared of goddesses.'

'I wouldn't go anywhere near that water – who knows what's still lurking in there.'

'Nothing, brother. I've been dangling above it for who knows how long, living in fear of the malice that emanated from it; but now it is gone and that is just a pool of hot water and I'm going to have a bath in it.'

'I'd sooner dunk my arse in a tub of boiling oil,' Magnus declared, looking suspiciously at the steaming, pinkish water. 'Less chance of letting in an unwelcome visitor, if you take my meaning?'

'Thank you, Magnus, if I ever need your opinions on hygiene I shall be sure to ask.'

Leaving Sabinus to his ablutions, Vespasian walked over to Yosef whose face was worn with fatigue.

'She nearly got the best of me,' Yosef said, leaning heavily on his staff.

'How did you defeat her?'

'I didn't defeat her, I helped her. I released her from the spell cast by Heylel that confined her to this valley. I took water from the pool that was heated by her wrath at being trapped and I invoked God's blessing on it. Once she was out of the pool the blessed water that I splashed on her face reconnected her to God, voiding Heylel's curse against which she has struggled for millennia. She wanted to go and was finally free to do so. By doing Good as Yeshua preached I was stronger than the druids who just fed off Sullis' malice; they couldn't pull her back into the pool although they tried. I was able to hold her long enough for her to leave the body she had manifested in and return to God.'

'Your god has proven his power but he had help from our gods; we were all praying that they would aid you. And Sullis manifest proves that they exist.'

Yosef chuckled. 'Believe what you will; all faith is good. My God doesn't need to prove His power.' He patted his bag. 'But Yeshua has. The cup I used was his; he used it to share wine with his followers on his last night. I keep it as a memento of him. His goodness seems somehow infused within it. When I asked God to bless the water, Yeshua's face burnt in my mind and I knew that he was answering his wife's and children's prayers and lending me strength. This cup is a very potent vessel and has the power to do great Good.'

'Kill every male you find down there, Maximus,' Vespasian ordered his prefect of the camp, looking back down into the valley soon after dawn.

Maximus saluted. 'What about the women and children, sir?'

Vespasian thought for a few moments. 'No, we'll spare them and sell them as slaves.'

'And then you should set to work cutting down every tree in the valley,' Yosef suggested. 'If you deprive the druids of their sacred groves you'll weaken them considerably.'

Cogidubnus nodded. 'I agree; we should cut down every grove that we come across. We need to drive the druids away west and north; then perhaps you can start negotiating with the chieftains that still resist Rome.'

'I would dearly love to capture a few alive,' Sabinus said, pulling his only garment, a cloak, tighter around his naked body. 'I'd hang them up in cages and feed them just enough to stay alive and keep them there for years. Most of all I'd like to find that bastard Alienus; think what he'd look like after five years in a cage.'

Vespasian looked apologetically at his brother. 'I'm afraid that won't be possible.'

'Why? Have you killed him?'

'No; we captured him.'

Sabinus' face brightened. 'Then I can hang him in a cage.'

'I'm afraid not; I gave him his life in return for information concerning your whereabouts. I gave my word.'

'Well, you'll have to go back on your word; I intend to have my vengeance on that treacherous little shit.'

'I can't, Sabinus, I—'

'I'm afraid that the situation has changed, sir,' Maximus put in.

'How? What do you mean?'

'Before we left we found one of the men guarding him with his neck broken and stripped of his uniform. I believe that Alienus walked out of the camp in the guise of a Gallic auxiliary.'

Vespasian checked himself from shouting at his veteran officer and then, as he closed his mouth, he smiled and turned to his brother. 'It seems that you're in luck, Sabinus; Alienus has been very stupid. Now he's escaped, our agreement is cancelled without me going back on my word.'

'That is very gratifying, brother; I'll have a cage commissioned. Now all I've got to do is find him.'

'Oh, I'm sure he'll turn up; he hates us too much to stay away.'

PART II

❧ ❧

BRITANNIA, SEPTEMBER AD 46

CHAPTER VII

THE BITE OF whips on the mud-grimed, bleeding shoulders of scores of manacled slaves caused the bireme to edge forward a further few paces, releasing four or five smooth, rounded logs from beneath its stern. Teams of slave boys, too young to be hauling on the four long ropes that powered the vessel overland, immediately lifted the freed rollers and ran with them up to the bow of the ship, taking licks from the whips of the legionary overseers they passed. They placed them ready for the ship to trundle onto after the next bout of exertion from the human beasts of burden treated no better than the bellowing oxen harnessed to great yokes in their midst.

The once-proud warriors of the Durotriges were using muscles more accustomed to martial exercise to power Roman ships towards the river estuary, now less than a ship's length away. Had the slaves been able to register anything but pain and misery they would have smelt the salt-tanged air and heard the gulls overhead crying as they circled the four ships already floated and now moored in a line down the middle of the hundred-pace-wide estuary. Long, low, wide-bellied rowing boats travelled to and fro from a couple of wooden jetties on the eastern bank, ferrying oarsmen and marines with their provisions out to their vessels to make them fit for sea.

Along the bank, north of the jetties, lay the rib-like skeletons of four triremes in various stages of construction surrounded by yet more Britons working under the direction of Roman shipwrights and guarded by two centuries of Cogidubnus' auxiliaries. Hammering, sawing, chiselling or carrying, these men were not manacled; they were free men having surrendered honourably to the II Augusta during its push westwards through the lands of the

Durotriges over the last two campaigning seasons. Now as free subjects of Rome they were being given the chance to earn citizenship by building the ships in which they would serve as rowers for the next twenty-six years.

Standing with Magnus and Sabinus outside the gates of the II Augusta's camp, overlooking the enterprise, Vespasian looked down the line of eight biremes still to be floated; in one huge convoy they had been hauled overland along the portage way from a river on the south coast of Britannia to this tidal estuary leading out to the sea on the northern coast of the peninsula running southwest out into the western ocean. The thirty-mile route was lined with crosses upon which were nailed those slaves who had fallen by the wayside too weak to carry on. They had been left to die in agony, as a warning to others, with their legs unbroken so that the instinct to survive would ensure that they would continually try to push up on the impaling nail through their feet in order to breathe, thus prolonging their death. The frequency of the crosses had increased as the days had gone by and although Vespasian regretted the financial loss he had condoned the executions in order to ensure that the operation was completed as quickly as possible.

'Just eight days,' Vespasian observed with satisfaction to Magnus next to him, 'it shows what can be achieved if you put your mind to it.'

'And if you've got the slaves to do it,' Magnus pointed out, watching an older slave who had collapsed to the ground receiving a beating that would probably finish him. 'I suppose he could be considered one of the lucky ones.'

'What?' Vespasian looked at the wretched slave; exhausted by his unremitting labours, he no longer cried out. 'Yes, I suppose so; still, none of them would have been in this position had they been sensible and surrendered, like the men working on the triremes, rather than fighting on and becoming captives.'

'You should be thankful that they weren't sensible; if they had you wouldn't have had the manpower to drag this squadron overland and then where would you be? Losing yet more vessels trying to sail hundreds of miles around this storm-riven island, rather than simply dragging them thirty miles to the north coast.'

'No, I'd have had them built like the triremes; but you're right, it's much easier and less effort to bring them overland; not to mention the time it's saved.'

'And lives,' Sabinus observed. He pointed to a smaller ship, a liburnian bobbing at anchor close to the shore, in which he had arrived the day before. He had sailed south from the XIIII Gemina's base, at General Plautius' orders, to take personal command of his half of the twelve biremes whose arduous overland journey was now coming to an end – he had only just recovered from two days' stomach-straining seasickness that morning. 'The *trierarchus* of my ship told me that he was the only one who made it round out of a flotilla of half a dozen. Apparently the tides and the wind are very rarely in the right conjunction; three of the ships were wrecked and two turned back.'

Magnus spat. 'Tides! *They* ain't natural.'

Vespasian chuckled. 'I'm afraid they are, Magnus. Anyway the main thing is that despite the tides we now have a naval presence on both sides of the peninsula ready for our push further west into the Dumnonii lands next season.'

With a flurry of scourging and a rise in the cacophony of agonised cries and bellows, both bestial and human, the next bireme rolled down the bank, plunging into the water, dipping its bow with a phenomenal splash that submerged many of the slaves toiling at its ropes in the river. The great vessel bounced gracefully back up as its full length floated; the resultant wave swept many of the captives from their ropes, out into midstream where they floundered, drawn down by the weight of their manacles.

'That's just stupid!' Vespasian exploded, striding forward with furious intent towards the nearest centurion commanding the legionary overseers. 'What the fuck do you think you're doing drowning decent livestock?'

The centurion snapped to attention in the face of his legate's wrath. 'We unhitched the oxen, sir!'

'I'm not talking about the oxen; I'm talking about the slaves!'

The man looked nonplussed for a few moments. 'It's unavoidable, sir.'

'Unavoidable! Do you have any idea how much each one of them is worth? Your annual pay, that's how much.' Vespasian gestured to a stoutly built, large stockade about a quarter of a mile away into which slaves who had completed their task were being led. 'And I make sure that every legionary and auxiliary gets their fair share of the profits for each one sold so what you're doing is throwing your money and mine away. I suggest that you find a way to make drowning them avoidable, centurion.'

'Yes, sir!' the centurion barked, snapping a crisp salute before turning and marching off to berate his men for bringing him to the attention of the legate.

'A very commendable and remunerative piece of advice, if I may say, legate,' a smooth voice observed from behind him.

Vespasian spun on his heel. He was in no mood for insolence. 'Theron!' he exclaimed, looking into the dark eyes of the Macedonian slave-trader from whom he had bought his body slave, Hormus. 'What are you doing so close to where the fighting is?'

Theron, a man only in his mid-thirties but already running to fat, bowed, bringing a hand across his ample chest; his voluminous saffron cloak wafted in the slight breeze and pendulous golden earrings glistened next to his trimmed and oiled black beard, which failed to conceal the beginnings of a double chin. Behind him stood a retinue of a dozen bulky men; their age, scars and muscles placed them unmistakably as ex-gladiators. Despite the absence of sun or rain a smooth-skinned eastern youth held a parasol, fringed with golden-threaded tassels, over his head. He was, Vespasian thought, almost a parody of the image that he tried to portray: a man whose wealth was based upon the sweat of others.

'Greetings, legate,' Theron said in a most deferential tone, 'allow me to pay my compliments to you for the magnificent victories that you have won since we last met.'

'What do you want?'

'The smallest of favours.'

'I doubt that.'

'In return for greatly adding to your personal fortune.'

Vespasian's experience of buying Hormus from Theron was in direct opposition to that statement. 'I find that very unlikely too.'

'Then you should hear me out, legate.'

Vespasian appraised the Macedonian for a few moments, the chance of profit fighting with his natural inclination to have the man run off military ground. 'Go on then.'

'May I suggest we retire to your tent and make ourselves comfortable?'

'No, you may not; you may enjoy comfort in the day but the art of leading men rather than selling them requires me to have different priorities. Say what you have to say here.'

'Your virtue does you credit. I am humbled by your sentiments.'

Vespasian found himself wanting to change his mind as the Macedonian oozed clichés; but knowing that his time, and therefore his money-making opportunities, must now be limited in the new province he overcame his scruples. 'Get on with it.'

Theron looked at Magnus and Sabinus questioningly.

'They stay as my witnesses.'

'Indeed, your honour.' Theron paused and cleared his throat as if he was embarking upon a carefully rehearsed speech. 'As the instigator of this great enterprise ...' He gestured expansively over the line of ships, surrounded by slaves and overseers; oarsmen from the recently floated bireme clambered into rowing boats, lined along the jetties, to make the short journey out to their vessel. 'As the instigator of this great enterprise now drawing to a glorious conclusion, much to your eternal credit, you are aware that the human cattle used as muscle are now, in the main, superfluous. I believe you are now having them taken to that holding stockade in readiness for their transportation back to the slave-markets in the east of Britannia. Please confirm to me that I'm not mistaken, excellency?'

Vespasian grunted his affirmation.

'That is gratifying. You know me to be an honest man of business with much experience in the line of trade that I pursue. It therefore should not come as a complete surprise to you to learn that I have recently acquired the contracts to supply three gladiatorial schools in Rome and a further two in Capua with Britannic livestock.'

Vespasian made no move to be either surprised or not.

'They have formed a consortium in order to buy in bulk at reasonable prices; their first order is for seventy-five men each of mixed builds, that's ...'

'Three hundred and seventy-five, I can do multiplication!'

Theron bowed deep. 'Humble apologies, your honour.'

'And stop talking in clichés!'

'Indeed, excel ... Indeed, legate.' He cleared his throat again. 'These *gentlemen* behind me are all former exponents of that noble profession and are here to assess the suitability of each slave for each gladiatorial role.'

'I see. So you want to have the first pick of the slaves before they get back to the licensed slave-markets.'

'I would describe it as a first assessment; being a law-abiding citizen I would not wish to make a purchase outside the jurisdiction and tax-net of the licensed slave-market.'

Vespasian felt a reluctant admiration for the man. 'But if you were allowed to take your pick here and choose the cream of the stock you would be more than happy to escort them, at your own expense, naturally ...'

Theron bowed his agreement.

'Back to the market and immediately make your purchase, without your rivals being able to outbid you, under the supervision of the proper authorities who would levy the correct amount of tax.'

'Your insight does you much credit.'

'And then you will transport them ...' Vespasian paused and raised his eyebrows.

Theron tilted his head, closing his eyes. 'Again at my own expense.'

'Naturally. Transport them back to Italia and share them out amongst the five schools.'

'You see the venture in its entirety.'

'Oh I do, Theron; I also see you taking bribes from each of the schools to provide them with the best of the excellent stock thus adding to your considerable profit.'

Theron shrugged in a 'wouldn't anyone behave that way' manner.

'And just why should I allow you to get such an advantage over your rivals?'

'Firstly because I had the initiative to travel out here to talk with you and share your dangers whilst my colleagues remained safely back east; and secondly because I'm offering you five per cent of the resale value of the stock in Italia.'

'Which means that you can afford to pay me fifteen.'

'Eight.'

'Ten and it's a deal.'

'But I get to keep any monies offered to me as an incentive for allocating the stock in a certain way, as you alluded to earlier.'

'I'm sure that you would do your best to keep those sums hidden from me even if I did demand a share.'

Theron bowed extravagantly. 'In which case ten per cent it will be. We shall keep this between ourselves as a verbal understanding.'

'Wrong, Theron; you won't get access to that stockade until I have a signed written contract from you.'

'But would that be wise? What we have agreed is slightly less than completely legal.'

'Wrong again, Theron. I'm obliged to sell these slaves once I have finished with them. The Emperor gets his share of the sale through the tax that is levied at the market; the rest is shared out amongst my legion and auxiliaries. The Emperor will also get his cut in tax from the resale in Italia. The fact that I'll also get money from the sale as well as the resale is irrelevant because the Emperor has had his due and is therefore happy. I'm just using my position to enrich myself like any sensible commander would do, and I want a contract from you so that you can't cheat me out of what's rightfully mine – as I'm sure you would, given the chance.'

'Never, your honour,' the slave-dealer crooned, bowing even lower.

'Stop fawning and go and draw one up.'

Theron righted himself. 'You shall have it by this evening, noble legate.' With a farewell oozing of obsequiousness he took his leave.

Magnus looked less than impressed. 'I wouldn't do business with the likes of him for all the whores on the Via Patricius.'

'Sometimes a business opportunity is worth more than a lot of whores,' Sabinus observed, watching the slave-trader and his retinue depart. 'Especially when one has no initial outlay.'

Vespasian turned his attention back to the biremes as the next one neared the water's edge. 'Exactly; I've got nothing to lose and everything to gain.'

Magnus scowled. 'I can see that – ten per cent of the value of the resale will be a lot of money which you wouldn't otherwise have got and it's probably your last opportunity to make a decent profit before you get recalled.'

'Which, after five years as legate of the Second Augusta, has got to be soon; so what's the problem?'

'He's going to cheat you, even if you have a contract.'

'I know he will and he's banking on me not taking him to court because the contract will show me publicly in a less than favourable light to my peers. Even though they all would do the same it's best not to be seen doing it, especially if one wants to be consul some day.'

'Exactly, you wouldn't risk that, would you?'

'Of course not.'

'So you're just going to let him make a fool of you?'

'No, Magnus, I'm going to let him make a fool of himself.'

'Well, good luck, because I can tell you that men like Theron ain't made fools of easily.'

The shrill blare of a lituus cavalry horn coming from within the camp ended the discussion. Vespasian turned towards the sound and looking up the Via Principalis saw a turma of cavalry dismounting outside the praetorium. Even at that distance he recognised the imposing figure and uniform of his commanding officer. 'Aulus Plautius! Saturn's stones, what's he doing here?'

*

'We have just a month, gentlemen!' Aulus Plautius bellowed at Vespasian and Sabinus, drowning out the cries and whip-cracks from outside the praetorium tent. 'No more than a month before our replacements arrive and we have to spend the winter briefing them and showing them around before we return to Rome. And if we want to come home covered in glory then I suggest that we take Caratacus in chains along with us.' Plautius fixed the two brothers sitting opposite him across the desk with an indignant, red-faced glare.

Vespasian shifted uncomfortably in his seat as he watched the veins throbbing in his commanding officer's bull-like neck; since his arrival at the II Augusta's camp Plautius had not been in the best of moods.

Plautius picked up a scroll and brandished it at the brothers. 'Narcissus has written to me stating that seeing as after three and a half years Caratacus remains at large, threatening our supply lines, ambushing columns and generally making a nuisance of himself, he feels the time has come to replace me and you two with men who own a degree of military competence. Military competence! The jumped-up little Greek shit! He wouldn't know military competence if it barged its way up his arse and saluted.' Plautius paused, breathing deeply through flaring nostrils, contemplating, Vespasian surmised, other more solid objects that he would like to see barging their way up that particular orifice. 'The trouble is, gentlemen,' Plautius continued with a degree of calm returning to his voice, 'that the soft-living bastard has got a point: why the fuck is Caratacus' head still on his shoulders and not decorating the end of a spike? How can I claim that the southern half of this dung-heap of an island is under Roman control when our lads have to go to the latrines in groups of eight so that they can hold each other's hands for fear of having their arses wiped by a Britannic spear rather than a decent Roman sponge?'

Vespasian felt it was best not to point out that this was a wild exaggeration. However, he could well appreciate Plautius' exasperation at the fact that, despite having taken the surrender of all the tribes in the south of Britannia – apart from the Dumnonii in the extreme southwest – he still had Caratacus at large with the ability to pop up with a considerable force and do humiliating damage. Apart from anything else, it was not good for trade and the occupied parts of the island were now swarming with fat merchants eager, like Theron, to squeeze as much cash out of the province as possible, whether it be in tin, lead, slaves, hunting dogs, pearls or any other commodity.

Vespasian glanced sidelong at his brother and now understood why Plautius had ordered him to come in person to pick up his ships, so far from the XIIII Gemina's camp on the east bank of the Sabrina River: this was a planned meeting to discuss a two legion offensive. The grating of wood on wood followed by a large splash and much shouting signified that another bireme had been launched.

'We should strike west in conjunction, sir,' Sabinus stated, having come to the same conclusion as Vespasian, 'and try to crush Caratacus between us.'

'No!' Plautius slammed his fist onto the desk. 'That's just what we shouldn't do, Sabinus; that's just what he wants us to do. He would dearly love to draw your legions into the wild hills beyond the Sabrina; we don't even know his whereabouts so we'd be blundering about on his terms. We've got to draw him to us.'

Feeling relieved that he had not made the suggestion that had seemed so obvious, Vespasian sat in silence hoping for the benefit of Plautius' military wisdom. The unmistakable screams of a man being nailed to a cross rode through the air.

Having glared at Sabinus for long enough to communicate his severe displeasure and disappointment, Plautius turned his attention to Vespasian. 'Well?'

Vespasian opened his mouth and then closed it.

'Come on, legate, you must have something sensible to say even if your brother hasn't!'

'About Caratacus, sir?'

'Of course about Caratacus; who else do you think we're talking about? How do we draw Caratacus to us rather than risk doing a Varus and marching a couple of legions into miserable terrain full of valleys, all damp as a whore's minge, that can only be described as ideal ambush country?'

'Attack something he values, sir.'

'Thank you; one of you at least has picked up a bit of soldiering whilst you've been here.'

Vespasian was aware of Sabinus bristling next to him. The crucified man's screaming suddenly stopped but the shifting clamour of massed exertion continued.

'So what does he value enough to make him risk venturing out of his gods-cursed hole across the Sabrina River?'

Vespasian glanced at his brother to give him a chance to make up for his earlier mistake.

'Well, we believe that he has his wife and children with him,' Sabinus ventured, 'so that's not an option. The rest of his family are either dead or have surrendered; his lands in the east are occupied and whatever wealth he had is now in our hands. It doesn't really leave much.'

'Of course it does, you fool! It leaves the one thing that he values most: his support. That's the only thing that's important to him; essential even. If he doesn't have support he ceases to matter and goes from being a king resisting a conquering army to being a mere brigand.'

'The druids!' Vespasian blurted.

'Precisely. The druids support his resistance because it's in their interests to do so and their continued backing gives him a legitimacy that transcends tribal loyalties amongst every savage on this island. Now, the policy of cutting down their groves has worked very well in the areas that we occupy and there are very few of those filthy, matted-haired sons of gorgons left; and whenever we do come across one we nail him up pretty sharpish. However, there are a few more nests of these vermin and if we threaten one of them then I believe that Caratacus will have to come to its aid. And we've got a month to do it in so that we can say "Fuck you and your military competence" – in the nicest possible way of course – to Narcissus when we get back to Rome.' Plautius referred to the map lying unrolled on the desk. 'Now, there are two breeding grounds of this druidical abomination.' He pointed to a small island just off the west coast, beyond the Roman sphere of influence. 'This is called Mona; apparently it's swarming with them. It would be ideal but it's too far behind their lines.'

'Not if we go by sea, sir,' Vespasian pointed out.

'It's a long way, the seas are treacherous and the coast is very rocky, according to the only survey ship that has ever come back from up there. Talking of ships: how are they doing, Vespasian?'

'They'll all be afloat by nightfall.'

'Good, because you're going to need them.' Plautius brought his finger down south on the map and rested it on the north coast of the southwestern peninsula of the island. 'Around here somewhere is Durocornavis, the main fortress of the Cornovii. They're a sub-tribe of the Dumnonii and may or may not be related to the Cornovii in the north of the island who are our buffer between us and the Brigantes. Just close by the fortress is a huge rock, almost an island that juts out into the sea. I'm told that this is a place of deep mysticism for the druids; they have many legends attached to it and it is of great importance to them.

'Now, it's too far into unconquered territory to risk a land assault in just a month but if we make Caratacus think that we're mad enough to try he'll come to the aid of the Cornovii and the druids, otherwise he'll lose all credibility. And he won't be able to resist the chance to cut a whole legion up.

'He'll either sail across the Sabrina channel or around it; or, perhaps, make his way there by land. Whichever way he chooses he can't take a big force with him, just a few followers; but to his mind that's irrelevant as there will be plenty of long-hairs down there ready to fight for him because of his reputation. He just needs to get there and we must capture him as he tries.'

Vespasian looked at the map; it was very vague, just a rough approximation of the coastline of the peninsula with the Cornovii marked towards its tip; and then to the north, across the widening Sabrina channel, another crude coastline with the Silures written in, seemingly at random. 'We have no idea of the distances, do we, sir?'

'None; the channel could be twenty miles wide or a hundred at any point, we just don't know; as I said, only one survey ship has ever returned. What we do know is that they are very treacherous waters and we've already lost too many ships trying to get round the peninsula, which is why we're bringing the smaller ships overland and building new big ones.'

'So we've no idea how long the news of our supposed attack on these druids will take to reach Caratacus; in which case he might judge that it's all over by the time he hears of it and it's not worth the risk coming.'

Plautius smiled for the first time since arriving, raising his eyebrows. 'That's why I've taken the trouble to inform him of our supposed intentions in advance by using one of his own weapons against him: Alienus.'

'Alienus!' Vespasian and Sabinus exclaimed simultaneously.

'Who better? After he escaped from your camp last year, Vespasian, he disappeared completely, probably judging, correctly, that his face was a bit too well known for his line of subterfuge. However, a couple of months ago he reappeared, masquerading as a Britannic merchant dealing in pearls. He's grown his hair and a long moustache but he was recognised by one of my slaves in the market at Camulodunum. I decided not to apprehend him but instead had him followed. It turned out that not all of his pearls were traded for money or goods, some he set aside to buy information with from one of the clerks who copies out my written orders. Having completed his business he sailed west up the Tamesis and then crossed into enemy territory. I countermanded the information that he was carrying and gave orders to let him go, hoping that he would be back. Sure enough five days ago, just after I received Narcissus' insulting letter, he arrives with more pearls. I immediately drafted orders for you, Vespasian, to take the II Augusta, destroy Durocornavis and kill all the druids that you find on the rock and that I would come down to take overall command; and to you, Sabinus, I wrote that you were not to proceed any further west this year and spend the time building defences. Needless to say I didn't send those orders to you, I just allowed Alienus to purchase them from the clerk.'

Vespasian looked at his commanding officer with admiration, thinking that, for all his ill-temper, he never tired of learning from him. 'So Caratacus thinks he's free to go to the druids' aid?'

'Not yet, but by tomorrow or the next day he will. I made sure that I left, very publicly, before Alienus; he's behind me and convinced that he's got vital information for his master so he'll be travelling fast.'

'We'd better get a move on then.'

'We'll be fine as long as you sail tomorrow with your six biremes. Find this place and then cut it off from the sea, intercept every ship or boat you see and patrol the coast further west so Caratacus doesn't land behind you. Use the marines and do some raiding; kill a few and stir them up a bit.' Plautius turned to Sabinus. 'Meanwhile, Sabinus, you sail back north around the coast with your ships, check every inlet and bay. I'll stay here with the legion and keep the countryside well patrolled. Between us we should snare him. Once we have Caratacus you return to your legion and await my orders to advance across the Sabrina and start securing territory, slowly but surely. Take no risks, it's not about quick victory, it's about convincing a good percentage of the Silures' chieftains that without Caratacus uniting them their defeat is inevitable and it's just a question of how many warriors they want left in their settlements under Roman rule. Do you understand?'

'Yes, sir. And what if I find Alienus? I've a score to settle with him and a nice idea of how to settle it.'

'You can have him and nail him up for all I care. I'm not going to leave a useful asset like that around for my replacement to use and help him to look as if he has more *military competence* than me.' The flush in Plautius' face returned as he spat out that loathed and insulting phrase.

'Thank you, sir; it'll be a pleasure to help preserve your reputation.'

Vespasian licked his fingers and then wiped them on the napkin spread out in front of him on the couch before helping himself to another of the fine local oysters. Hormus refilled Sabinus' proffered cup and then stepped back into the shadows.

'And as to who my replacement will be,' Aulus Plautius continued, breaking a duck leg in two and dripping thick, brown sauce onto his napkin, 'I neither know nor care; he's welcome to this province as far as I'm concerned, with all the *military competence* that he can muster.' He drained his wine – his fifth cup of the dinner – before taking his anger out on his duck leg, gnawing noisily on it and then pointing it at Vespasian. 'But mind you, according to my wife's letters, the Rome that we'll be returning to is not the same as the one we all left at the beginning of Claudius' reign. The in-fighting for the mastery of Rome between his freedmen and the Empress rages on whilst Claudius, having celebrated his Triumph for his *glorious victory* in Britannia and having just annexed the client-kingdom of Thracia to further prove his military competence, now immerses himself in public projects and the law courts trying to create a legacy for himself. He's busy building a new port at Ostia, two new aqueducts – as well as repairing the Aqua Virgo – and this year he's started a project to drain the Fucine Lake. Meanwhile the business of government has been completely centralised and anyone who wants a position has to petition either one of the three ex-slaves or a vicious vixen with a sexual appetite that would have made Cleopatra blush.' He held out his cup for Hormus to refill and refused the offer of water.

Vespasian glanced in concern at Sabinus, on the couch to his left, whilst their commanding officer's attention was devoted to the contents of his filled cup; Sabinus put his hand to his mouth, understanding that he should not join in a conversation that was approaching the realms of treason.

'The Senate still administer their provinces,' Plautius continued, ripping more flesh from the thigh, 'but increasingly their appointments have gone to the Empress's worn-out lovers who now outnumber those in that *august* body who haven't had the pleasure of ingress into one or all of the imperial orifices. And what's worse is that the Emperor's provinces now seem to be the personal fiefdom of Narcissus and his cronies and to receive an appointment in one of those you have to denounce a supporter of Messalina's in open court.' He paused to down the rest of his cup and signal for a refill. 'And anyone who has the stupidity to complain about the situation is immediately charged with treason by both Messalina's faction and the supporters of that idiot Emperor's freedm—' Plautius stopped himself and looked with alarm at the two brothers; he put his full cup down on the table, careful not to spill a drop. 'Forgive my foolishness, gentlemen, I've been too long on campaign with you and my tongue has grown loose.' He glanced at Hormus now back in his position in the shadows.

'My slave is loyal, sir,' Vespasian assured him, relieved that Plautius had stopped his tirade before he had suggested a solution to the situation; his voice may well have been loud enough to carry outside the tent. 'I too am aware from letters of the situation back home.'

'Quite so; and it's best not to dwell on it. It's always hard to return to being a politician after a few years of being a blunt, plain-speaking soldier.'

And that very thought had been revolving around Vespasian's mind repeatedly for the last couple of months as his inevitable return to Rome approached: how would he adapt back into the narrow confines of imperial politics, keeping his opinions to a minimum and well hidden whilst being subject to the will of others? How would he cope after so long in the field commanding his own legion and auxiliaries? That he would be sucked back down into the schemes of Claudius' freedmen upon his return as they struggled for the mastery of Rome, he was in no doubt. Their plotting had even followed him to the very limits of the Empire by way of Pallas' letter, the previous year, demanding – in the form of a polite request – that he send Paetus back to Rome. However, this time he would not just be acting to further the ambition of others; this time he would have an objective of his own in mind; this time he would have a price and that price would be the removal of Flavia and the children from the imperial palace and out of the reach of the Empress Messalina and her brother, Corvinus. But he knew that the transition from soldier to politician would be difficult and he inclined his head to indicate to Plautius his sympathy. 'I imagine that keeping one's political thoughts to oneself after four years of saying exactly what you think militarily will be a challenge.'

'Thank you for your understanding, Vespasian.' Plautius looked at Sabinus. 'And yours too, I hope, Sabinus.'

A scratching on the leather door prevented Sabinus from replying immediately; Vespasian signalled Hormus to find out from the guards who wanted to see him.

'I think that it is fair to say that it would be hypocritical of my brother and me to condemn the views that you may have expressed, sir,' Sabinus observed as Hormus glanced around the door.

Plautius burst into laughter. 'And when did hypocrisy stop anyone from doing anything?'

With a relieved glance at Sabinus in thanks for defusing the situation, Vespasian motioned to Hormus to speak.

'Theron, the slave-trader,' Hormus said with palpable tension in his voice.

'Show him in.'

Hormus pulled the door aside and ushered in his former owner.

'Greetings, most noble Vespasian,' the Macedonian crooned, bowing unnecessarily low whilst keeping his eyes raised, taking in everyone else in the room. As they rested on Plautius they widened in alarm and his body became rigid, frozen mid-bow.

'Good evening, Theron,' Vespasian said, suppressing his amusement. 'Have you brought that contract for me?'

Pulling himself upright, Theron did his best to cover his consternation at having the Governor, the Emperor's representative in the province, overhearing their conversation. 'Er, yes, your honour ...'

'Just address me as "legate"!'

'Y-y-yes, legate. And greetings to you, most exalted Governor Plautius; may I say what an honour it is to meet you again?'

Plautius looked at the slave-trader with abject disgust and disdained to give an opinion as to whether he was at liberty to say that or not.

'Give it to Hormus and I'll look at it later; come back at dawn.'

Theron handed the scroll to Hormus who trembled visibly. 'I trust that you are getting, er,' he smiled knowingly, '*satisfaction* from this fine specimen that I sold to you at such generous terms, legate?'

Vespasian jumped to his feet and hurled his half-full wine cup at the slave-dealer, staining his saffron cloak red. 'Get out, you filth! And take your contract with you. If you want me to sign it then bring it back in the morning with ten per cent crossed out and replaced by twelve.'

Theron looked in horror at Vespasian. 'My humblest apologies, most noble legate, I meant no insult, I was merely making pleasant conversation.'

'Hormus, you have permission to physically kick the man out.'

Hormus looked from his master to his former owner with timid uncertainty all over his face. Theron grabbed the contract from the immobile slave's hand and bowed his way backwards from the tent with a flurry of unctuous apologies.

'You'll regret doing business with that man, Vespasian,' Plautius informed him. 'I was forced to use some rather persuasive methods to extract what he owed me for allowing the slave-traders to act as a cartel and fix the price they pay for new stock. All the others paid up reasonably promptly. I ended up throwing him out of the province last year once I got my money. I didn't know that he was back.'

'He turned up this morning and offered me a business proposition, which I accepted.'

'Very wise; four years serving Rome with no reward other than the satisfaction of doing one's duty – despite one's lack of *military prowess* – can be a drain on the coffers and we don't have long left to refill them. Just keep an eye on him, that's all.'

'Oh, I will, in fact I'll do—'

A bucina's blare from outside cut him off; the door was suddenly pushed open and Camp Prefect Maximus burst in. 'You'd better come quickly, sir; there's at least two dozen small boats in the estuary. They're trying to torch the biremes.'

CHAPTER VIII

'GET GLAUCIUS AND his Hamians down to the river now, Maximus!' Vespasian shouted, sprinting out into the camp, slinging his sword's baldric over his shoulder. 'And then have Ansigar and three turmae of his Batavians meet me at the gates.'

In amongst all the tents, legionaries and auxiliaries, some still chewing on their last mouthfuls of supper, were struggling to tie on their *lorica segmentata* or wriggle into their chain mail, cramming helmets on their heads, fastening belts and then grabbing weapons and shields before forming up by centuries and then cohorts along the hundred-foot gap running between the palisade and the tent lines. Burnished iron glinted with torch-light, steam wafted into the air as slaves poured water onto cooking fires; centurions and optiones, themselves trying to remedy their various states of undress, bellowed at their men for more urgency as bucina calls rent the air, unnecessarily re-sounding the alarm.

Vespasian sprinted the length of the Via Principalis, through the gates, past the two guard-duty centuries forming up beyond them, and cursed vociferously as he came out into the golden, flickering glow of a bireme burning like a beacon in the middle of the estuary. Silhouetted by the flames, scores of figures struggled in the water, splashing to stay afloat or, if capable, swimming to shore away from the ship in which they rowed and slept, and that had now become a blazing tomb.

Small boats, fifteen to twenty feet long, under oars, circled around the next two biremes in the line, their crews lobbing lit torches onto the decks and through the oar-ports and hurling fire-spears into the hulls. Sailors fought with buckets of water to

146

prevent the flames catching the dry planking and the pitch-sealed horsehair with which they were caulked. Other oarsmen heaved javelins, broken out from the weapons boxes at the base of the mainmasts, at their attackers, driving them off but not before many of their incendiary weapons had struck their mark.

In the few moments that Vespasian surveyed the scene, flames burst forth from the bow of a second bireme, next in line; the faint-hearts amongst its crew dived into the water whilst the steadier members renewed their fire-fighting efforts – to little visible effect.

'Centurions, with me!' Vespasian roared at the officers of the two guard-duty centuries. He set off down the slope towards the triremes under construction along the riverbank, just a hundred paces away. Easily outpacing the men doubling behind him, Vespasian arrived at the skeletal frames of the great ships; a dozen of the attacking boats now steered towards them. With five or six sweeps pulling on either side their speed gradually increased as they closed on their objective. Standing at their bows and sterns, fire-wielding warriors roared their rowing comrades on, eager to spread destruction through the makeshift shipyard.

Vespasian looked back; the centuries were arriving. 'Form up on the bank; we must stop them from landing!'

The legionaries funnelled through the gaps between the partially constructed hulks and fanned out two lines deep at the water's edge.

'Prepare to release!' Vespasian shouted as the line was completed. The attacking vessels were barely ten paces out.

Gauging the distance to their target, one hundred and sixty legionaries slung their right arms back, feeling the weight of their pila.

'And release!'

Black against the glowing background, the sleek, weighted weapons tore towards the oncoming boats and punched into the upper bodies of the men within or ripped through the hide-covered hulls and on into the crews' legs. Warriors were flung back and overboard, oarsmen were skewered to the backs of the men in front of them; the rapid changing of the weight distribution caused many of the craft to rock violently. Four of the vessels immediately capsized, spilling their screaming crews into the water; but the rest righted themselves and came on with foolhardy valour, their crews intent upon firing the ships that would make Rome masters of the sea in these waters.

'Hold them off, Placidus,' Vespasian ordered the centurion nearest him, recognising the man's face in the increasing glow; out in the estuary a third bireme, adjacent to the other two, now spouted flames from three of its oar-ports. 'I'll send you reinforcements as soon as they're available, in case more boats come.'

With no time to acknowledge his legate, Placidus roared at his men to prepare to receive as Vespasian turned and, with confidence in the men, left the two centuries to beat off half their number.

'I brought you a horse, sir,' Magnus shouted, bringing his mount to a halt, 'but I didn't have time to saddle it, I just threw a bridle over it.'

'Thank you, Magnus,' Vespasian said, raising his voice over the familiar clamour of mortal combat behind him. 'Ride along the bank to the jetties and start untying the boats.' Vaulting onto the animal's bare back, he turned it with a vicious tug of the reins and kicked it away back up the hill as Magnus headed off along the bank.

The Hamians streamed out of the gate in an eight-man-wide column as Vespasian approached; wheeling his mount to the right he accelerated along the formation of bow-armed auxiliaries to their prefect riding at their head. 'Send a century of your lads down to the jetties and have eight loaded into each of the boats. You know what to do then, Glaucius.'

'Get as close to the bastards as possible and then do what my boys are best at, sir.'

'Exactly; and be quick about it.' He pulled away and headed back towards the gates. Ansigar was waiting for him with ninety of his troopers. 'I hope these lads can row, Ansigar.'

'They're Batavians, sir,' Ansigar replied with a grin. 'They swim, row, ride and kill Britons.'

'Hopefully they won't need that first talent tonight; follow me.'

Magnus and the Hamian centurion were supervising the archers' embarkation into ten boats as Vespasian arrived with the Batavians at the jetties. Ansigar needed no orders and, shouting in his guttural language, assigned his men eight to each craft; the remainder he left minding the horses. Along the bank the main body of the Hamians had begun loosing volley after volley towards those attacking boats clear of the biremes; hundreds of shafts hissed into them, annihilating entire crews in moments and churning up the flame-red water around them as if a brutal hail storm had hit.

Jumping into the lead boat as soon as it was loaded, Vespasian grabbed the steering oar. He looked up at Magnus. 'Coming?'

'What, get in a boat when I don't have to? Bollocks!'

Vespasian shrugged and cast off.

The nearside Batavians pushed their oars against the jetty and, once clear, all eight of them pulled a stroke as one without a word of command; the wooden craft surged forward.

Out in the estuary the few surviving Britannic boats were seeking relative safety in the lee of the burning biremes out of sight of the Hamians. Along the bank, Placidus' men had beaten off the attempt to fire the shipyard; all down their line empty boats bobbed amongst the dark shapes of their former crews floating in the shallows. Just three of the erstwhile attackers' boats had the manpower remaining to flee back out into the estuary; the Hamians used them for target practice and ceased their volleys as the last one capsized.

Vespasian steered his boat towards the three blazing ships, now consumed with flames and wreathed in smoke; behind him the other crews strained at their sweeps, keeping pace. The heat from the raging infernos scorched his skin as they drew closer; sweat poured down the labouring oarsmen's faces and into their beards, and noxious fumes ravaged their gasping throats.

'Ansigar,' Vespasian shouted over his shoulder, 'take five of the boats and pass on the other side of the burning ships; we'll try and cut off the survivors. I want prisoners.'

Ansigar acknowledged the order with a wave and veered his craft away to the left, taking four of the others with him.

Passing the blazing bow of the first stricken bireme, Vespasian looked down the gap between it and the next; through the wafting smoke he could see no sign of the enemy, only bodies floating on the surface. He kept his course straight, passing the next ship and peered left, with stinging eyes, into the thirty-pace-wide lane between it and the final fired vessel. Again there was nothing; through the smoke he could just make out the shadowy form of Ansigar's boat powering by the other end.

Vespasian's crew rowed on, eyes squinting against fumes and sweat, past the final burning ship, now listing heavily; beyond it was open water. Vespasian swung the steering oar to the right, slewing his boat in the opposite direction around the doomed vessel as Ansigar appeared around the stern; between them was nothing but smoke and flotsam and jetsam.

'Shit!' Vespasian swore as he veered his boat back to its original course; Ansigar did the same coming alongside. The oarsmen kept up their pace, groaning with the effort of each pull and soon they were clear of the smoke; and then he saw them. They were mere outlines a hundred or so paces distant but they were unmistakably boats, six of them, heading down the estuary towards the sea. 'Put your backs into it, lads, and we'll have them; they'll tire before you will.'

The Batavians renewed their efforts in response to his call whilst the archers, seated forward of them, nocked arrows and tried to gauge the distance in the gloom. Behind them the rest of the small flotilla increased their pace at the sight of their quarry.

Then a new sound, shrill and regular, pierced through the grunts of exertion and the creak and splash of oars; Vespasian turned his head. From out of the bank of fire-lit smoke a ship emerged, its blades dipping in time to the stroke-master's piped beat: Sabinus' liburnian. Two men pulled on each of the eighteen oars protruding from either side of its streamlined hull forcing the bronze-headed ram extending from its bow through the foaming water at a speed that Vespasian's craft could not hope to match; but nor could the Britons. Within a few score strokes the ship had drawn level; Sabinus stood in its stern, next to the trier-archus, encouraging the oarsmen in the open rowing deck to greater efforts. On a platform in its bow a party of marines loaded a small carroballista; winching back the torsioned arms of the artillery piece they placed the three-foot-long iron-headed wooden bolt in the shooting-groove before sighting the weapon. Up ahead the Britons had seen the new threat looming dark against the glowing background and their shouts of dismay carried over the water; but their speed did not increase; they were already at the limits of their power.

'We need prisoners!' Vespasian yelled at his brother as he passed. Sabinus waved in acknowledgement as, with a rasping twang followed by the dull thump of the arms hitting the padded restraining bars, the bolt accelerated from the carroballista into the night; the whisper of air rushing past its leather flights marked its passing. The marines hurried to reload as the liburnian ploughed on, overtaking Vespasian's flotilla and gaining with every oar-straining stroke on the six fleeing boats.

'What are you waiting for?' Vespasian shouted at his archers. On unsteady legs the eight Hamians in the bow stood and released a speculative volley from the rocking craft; their comrades in the other boats followed their lead and were rewarded, more by luck than judgement, by a couple of cries of pain and a shadowy figure falling overboard. Then the carroballista spat a second missile; within a heartbeat shrieks rang through the air and a boat disintegrated into foaming water. The Hamians kept up a quick rate of release, peppering the Britons and reducing their rowing power so that their overhaul became inevitable. A third shot from the bolt-shooter, almost at point-blank range, took the head off one warrior before passing through the chest of the next and finally skewering a third by his belly to the pierced hull of the vessel. With the distance closing so that visibility became less of an issue the Hamians set about their work with relish and their kill-rate increased. As oarsmen perished and their sweeps fouled, the boats began to slew and it was almost at a broadside that the merciless ram of the liburnian crashed through the nearest, tossing its crew aside like dolls to be sucked under its hull or pounded down by its weighty wooden blades.

The liburnian drove relentlessly on towards its next victim, blocking the Hamians' line of sight; Vespasian steered his boat through its choppy wake, searching the surface for survivors. As another fleeing boat was ploughed beneath the bow of the liburnian, a warrior bobbed up from under its stern, coughing and spluttering and making frantic movements with his arms to stay afloat.

Vespasian changed course towards the floundering man, bringing the boat alongside him. With the drawn bows of a couple of the Hamians aimed at his face, he grabbed an oar and was hauled in; he scrambled aboard, his chest heaving and blood streaming down his face from a gash on his forehead. Sweeping his sword from its scabbard, Vespasian brought the flat of the blade cracking down on the man's skull; he slumped, unconscious, into the shallow water slopping in the bilge as the screams of the last of his comrades were silenced beneath the liburnian's hull.

'He says that he comes from Durocornavis,' Cogidubnus informed Vespasian, Sabinus and Plautius, 'and I believe him; he has the uncouth accent of the Cornovii of the southwest.'

Vespasian looked down at the terrified warrior, splayed out on a cross on the ground, his arms and legs held in place by legionaries with mallets in their belts and long nails gripped in their teeth. 'I can't think of any reason why he would choose to lie at this moment.'

'Ask him whether this was Caratacus' idea,' Plautius ordered, 'or whether they just took it upon themselves to try to burn our ships.'

After the question had been put the warrior spoke quickly, his eyes flicking between all the nails that might soon be pounded through his wrists and feet.

Cogidubnus listened, the glow of the three dying fires out in the estuary playing on his face, and then nodded, as if satisfied by the answer, before translating. 'It was their chieftain, Judoc, who ordered the attack once he'd received news from Arvirargus, King of the Dumnonii, of the ships being dragged across the portage way. The druids told him that they'd read in the entrails of a shipwrecked Roman sailor that the gods would favour them.'

'They were mistaken on that point,' Sabinus observed unnecessarily.

Vespasian raised an eyebrow. 'It goes to show that you should never believe everything you read.'

'Thank you, legate!' Plautius snapped. 'There's no place for wit in my army. Ask him what he knows about Caratacus.'

Again Cogidubnus posed the question; this time the answer was more hesitant. 'He claims that they have had no contact with Caratacus.'

'Bollocks! He's lying.'

'Yes, I agree; Caratacus would have sent emissaries to every tribe and sub-tribe not yet under Roman rule.'

Plautius looked at the legionary holding the captive's right arm. 'Soldier, put your nail ready to hammer it home.'

The legionary took the six-inch nail from his mouth, placed it on the warrior's wrist, just below the base of the thumb, took his mallet from his belt and held it ready. The captive's chest started heaving with terrified anticipation and he spoke breathlessly with a pleading timbre to his voice.

Cogidubnus smiled, his eyes glinting in the glow. 'That's more like it. What he meant to say was that they have had no *direct* contact with Caratacus; he hasn't crossed the water to hold counsel with his chieftain, but his representative did, in the summer of this year, and met with Arvirargus and all the chieftains of the sub-tribes.'

Plautius was interested. 'When exactly did this man arrive?'

'A month after the summer solstice,' was the translated reply.

'Towards the end of July, just under a couple of months ago; that fits with Alienus leaving Camulodunum the first time and taking my cancelled orders back to Caratacus. What was discussed at this meeting?'

'He doesn't know all that was said,' Cogidubnus translated, having listened to the reply. 'He's just a warrior and doesn't share in the counsels of the great; but after the man left, Arvirargus declared that there would be a muster of the Dumnonii on the first full moon after the harvest had been brought in. He also ordered the Cornovii to build more *currachs* – they're the boats that they used tonight. They were told to make them longer and wider so that they could hold more men.'

Vespasian looked at his superior. 'What were the written orders that Alienus purchased from your clerk, sir?'

Plautius thought for a few moments. 'They were for you: I'd been considering for a while not advancing any further south-west for the time being, seeing as apart from some tin there's very little of value down there; the Dumnonii don't even mint their own coins. So I issued orders for you to negotiate honourable terms with Arvirargus whereby he keeps his crown and independence but gives us access to his tin mines. Once done, you were to hold this line that we're now on with garrisons of auxiliaries whilst the legion moved to relieve the Fourteenth Gemina. They would then, along with half of the Twentieth Legion, called up from reserve, have gone north into the northern Cornovii's territory to threaten the lands of the Brigantes and force their bitch of a queen, Cartimandua, to make a decision one way or another instead of telling both me and Caratacus that she supports us entirely and would be only too happy to bear our children.'

'So Caratacus was going to take advantage of our weakened presence down here and send the army of the Dumnonii against us, without telling Arvirargus that you were willing to negotiate.'

'Which is exactly what I would have done in his position; he would have forced me to abort my move against the Brigantes and would have been able to claim to Cartimandua, with some justification, that he had saved her people from invasion, thereby claiming her loyalty. Only it didn't happen because I rescinded the orders.' Plautius looked back down at the captive. 'Cogidubnus, ask him what happened to the army after it was mustered.'

The King translated the brief reply. 'It was disbanded after half a moon.'

'Because the Second Augusta did not move north, which tells us that the Dumnonii have not got the strength or inclination to face a full legion, which means that they could be open to negotiation. And yet the druids persuaded one of the sub-tribes to launch an attack on us, which is bound to bring reprisals, if not an all-out invasion of their worthless territory which hitherto we have left untouched.'

Sabinus ran a hand through his hair, shaking his head, incredulous. 'They want us to attack them?'

'No, brother,' Vespasian said softly, 'Caratacus wants us to attack them. He's willing to sacrifice the Dumnonii knowing that their conquest will keep a whole legion busy for at least a year or two. And to what end? Some tin mines in a peninsula that leads nowhere; strategically it's irrelevant and he knows it. The druids helped him to try and trigger the attack because it's also in their best interests. Don't forget they have no tribal loyalties, they're not Dumnonii druids or Cornovii druids; their loyalty is only to their gods and they see Caratacus as the man who will preserve their ways and, hence, the druids' power.'

'Judoc is not going to be very pleased with the druids or Caratacus if he finds that out,' Cogidubnus observed; his face revelled in the pleasure of the thought.

Plautius looked equally pleased. 'No, he won't; and nor will Arvirargus. I believe that you should be the one to tell them. Vespasian, I think we should revise your part of the plan slightly: Cogidubnus will now go with you and whilst you wait to intercept Caratacus' arrival do nothing to upset the Cornovii; instead, Cogidubnus will go ashore and meet with this Judoc and explain to him that I'm willing to overlook his raid on our ships because he was obviously manoeuvred into it by self-serving priests. If we can turn the Cornovii against the druids they could do our job for us.'

'Very good, sir. What about Arvirargus?'

'I'm going to deal with him later. Once the druids are disposed of and Caratacus captured, we'll take the legion a few miles into Dumnonii territory, burn some settlements and then summon the King for a meeting. I'll just ask him one question: does he want to keep his crown and lands? Without the druids' self-serving advice and Caratacus' false counsel being poured into his ear, I think I can guess what the answer will be.'

'That's two big assumptions, sir.'

'Not really; you'll deal with the druids if the Cornovii won't. And Caratacus acted on the false information that Alienus gave him last time and so he will this time; he'll come. You'll sail with the tide at the third hour of the day; so I suggest that you get some sleep. Any questions?'

Vespasian looked down at the captive still lying on his cross. 'What about him, sir?'

'What?' Plautius glanced down at the man. 'Oh, him; nail him up.'

'I'd rather take him with me; he could be useful. For a start he knows where this nest of druids is.'

'Will we be ready by the time the tide turns, Maximus?' Vespasian asked, stifling a yawn as they walked through the gates and surveyed the boats rowing back and forth to the nine surviving biremes with the last of the crews and provisions. The burnt-out remains of the three fired ships protruded from the river's surface as they were gradually submerged by the rising tide.

'I spoke to all the trierarchi an hour ago at dawn and they were confident we would be, sir. The oarsmen are all aboard and it's just the last of the marines and provisions being ferried across now.'

Vespasian grunted his satisfaction, stifling another yawn. 'How many of those currachs did we manage to salvage?'

'Currachs?'

'It's what the Britons call those boats that they were using last night.'

'Oh, I see; eight so far, but with only enough oars for five.'

'That'll be enough; have them tied off to my biremes, we'll take them with us.'

'Who's going to handle them? They're completely different to our small boats.'

'Speak to Cogidubnus and tell him to choose the men he's taking with him on their ability to row. That'll be all.'

Maximus saluted, his distrust of anything un-Roman barely concealed on his face. Vespasian watched him go wondering whether Plautius had got his plan right.

'You've got that constipated expression on your face again, sir,' Magnus informed him, walking through the gates with a steaming bowl in his hand. 'Are you worried about something again or have you genuinely got a blockage? If it's the latter, this'll help.' He handed the bowl and a spoon to Vespasian. 'Lentils – with pork and lovage; Hormus is getting the knack of it, slowly that is. Now that you've managed to force yourself to buy a body-slave I do think you should have a go at purchasing a cook. Perhaps some high-class cooking will stop you looking like you're trying to pass a ballista bolt, if you take my meaning?'

Vespasian took the bowl and helped himself to a mouthful. 'It's not the standard of Hormus' cooking but rather the standard of Plautius' planning that I'm finding hard to pass.'

'What do you mean?'

Vespasian sat on the ground and explained Plautius' plan whilst eating his breakfast.

'Well, it seems to me,' Magnus said after a few moments' rumination to digest the information, 'that it all relies on Caratacus reacting to the information that Alienus brings him even though the last time he did so that information turned out to be wrong.'

'Exactly. I didn't realise that yesterday afternoon when Plautius explained to me and Sabinus what he planned, but then last night, after he told us that Caratacus had made moves to counter Plautius' cancelled orders, I seriously wondered if Caratacus would fall for the same ruse twice.'

'Does it matter? Look at it this way: if he does think that the risk to his credibility is too much to hazard, then he will come, even if he's suspicious about the information. He can't afford not to and then it's down to us to catch him and Plautius' plan will hinge on us doing so. However, if he believes the whole thing to be a trap to lure him into the open – which is what I'd put my money on – then what'll happen? Bugger all. He won't move, you'll sail up and down the coast for a while whilst Cogidubnus tries to convince Judoc to kill the druids for us and if he doesn't succeed you'll have that pleasure; but whoever does it, the druids will be dead, Caratacus' reputation as a defender of all things Britannic will be tarnished and Arvirargus will have no one to argue him out of doing a deal with Plautius.'

Vespasian scraped out the last of his lentils and chewed on them thoughtfully. 'I suppose you're right: whatever happens, the plan should work; it's just that we might not end up capturing Caratacus and taking him back to Rome.'

'Ah! So that's what's making you look like you could do with a good couple of hours thrashing about in the latrines: you're worried that our masters back in Rome ain't going to give you the recognition you feel that you deserve because you've left unfinished business in this gods-cursed island.'

'Wouldn't you be?'

'Of course not. Whether you go back with or without Caratacus, Claudius' freedmen will make sure that you're feted. They have to. It's vitally important to them to keep Claudius' great conquest firmly fixed in the Senate's and people's minds. Claudius will drool and slobber all over you in public because the more glory he bestows on you the better he looks as being the instigator of this heroic enterprise. You'll be paraded in your Triumphal Regalia; Plautius may even be granted an Ovation just so the Emperor can share it and remind everyone of his Triumph when he returned as the conquering hero three years ago, having *saved* Plautius' beleaguered legions. Sabinus will be made consul next year when he's forty-two and you'll be promised the consulship in five years' time when you reach that age, and the fact that Caratacus is still at liberty to run around and lop our lads' heads off whenever he gets the chance will be quietly forgotten.'

Vespasian smiled ruefully at his friend's blunt assessment of the realities of keeping up imperial appearances and handed back his bowl. 'Yes, that makes sense; this invasion was always about keeping Claudius and his freedmen in power.'

'Exactly; and if you're not seen to be rewarded there'll be rumblings in all classes of society that the Emperor is an ungrateful cripple who refuses to honour men who make him look good. It's the same thing for me as leader of my Crossroads Brotherhood: if one of the lads does something which benefits the community we look after and therefore makes me look good in their eyes ...'

'Like knifing a persistent thief in a back alley, for example?'

'Now there you go mocking again. I'm just trying to say that my position's no different to the Emperor's except on a far smaller scale, but yes, you're right: if one of the lads did that then I would publicly praise him and we'd all forget that he'd committed—'

'Excuse me, most honoured legate,' a smooth voice cut in.

Vespasian looked up and remained seated. 'What is it, Theron?'

The slave-dealer bowed with sycophantic reverence as if presenting himself to an eastern potentate. 'Your contract, excellency.' He proffered a scroll towards Vespasian. 'With the, er, amendment that you suggested, plus an extra half of one per cent to clear up that silly misunderstanding that we had last night.'

Vespasian took the contract and unrolled it. 'It wasn't a *silly* misunderstanding, Theron; I understood you very well. Just because you bugger your male slaves doesn't mean I do; nor do I have them fellate me.'

'Indeed not, noble legate, that would be a dangerous position to put oneself in.'

'You're disgusting; get out of my sight.'

'This instant, your mag—'

'Go!'

'And our agreement?'

Vespasian looked at the contract and then back at Theron. 'All right, go and wait by the slave compound; I'll read this and if it suits me I'll send word to the slave-master that you're to pick three hundred and fifty of them.'

Theron tried but failed to suppress a profit-motivated smile as he bowed his way backwards. 'Most gracious, your legateship, my eternal—'

'Theron!'

'Yes, your—'

'Not another word!'

'Of course not, y—'

Vespasian's glare finally reduced the slave-dealer to silence. 'I shall be back in Rome in spring next year; I expect *you* to find *me* and bring me my money.'

'With utmost pleasure, excellency.'

'That's the last time you'll see him,' Magnus said, getting to his feet as Theron turned and left.

'Oh no, he and I are going to become very close friends,' Vespasian replied, going through the contract. 'Twelve and a half per cent of the resale value, how generous; he must really like me.'

'It's easy to be generous to friends whom you have no intention of paying.'

CHAPTER VIIII

THE SWELL HAD grown to the point that rowing was unfeasible as the oars could no longer be guaranteed to bite into the sea's undulating surface. The flotilla's leather sails, however, were full-bellied with a brisk northerly wind that, with muscle-straining coaxing by the steersmen on their oars, was driving the five biremes along the rugged coastline of the peninsula, a couple of miles off their larboard side.

Vespasian held onto the rail on the windward side, enjoying the sea air and the spray thrown up by the ship's bucking ram blowing into his face. Ahead of him, along the deck the half-century of marines and Cogidubnus' thirty followers sat glumly looking out to sea; many of the Britons' faces betrayed how unsuited they were to a mariner's life.

'I don't suppose Sabinus is looking as cheerful as you are,' Magnus mused, arriving at the rail on unsteady legs and looking slightly pale.

Vespasian chuckled. 'He'll be prostrate in his cabin; he's the worst sailor I know. I think it broke his heart when Plautius ordered him to come and personally take command of his biremes; three days at sea and then back again. He's convinced that Plautius did it as a punishment for getting himself captured last year. This wind is certainly paying him out for his stupidity.'

Vespasian chuckled again at the thought of his brother's discomfort and thanked Neptune for the wind with which they were finally making some progress. They had sailed out of the estuary two days earlier and had made little headway, rowing into a stiff breeze. The following day they had fared slightly better as they rowed past a moor perched high on precipitous cliffs and then finally rounded a point and turned from due west to southwest.

Having spent the night in the shelter of a river estuary, to which the captive Briton had guided them, they had set out that morning with the tide and their progress had been good; the captive had assured Vespasian and Cogidubnus that they would reach their destination by sunset. During the whole three days of the voyage there had been no sign of any other vessels nor had any figures been spotted on the cliffs or shore. The only life they had come across had been the occasional settlement in an inlet and a small fishing village in the estuary the night before; Vespasian had ordered the inhabitants to be rounded up to prevent them from sending a boat off in the night to warn of their journey. In compliance with Plautius' orders not to upset the Cornovii, the villagers had been released unharmed that morning.

Looking at the deserted coastline backed by forested hills, Vespasian could quite understand Plautius' reluctance to move into the peninsula aggressively; the little there was down here would be hard to hold by a force small enough to justify its secondment to such a poor and irrelevant part of the island.

A shout from the trierarchus brought Vespasian back to the moment; bare-footed sailors scampered across the deck and began to climb the mainmast whilst others performed complicated nautical manoeuvres with ropes. Cogidubnus strode over to him, as firm and steady as if he were on a paved road. 'The captive says that it's time for us to risk going inshore otherwise we'll be spotted from the lookouts around Durocornavis, which he claims is only three bays away.'

'Do you trust him?'

The King shrugged. 'If we drown, he'll drown.'

'It's not him I'm worried about.'

'Well, either we take his advice or we announce our arrival.'

Vespasian was forced to agree.

'He says that the bay before our objective has a natural harbour where we could land in the currachs; it's about two and a half miles from Durocornavis and is the only safe landing place within seven miles of the settlement. His people keep their boats there; there are some huts but everyone spends the night within the walls of the settlement.'

'He can pilot us in there at night?'

'He says that he can. Why did you say "us"?'

'Yeah, I picked up on that,' Magnus muttered.

'Because I'm going ashore to have a look at that rock; if you can only get to it by land then it's pointless looking at it from the sea.'

'You won't have to look at it at all if Cogidubnus persuades the Cornovii to clean off all the vermin from that rock.'

'Yes, but if he doesn't then we'll have to do it and we'll need to do it quickly; so I have to have some sort of plan in my head. Tomorrow I'll be sending three of the ships on patrol down the coast to keep an eye out for Caratacus so our presence here will be noted; tonight is my only chance to go ashore and back again in secret. It won't take long to cover the five miles there and back; I'll be back by dawn.'

'I can't think of anything that I'd like to do less than go and spy on a load of druids.'

'Which is exactly why I'm not taking you – I couldn't bear you moaning about it all the time.'

Vespasian blew into his cupped hands, warming them, as Cogidubnus' men rowed the currach, guided by the captive, towards the natural harbour along a rugged coastline pounded by crashing waves whose spray, caught in the moonlight, rose like repeated explosions of pearls to dissipate into a fine silver mist.

Uneasy at once again coming close to a druidical centre and the horror that he knew could be lurking there, Vespasian tried to console himself with the knowledge that their presence on this coast was still undetected – at least he hoped that it was. To stop himself worrying about it he turned to Cogidubnus, seated next to him in the stern of the small craft. 'How do you plan to get to see Judoc?'

'We'll make our way to his settlement tonight and then wait until dawn when the gates open and we'll walk in under a branch of truce; he'll be honour-bound to respect that. No one can kill a man who has come to parley before he has heard what he has to say.'

'And after?'

'Then he's free to do whatever he wishes, but I don't think that I'll be in any danger because he'll understand that in killing me, or handing me over to the druids, he'll be signing his eventual death warrant.'

'I hope you're right.'

'I am, Vespasian, don't worry about me; you just concentrate on getting to the harbour before dawn so that my men can take you back to the ship. With luck I'll be waiting for them at the harbour when they return in the evening.'

Vespasian could see the logic of the argument and grimaced as he realised that in all likelihood he would be in more danger than the King. He grasped the hilt of his gladius and checked that the weapon was loose in its scabbard whilst trying to calm his growing fear. He looked over to the two marines sitting in the bow with the four men who would accompany Cogidubnus and prayed that he had chosen steady, stealthy, hard men as his companions.

The captive spoke to the oarsmen in their own tongue and pointed towards the shore; the rocks had started to fall away and Vespasian could see the sea, dappled by moonlight, curl inland. As the currach turned to larboard into the harbour he felt the swell decrease markedly and saw the dim outline of a small island, away to his right, planted squarely in front of the inlet's mouth, sheltering it from the worst ravages of the sea. The oarsmen pulled with vigour, their oars biting into the calmer surface, propelling the boat faster as it snaked left and then right around the rocks, following the looping inlet. As the boat straightened out after the right turn they came to a long thin harbour with no view back out to sea; the rock wall that protected it dulled the constant roar of breaking waves and the creak of the oars seemed to be magnified in this strangely quiet haven. Vespasian felt a chill in the eerie silence as he looked up at the surrounding hills that tumbled down to the water's edge; it was the same chill that had affected him on his approach to the Vale of Sullis. The power of the druids was near.

The oarsmen raised their sweeps and let the currach glide onto the shingle beach at the head of the harbour. The captive jumped out and steadied the craft as Vespasian, Cogidubnus and their companions splashed into the shallow water.

'Stay out in the middle of the harbour whilst you wait for me to return,' Vespasian ordered the oarsmen as the currach was pushed back out into the water.

Crunching across the shingle they passed through the collection of currachs drawn up on the pebbles and crossed the wide but low-running river that fed the inlet. Once on firmer, quieter ground, Cogidubnus exchanged a few words with the captive before turning to Vespasian. 'He says that our paths lie together for the first couple of miles and then we'll veer south to the settlement just before we reach the rock that he says is called Tagell by his people – it means "throat".'

Vespasian forced a half-smile. 'Then I pray that I don't get swallowed.'

'Don't joke about it; that was my thought when he told me.'

Vespasian looked at the captive and signalled him to lead off, following the course of the river inland. Wrapping his dark cloak around his shoulders he hurried after the man, but then stopped abruptly, his hand flying to his sword hilt, as shouts came out of the gloom from all about, followed by rushing, shadowy figures.

He spun around looking for the boat but it had passed out into the middle of the harbour, too far to reach in time. 'Go!' he yelled at the oarsmen. 'It's a trap; get back to—' Pain sheared through his skull and a blinding light flashed across his inner vision; then all was darkness.

Vespasian woke to see the half-moon shining down upon him from a sky alive with stars. He felt himself swaying gently; he tried to move his arms but found them to be constricted, pressed into his body. He realised that he was lying in a makeshift stretcher of a blanket or cloak tied onto two spears. He raised his head slightly, grimacing in pain, and could make out the huge form of Cogidubnus walking ahead of him, his arms behind his back – presumably tied there. He cursed inwardly and wondered how the Cornovii had known to expect them. But it was a futile exercise and he closed his eyes and succumbed once more to darkness.

*

Shouting, the grate of iron hinges and creaking of wood woke him and he looked up to see that he was passing through a gateway; the reek of unsanitised habitation sweetened by wood-smoke assaulted his nostrils. After a few score paces his bearers stopped and he heard the rasp of a heavy bolt being pulled back, then a door scraped open and he was carried into a dimly lit hut whose walls were covered with animal skins. Without much consideration for his comfort he was lowered to the ground; he was surrounded by half a dozen warriors, the tips of their spears a couple of feet from his face. One shouted at him incomprehensibly and gestured to the ground; Vespasian sat up and looked to where the man was pointing and saw the gaping mouth of a pit with an iron grille with a rope attached lying next to it. With no choice other than to comply he shuffled forward and, grabbing the rope, lowered himself down its ten-foot length. As he reached the bottom he looked back up; the warriors surrounded the pit's rim, but then two moved aside and Cogidubnus was shoved into view and his bonds were cut. With what sounded like the most virulent of curses the King lowered himself down. The rope was withdrawn, the grille was placed over the entrance and then two huge logs were rolled onto it to hold it firm.

'Where're our men?' Vespasian asked.

'I don't know. They're still alive, though; they were taken away as we entered the settlement.'

'How did they know to expect us?'

'Again, I don't know.'

'We'll just have to hope that Judoc listens to you before he does anything rash.'

'He's under no obligation to parley now as I didn't enter the settlement under a branch of truce and I also came with an invader. He would be well within his rights to disembowel me, take out my tongue and eyes and leave me to die.'

Vespasian winced at the image as voices came from above and someone entered the hut. 'Well, perhaps this is him; we'll find out how amenable he is to negotiation.'

He looked up; a figure walked into view and squatted down by the grille, holding a flaming torch to illuminate the pit.

Vespasian's heart jumped as he looked into the triumphant, malicious eyes of Alienus.

'I'm gratified that you look so surprised to see me, legate,' the spy said with a smile spreading across his face. 'No doubt you thought that I'd be running back to Caratacus with my copies of Plautius' orders?'

'It was assumed that was what you would do.'

'Ah, assumptions; dangerous things, wouldn't you agree, legate, seeing as you're in your present predicament because of one? Did Plautius really think that he could cancel the orders that I purloined and I wouldn't realise that he knew I had them – that he must have let me have them?'

'It had crossed my mind.'

'And yet here you are as I knew you would be when I read Plautius' obvious attempt to lure Caratacus out into the open. I was intrigued to know what he would try to set up if I went back to get more of his misinformation and he didn't disappoint me; it might even have been construed as clever had he tried it on a lesser mind than mine. Unfortunately for him and you I didn't waste time taking the rubbish to Caratacus but instead rushed straight here to await your arrival. And you've duly obliged me; more than that, you've brought my usurping cousin with you. That, I confess, I didn't expect; it's almost too delicious to be true.'

Cogidubnus showed no emotion as he stared steadily at his cousin. 'Don't let your enjoyment run away with itself and cloud your already suspect judgement, Alienus; if I were you I would think carefully before deciding how to treat us. Judoc won't thank you for killing us and bringing down Roman retribution upon him and his people.'

'Judoc!' Alienus sneered. 'What does he know? As far as he's concerned you were sent here to kill him.'

'Is that what you told him?'

'Of course; and your prompt arrival proved me to be correct and he's got no reason to disbelieve my assertion that he's not the only leader who's been targeted. At dawn he's going to send a message to Arvirargus warning him that assassins in Rome's pay are on their way to kill him; your comrades' heads are, as we speak, being removed from their bodies to send as proof of the attempt on Judoc's life. Arvirargus and Judoc will now fight because they think that they have no alternative if they wish to remain alive; so unless Rome wants a permanent thorn in her southwestern flank, she'll have to commit a legion to subduing the area.

'How are you going to progress north and west with only three legions whilst at the same time holding the lands that you've already gained and keeping those tribes down now that your rapacious tax-farmers have been let loose amongst them? Move yet more troops from the Rhenus and leave Gaul even more open to all those nasty Germans? I think not.' Alienus stood and assumed a look of innocence. 'My game, I believe. I shall see you later, gentlemen, once I've composed a suitably disconcerting message for Judoc to send to his king concerning Roman assassination attempts. I've a little score to settle with the legate before Judoc hands you over to the druids so that Myrddin can decide what to do with you. I don't know about you but I've a curious feeling that Myrddin's going to get his sacrifice after all.' He raised his eyebrows and pursed his lips. 'But then again, Myrddin always gets what he wants.'

Vespasian sat hunched against the pit wall and drifted in and out of uneasy sleep during the next few hours of the night whilst Cogidubnus paced back and forth. Their attempts at shifting the logs weighing down the grille had proved fruitless: the guards had laughed at them and had not even bothered to crack their spear shafts down on Vespasian's exposed fingers as he sat on Cogidubnus' shoulders.

The imminent arrival of dawn was heralded by sporadic bird-song and a persistent cockerel close by; a torch flickered overhead and a stale loaf of bread and some meat of unknown provenance were thrown down through the grille.

'What do you think the chances are of a rescue party making it ashore during the night?' Cogidubnus asked, doing his best with a lump of gristle.

Vespasian shook his head. 'They've got five currachs plus the launches on each of the biremes but where would they land? Alienus would have left a force watching the harbour, and the last beach that I noticed that was suitable for a landing was at least twenty miles back.'

Cogidubnus gave up the struggle and spat out a semi-chewed mess. 'Yes, that's how I figured it; even if they did that there's no way they would get here overland before we're handed over to the druids. And without a local pilot they wouldn't know where was safe to land further southwest until daybreak. I'm afraid that we have to find our own way out of this. I don't fancy a meeting with these druids: Myrddin will have heard that it was me who killed his brethren in the Vale of Sullis and I'm sure that he'll enjoy his revenge.'

Vespasian did not bother to voice his agreement. 'Who is Myrddin?'

Cogidubnus betrayed the first sign of fear that Vespasian had ever seen on his face. 'He's the chief druid in Britannia; the man who possesses all the secrets of their power, which he will hand on to his successor along with his name once he has been found.'

'Found?'

'Yes, the druids believe that when they die they are reincarnated in another body, that's why they don't fear death; therefore previous Myrddins are always being reborn. It's the present Myrddin's duty to identify a previous Myrddin amongst all the new initiates so that he can train him and pass on his lore so that Myrddin is, to all intents and purposes, immortal. The present one is probably here to judge the new initiates.'

'Immortal like a god.'

'Yes, sort of like a god.'

'Do these druids have another god like Sullis?'

'I've no idea but they'll have something to keep them there, otherwise there wouldn't be so many of them clustered on that rock.'

Vespasian felt his stomach turn and knew that it was not due to the poor quality of the food. A noise from above diverted his attention.

'I expect that you're regretting keeping your word and letting me live, legate?' Alienus mused, looking down from above, holding in a leather-gloved hand an iron, glowing like the dawn sun, soon to rise outside.

Vespasian struggled against the four men who pinned his shoulders and legs to the wooden table as he had struggled against everything that had happened to him since being forced at spearpoint out of the pit. He had fought against the warriors who had eventually managed to tie his hands behind his back; he had kicked out at the men who had secured his legs together with leather thongs. Blood dripped down his forehead from where he had managed to head-butt the first man who had attempted to rip his tunic off – a second man had succeeded with no more than teeth-marks in his hand – and the warrior who had removed his loincloth now had a broken jaw from a double knee-jerk that had left both him and Vespasian sprawling on the floor. But now he had been lifted, writhing and bucking, onto the table and, despite his efforts, he realised that he was now helpless; he ceased to battle and lay, his chest heaving, naked apart from his sandals, looking at Alienus and the red-hot terror in his hand.

'Well, legate, you seem to be even less keen to have your flesh burnt than I was,' Alienus observed, thrusting the iron back into the heart of a mobile brazier. 'Perhaps it would make it easier for you if you were given some questions to answer, as I had to; then it wouldn't be just mindless torture for the sake of it. Yes, answering questions will give a sort of validity to the exercise – an air of respectability, if you will – and it'll give us both a purpose; me to find out what you know and you to withhold the information like a soldier should.'

Vespasian spat at the spy but missed.

'I wouldn't try to make me cross if I were you; it might jog my memory about which part of my anatomy you threatened to sear off. Now, where were we? Ah yes, questions. What to ask? The trouble is that there are very few things that I need to know from you.' He pulled the iron from the fire, its tip now as yellow as the midday sun, and brought it close enough to the outside of

Vespasian's right thigh for it to singe the hairs upon it. 'I know what I want you to tell me: on the morning that you sailed out of the estuary,' he leant in closer, 'what did you have for breakfast?'

Vespasian looked at his tormentor, wondering if this was some trick, and then a scorching heat raged up his body. The glowing iron seared through the skin and into the muscle of his thigh and he convulsed in unimagined pain.

'Well?' Alienus roared in his ear. 'What did you have for breakfast?' He pulled the iron away from the charred flesh, smoke rising from the burn, and repeated his question in a pleasant, friendly tone: 'What did you have for breakfast on the morning you sailed?'

Vespasian hyperventilated as he tried to work out whether he had heard correctly; another repetition of the question convinced him that he had. With a hiss, the pain hit again. 'Lentils,' he muttered through gritted teeth.

Alienus smiled with regret. 'Lentils? Oh legate, you disappoint me; I would have thought that a man of your rank and *dignitas* would have held onto such vital information for much longer. I can see that I'm going to have to ask some tougher questions.'

'Spare me the little games, Alienus; burn me if you want but don't try and pretend that it's anything other than revenge for the humiliation that you must still feel because I made you talk.'

'You gave me no choice!' Alienus' jaw clenched and his mouth set firm and he drew the iron slowly down the inside of Vespasian's thigh.

This time Vespasian resisted the pain as his mind raced and he realised that he had unwittingly hit the mark; he squinted up through watering eyes at the spy. 'It was you who told me where Sabinus was, remember?'

The iron stopped and Alienus pressed it hard against the soft flesh.

'Does Myrddin know?' Vespasian roared, converting the scream that welled up within him into words. 'Does he know that because of you Sabinus was found and released?'

Alienus thrust his iron back into the fire. 'And what's that to do with you?'

Vespasian took a shuddering breath through his nose as the pain subsided; the stink of his burnt flesh clung to the inside of his nostrils. He closed his eyes. 'It's nothing to me. But if Myrddin found out that he lost the chance to sacrifice a legate because you told me where to find him in exchange for your life I can't imagine that he would be that pleased. And if you kill me to prevent me from telling him, then that'll be another legate that you've deprived his altars of.'

Alienus' fist crashed into Vespasian's jaw, lashing his head to one side.

Vespasian tasted blood in his mouth; he turned his head back and gave a low, mirthless chuckle. 'Tricky, isn't it? Even for a mind like yours.'

Alienus grabbed the iron and thrust it towards Vespasian's bleeding mouth. 'I'll burn your tongue out and then enjoy the sight of you trying to tell your nasty little tale to Myrddin.'

'I don't think that you will, Alienus, because you would also have to do the same to Cogidubnus, and Myrddin wouldn't like that. He knows that Cogidubnus killed the druids in the Vale of Sullis and he will want the King who has defied him in one piece as he will want me in one piece; what use are we as sacrifices if we're missing bits?' The glowing tip wavered; there was uncertainty in Alienus' eyes. 'You don't have the authority to do anything to us before Myrddin gets his hands on us and you know it, don't you?'

'I should kill you now!'

'I know you should but you can't, you can't even hurt me too badly. I realised that when you just confined your attentions to my thighs. But I can hurt you before I die and I will; Myrddin will know that you betrayed him and he'll want his revenge. And as you pointed out, Myrddin always gets what he wants.'

Alienus' eyes narrowed as hatred exuded from them; he pressed the glowing iron hard down onto Vespasian's shoulder and smoke spiralled up from the cauterising flesh.

Vespasian clenched his teeth and managed to growl, 'I'd run if I were you. Start looking for a place where you'll be safe from Myrddin's wrath because that will be my dying gift to you.'

Alienus pressed harder; Vespasian rode the pain and forced a hard-eyed smile. 'Where will you be safe from both Rome and the druids?'

Alienus threw his iron to the ground and shouted in his own tongue at the men restraining Vespasian before barging his way out of the hut.

Vespasian was lifted from the table and thrown feet first back down into the pit to land with a spine-jarring thump.

Cogidubnus rolled him over and began untying his hands as the grille was replaced. 'You were absolutely right: how did you work that out?'

'When he pretended to be so disappointed with me for telling him so easily what I had for breakfast.' Vespasian pulled his hands free, spat on them and then placed them gently on the burns on his thigh; he breathed deeply, forcing the pain down. 'I realised that what I had told him was irrelevant compared to the information that he had given us.'

Cogidubnus started to work on the leather thong binding his ankles. 'And you guessed that was something that he wouldn't have boasted about.'

'Yes, I imagine that he's never even told anybody that he'd been captured and then escaped.'

A scream from not far off cut through the air, followed by a second and then scores of voices were raised in cries and shouts.

'It sounds like our friend has just left the settlement,' Vespasian observed, pulling his feet apart and gritting his teeth at the movement, 'and I don't think his hosts were too keen on him leaving so suddenly.'

Cogidubnus lifted his head and listened for a moment; the noise escalated. 'That's not the sound of one man escaping; they're shouting "fire". Someone's torching the settlement.'

'Our men?'

'Who cares?'

Vespasian felt a surge of hope and the pain in his wounds was pushed aside as the shouting increased and he looked up to see the guards rush off; the first log was in place but the second had only been rolled to the edge of the grille. The tell-tale glow of burning seeped through cracks between the walls and the thatched roof. 'Now's our chance; let me get onto your shoulders.'

Cogidubnus squatted and Vespasian swung a leg around his neck; with a grunt the King strained upright and Vespasian grasped the edge of the grille and pushed up. It shifted slightly; he increased the pressure, ignoring the sharp pain from the burn on the inside of his thigh rubbing against Cogidubnus' unshaven chin. The grille rose up a couple more inches and the single log across it rolled a hand's breadth; with another mighty effort Vespasian forced his arms up and the log rolled away, leaving the grille free as the sound of fire-fighting grew more intense. He pushed it aside and scrambled out of the pit; after a quick search of the floor he found the rope and threw one end down. Cogidubnus scaled it quickly and then coiled it and slung it over his shoulder; they moved towards the door and pulled it open a fraction. A handful of warriors hurtled past in the narrow lane outside, all heading in one direction.

Vespasian closed the door. 'We need to get out and then find a way to talk to Judoc.'

'You can't go anywhere like that,' Cogidubnus stated, looking at him.

Vespasian looked about for his tunic and found it, along with his belt and sword, under the table, ripped beyond use; his cloak, however, was still attached to the two spears that had made up the makeshift stretcher. With his sword he cut two armholes in it and flung it around his shoulders securing it at the neck, tied on his discarded loincloth and then fastened his belt about his waist. 'This'll have to do.' He threw one of the spears to Cogidubnus and then kicked over the brazier against the wall; the glowing charcoal scattered along it causing the animal skins to smoulder. 'The more distractions the Cornovii have the better in the circumstances, I think.'

'Agreed; pass me that tunic.'

Vespasian chucked the ruined garment over as the first hide ignited.

Cogidubnus held the tunic in the flames; as it too caught fire, he pulled the door ajar, and lobbed it, underarm, through the narrow opening and onto the dry thatch of the hut opposite. Fresh air, sucked in through the gap, fed the fire climbing up the skins, filling the hut with smoke. Cogidubnus waited for a few moments for the fumes to thicken and then flung the door wide, releasing them to the outside. 'Time to go!'

Vespasian followed the King out, unnoticed under the cover of the smoke belching from the doorway and the flames now raging across the lane. He raced after Cogidubnus, past other blazing, circular huts, surrounded by men trying to combat the flames with buckets of water, and then away from the confla-gration into a maze of dark, narrow lanes. The burns on his thigh and shoulder smarted as the muscles worked beneath them and the blood pumping through his veins caused the swelling on his head to throb. The sound of the fire-fighting grew and the narrow lanes became congested with warriors anxious to join the effort. Cogidubnus stepped off to the left, ducking into what was no more than a drainage alley between two lines of huts, and moved along it as fast as the slimy, noisome surface would allow. Emerging from the other end, scattering some panicking chickens, they saw the palisade just thirty paces away; a dark shadow against the bluing sky. With a mutual look of agreement they headed towards it, passing only a few women rounding up errant children and hustling them into the relative safety of their huts. Behind the last abode they spotted a ladder leading up to the walkway, just less than a man's height from the top of the palisade. Within moments they had scaled it to look down in the direction whence the clamour came; and then another noise from a different direc-tion attracted their attention.

'Mars' arse!' Vespasian exclaimed. 'It's not just the fire that has got the Cornovii excited. How did they get here so quickly?'

Fifty paces away, just visible in the weak dawn light, were the two and a half centuries of marines from the flotilla, approaching the open gateway. With an eight-man-wide frontage and protected by a roof and wall of shields, they stamped forward with blades flicking out between their shields, towards a mass of warriors forming up at the gates.

Vespasian slammed his fist against the palisade. 'The idiots! Who's the fool leading them? If they get in they'll be surrounded and hacked to death. We've got to stop this.'

Cogidubnus unslung the rope and tied it to the top of the palisade. 'It's not long enough but there shouldn't be more than a six- to eight-foot drop to the bottom of the ditch. Watch out for the stakes.' He clambered up and over and let himself down; the noise was intensifying as the marines made contact. A mile or so beyond them, a solid shadow in the gloom, the rock of Tagell projected into the sea.

Vespasian glanced over his shoulder – the fire was growing, fanned by a strong breeze coming off the sea – before following Cogidubnus down. The rope reached to just above where the wooden poles of the palisade were buried in the banked earth dug from the surrounding ditch. He let go and slid down the steep bank; Cogidubnus grabbed him as he hit the bottom, preventing him from toppling backwards. Without a word they made their way through the stakes and clambered up the other side and then down into the second of the two ditches that comprised the settlement's earthworks. Keeping low as visibility grew with the light they scuttled along until they were within ten paces of the rear of the Roman formation. Slingshot ricocheted off the marines' javelin-studded shields as they advanced steadily towards the gate.

Grasping a sapling growing at the top of the bank, Vespasian hauled himself out of the ditch; Cogidubnus made to follow but the young tree's roots were not strong enough and he fell back. Vespasian lay down and held out his arm; the King grabbed it as a javelin slammed into the bank next to him; slingshot followed.

'Get away!' Cogidubnus yelled, throwing himself to the far side of the ditch out of sight of the warriors on the palisade. 'I'll make my own way up.'

Feeling a stone fizz past his head, Vespasian scrambled to his feet and sprinted to the rear of the marines' formation and barged into the middle of the back rank.

'Let me through! Let me through!' he ordered, pushing his way into the second and then third ranks. The startled marines parted just enough for him to squeeze forward without compromising the roof of shields over their heads.

'Stand by to fall back!'

On he drove, up through the heart of the enclosed formation, repeating the warning, raising his voice against the drumming of slingshot and the growing resonance of combat as he neared the front.

'On my mark, fall back!' he yelled upon reaching the cornicen huddled just behind the forward ranks; the marine glanced at him and, recognising his commanding officer, set his lips to the mouthpiece.

'Now!

The three descending notes of the signal rumbled out and the formation took a step back.

'Keep a steady, slow beat,' Vespasian ordered.

The cornicen blew a single note and they retreated another pace followed by another in time to the instrument's call. Gradually they passed back through the gates, still under a sustained but ineffectual slingshot barrage and still in contact with the enemy on three sides in the forward ranks. But as the foremost rank passed onto the track leading away from the gates the precipitous drops to either side meant the only contact was to the front and the superior fighting technique of the legionaries of the sea began to tell. Fewer warriors were willing to throw themselves at the shield-wall bristling with blood-dripping blades, and by the time the marines had fallen back to the second ditch contact had been broken and Vespasian ordered an increase in pace to the jeers of the defenders.

'Form line!' Vespasian ordered as they cleared the second ditch and arrived back on open ground.

Within moments the rear ranks had flooded forward, fanning out to either side to make a block four men deep and sixty across. The defenders pulled back to the gates and the slingshot ceased: stalemate.

In the settlement the fire raged.

Vespasian pushed his way through to the front rank and looked around, fuming. 'Who ordered this madness?'

An ordinary marine stepped forward and stood smartly to attention, his sword arm smeared with blood. 'I did, sir.'

Vespasian sighed. 'I might have known it. On whose authority did you do it, Magnus?'

'Well, the lads all agreed with me. When the boatmen came back and said that you'd all been captured we reckoned that we wouldn't be able to get ashore in the same place. However, I heard Cogidubnus mention that the captive had said this was the closest safe place to land within seven miles and seeing as we hadn't passed a landing place I assumed that there must be one seven miles ahead. So we sailed along the coast not worrying about being seen since they already knew we were here and found the inlet that the captive must have mentioned to Cogidubnus. Then we rowed ashore in two trips and doubled the seven miles back in quick time and managed to get here under cover of darkness ready to storm the gates when they opened at dawn. The rest of Cogidubnus' men have gone on down to secure the haven for when the ships get back, just in case we have to leave here sharpish.'

'As I expect we will, now that you've managed to piss the Cornovii off by setting fire to their settlement and then trying to kill them.'

'We didn't set the fire, sir; that was just a piece of luck.'

'Luck? Then it's a weird coincidence.'

'It is. Anyway it helped to cover your escape. What do you suggest we do now?'

'Talk to them,' Cogidubnus said, walking forward with the uprooted sapling, 'seeing as that's what we originally came for.' He strode past Vespasian and on up the track holding the branch of truce and shouting, 'Judoc!'

There was a stirring amongst the Cornovii and a squat, powerfully built man with a magnificent drooping, ginger moustache and a mane of hair to match pushed his way to the front; he called out in his own language and ostentatiously laid down his sword before walking to meet Cogidubnus between the first and second ditches. Behind Judoc, his followers thinned out as many fell back to fight the fires; but a sizable force of warriors remained to defend the gates.

As the two men started to talk, Vespasian turned to Magnus and said, 'I suppose you think that barging in through their front door heavily outnumbered was a good idea?'

Magnus shrugged, looking pleased with himself. 'We came to get you out and here you are, so it must have been.'

'But now we've given away our actual strength and so are negotiating from a very weak position, whereas if you had sent some of Cogidubnus' men in they might have been able to pass unnoticed through the fires.'

'But they might not have and by that time it would have been broad daylight with no chance of a surprise assault; so the front door before dawn seemed to be the only option.'

Vespasian found himself unable to argue and he slapped his friend on the back. 'We'll just have to make the best of it then.'

'Legate!' Cogidubnus called over his shoulder. 'Judoc wishes to speak with you.'

'Better go and see what he wants, sir, but I'd dress a little more formally if I was you,' Magnus suggested helpfully.

'Yes, all right! Tell centurions Glaubus and Balbus to keep their men alert and then resume your duties as a private citizen.'

'Anything else?'

'Yes; thank you, Magnus.'

'Ah! I was wondering when you were going to get around to saying that.'

Vespasian pulled the cloak tighter around his body and walked towards the two Britons, well aware that his appearance did not come up to what was expected of a legate of one of Rome's legions.

'Legate Titus Flavius Vespasianus,' Cogidubnus said formally, still holding the sapling aloft, 'this is Judoc, chieftain of the Cornovii, a sub-tribe of the Dumnonii.'

Vespasian stood straight and looked the man directly in the eye. 'I'm pleased to make your acquaintance finally, having already *enjoyed* your hospitality.'

'The pleasure is mine,' Judoc replied, pulling his windswept hair from out of his hard eyes, 'and it's made more enjoyable by your expression, which tells me that you didn't expect me to speak Latin and therefore understand the sarcasm in your greeting.'

Vespasian caught himself before he blustered an apology and continued to hold Judoc's cold gaze.

'Your treatment was not of my doing, nor did I condone it, and, as yet, I am not willing to apologise for it unless you can disprove the assertion that you were here to kill me. I grant you the privilege to speak under a branch of truce out of respect for Cogidubnus, King of the Atrebates and Regni, even though I regard him as a traitor to our people.'

Vespasian gathered his thoughts, knowing that he had very little time to make an impression upon the man who now held his fate and those of his men in his hand. 'You have my thanks, Judoc, as well as my sympathy.'

'Sympathy? Why?'

'Because you are in an extremely dangerous situation.'

The chieftain burst into laughter, cold and guttural. 'I have heard of the arrogance of the Romans. You stand here, half naked, on the brink of death, and tell me that I'm in an extremely dangerous situation.'

'I don't mean at this moment but in the very near future. Yes, you could unleash your warriors and no doubt in an hour or so they'll kill or capture all my men, but not before they kill twice their number or more and your settlement has burnt to the ground. And where will that leave you? As a hunted enemy of Rome, and believe me, Rome will not stop until the whole of the Cornovii are either dead or in chains working in your own tin mines, adding to Rome's wealth.' He paused whilst Judoc took in the threat. 'We did not come here to kill you; that was a lie fed to you by a man whom I know as Alienus but you probably know as Verica, grandson of his namesake, the previous King of the Atrebates and Regni. He wants you to fight Rome and lose everything; he, Caratacus and the druids are willing to sacrifice the Cornovii and the whole of the Dumnonii solely to delay the inevitable. Your subjugation will take a year or perhaps two but in the end you will be crushed and you, Judoc, will be dead.

'But it doesn't have to be that way; Rome is offering you the chance to keep your freedom in return for two things: an annual tribute of tin and the removal of the druids on Tagell. The raid on our ships will be forgotten because you were pushed into it by the poisonous counsels of your vile priests who serve nobody but themselves. There will be no tax-farmers down here but you will be able to trade in the Roman sphere and your men will be free to join the Britannic auxiliary cohorts and earn citizenship. You are being offered the best of both worlds, Judoc; you can enjoy the fruits of the Roman Empire without feeling the weight of our swords. That's what Cogidubnus is here to offer you; and I am here to kill the druids if you refuse to do that yourself. We are not here to murder you but, rather, to ask for your friendship. What do you say?'

Judoc was silent for a short while and then turned to Cogidubnus. 'I heard that before you submitted to Rome you first fought against her, so that it would be said amongst the tribes that the terms of your surrender were written in Roman blood. Is that true?'

'I wouldn't have been accepted by the Atrebates as Verica's heir had I not shown that I was willing to resist the invaders.'

'And if I submit without showing any defiance then how long do you think I'll remain chieftain of the Cornovii?'

'Your honour has already been satisfied; your men destroyed three of Rome's biremes. No tribe can claim to have sunk even one of her ships.'

'Three, eh? So it's true what the only man who returned from the raid claimed before I had him executed for leading you here; and now Rome asks for my friendship because she fears me?'

Vespasian tried to look as solemn as he could, given his attire. 'Rome does fear a man who can reap such destruction on her fleet and Rome respects such a man. We could in time crush you but we know that it would be a long struggle, so we would prefer, instead, to beg for your friendship; we would honour the man who has fought so bravely against us, with his freedom and independence as well as the title of friend and ally of Rome.'

Judoc visibly swelled. 'Rome begs for my friendship? Then let it be so, legate.' He turned and addressed his warriors in what were, Vespasian recognised, boastful tones.

'He's claiming victory over Rome,' Cogidubnus muttered.

'Let him claim anything he likes so long as it's not our lives.'

'He's now telling his people that they have a choice: either to carry on their valiant struggle for which the warriors on the boat raid gave their lives; or to accept Rome's plea for a cessation of hostilities in return for the guarantee of independence.'

Vespasian suppressed a grin. 'It's the same everywhere: what leader is ever truthful with his people?'

'With power, truth becomes a luxury and, like all luxuries, it should be used sparingly.'

Vespasian sighed and his mind turned to the imperial politics of Rome. 'That's something that I have learnt only too well.'

A cheer erupted and Judoc punched his arms into the air, acknowledging his warriors.

'I think the Cornovii have graciously consented not to threaten the Roman Empire any more,' Cogidubnus observed.

Vespasian felt a surge of relief but kept his face neutral. 'Thank the gods that men can always be relied upon to find a face-saving way to look after their best interests.'

Judoc turned, beaming broadly, and opened his arms to Vespasian, who felt that he had no option but to subject himself to the chieftain's embrace. 'My friend, the Cornovii will no longer make war on Rome. However, there is one condition: I cannot be responsible for the deaths of the druids on Tagell but I would welcome their disappearance as they interfere with my people.'

And lessen your power, Vespasian thought. 'So you won't hinder us?'

'I would never hinder a friend.' Judoc signalled over his shoulder. 'And to prove what a good friend I am I shall give you a gift when the druids are dead.' From within the crowd two warriors stepped forward with Alienus, bound and gagged, but walking with pride. 'This I hope will make up for the execution, on his recommendation, of the men that you brought with you.

Their heads will no longer be sent to Arvirargus; instead my message will be that I've accepted Rome's friendship and will explain the terms and suggest that he does likewise. He's a pragmatic man and dearly loves his horses; I'm sure that he would hate to lose them.'

'I'm sure he would.' Vespasian looked at Alienus; defiance burnt in the young spy's eyes, but he did not struggle. 'Thank you for this gift, Judoc, I shall be back to claim it. My brother has got just the right place to keep him; he's going to be very well looked after for the next few years. Who knows, he may even survive into his thirties.' He indicated over his shoulder to the rocky mound of Tagell. 'Which is far longer than that filth over there can expect.'

'I must warn you, legate, that the druids on Tagell have their own protection, and it can freeze the soul. But more than that, Myrddin arrived with them a few days ago and Myrddin is like no other man. He has great foresight and I believe that he's here because he's expecting you.' Judoc pointed in the direction of Tagell. 'Look.'

Vespasian turned and saw a sight that chilled him to the core: standing tall amongst the few scattered huts on the rock of Tagell, lit by the soft red rays of the newly risen sun, stood a giant, five or six times the height of a man, with a stag's head and towering horns.

'That's been built for you.'

Vespasian stared in awe at the wicker man.

CHAPTER X

'THEY MAKE THEM a lot bigger here than they do in Germania,' Magnus grumbled, looking at the huge figure on the Tagell peninsula just across the isthmus of bare rock connecting it to the mainland. 'I doubt that the lads are going to want to go anywhere near it.'

'Getting them there is going to be the first problem,' Vespasian observed, looking at the sheer cliff-face at the end of the isthmus. 'There doesn't seem to be any path. We'll just have to scramble down and across.'

'I can't see anyone over there; where are they all?' Cogidubnus shaded his eyes from the strengthening sun. 'They'll have seen us coming and, if Judoc is right and they're expecting us, then no doubt they'll appear at some point with a few unpleasant surprises.'

Vespasian felt his unease grow at the marked lack of panic amongst the druids, faced with the imminent arrival of more than two hundred more troops; although smoke rose from the half a dozen huts around the wicker man the only life that he could see was a few sheep grazing on the rough grass at the giant's feet. He turned to the two marine centurions waiting behind him for orders. 'Glaubus, take your men across to the peninsula and try to find a way up along the south side. Cogidubnus will go with you; kill anyone you find over there. Balbus, you and your men will come with me and we'll try the north side.'

The centurions snapped brisk salutes but the mutual look of disquiet that they shared as they turned to go gave Vespasian cause for concern. 'I think you were right, Magnus: if the centurions are nervous about going over there how can I hope that their men will follow them?'

'Then let's just get back to the ships instead. Let's face it, sir, Caratacus ain't coming because Alienus didn't tell him that we were here. You've succeeded in bringing the Cornovii over to us, which was the only other thing you had to achieve down here, so why don't we just sail away and leave the druids to their own devices?'

'There's nothing that I'd like to do more; having faced the druids twice now I'll not willingly do so again. But within a day or two of us leaving they'll have turned Judoc against us or had him killed and replaced with someone more amenable to their cause.'

Cogidubnus nodded in agreement. 'They've all got to die, otherwise there'll never be any peace on this island. We've got the chance of killing Myrddin perhaps even before his successor has been found and that's something that we mustn't pass up.'

Magnus scowled and looked again at the wicker man. 'It seems to me that the druids believe that if there is any killing to be done, they're going to be the ones doing it.'

Spray flew on the strengthening wind, soaking their hair and making the bare rocks of the isthmus slippery and treacherous as Vespasian led Balbus and his men across. Just ten paces to his left Cogidubnus with Glaubus' century kept level as they too slowly negotiated the passage in ones and twos. Above them the mound of Tagell soared to the sky, a dark, looming place filling their hearts with foreboding.

The roar of crashing waves intensified as they reached the lowest point of the isthmus; great rollers thundered in, pummelling a narrow beach below, to Vespasian's right, and pulling on a currach turned upside down amongst the rocks at its head.

With no obvious pathway to follow, Vespasian picked his way through boulders and driftwood, using his hands to balance; the marines followed behind him in a random, dispersed order, struggling with their shields and pila. As they started to ascend the broken-up slopes of the peninsula itself, working their way around it away from the cliff-face, the wind speed picked up, whistling through the crags, tugging at their garments and increasing the sea's rage. Magnus struggled at Vespasian's side, muttering prayers and obscenities in equal measure as they slowly gained height and the head of the wicker man came back into view, gradually followed by its shoulders and chest. Vespasian scrambled on up, dislodging loose scree onto the marines below, as the noise of the wind's fury grew, mixed with the crash of waves rising up from below, and now augmented by a new sound, a chilling sound: a high-pitched, bestial howling. He looked in alarm at Magnus. 'Wolves?'

'I actually hope so; I don't know of any other animal that makes that sound, and if there is one then I wouldn't like to meet it.'

'Me neither; I'd rather face a wolf than the unknown.' Vespasian looked back at the men following; their expressions were less than keen and Balbus and his optio were doing their best to urge them on, although with each new baying cry they too looked fearfully up the hill. The howling got louder as they climbed off the rocks and onto the steep, grassed hillside; the wicker man, visible down to its thighs, swayed in the gale but was kept upright by four ropes extending at right-angles from its neck. The ground was firmer and the going became easier, but Vespasian felt his reluctance to move forward grow with every step he took up the hill towards the source of the howling, yet he drew his sword and pressed on, conquering his powerful urge to turn back. Behind him the shouts of Balbus and his optio forming their men into a column were almost lost on the wind. Cutting back and forth diagonally to reduce the incline, his breath short and his heart pounding, he came to the final steep escarpment before the summit. The huts were still obscured from view but the wicker man towered above, totally visible apart from its lower legs: a brooding, malevolent colossus.

Pausing, he looked back to Balbus. 'Have your men form line, centurion!'

Within a few moments the column had fanned out into four lines of twenty; many of the marines looked uneasily around at the steep drop behind them and then at the unknown over the brow of the hill. Not wanting to give the men too much time to fret over their situation, Vespasian moved forward and began to scramble up the escarpment, his hobnailed sandals struggling for purchase in the looser, grassless earth. As his hands reached the summit the howling ceased and was abruptly replaced by a series of rumbling growls; he thrust his legs down and propelled his body up so that his head crested the ridge. A light shape flew at his face; he managed to duck in time and it passed over him as similar forms flicked by to both sides. Behind Vespasian the screaming started instantaneously and was mixed with the throaty snarls of wild beasts ravaging flesh. He kicked a leg over the rim and hauled himself up; Magnus made it up next to him with Balbus and a few others who had been fortunate enough to slip under the pounce of the wolves – white wolves. But, below, carnage ensued as man fought beast in a savage battle of iron, teeth, fist and claw. Many of the marines had bolted, tumbling headlong down the incline, a few rolling uncontrollably towards a shattered-bone death on the rocks below. Others engaged in combat that would have delighted the crowd in any arena for its savagery as at least twenty beasts tore their way through the remaining terrified marines, clamping blood-stained teeth on sword arms, throats and thighs, ripping flesh and muscle as the wind blew ripples along their sleek, off-white coats in a strange juxtaposition of beauty and horror. Wrenching his eyes away from the slaughter, Vespasian looked around for the beasts' handlers or the druids who had set this fearsome attack in motion; but on the summit of Tagell there was no one and nothing to be seen apart from the sheep, that had somehow escaped the attentions of the wolves. They grazed peacefully beneath the monstrosity whose magnitude could only now be appreciated. Vespasian led the dozen survivors towards the huts, knowing that they could not help their comrades against the fury of the wolves, which, although they had been reduced in number, were mauling their way through the very few marines still prepared to stand against them; a few men had been hauled to safety by their mates but the remainder were now scattered and beyond rallying.

A search of each of the half a dozen thatched shelters turned up nothing apart from burning fires in their central hearths; animal skins, boar tusks and antlers lined their walls and pots and bowls full of strange ingredients were formed up in neat lines on their floors. Each had four beds but not all seemed to have been slept in.

'Where in Hades are they?' Vespasian shouted against the wind, coming out of the last hut having checked the floor for trapdoors.

Magnus glanced nervously over his shoulder in the direction of the wolves. 'They evidently ain't here so I suggest we should find a way off this rock that doesn't involve feeding ourselves to wild beasts.'

'Yes, sir, we should go,' Balbus affirmed, his eyes still registering the shock of losing so many men.

Vespasian looked up at the wicker man. Thirty feet above him its stag-like head and huge wooden antlers rocked back and forth against its restraining ropes in the howling wind, as if it were a beast on a leash straining to lurch forward; he wanted nothing more than to be away from it and everything else that was strange and unnatural on this windswept lump of bleak rock. 'Yes, we'll go.' He turned to make his way back down in the opposite direction from the wolves and stopped suddenly in his tracks. Cogidubnus, Glaubus and a few marines were running in ragged formation towards him as if the Furies themselves were after them.

Magnus spat. 'There seem to be a lot of wolves on this rock.'

'Where are the rest of your men, Glaubus?' Vespasian asked as the centurion came to a chest-heaving halt.

Glaubus took in the very few marines left from Balbus' century. 'Gone, the same as yours; although how I don't know. It was like they were just plucked off the rock by invisible hands.'

'Myrddin,' Cogidubnus wheezed. 'I've heard it said, although I've never believed it, that he has the power to call upon the spirits of the Lost Dead.'

Vespasian glanced nervously over the King's shoulder. 'The Lost Dead? Who in Hades are they?'

'That's just the point: they're not in Hades or any other afterlife; the druids believe them to be the dead that have missed the chance to be reborn into another body and so are condemned to wander the land. They hate everything that lives. They congregate in barren places such as the plain to the east with the Great Henge of stone and, evidently, here. If Myrddin really does have the power to control them then we must leave. We are in great danger.'

'I don't think that Plautius understood just what he was asking us to do by coming here.'

Cogidubnus looked around with darting, nervous eyes. 'How could he have? I didn't even know.'

Magnus clenched his thumb and spat to ward off the evil-eye. 'I've heard enough. Let's get back to the ships, sir.'

'I agree,' Vespasian said, 'but which way? Through the wolves to the north or the Lost Dead to the south or over the precipice to the east?'

Cogidubnus' eyes widened with fear as he looked past Vespasian, towards the wolves. 'The north is closed to us.'

Vespasian turned and froze. It was not wolves that he saw coming back towards him, but druids; druids with robes, hair and beards covered in blood as if they had just been in battle.

'Hold, Romans!' a druid called out in Greek. 'You are surrounded.'

Curtailed screams pierced the wind and, turning to their source, Vespasian saw that it was true: they were surrounded. Eight marines buckled to the ground with their throats gushing blood to reveal a similar number of druids with vicious curved blades staring at him with no emotion in their dark eyes. 'Where the fuck did they come from?'

'And where did the sheep go?' Magnus asked in a slow thick voice, looking with drooping eyelids at the deserted grazing beneath the wicker man's legs.

Vespasian tried to recall how many sheep there had been but his mind was becoming sluggish; he felt a hand on his shoulder but saw nothing there, and then a cold pressure pushed into his back and icy fingers squeezed his heart. He managed to focus on the eight druids as his knees sank to the ground and then the image of the same number of sheep grazing beneath the wicker man came to his fading consciousness. 'That's impossible,' he murmured as the wind-flattened grass came rushing towards him.

*

The mist cleared from Vespasian's eyes to reveal spots of blue sky through a myriad of cracks in a tightly woven lattice of branches encompassing him. His hands were tied behind his back; he pressed his fingers down and found a gap in the weave of wood; probing it he felt grass. He raised his head and saw that Magnus and Cogidubnus were imprisoned with him in a confined area just long enough for them to lie in full length; a thick pole ran through the centre of the cage, above him, from wall to wall.

'The legate wakes,' a voice said in Greek from outside the cage. 'We can soon begin.'

Squinting, Vespasian could make out a figure looking down at him through the weave; his face was indistinct but one dark eye peered through a crack, cold as a midwinter's night and just as deep. 'Myrddin?'

'So you know our name. If you knew that why did you come here on your own volition?'

'To kill you.'

'To kill us? But don't you know that we can't die? Myrddin will always live on this island. We will still be here when you Romans are gone and the new invaders come from across the cold northern sea in their fat boats and then we shall laugh as they too lose our Lost Lands to an army less than the size of one of your legions.

'We will still be here even if your death fails to prevent a power greater than those legions, which now spawns in the heart of your Empire, from coming to fruition. Even if another takes the place that you were destined to occupy and he allows this canker to be nurtured so that eventually it sweeps everything old and true before it – in a way that Rome could now only imagine doing with her armies – we will still be here. If the time comes when knowledge is forbidden, forcing us to hide in the forests to practise the true religion, we will still be here. Can you really believe that you can kill us when we know all this?'

Vespasian struggled to his knees. 'You're still just a man.'

'Are we? If we were "just a man" do you think that we could have disguised what you saw? You heard wolves, you expected wolves, in fact, you even wanted wolves for fear of something worse, so when our druids came at you it was easy for us to make your simple minds see wolves, white wolves, the same colour as our robes, with a *simple* hex. And the same with the sheep: you had seen real sheep from afar so expected real sheep to still be there. But think: if there had been sheep and wolves together, wouldn't nature have taken its course?'

'So those sheep didn't change into druids, we just couldn't see them for what they really were.'

'Exactly.' Myrddin's throat rasped in what sounded like sneering amusement. 'Not even we have the power to change form, but we can make you see white sheep rather than white-robed druids. Our power is not about what we can do to ourselves, it's about what we can make other people think we've done. Your men thought that they went to their deaths ripped apart by tooth and claw but if you were to look at their bodies you would only see slashes and punctures of blades. But you won't get that opportunity, Titus Flavius Vespasianus, because once this *King* lying next to you is conscious we will have our sacrifice that you've tried to deny us. And what is more, you will die in the flames of our gods despite what has been prophesied for you because you have come here willingly.'

Vespasian felt suddenly alert. 'What do you mean?'

'Few men's destinies are preordained and those that are can be changed if that man voluntarily accepts an early death. We can see the fate that your guardian god, Mars, had waiting for you, but that will not come to pass because Judoc played his part well.'

'Judoc was false?'

'Of course. When the man you know as Alienus came and told us that you were on your way here we had to work out how best to have you deliver yourself up to us. Alienus we couldn't trust because we're sure that he was the one who betrayed us before.'

'It was; in return for his life.'

'Then we shall take that from him. He was never going to be given to you, that was just a pretence by Judoc to make you trust him. Judoc respects the gods and will give his life and those of his people to preserve their ways. He set the fire in his settlement and allowed you to escape; it was fortunate, but not unforeseen, that your men turned up so that you wouldn't realise how easy your escape was. You see, if you had been delivered to us in chains then you would not have willingly come to your death. In that case the prophecy from your birth would have been stronger than our will and you would have survived – somehow. So Judoc pretended friendship but refused to help you against us; he told you that we were expecting you; he told you that this wicker man was built for you and he warned you of our power and yet you still came of your own accord.'

Cogidubnus let out a groan.

'Ah, the King stirs; we can begin. You're a dead man, legate, and a worthy sacrifice to our gods.'

'You're wrong, Myrddin.'

'We're never wrong.' Myrddin turned and walked away, shouting at his followers.

Vespasian yelled after him, 'You are this time, Myrddin; I didn't come here of my own accord. I came because it was my duty to Rome to do so; but I had to force myself to take every step towards you, do you understand? Every step was unwillingly taken; every part of my being rebelled against coming here except my sense of duty. I, Myrddin, am not here of my own free will!'

A sudden jerk unbalanced him and he sprawled onto Magnus. 'That was some weird conversation you were having.'

'You heard it?'

'Most of it; and I reckon that you made a fairly decent point at the end.' Another jerk and they felt themselves rise slightly off the ground; cries of terror came from close by accompanied by the bleating of sheep. 'Although I don't see how that's going to help us now.'

Vespasian suddenly took in his surroundings. 'Shit! We're in the wicker man!'

'Well, where else did you think we were?'

'I thought that we were just in some sort of cage.'

'And why would they put us in a cage when they've got a perfectly good wicker man waiting for us?'

They felt the wicker man rise again; the cries intensified and wind whistled through the gaps in the weave. 'Of course! That settles it, I was put here without my knowledge and there's no way that can be construed as willing. Let's pray that Myrddin is as right about the prophecy meaning that I will survive as he is wrong about me being here of my own accord.'

'I'd prefer it if you said "us", "we" and "our" rather than "I", "me" and "my". Now get behind me and let's try and loosen these knots.'

Vespasian crawled into place and Magnus began to work his binding with his fingers. Another jolt raised their prison further; white-robed figures placed themselves underneath and began heaving at the wicker framework with their hands and backs, helping their colleagues hauling on the four ropes. The ascent became smoother and steadier.

Cogidubnus opened his eyes; he groaned as he registered where he was and began struggling against the rope binding his wrists. 'You shouldn't have talked about being swallowed, Vespasian.'

'What?'

'Look where we are: at the top of the chest, just below the throat.'

With Magnus working behind him, Vespasian leant his head against the central pole and put his eye to a crack in what would soon become their floor; he could see down into the next compartment in the belly of the wicker man where Glaubus and Balbus were sitting back to back also fumbling with one another's bonds, surrounded by bleating sheep. Beyond them the central pole split into a 'Y' shape; each branch headed into one of the legs, whence the cries emanated. He could just make out figures through the wall: the last few marines. He was, indeed, just below the throat; he felt the bile rise in his.

Then a vague hope came to him. 'The four ropes came out of the throat; they must be tied off to this pole just above us. If we can break through into it we might be able to release them, and then with this wind the man would fall.'

'And we'll break our necks,' Magnus complained, still pulling at the knot.

'Better than being burnt alive; but we might not if we brace ourselves between the walls and try to land on our feet.'

'I can't think of a better option,' Cogidubnus agreed. 'And we have a bit of time; there'll be prayers of dedication before they set the thing on fire.'

Magnus turned around to examine his progress. 'This plan works upon yet another assumption: that I can get this bastard knot undone.'

Cogidubnus crawled over. 'You use your teeth and I'll pull at it; stop me if I've got hold of the wrong bit.'

The wicker man continued to rise; it was now beyond the height of the druids below who had resorted to long poles to help erect it.

The wind strengthened the higher they went, whistling through the different sized and shaped cracks, producing various tones and pitches as if scores of pan pipes were being blown at once. The angle grew steeper and Vespasian's face was forced against the wall that would soon become the floor of the chest section, but he stayed where he was and prayed to Mars that this was how he would survive to fulfil the prophecy made at his birth.

'It's coming,' Magnus growled through teeth clenched around the rope. 'Pull yourself away slowly, sir.'

Vespasian arched his back, pulling his wrists away from Magnus and Cogidubnus; he felt the pressure of the rope around his wrists tighten and then, a moment later, give a little.

'Stop,' Magnus ordered. He opened his mouth and let go of the rope. 'I've made a loop; put your fingers to my chin, Cogidubnus, and I'll guide you to it.'

The King did as he was told and Vespasian felt a finger push next to his wrist.

'Got it!' Magnus exclaimed. 'All right, pull again, sir.'

This time he sensed the rope giving gradually; Magnus leant forward and yanked with his head and neck. Vespasian felt the constriction around his wrists lessen and began to work them apart until, with a sharp pull of his right hand, the rope fell away.

He hauled himself up as the angle increased; Magnus and Cogidubnus floundered forward unable to support themselves. Pulling Magnus towards him, Vespasian worked on his knot; within a few moments it was loose. The wicker man was almost upright; through the gaps he saw two of the four ropes pulled around to the other side to prevent the colossus toppling as it reached the vertical. Cogidubnus' wrists were released as the wicker man settled upright, rocking back and forth and making Vespasian feel sick as he looked down from his swaying prison.

Cogidubnus began to scrabble at the wickerwork's weak point where the central pole cut through the ceiling. It was just within his reach. 'It's giving a bit.' He stuck his fingers through the gaps and pulled up his body with his arms so that his full weight was suspended from the ceiling; he hung there for a moment and then began to bounce. 'Add your weight to mine!'

Vespasian and Magnus each grabbed one of the King's shoulders and pulled down; the woven wood began to creak and bend. Below, the druids had tied off the four ropes and were now forming a circle around the base.

Still Cogidubnus bounced as the wind howled around them and still the extra weight of Vespasian and Magnus produced nothing more than the groaning of supple wood. Their efforts became more frantic as it became clear from the raising of their hands that the druids had started to dedicate their sacrifice.

Cogidubnus heaved down once again and this time a small gap appeared between the ceiling and the pole; clinging on with one hand he forced the other into it, grazing his knuckles. Once he had a grip he slipped the other hand in next to it and then pulled himself up with all his strength as Vespasian and Magnus pulled down with all theirs. A loud crack caused their hopes to surge.

'And again!' Cogidubnus shouted as the cries of terror from below reached a new high.

They pulled down and, with another series of cracks, the gap grew. Vespasian glanced below and saw the cause of the intensified screaming: a brazier, glowing with burning charcoal, had been brought out of one of the huts. His pulse quickened as they wrenched down again; the gap was now wide enough for a head.

'A couple more!' Cogidubnus cried; blood trickled down both his arms.

Vespasian closed his eyes as he put his whole force into the effort; Magnus snarled like a beast at bay. With multiple snaps Cogidubnus fell back and all three of them collapsed to the floor causing the wicker man to sway and then jerk against the supporting ropes.

The gap was now a hole and through it could be seen the knots.

'Give me a hand up,' Magnus said, getting to his feet and clambering onto the pole. 'I'll undo the two seaward ones so we fall inland.'

The desperate noise continued to rise from below but now it came with something else: the smell of burning straw. Vespasian and Cogidubnus pushed Magnus without ceremony up through the hole as fingers appeared through the gaps in the floor.

'Break it down!' Balbus bellowed, tearing at the wicker with Glaubus; below them the sheep ran in circles bleating fearfully.

Vespasian and Cogidubnus both began to stamp and jump on the area around the pole as smoke fumed upwards from the legs along with screams that were no longer of terror but of anguish.

As Vespasian worked he glanced out to sea; the biremes were making their way north, under oars on a heavy swell. 'We'll head for the haven, if we make it.' Cogidubnus' expression indicated that he thought that was a remote possibility; the tang of roasting human flesh wafting on the wind seemed to confirm his doubts.

'Catch!' Magnus shouted from above and threw down the end of the first rope; the wicker man swayed precariously for an instant before Vespasian managed to take up the strain. 'I'll untie one more and that'll do it.'

Vespasian coughed as the smoke started to rasp in the back of his throat; he held on to the rope whilst still trying to trample a hole in the weakening floor. Horrific animal cries rose even above the human agony as, below Balbus and Glaubus, the sheep began to ignite and race around the base of the belly like four-legged torches.

'And again!' Magnus shouted, chucking the second rope's end down for Cogidubnus to catch. Magnus followed it down as Vespasian's foot finally went through the floor. 'We're going down!' Vespasian shouted at the two centurions as they scrambled to enlarge the hole. He looked below; through the wafting smoke he could see faint figures running this way and that and it seemed to him that there was a different human sound in the air and it was not one of pain. The heat started to scorch his legs; he, Cogidubnus and Magnus looked at each other for a second, as if to say "what choice do we have?", before letting go of the ropes and then throwing themselves onto their backs on the floor, gripping onto the wall that would end up as their ceiling.

They felt the wicker man sway and then roll; below them Balbus and Glaubus clung on for their lives as the sheep, now balls of fire, threw themselves at the walls, maddened by pain.

The construction lurched and teetered for an instant, as if held up by one of the gods to whom the sacrifice was dedicated, before groaning forward just a few hands' breadths; then, with a stomach-lurching inevitability, momentum took over and the colossus fell, uncontrolled, sickeningly fast, funnelling the smoke up through the wicker to blind Vespasian.

'Bend your legs!' Magnus yelled as they were at forty-five degrees; the sudden impact came an instant later and a mighty crash filled Vespasian's ears as he was propelled forward face first into the jagged wooden weave that separated them from the throat before crumpling to the ground.

The clash of iron against iron broke through Vespasian's reeling senses; he opened his eyes but his vision was still obscured by stinging smoke. A low groan next to him caused him to turn; Magnus was on his knees clutching at his face with blood seeping through his fingers. 'Are you all right?'

'I can run.' He wiped the blood from his face, contorted with pain, to reveal a gore-dripping mush in place of his left eye, which hung, impaled, on a shard of wood protruding from the broken weave. He blinked his other eye. 'And I can see, just; let's get out.'

Cogidubnus picked himself up, unscathed, a flicker of hope on his face. 'The head broke off in the impact; we're clear!' He climbed through the hole, dislodging Magnus' eye.

Vespasian helped Magnus through the gap as Balbus and Glaubus scrambled out of their compartment with tunics smouldering and legs blackened with burns; behind them the sheep blazed and crackled.

Focused only on following Cogidubnus and Magnus out of the growing inferno, Vespasian made his way, crouching low, up the throat out into the open; figures ran towards them through the eddying smoke, shouting war cries, across ground strewn with the bodies of druids.

'Cogidubnus!' the King bellowed; the figures slowed and Vespasian almost stumbled to the ground with unexpected relief as he recognised them as Cogidubnus' followers whom Magnus had sent to secure the haven.

After a brief conversation with his men, Cogidubnus turned to Vespasian. 'We must hurry.' He ran off in the direction whence they had come. Vespasian followed, helping Magnus who held a piece of material ripped from his tunic over his bleeding socket. Cogidubnus' men, carrying the two marine centurions and a couple of their own wounded, maintained a rearguard as they raced away from the wicker man. Horizontal, blazing uncontrollably, it consumed the remains of the marines and the sheep. Only its great stag-like head remained untouched by the flames, looking up towards the gods who had been deprived of the most potent part of their sacrifice.

'How did your men know to come here?' Vespasian asked as they climbed down the escarpment where the wolves had attacked.

'Some of the marines made it back to the haven and told them what had happened and that they thought we were dead. As my men are sworn to me unto death they were oath-bound to come to avenge me and reclaim my body. They say the way back is clear; the marines are holding the haven.'

'The druids?'

'Dead or scattered; my men came at them through the smoke and caught them unawares. We must be off the peninsula before they regroup.'

'That gets my vote,' Magnus croaked, struggling to keep on his stumbling feet as they passed through the bodies of the dead marines; all had wounds inflicted by blades. 'I've just about had my fill of their company.'

'I've a feeling that's not a mutual sentiment,' Vespasian observed, placing a supporting arm around his friend's shoulders as they descended, as fast as the gradient would allow, diagonally down the steep flank of Tagell.

Reaching the bottom they began to scramble along the rocks back to the isthmus. As they negotiated the treacherous slabs of rock, Vespasian felt the urge to stop and look back at the sheer cliff above; seeing Myrddin standing there, he knew that the thought had been placed in his mind.

'Vespasian!' the druid cried. 'We will let you go. Your guardian god's will has proven too strong for us and our power cannot fight it – this time. Go! Leave this island and return to Rome where you may yet fulfil the prophecy laid out for you. But remember, nothing is absolute; there are many ways for a man to accept death willingly without him realising. We failed to secure yours because we made the mistake of allowing you to see the true extent of our power before you came here. Therefore you feared us. We see that now; Alienus will pay dearly for leading you to Sullis. We pray that another will succeed where we have not and by your death, which we still demand, help to bring to an early end the abomination that threatens the freedom of us all that, even now, grows in the bosom of Rome. The abomination that, although you will have the power to do so, you will not crush.' Myrddin extended his right arm and held his palm towards Vespasian for a few moments before walking backwards to disappear behind the brow of the cliff.

'What was that all about?' Magnus asked.

'I've no idea; what he said made no sense to me whatsoever.'

'Said? He didn't say a word; you just stared at each other. And none of us could move.'

Vespasian looked into Magnus' one remaining eye and saw he was in earnest. 'I've had enough of this; let's get away from here.'

Vespasian's chest was tight by the time they descended into the haven, following the downhill path of the stream that flowed into the inlet. A marine optio met them, looking nervous to see his commanding officer whom he had left to die.

'It's all right, optio,' Vespasian reassured him, 'I can't blame any man for running from that horror.' He looked over the man's shoulder to his men who were busy floating the Cornovii's currachs. 'Have you sighted the ships?'

The tension on the optio's face cleared and he looked mightily relieved. 'Yes, sir; they're about a quarter of a mile offshore.'

Four of Cogidubnus' followers pushed a currach over and held it steady for Vespasian to climb in. 'Good; how many men have you got here?'

'Just seventy-four, sir.'

'Seventy-four! That's worse than I thought.'

'Well, it's seventy-six actually.' The optio nodded to the men holding the boat as Magnus got reluctantly aboard. 'But a couple rowed one of Cogidubnus' men with your message out to the master trierarchus about half an hour ago.'

'I didn't send any messages.' Vespasian turned to Cogidubnus. 'Did you?'

'No.' The King shook his head and raised his eyebrows in admiration as he swung himself into the currach. 'But you've got to hand it to the man; he's got balls.'

'I don't suppose the two lads floating with their throats cut are feeling that complimentary about him right now,' Magnus pointed out, settling heavily in the bow.

'We could chase him.'

Vespasian sighed in resignation as Cogidubnus' men pushed the boat out before jumping in to man the oars. 'No, he'll have headed further southwest. By the time we're all aboard he'll have a two-hour head start; we'll never catch him. I'd like to know how he escaped from Judoc, though.'

Cogidubnus took up the steering-oar. 'There seems to be

nothing that can hold him; best just to kill him as soon as you have him.'

'Well, that's down to you now, Cogidubnus. Kill Alienus when you find him. Although where he will go with Rome, you and Myrddin all wanting him, I don't know.'

The King's florid, round face cracked into a smile as his men pulled on the sweeps, propelling the boat out into the harbour. 'He'll turn up. Men who want vengeance always do.'

'Yes,' Magnus muttered, dabbing at his seeping socket, 'and normally they turn up just when you least expect them to.'

'Oh, I'll be expecting him every day; it'll give me great pleasure to send his head to you in Rome.'

Vespasian patted the Britannic King's shoulder. 'Cogidubnus, my friend, when I'm back in Rome the last thing I shall want to receive is a souvenir of this island, however pretty it might be.'

PART III

❧ ❧

ROME, JUNE AD 47

CHAPTER XI

THE SEA, CALM and azure, reflected a myriad of tiny, transient suns off its gentle undulations. Vespasian squinted and pulled his face into an expression even more strained than had become the norm during his last six years under the Eagle of the II Augusta. Above, the cause of each fleeting flash of golden light burnt down from its midday high onto his uncovered, thinning hair with an intensity that had been just a memory to him after so long in northern climes far away from Rome. Feeling the strength of the sun warming his body warmed his heart in equal measure as he watched the warehouses, cranes and tenements surrounding the ship-lined harbour of Ostia, just a mile away on the southern bank of the Tiber mouth, come closer with every shrill-piped pull of the trireme's one hundred and twenty oars.

The flitting shadows of gulls played on the wooden deck, bleached by sun and salt and worn smooth by sailors' calloused feet; swooping and soaring above, they serenaded the ship with their mournful cries as they escorted it on its final leg of the six-day voyage from Massalia via Corsica. Vespasian turned his head left, shading his eyes, and tried to focus on the huge construction site a couple of miles north of the Tiber and Ostia; two great curving moles extended into the sea enclosing what would be a spacious harbour at whose centre, on a rectangular man-made island, stood the beginnings of a lighthouse.

The trierarchus, standing next to him, saw the direction of his gaze. 'Claudius had one of the great ships that Caligula built to transport obelisks from Egypt filled with rocks and concrete and then sunk to provide the foundations for the lighthouse.'

Vespasian whistled softly as he surveyed the thousands of tiny figures slaving away – literally – on the new port and the buildings surrounding it. 'That is a massive undertaking.'

'It's even bigger than what you can see; Claudius has ordered that a canal be cut to the southeast to link the port to the Tiber. That way the river transports won't have to brave the open sea with the prevailing wind blowing straight up the river mouth as they have to when coming to and from Ostia.'

'It'll put Ostia out of business.'

'I doubt it; Rome is becoming so big that she needs two mouths to feed her.' Laughing at his wit, the trierarchus began to issue incomprehensible orders of a nautical nature, sending bare-footed sailors scurrying around the deck in preparation for docking.

Vespasian adjusted his toga and walked over to join Magnus, leaning on the larboard rail and admiring the scale of the project. 'Do you remember when we sailed into Alexandria and saw the Pharos, and I said that's the way to be remembered: build something that benefits the people?'

'What of it?' Magnus asked, not bothering to turn his blind eye to Vespasian.

'You asked who built the Circus Maximus and when I didn't know you said, "See, it doesn't always work." Well, this time it will work: Claudius will be remembered as the Emperor who built Rome's great harbour and not the drooling fool who invaded an irrelevant island to fake a victory that will never and can never be complete because the inland tribes have little interest in the benefits of becoming Roman.'

'You're wrong, sir; he'll always be remembered for that and future emperors will curse him for giving them a thorn in their side that they can't walk away from without losing face and endangering their position. And Claudius has chosen the wrong project to be remembered by: the Pharos is finite; it's as big as it's going to be. That port, however, can always be improved upon. I'll bet whatever you like that the next few emperors, whoever they are, will expand it or just change its name out of spite as they struggle to put down another expensive rebellion in Britannia.'

'Just to diminish Claudius' legacy?' Vespasian considered that for a moment. 'I suppose so; that's what I'd do. After four years in Britannia I can see that the money spent holding those parts already pacified and expanding the frontiers until the whole island is under our control is going to be far more than the tax revenue for many years to come. You're right, Magnus: if Claudius wants to divert attention from his folly then he should have chosen something else, because there is a lot of folly to mask.'

Vespasian fell silent as he contemplated the immensity of the task that he, Sabinus and Plautius had left unfinished in Britannia. Having returned to the Roman sphere of influence, leaving the druids depleted but still in place and Judoc unpunished for his treachery, Vespasian had spent the next month, before the arrival of his replacement, probing into Dumnonii territory in strength, destroying everything that could be destroyed until Arvirargus had seen sense and realised that if he wanted to keep his kingdom and his precious horses then he had to come to an accommodation with Rome. This had cost him far more than it would have done a couple of months earlier: not only did Plautius oblige him to pay a greater annual tribute in tin than might be considered fair but also, at the request of Vespasian and Cogidubnus, he was obliged to ensure that a hundred of Judoc's followers lived out the rest of their lives mining that tin. Judoc himself was to work in the mines until the time came for him to be transported to Rome to be displayed in Plautius' Ovation, which the Senate had recently voted him – at Claudius', or rather Narcissus', request.

Most gratifyingly for Vespasian had been Plautius' insistence that Arvirargus clear the remaining druids off Tagell and ensure that it remained unoccupied – apart, of course, from the Lost Dead. Vespasian shivered as he remembered the cold grip of an unseen hand and then the squeezing of his heart as if another hand constricted it; the Lost Dead were welcome to that forsaken spit of land.

The arrival, in November, of Publius Ostorius Scapula, the next Governor of the infant province, along with the new legates, had meant that Vespasian's work was complete and all that remained for him to do was to brief his replacement, Titus

Curtius Ciltus, thoroughly in the geography, people and politics of the II Augusta's theatre of operations. Finding Ciltus to be a nonentity with a very limited capacity for independent thought and hearing Plautius' assessment of Scapula as a man who made him seem calm in temper but reckless in action, Vespasian had left Britannia with the feeling that it was a problem never to be solved and he wanted no more part in it. He was put in mind of the legend of Pandora's box – but without, at the end, Hope flying out of the casket that should never have been opened.

With Caratacus still at large and resentment building as the tax-farmers ploughed their fresh fields, Britannia was far from pacified. Indeed, news had reached him on his way home, during his two-month sojourn at Aventicum to complete the sale of his parents' estate, that the Iceni, who had hitherto been an independent client-kingdom, ruled by their king Prasutagus, had revolted after Scapula had tried to disarm them. The foolishness of needlessly provoking a peaceful ally into rebellion summed up for Vespasian everything that had been wrong about Rome's approach to her reluctant province: they had been too tough on their friends and allies in their attempts to keep them subdued and to extract the taxes to pay for the invasion; yet they had failed to crush their enemies because, quite simply, there was not the manpower to fight an aggressive campaign and at the same time police what had already been won.

The multifarious odours of a port in high summer cutting through the salt-tanged sea air and the ship's smells of musky warmed wood, pitch and hemp rope brought Vespasian back to the present as the trireme entered the harbour mouth with its oars dipping in slow and steady time. He was almost home after his longest ever absence; and, what was more, he had made it in time for Aulus Plautius' Ovation and then his brother's inauguration as suffect-consul for the last six months of the year, which was to be on the day after: the calends of July.

As the ship manoeuvred, with much shouting from the trier-archus, in preparation for berthing, Hormus appeared on deck with Vespasian's travelling luggage, the main bulk of his possessions having been sent overland in the spring.

'Find a carriage to take us to Rome as soon as we dock, Hormus,' Vespasian ordered.

With a bow, Hormus went to stand by the gangplank waiting for it to be lowered; down on the quay a crowd of traders and whores had started to gather, eager to sell their wares to voyage-weary sailors.

'I think I'll go to my uncle's house first,' Vespasian informed Magnus, 'before going to the palace to see Flavia and the children.'

'Very wise, sir; he'll have a good idea of how things stand between the imperial family and yours.'

Vespasian steadied himself on the rail as the trireme nudged the dock. 'And, more to the point, how I can expect to be received by Rome's true masters.'

'I wouldn't worry about that; Sabinus has been nominated as consul and I'm sure that Claudius didn't do that without his freedmen's consent. So I'd imagine that you're in their favour.'

'You'd think so, wouldn't you? But what I also need to know is whether Messalina and Corvinus made any objections to Sabinus' appointment, because if there's one thing that I must do for sure it's to find some way of getting Corvinus into my debt. Only once I've done that will I stand a chance of getting Flavia and the children out of the palace and into the relative safety of my own home in Rome.'

'Oh, so you've finally got one now, have you?'

Vespasian watched the gangplank being lowered and Hormus make his way down and through the crowd of vendors. 'I don't know; I wrote to Gaius from Aventicum asking him to find me something suitable near him on the Quirinal.'

'And near Caenis.'

'Well, yes; it would make matters simpler all round.'

'I wouldn't describe moving my wife into a house that's been chosen for its proximity to my mistress as "making matters simpler all round".'

'How would you describe it then?'

'As the complete opposite, and the action of a madman; especially when you consider that your mother is living with your uncle. Are you seriously going to put all the women in your life close enough to each other to fight on a daily basis?'

'But Caenis and Flavia get on very well.'

'Whilst you were away they did; but now that you're back they're going to be vying with one another for your attention – as will your mother. And when that sort of competition arises whoever's winning will make the other two deeply jealous; until, that is, they get tired of fighting and realise that you're the cause of it and they unite against you as their common enemy – which will probably happen on a monthly basis.'

Vespasian's face became even more strained. 'I hadn't thought about it like that; still, it's too late, it's done now.' He tried to lighten his expression. 'I guess I'll just have to spend a lot of time concentrating on getting more money out of the estates.'

'What? And leave the women unsupervised with none of them getting any attention? That really would be the act of the rashest of fools.'

'And what makes you such an expert on women all of a sudden? You don't even have one of your own.'

'It's because I'm an expert on the subject that I've chosen never to get embroiled with one on any basis more permanent than an exchange of coinage and bodily fluids.'

'Very romantic!'

'It may not be romantic but it certainly does make matters simpler all round.'

Hormus' reappearance on the quay walking next to a four-wheeled, two-horse open carriage took Vespasian's mind off his complicated domestic situation. Having made his farewells to the trierarchus, whom he left muttering about tight-fisted senators having not given him a tip, Vespasian descended the gangplank behind Magnus, who proceeded to clear a path through the sweating traders and sickly sweet-perfumed whores without any consideration for their ability to remain upright. Hormus followed with the baggage as best he could through the now irate crowd who saw him as an easy target for their indignant wrath; he had a few fresh bruises on his arms and legs before he managed to stow the baggage on the rear of the carriage and take his place perched atop it.

Vespasian leant back in his seat, stretching his legs as the driver whipped his charges into reluctant action, again without any consideration for the ability of those nearby to get out of the way; the carriage did a hundred and eighty degree turn and headed off down the quay bustling with dock-slaves loading and off-loading goods from all corners of the Empire. Upon reaching the end it turned left onto the waterfront, heading towards the arterial road that would take them to the main gate and onto the Via Ostiensis, at the same time as a party preceded by lictors turned the corner coming in the opposite direction.

'I wonder who that is?' Vespasian mused, counting the fasces, the bundle of rods tied around an axe that symbolised the magistrates' power. 'Eleven lictors – so it's a proconsul on his way to his province.'

'Poor sod has probably been sent somewhere terrible,' Magnus said with a grin, 'but is so pompous that he thinks it's an honour.'

'It is an honour, wherever you get sent to govern.'

Magnus' eyes widened as the party came nearer and he could make out their features. 'But this one's so pompous you could send him to govern Hades and he'd still puff up with pomposity.'

'Germania Inferior,' Gnaeus Domitius Corbulo replied in answer to Vespasian's question. 'It's a great honour and a challenge; I was specifically chosen for my military abilities.' He snorted in contentment and looked down his long nose at Vespasian as they sat under a hastily erected awning on the waterfront, sipping a fine Falernian wine broken out from Corbulo's extensive baggage.

Vespasian suppressed a smile as he studied his old acquaintance's haughty, horse-like face; it had seemed middle-aged even when they had first met in Thracia when they had been military tribunes together in the IIII Scythica. Now, over twenty years later, it was as if his age had finally caught up with his appearance. 'Do you believe that you'll get much fighting?'

'Without a doubt; now that our presence on the Rhenus has been weakened by the ...' He dropped his voice and looked conspiratorially at Vespasian. 'Shall we say "ill-conceived" invasion of Britannia?'

Vespasian inclined his head. 'Just between us two we could use that term.'

'Indeed, Vespasian. And also, just between us two, our weakened presence on the Rhenus has caused a few of the tribes across the river to think that they no longer have to pay their annual tribute.'

'I see; and you've been ordered to make them think otherwise?'

'A great honour, don't you think?' He paused for another snort of contentment. 'Now that the stain on my character left by my wanton half-sister's lustful cavortings as Caligula's wife has been removed I'm finally free to carry on my career.'

'I had heard that there was a price for the removal of that stain.'

'What? You have good ears. But you're right: I had to threaten to bring a prosecution.'

'Against Corvinus?'

'You are well informed, seeing as it came to nothing.'

'What do you mean?'

'Well, last year Pallas asked me to prepare a case against Corvinus, in secret, accusing him of treason during the ill-conceived invasion. This I did despite the fact that I had to work in conjunction with that arrogant young puppy, Lucius Paetus; he would have been the star witness who could attest to Corvinus exceeding his orders in pushing further north of the Tamesis than he should have. Pallas managed to have Paetus come first in the quaestor elections so the little snob was made an Urban quaestor like his father before him, which would have given his testimony added weight.'

'But he never had to testify.'

'No, that was the strange thing.' Corbulo lowered his voice even more and leant towards Vespasian. 'Now, I try not to take too close an interest in imperial politics and I certainly never gossip about the subject but I'm not unaware of what the Empress is like, having been ... well, you know.'

'I'm afraid I don't know, Corbulo.'

'Well, sucked into her circle, as it were.' A repeated harsh bleat, much like a ram in distress, followed by yet another snort indicated to Vespasian, who knew the signs, that Corbulo had essayed humour.

'You as well, Corbulo, surely not?'

'No one has any choice in the matter; if the Empress summons you then obviously you have to obey. Then if she demands that you perform certain acts, only a suicidal fool would refuse. But it is very difficult to refuse her anything; such is the power of her allure that most people would find themselves unable to resist her even if their lives were not under threat. My wife was very displeased.'

'You didn't tell her, did you?'

'Of course I did; a Roman senator should share everything with his wife.'

'I would differ on that.'

'But then you're a New Man, Vespasian, and can't be expected to act with the same code of honour as those of us who come from far older families.'

Vespasian ignored the insult knowing that it was not meant as such but, rather, as a bald statement of fact based on Corbulo's patrician view of the world. 'So the Empress is as promiscuous as the rumours would suggest?'

'Worse than the rumours, believe me, she made me ... Well, no matter; suffice it to say that my eyes watered more than once. Anyway, for obvious reasons Claudius' freedmen are trying to remove her and this court case was to be a step in that direction by disgracing her brother. At the end of last year I finally showed the case to Narcissus, Pallas and Callistus once I'd assembled all the evidence, and both Narcissus and Pallas were very impressed.'

'But Callistus, in his capacity as secretary to the courts, dismissed it as being too flimsy?'

'How do you know?'

'Just a guess, Corbulo.'

'Well, it was a very good one. That's exactly what happened; he tore it up and left the room saying that to get rid of this harpy was going to take more than the feeble work of a ... Well, I won't say what he called me as I didn't deign to acknowledge the little man's insult. I expected Narcissus and Pallas to be furious with me, although it offends my dignitas to worry about ex-slaves' feelings, but, on the contrary, they were very pleased and promised to ensure that the Emperor appointed me Governor of Germania Inferior seeing as I was obviously the right choice.'

'And no one tried to block the appointment?'

'Not to my knowledge.'

'Now that is interesting.'

'Is it? Anyway, I've told you this in confidence as an old er ... er, person that I've known for a long time, to illustrate just how precarious patronage is in Rome under Claudius. My advice is to avoid contact with the Empress and Claudius' freedmen until their feud has been played out one way or another because until then it'll be very difficult to judge who to cultivate for advancement.'

'Thanks for the advice, Corbulo; however, I think that you've confirmed for me who, happily, has the ascendancy.' Vespasian drained his cup; Corbulo signalled to a slave attending them to refill it but Vespasian held up his hand, getting to his feet. 'I should be getting on; I want to be in the city well before nightfall.'

'Quite so. I'm pleased to have seen you, albeit briefly. I believe your brother is to become suffect-consul next month?'

'He is.'

'Astounding, really, isn't it? Second generation senators becoming consuls; where will it all end?'

'With pompous arseholes becoming governors,' Magnus muttered not entirely to himself as he came forward to pick up Vespasian's folding chair. 'Silly me, they've been doing that for ages.'

Corbulo bristled, rising to his feet, but refused to acknowledge the words of someone so far beneath him. 'I wish you luck, Vespasian; no doubt you will be nominated as a consul in these strange times.'

Vespasian grinned, taking Corbulo's proffered arm. 'I fully intend to be; if only for the look on your face when you have to give way to me in the street.'

Corbulo shook his head in regret. 'Indebted to freedmen, ordered about by lewd women and surpassed by New Men; I'm thoroughly looking forward to getting back to the certainties of a military camp.'

'And I'm sure the men will welcome you, knowing how much they love strict discipline.'

Corbulo looked wistful. 'Yes, at least in the legions decent ancient Roman values still prevail.'

Rome stood before them, her cluttered skyline glowing in the warm evening sun and crowned with a pall of thin, brown haze: the fumes of countless cooking fires, forges, tanneries and bakers' ovens.

Vespasian stared with greedy eyes at the mistress of the world lying languidly on her seven hills, open to all who wished to enter her and share in her pleasures, her wealth and her power, provided they honour her. 'Six years is too long to be away.'

Magnus roused himself from the slouched doze into which he had been falling sporadically throughout the twenty-mile journey from Ostia. 'Mmm? Yes, I suppose so; six years is a long time. However, I've only been away for just over two and I'm wondering whether that's enough, if you take my meaning?'

'I'm sure that my uncle would have done everything within his power to sort out that misunderstanding over the burnt-out tenements.'

'I hope so; but it'll have cost him a few denarii in blood money and bribes so he'll be wanting a good return on his investment. I reckon that I'm going to be very busy for him.'

'And I reckon that you're right; with Sabinus consul this could be a very good few months for the family.'

'It's always helpful to have a tame consul.'

Vespasian glanced at the long row of granaries lining the Via Ostiensis, blocking off the view of the Tiber, to his left. 'And with reports of a good harvest the city should be peaceful and very conducive to business. I intend to make a lot of money.'

The carriage slowed as beggars gathered around it, thrusting their bowls, clutched in filthy fingers or between stumps, towards

Vespasian, attracted by the broad purple senatorial stripe on his toga. A couple of lashes of the driver's whip cleared the path and the carriage moved on towards the Porta Trigemina in the shade of the Aventine, rising up on the other side of the Servian Walls to their right.

Paying off the carriage driver – and almost giving him a tip for fighting off the beggars, but then thinking better of it – Vespasian stepped down and, as wheeled transport was forbidden in the city during daylight hours, walked through the open gates and entered Rome. Magnus followed with his own bag over his shoulder and Hormus brought up the rear, struggling with Vespasian's baggage whilst jerking his head this way and that, looking with goggle eyes at the multitude of architectural wonders within the city.

A huge roar of an excited crowd from their right, emanating from behind the high frontage of the Circus Maximus, surprised Vespasian and Magnus as they turned a corner into the Forum Boarium, which was awash with chariots, teams of horses and scores of men all bearing one of the four racing faction colours.

'A race day?' Magnus questioned. 'That's unusual only a few days before the festival of Apollo.'

'It's also inconvenient,' Vespasian observed, looking at the fenced-off forum filled with the bustling activity of teams preparing for the next race or rubbing down sweating horses who had managed to survive the ordeal of the last. 'How do we get past?'

'Wait here, sir. There's bound to be someone here that I know and they can escort us through; no one is going to stop a senator.' He followed the fence around, looking for an acquaintance from his favoured Green team, leaving Vespasian and a visibly over-whelmed Hormus to wait amongst the crowds of onlookers studying the racehorses.

'Have you ever seen a chariot race, Hormus?' Vespasian asked with mild interest.

Hormus looked surprised at being addressed directly in public. 'Never, master.'

'Then, during the festival of Apollo at the beginning of July, you should go.'

'Go, master? Me? How can I?'

'By walking to the Circus Maximus.'

'But I'm your slave; I can't leave your house.'

'Of course you can – if I say so. We have a relaxed attitude to personal slaves here in Rome: if they aren't needed by their masters, they're free to come and go. You can go to the circus, the theatre, the arenas, wherever you like, so long as you have my permission. You must remember, Hormus, that we free our slaves so that they become freedmen who owe us total allegiance; they can be very useful in setting up businesses by proxy and circumventing certain laws that forbid senators from profiting from trade. If you serve me well I will free you one day; but what use will you be to me if you've never been outside of the house and have no contacts and know nothing of the city?'

Hormus raised his eyes a fraction, almost meeting his master's. 'Do you mean, master, that I will not always be a slave?'

'Of course you won't.'

'But, then how will I live?'

'We'll talk about that when the time comes; in the meanwhile when you're not busy you should get to know the city.' The corners of Hormus' mouth twitched and timidity flickered in his eyes; Vespasian felt a twinge of contempt. He subdued it and continued: 'If you want to be of use to me then you should ignore your fear and do as I suggest.'

'Yes, master.' Hormus' tone was less than convincing.

'You'll never guess who I've found, sir,' Magnus announced, shoving through the crowd.

'I'm sure you're right, Magnus.'

'Follow me.' Magnus headed off towards the Tiber. 'My mate, Lucius; remember? You saved him from execution in Thracia and then him and a few mates helped us get that disgusting weasel-like priest out of the fortress at Sagadava in Moesia.'

'I recall the incident but I don't remember him.'

'His dad used to be the Greens' stable-master and Lucius was a stable lad before he joined up.'

'I remember you getting excited about someone being able to give you decent tips.'

'Exactly; and fifteen years ago he was able to help me with quite a tricky situation involving a dodgy bookmaker, a monstrous consul and your brother's inability to get elected as a quaestor. Very helpful he was too. Well, he's finished his time with the IIII Scythica and he's back working for the Greens as, er ... sort of muscle for the faction-master, if you take my meaning?'

'I do; very responsible work, I'm sure.'

'That's you mocking again. Anyway, he's meeting us by the gates next to the Aurelian Bridge and he'll see us through.'

'I'm pleased to hear it.'

Vespasian did not recollect the face nor did he recognise it when Magnus and Lucius embraced in a joyful reunion under the watchful eye of a *contubernium* of eight men from an Urban Cohort on duty at the gate.

'It's an honour to see you again, sir,' Lucius said, bowing his head to Vespasian once he had got them through the gate. 'I will always be beholden to you for my life.'

'Then I would suggest that you come to my morning *salutio* each day and greet me as your patron.'

'I will do that with great pleasure, sir, and I will try to be as useful as possible to you.'

'You can start by telling me why we're having a day of racing; there's no festival today.'

'But there is now. Claudius is celebrating the Secular Games.'

'The Secular Games? But they're meant to be once every hundred years. Augustus only celebrated them just over sixty years ago.'

Lucius shrugged as he led them through the racing activity. 'Well, we're having them again at the moment.'

Magnus looked at Vespasian and chuckled. 'The fool evidently can't count.'

'Either that or he's really working hard to create a legacy. I wonder what my uncle's got to say about it.'

Vespasian knocked on the familiar door of his uncle's house on the Quirinal Hill and was unsurprised to see it opened by the most beautiful teenage boy with long flaxen hair and lithe limbs that were barely concealed by the flimsiest of light tunics. 'Announce me to your master; I'm his nephew, Vespasian.'

The boy scampered off and Vespasian followed him through the vestibule and on into the atrium dominated by a large homo-erotic mosaic of a naked Achilles despatching a doe-eyed Hector.

'Dear boy!' Senator Gaius Vespasius Pollo boomed, waddling out of his study in a flurry of black-dyed, tonged ringlets and wobbling jowls. 'Sabinus told me to expect you before his inauguration; I was getting worried that you were not going to make it.' He enveloped Vespasian in an amply fleshed embrace and planted a moist-lipped kiss on each of his cheeks. 'It's in eight days' time, you know. Have you been to the palace to see Flavia?'

'Not yet, Uncle; I thought that I'd talk to you first. Where's my mother?'

A hint of displeasure crossed Gaius' face. 'She's visiting Flavia and the children at the palace, before travelling on up to Aquae Cutillae; she expects to see you there very soon. The owner of one of the neighbouring estates has fallen ill and is not expected to live and she's concerned as to who will inherit.'

Vespasian shook his head, sighing. 'Typical of her to worry about the neighbours' business. I'll not go up there to pry; I'll let her get on with it and see her when she's back in Rome. How is Flavia?'

'Your mother has been visiting, which means Flavia is in a foul temper. They always have an exchange of views about something – some petty feminine subject, I imagine. Take my advice and don't go and see her until tomorrow when she will hopefully have got over your mother's visit.'

'As bad as that, is it?'

Gaius rolled his eyes and pulled his face into a picture of resigned exasperation and then turned to Magnus and grasped his forearm. 'What happened to your eye, Magnus?'

'I left it in Britannia after examining a wicker man too closely.'

'Well, I hope it won't affect your usefulness; I've been missing your services, my friend, and I'm glad to have you back.'

'It's good to be back, senator; but I was wondering if it's safe to be back, if you take my meaning?'

'Indeed I do; and the answer is yes.'

'I'm relieved to hear it. It weren't too expensive, I hope.'

'Surprisingly cheap. I managed to persuade your friend, Paetus, in his capacity as an Urban quaestor last year, to delete all mention of the incident from the city's records. He was very happy to do it without a substantial bribe; which is as well seeing as he is now soon to become family.'

'I'm grateful, sir.'

'And I know you'll show it in the near future.'

'Indeed. I'll be off to the Crossroads Brotherhood now to give them the good news. I'll be back at dawn.'

'Paetus to become family?' Vespasian queried as Magnus left.

'Yes; a few days ago Sabinus offered him his daughter, young Flavia, in marriage. She's fifteen now, more than old enough. Paetus has accepted and it's a good match for everybody. We've made a connection with the Junii and Paetus gets to marry a sitting consul's daughter, which will naturally associate him with the office and stand him in good stead in the future. But come, dear boy, let's take a seat out in the garden and have some refreshment before we go and dine; Valerius Asiaticus has invited me. I'll send a message and ask if it will be all right to bring you; I'm sure it will be fine, he's disgustingly rich now. Did you know that he bought the Gardens of Lucullus about five years ago?'

'Yes, I heard. Narcissus told me when he came north for the invasion.'

'It's one thing for a Gaul to become a senator and then be the first of his race to make it to the consulship, but then to own the most beautiful gardens in Rome? It's been the cause of much jealousy.' Gaius clapped his hands and an elder boy appeared, more mature but equally as beautiful as the doorkeeper. 'Ortwin, bring some wine and honeyed cakes.' For the first time Gaius noticed Hormus standing in the doorway to the vestibule. 'Who's that?'

'That's Hormus, my body slave.'

Gaius raised a well-plucked eyebrow. 'So you've finally gone to the expense of purchasing your own slave? Well done, dear boy; you're going to have to get used to expenditure now that you have your own house. I'll have Ortwin show him where to put your things and find him a bed in the slave quarters for the night before you move into the house I've found you tomorrow.'

'Of course, they had to give Sabinus the consulship,' Gaius said, licking crumbs from his fingers. 'He's forty-two so it would have been difficult not to have rewarded one of the heroes of Britannia with that honour when he has reached the prescribed age; especially as he's going to be useful to Narcissus, Pallas and Callistus in countering his senior colleague who, incidentally, will be technically too young for the position.'

Vespasian passed the plate of cakes over to his uncle. 'Who's that?'

'Gnaeus Hosidius Geta.'

'Geta! He's younger than me by at least a year.'

'But he's Messalina's choice and Claudius will deny her nothing. So Sabinus is going to have a hard time of it fighting Geta and keeping Messalina's agenda from dominating the Senate's business. However, if he does that competently he will earn a lot of favour from the three freedmen, which can only benefit us.'

'Two freedmen, Uncle.'

'Two? What makes you say that?'

Vespasian recounted the story of Pallas' ruse to expose Callistus' true loyalties and how, as far as he could judge from what Corbulo had told him, it seemed to have worked.

'So Callistus is protecting Corvinus,' Gaius mumbled through a mouthful of cake, having heard Vespasian's short tale, 'now that is strange.'

'No it's not; if Callistus really is secretly supporting Messalina against his colleagues then it's only natural that he should protect her brother from prosecution.'

'I'd agree if it wasn't for one fact: Corvinus and Messalina have fallen out.'

'Over what?'

'Power, what else? She loves having it and hates to share it, even with her own kin. Yet, as she has no access to the Senate other than by proxy it's always vitally important to her that at least one of the Consuls is her creature.'

Vespasian's eyes widened with comprehension. 'I see: Corvinus is still too young, technically, to become consul and yet he sees his sister favour Geta and have Claudius nominate him well before his time.'

'Exactly so, dear boy; Messalina didn't want her dear brother to have the consulship because she was fearful of the influence that he might try and exert over Claudius, which he would use for his own gain and not hers. The way she sees it is that it's bad enough having Narcissus influencing the Emperor without risking setting a third party to compete for Claudius' attention.'

'So Corvinus' dignitas must be feeling very bruised.'

'It's throbbing painfully, dear boy, and not just because of that slight. Messalina has been having an affair with an equestrian called Gaius Silius and has persuaded Claudius to raise him to the Senate, which the old fool, in his capacity as censor, did with pleasure for his darling wife. Now the rumour is that she's trying to get Claudius to nominate him as suffect-consul next year.'

'Becoming consul so soon after entering the Senate?'

'You would have thought it impossible but the precedent was set by Claudius himself, remember; he was only an equestrian before Caligula made him a senator so that he could be his colleague in the consulship. Obviously, he did it as a joke, as well as to show the Senate exactly what he thought of us. This time, however, Claudius will have no idea that the joke's on him if he honours his wife's lover.'

'So Corvinus has been passed over for someone too young to be consul and may be so again by a lover of his sister who this time last year wasn't even eligible to become consul.'

Gaius' smile was laden with false sympathy. 'I know; it's tragic for Corvinus. He must be so hurt by his sister; but that's just the way she is: always alienating the people close to her through arrogance and a belief that her power is such that she needs no support. Take Asiaticus, with whom we're dining later, for example: as you know he was always on very good terms with

Claudius, being a favourite of his mother, Antonia – may the gods hold their hands over her shade – as he proved by being so helpful when he was consul by affecting to discover Poppaeus dead in his litter.'

'I prefer not to be reminded of that, Uncle.' The murder of Poppaeus that, at the request of Antonia, he and Corbulo had committed with Magnus' help, twelve years before, was not a memory that Vespasian felt proud of.

'Of course you don't but it has to be remembered that killing Poppaeus left Claudius extremely rich. Everyone involved in the act, either directly or indirectly, has benefited in various ways. Pallas and Narcissus are now the two most powerful men in the Empire, Corbulo wasn't executed for being the half-brother of Caligula's Empress, you earned Narcissus' gratitude and with it furthered your career and saved Sabinus' life, and Asiaticus helped Claudius invest that unexpected windfall and in the process has become fabulously wealthy.'

'Wealthy enough to purchase the Gardens of Lucullus?'

'Exactly; and wealthy enough to improve them in a lavish manner. Now, being a good friend of Claudius' he took care to ingratiate himself with Messalina, promoting her business in the Senate last year when he was consul for the second time and offering her the use of his beautiful gardens whenever she feels like it. But, of course, that's not enough for her; she wants them for herself now. She tried to make him sell them to her and when he refused she told him that the best that he could hope for now was to give them to her.'

'That's a nasty threat.'

'Yes, very sinister. Asiaticus has declined the offer and has declared that he would rather die than give up his gardens – which, I pray, will not be necessary.'

'They must be very beautiful to risk so much.'

'Oh, they are, dear boy; and you'll see them this evening – Asiaticus is holding his dinner there.'

CHAPTER XII

VESPASIAN BREATHED IN deeply the lush scents of a garden in full bloom. Enclosed by a high wall and set on the south-western slope of the Pincian Hill, just beyond the Quirinal Gate, north of the Campus Martius, the Gardens of Lucullus offered the perfect retreat from the noise and bustle of the streets of Rome. Here, Vespasian noticed, the loudest sounds to be heard were the cicadas' relentless creaking and the patter of water flowing from the fountains that stood in the centre of each of the many themed areas of the gardens laid out around the villa, which was accounted to be one of the most luxurious in Rome.

'Claudius has used rather a clever trick to enable him to put on the Secular Games,' Gaius informed Vespasian as they walked up a red-peony-lined path made of a fine mosaic illustrating the various forms of flora and fauna to be found in the gardens. A couple of other guests walked leisurely before them. 'He reckoned on them being held every hundred and ten years as in the traditional Etruscan method of calculation rather than every hundred years as Augustus did when he revived them. It probably means that we'll end up with two cycles, one every hundred years and another every hundred and ten, as no emperor would want to turn down the chance of holding such a prestigious event. However, Claudius has made himself very popular with the masses for his bit of false accounting and I haven't heard any mumblings against it in the Senate. In fact, I've hardly heard anything in the Senate as opinions have become rather dangerous things to own since Messalina has persuaded her husband that every senator harbours treasonous thoughts.'

'How has Messalina treated Flavia?'

ROBERT FABBRI

'Strangely enough, they get on very well and Flavia is as close a thing to a friend that a harpy like Messalina could have. Flavia, of course, has no idea of the potential danger that she's in and spends her time flaunting her exalted position as the Empress's companion to every other woman in Rome. I can't say that's gone down too well; you know what they're like.'

Vespasian grunted, well able to imagine Flavia behaving like that.

'I think that you'll find this will make up for not seeing Flavia this evening.'

Vespasian breathed in deeply again, enjoying the warm evening sun on the back of his head and neck, and found himself agreeing with his uncle: it was much better than a reunion after six years with a wife who was liable to be in a foul temper. 'I do feel a bit guilty about delaying seeing Titus and Domitilla, though.'

'Nonsense, dear boy; you've never met Domitilla and Titus was just over a year old when you left so he won't recognise you. What difference are a few more hours going to make?'

'None, I suppose; but I am nervous about seeing Titus again.'

'Don't worry about him, he worships the memory of his father. Flavia, your mother and Caenis have all seen to that.'

Vespasian felt a certain relief as he admired a Pan-themed area to his left, surrounding a fountain of the goat-legged demi-god spurting water from his pipes into a pool in which grew the reeds from which the pipes were made. His imminent reunion with his son had been playing on his mind: the boy was almost eight and would already have his own character and opinions; if he was to mould the child he would have to make a big impact on him to make up for the lost time.

A shrill cry erupting from close by cut through Vespasian's thoughts; he turned to see a bird, bigger than a cockerel but with similar legs and feet and with a long neck of intense blue plumage upon which was perched a tiny, crested head coloured blue, black and white. As Vespasian looked at the creature it cried again and then spread its magnificent tail feathers into a huge semi-circle, framing its body with colour: light and dark blues, turquoise, pale green and soft yellow-browns. Each feather was of a differing length but tipped with the same bright design that was like an eye with a dark blue iris within a turquoise, rather than white, sclera. 'What's that?'

'I don't know what it's called but Asiaticus had three pairs of them imported at great expense from India, I believe. It's only the male that has such a striking tail; the female is drab in comparison.'

'They make a horrible noise.'

'Yes; I'm sure that they would taste far better than they sound,' Gaius opined as they passed through the warm shade of an apricot orchard, the descendants of the original trees imported from Armenia by Lucullus when he laid out his gardens over a hundred years before. As they cleared the last of the fruit-laden trees filled with songbirds celebrating the waning sun, the villa came into view: single storey with sloping terracotta-tiled roofs leaning upon elegant, towering columns painted yellow and red to contrast the umber and golden hues that adorned the walls. It was the height of refined taste and Vespasian understood why Asiaticus would rather die than give up this paradise – as they would say in Parthia – so close to the stews of Rome.

'Vespasian, it is good to see you back in Rome,' Decimus Valerius Asiaticus said, clutching Vespasian's forearm with a huge hand as he and Gaius mounted the steps to the marbled terrace in front of the villa. 'When I got your uncle's message that you were here I was only too pleased to offer my hospitality.'

'It's good to see you again too, proconsul,' Vespasian replied with genuine feeling, whilst suppressing surprise at Asiaticus' appearance: he had lost all his hair since he had last seen him, which made his round, ruddy face with its pudgy nose and broad mouth seem even more Gallic now that it lacked a civilised Roman hairstyle. Despite having been consul twice, he now looked like what he essentially was: an old Gallic chieftain in a toga. 'And it's a great honour to able to admire what has to be the most beautiful place in the whole of Rome.'

'But beauty always has a price, Vespasian, and in this case the price could be as high as my life.'

'Surely Messalina won't go that far,' Gaius put in, taking his turn to grasp his host's well-muscled forearm, whilst Vespasian took two cups of chilled wine from a passing slave. 'She can't be seen to have you killed and then steal your property.'

'Why not? Emperors have always done that in the past so why not the Empress? What does she care how she looks to others? Everyone knows that she's the biggest whore in Rome – mostly, like me, from experience – so why not add thief to whore?'

'And murderer?' Gaius asked, taking his drink from Vespasian with a nod of thanks.

'No, she won't go that far. She's going to force me to take my life instead; in fact she's already started the slanderous whisperings to her husband that will finish me, which is why I've started sending a lot of my wealth back to Gaul. That extortionist, Publius Suillius Rufus, is preparing capital charges against me – and he doesn't even know how ironic one of the accusations is.' He leant in closer so as not to be overheard by his other guests on the terrace. 'He's going to accuse me of adultery with Poppaea Sabina.' He tried but failed to force down a guffaw, causing more than a few heads to turn in his direction. 'Can you imagine it? I'm being accused of ploughing Poppaeus' daughter after I was part of Antonia's conspiracy, along with you, Vespasian, to murder him. Isn't that rich? It's almost as if Poppaeus is having his revenge from beyond the grave.'

Vespasian smiled despite being once again reminded of that ignoble deed. 'But that's not a capital crime.'

'Not in itself it's not; he's also preparing a case accusing me of passive homosexuality. Me, of Gallic descent, taking it up the arse like some Greek after two cups of wine! Ludicrous! But he's been clever; he's claiming that whilst I was in Britannia with the reinforcements that Claudius brought, I let common legionaries do that in return for exempting them from the more arduous duties of the camp.'

'But corrupting legionaries is still not a capital crime – although it's a humiliation to be accused of it.'

'I agree. But a few days ago I heard, from my good friend Pallas, what I was really going to be accused of. That's why I rushed back from my estates at Baiae so that I can be arrested in Rome in front of witnesses – which I fully expect to happen this evening.'

Gaius' jowls wobbled as he clenched his jaw nervously. 'Arrested here, this evening; what makes you say that?'

'Pallas sent me word that Messalina has paid Sosibius – who is Britannicus' tutor and therefore has unfettered access to the Emperor when he comes to see how his son is progressing at his lessons – to tell Claudius that I was the unidentified man who helped assassinate Caligula.'

Vespasian felt himself go pale and snatched a quick, sideways glance at his uncle whose jowls were now in a state of constant motion.

Asiaticus picked up on his unease. 'What, Vespasian? It's always been known that there was another conspirator whom Herod Agrippa and Claudius himself both saw just prior to Caligula's murder. Claudius never saw his face and Herod glimpsed it only fleetingly.'

'It's not that,' Vespasian replied quickly. 'My son, Titus, is being educated with Britannicus; I don't like the idea that his tutor is so ... er ...'

'So what? Of course he's Messalina's to command, she's Britannicus' mother so he's beholden to her for his very influential job.'

Vespasian managed to conceal the relief that he felt at Asiaticus swallowing his not entirely untruthful excuse. 'Of course he is.'

'With all the other conspirators executed and Herod Agrippa dead from a pleasingly vile disease – when was it, three years ago? – there's no one left who could identify me as the man or not. Which means there is no way that I can *dis*prove it was me.'

'But neither can they prove it was you.'

'They don't need to; Sosibius has sworn to Claudius that he heard me boasting about it and Claudius believes it because he's recently become obsessed with uncovering who was the masked man who so nearly killed him. It's a perfect charge and, backed up by Suillius' lesser ones spells my death as surely as if I had been caught in the act of assassinating an emperor. The only thing that can save me is if it became known exactly who this mystery man was. So come, gentlemen, and enjoy what may be my last night not under a sentence of death.'

Vespasian took a pork, leek and cumin sausage from the platter on the table in front of him and chewed on it without the enthusiasm that its well-balanced flavours deserved. The meal had been exemplary, so far; the musical entertainment gentle and unobtrusive; the surroundings magnificent and the view from the terrace over Rome, with the sun setting behind it, unparalleled. But none of this could assuage his unease at the thought that Claudius was now obsessed with trying to identify the man who had helped to kill his predecessor.

Apart from himself and the close members of his family, Vespasian was aware of only four people of consequence alive in Rome who knew the masked man had been his brother, Sabinus; he had taken part in the assassination to avenge the brutal rape of his wife, Clementina, by Caligula. Magnus and a couple of his crossroads brethren also knew, as it was in their tavern that Sabinus, wounded in the violent aftermath of the killing, had sought refuge; they could be trusted, but what of the four? The first, Caenis, he could rely on implicitly; she would never betray Sabinus. But then there were Claudius' three freedmen: they had promised to cover up Sabinus' part in return for his and Vespasian's efforts to secure their newly elevated patron in his position by retrieving the Eagle of the XVII Legion; this they had done and they had been rewarded by Sabinus being made legate of the XIIII Gemina and all mention of his role in Caligula's death being dropped. But that had been six years ago and Vespasian was all too aware that promises, however iron-clad they may seem at the time, could rust away as easily as the metal from which they symbolically gained their strength.

He carried on picking at the ever-changing plates of food in front of him, whilst half-heartedly joining in the conversation around his table. Torches were lit around the terrace and throughout the gardens and the whole complex was bathed in shimmering firelight, giving the open blooms and lush foliage an artificial, gilded hue that, contrasted with the deep shadow of night, made it seem that Lucullus had sown his garden with seeds of fertile gold. That so much cultivated beauty could reside in one small area and yet be unable to repel the ugliness that surrounded it was an irony that Vespasian appreciated with a hardened heart and a resigned sigh as he watched Rufrius Crispinus, the Praetorian prefect, lead an unnecessary number of his men up through the gilt garden to fulfil Asiaticus' prediction.

'Decimus Valerius Asiaticus,' the prefect proclaimed as he reached the top of the steps to the terrace, 'I arrest you in the Emperor's name.'

Asiaticus got to his feet and wiped his lips with a napkin. 'Don't you mean, Crispinus, that you arrest me in Messalina's name? Are you fresh from her bed or has it been promised to you when you return with her prize? Whichever one it is, remember that I too have been there and I know that it doesn't stay warm for long.'

'It is only the Emperor who has the power to order your arrest.'

'Don't pretend to be more stupid than you really are; we both know how things work. What is the charge?'

'Treason,' Crispinus replied in a low voice.

'Speak up, Crispinus, so that my guests can all hear why I'm being dragged from my dinner table.'

'Treason!'

'Treason? Then I shall argue my case before the Senate and the Emperor, as is my right.'

'There will be no trial before the Senate; you will appear before the Emperor in the morning.'

'I'm to be disposed of in secret; very well, upon what ground is the charge based?'

'You will find out when you—'

Asiaticus threw his head back and cut Crispinus off with a slow, false laugh. 'You don't know, do you, message boy? You don't know because a beast like you just does what it's told.' He stepped forward. 'Come, beast, take me to your handler.'

*

'I can't say that I was thrilled at being present at Asiaticus' arrest,' Gaius muttered as he and Vespasian made their way down through the torch-strewn gardens. 'I'm sure Crispinus saw my face even though I tried to keep it in my neighbour's shadow.'

'That's the least of our problems at the moment, Uncle,' Vespasian replied, keeping his voice below the chatter of the senators around them. 'The question is, will Narcissus or Pallas want to defy Messalina by denying her Asiaticus?'

Gaius stopped momentarily, putting his hand to his mouth. 'Oh! I see; I hadn't looked at it that way. I just thought that Callistus wouldn't reveal Sabinus' name because he would have no interest in proving Asiaticus' innocence.'

'And I don't think that Pallas would because of the long-standing relationship with our family.'

'You'd have hoped so; but political expediency often outweighs loyalty.'

'I don't think he'd sacrifice Sabinus for this; but Narcissus?'

'Narcissus? Narcissus is capable of anything, especially when it comes to fighting Messalina.'

'But would he sacrifice his nomination as suffect-consul?'

'There're plenty more like Sabinus and if he's finally exposed then that could put us both in great danger.'

'So what do we do, Uncle?'

'The only thing we can do: we have to see Narcissus – now.'

'That was sooner than I expected,' Narcissus crooned from behind his desk as Vespasian and Gaius were shown into his chamber; he did not get up. 'When I heard that you two were amongst Asiaticus' guests I knew that you would come to me but I confess I didn't expect you to see the danger that you're in quite so quickly. I congratulate you both as I only realised that possible course was open to me a short while ago.'

'It was good of you to receive us at this late hour, imperial secretary,' Gaius said, hiding any irritation that he might have felt at being kept waiting for two hours.

'Had my secretary not been still here then I might not have seen you at all, but Caenis is very persuasive on behalf of her very good friends. I imagine she's gone home to warm up the bed, Vespasian.'

Vespasian gave a weak smile; his meeting with Caenis had been brief and tempting but he knew where honour dictated he would have to spend the night now that he was in the palace and so close to Flavia.

'Anyway, it's only halfway through the third hour of the night; the Emperor's affairs keep me up late and this business with Asiaticus is most taxing.' Narcissus indicated to the two hard wooden chairs opposite him. 'So, please be seated, gentlemen.'

Vespasian glanced around the room, predominantly decorated in shades of red and lit by four identical ten-armed candelabras each placed in front of a bronze mirror, and he shivered internally despite the warmth and beautiful light. The last time he had been in this room, six years before, had been to plead for Sabinus' life and now it seemed that he was about to do the same thing; but this time his own life might also be in the balance. 'Thank you, imperial secretary.'

'Welcome back, Vespasian; although not covered in glory, it would seem that you did adequately. The Emperor has read all Plautius' rather feeble excuses in his despatches as to why more of that sodden, cold island is not feeling the warm and kindly hand of Rome, but he has decided to award him an Ovation anyway, as you know. Can you tell me why?'

Vespasian knew from past experience that with Narcissus straight-talking was appreciated. 'Because it wouldn't do to have the people think that anything other than constant glorious conquest was happening in Britannia; giving Plautius the first Ovation for decades awarded to someone who is not a member of the imperial family confirms that must be so. Also the Emperor will share Plautius' moment of glory and bring the attention back onto himself.'

Narcissus twitched an eyebrow in appreciation of the assessment as he toyed with his neat, pointed black beard; two weighty gold earrings glinted on either side of it. 'Very good, Vespasian;

indeed, Claudius will hijack the whole affair so he can celebrate his glorious conquest twice without the people noticing.'

'But Plautius will; as will the Senate.'

Narcissus slowly hunched his shoulders and opened his arms, half closing his eyes. 'And how do you think I consider that?'

'As an irrelevance barely worth mentioning, imperial secretary?'

'Please, we're all old friends here, Vespasian; you may be familiar.'

'That's good of you, Narcissus, I'm honoured.'

Narcissus acknowledged the compliment with a dismissive wave. 'That is most gratifying but hardly of concern to me at the moment. So, gentlemen, to business.' He picked up a scroll from the desk and turned it over in his hands. 'How do I counter Sosibius' sworn claim that Asiaticus boasted of being the unidentified man who took part in Caligula's murder without revealing the truth and condemning Sabinus in his place?'

'Do you need to counter it?' Gaius asked, wiping a bead of nervous sweat from his brow.

'A very good question, Gaius, but one that shouldn't be asked in isolation.'

Vespasian's heart sank as he realised what Narcissus was driving at: as he had foreseen he was, once again, being drawn into the tangled world of imperial politics. 'Do you need to counter it, and if you don't what can we do to help you?'

Narcissus steepled his hands and pressed them to his lips whilst regarding Vespasian with ice-blue eyes. 'What indeed?'

Narcissus let the question hang and Vespasian knew that this master of Rome's politics already knew the answer; he waited with a quickening pulse to hear it. An abrupt knock at the door almost made him jump.

'Ah! At last,' Narcissus exclaimed as if he had been awaiting the interruption. 'Enter!'

Pallas arrived, followed by Sabinus. Convenient, Vespasian thought: Narcissus must indeed have been expecting them. A slave followed them in with two chairs.

'Good evening, secretary to the Treasury,' Narcissus enthused with hollow enthusiasm, 'and our consul-designate, Titus Flavius

Sabinus, the man behind the mask. We all know each other so let's dispense with the formalities; please be seated.'

As the slave placed the chairs for the new arrivals and then retreated, Vespasian tried to read Pallas' face, but, as always, it was expressionless, if somewhat more lined than when he had last seen it four years previously. His wavy black hair and full beard were now flecked with grey in accordance with his forty-seven years but his bearing was still that of a younger man. His dark eyes betrayed no weariness, in fact they betrayed nothing at all; whereas Sabinus' eyes darted around the occupants of the room with barely concealed unease.

'I take it by Sabinus' demeanour that you have apprised him of the delicacy of his present situation, esteemed colleague?' Narcissus asked, unnecessarily in Vespasian's opinion.

Pallas inclined his head a fraction. 'Indeed, Narcissus.'

'But we had a deal!' Sabinus exploded.

Narcissus raised a warning hand. 'Hush, my friend; the operative word in that sentence was "had". We *had* a deal but now what we have is a difficult issue to resolve, and if we are to stay with that deal the terms of it may need to be strengthened on your part.'

Vespasian kept his expression as neutral as possible as he once again found himself disappointed but unsurprised by the ruthlessness of those with power. But then was he any better? Was he not willing to let an innocent man take the place of his brother? That was what he was here to negotiate after all. 'We're in no position to bargain, Sabinus; we should just sit and listen.'

Narcissus watched Sabinus gather himself and, once satisfied that he was paying attention, continued: 'To put it bluntly, I have two things to balance here: Asiaticus' usefulness compared to that of your family's in my struggle with the Empress and then, more importantly, once that is decided, how it affects mine and my esteemed colleague Pallas' standing with the Emperor.

'Asiaticus is to appear before Claudius in the morning to face the accusations that we all know are false. Messalina has persuaded her husband that she too should attend to help shoulder the burden of judgement of a man who was hitherto a friend of his. Unfortunately for Asiaticus, I was not there when she made the request, so naturally Claudius has agreed, believing that Messalina is just being a considerate wife. Lucius Vitellius, who as you know is Claudius' other great friend, will appear for Asiaticus against Suillius and Sosibius.

'Now, I have two choices: firstly to tear the case against Asiaticus apart by naming Sabinus and thereby admitting that I knew this all along and kept it from my patron; not a happy admission, I think you'll agree. Or I could go the other way and save my face by making the case against Asiaticus irrefutable.' He paused and looked meaningfully at Sabinus.

'How do you mean, "irrefutable"?' Sabinus asked, looking justifiably nervous.

'By having you testify that when you served in Britannia with Asiaticus you too heard him boast that he was the man behind the mask.'

There was silence in the room, a long silence, as the enormity of the lie was contemplated. Sabinus opened his mouth and closed it a couple of times before realising that there was nothing he could say: to argue against it was to argue for death.

'I see you understand, Sabinus,' Narcissus said with a hint of a smile and an even colder glint in his ice eyes. He turned to Vespasian. 'You would naturally be on hand to corroborate your brother's statement by saying that he told you of this; you will also beg forgiveness for not having brought the matter to my attention to pass on to the Emperor and I will support you in that.'

Vespasian nodded dumbly, wondering if Narcissus would really stick his neck out that far for them; but he could see no option but to take that risk.

'This course of action has, obviously, one possible disastrous side effect: Asiaticus may well denounce the Emperor and us for the murder of Poppaeus.'

Vespasian's blood chilled; was that dishonourable deed always going to come back and haunt him? But then, would this equally as unworthy act also prove to be the cause of years of unease and guilt? Or would he be able to reconcile himself to it as the only option to protect his brother as well as the whole family?

'But surely if he is condemned and despatched quickly he won't be able to make the accusation,' Gaius pointed out.

'Not so. If I were Asiaticus I would be writing a new will tonight and depositing it with the Vestals.'

'Ah!'

'Ah, indeed. I could get access to that will before it was read but I'm sure that Asiaticus will have thought of that and will have ensured that another copy exists to be read by persons unknown at a time unknown. The Emperor will naturally deny he had any part in the affair and place the blame solely on us.' He paused to contemplate the problem and then turned to Pallas. 'Do you have any observations on the matter, dear colleague?'

'Only this: as I'm sure that these gentlemen have noticed, our third colleague, Callistus, is not present: and I'm sure they've worked out why.'

Vespasian realised that an explanation was required. 'Because you no longer trust him after he revealed where he stood by rejecting Corbulo's case against Corvinus?'

'Exactly. So, imperial secretary, we have also got to balance which of these two courses of action will also do the most harm to our former trusted associate.'

'How right you are, secretary to the Treasury. Obviously, as secretary of Justice and the Law Courts, Callistus will wish to be present at tomorrow's hearing; how he acts will be an added factor in making my decision.'

Vespasian realised the truth of the matter. 'There's nothing that we can do or say to persuade you, is there, Narcissus? You're not going to make up your mind until tomorrow during the case, are you?'

'Of course not; would you? How can I make a decision without all the relevant information? And that won't be apparent until I see what the Emperor and, more importantly, Messalina and Asiaticus have to say. I'm a cautious man, as all politicians should be; only once I know what position everyone else is taking will I commit myself to either course of action. Therefore I expect all three of you back here at the second hour of the morning.'

'Why me?' Gaius asked. 'What use do you have for me?'

'That may become apparent tomorrow, senator. In the meantime, if you'll take my advice, have a good night's sleep.'

CHAPTER XIII

'IT'S OUT OF my hands,' Pallas repeated in a voice barely audible above the clatter of four sets of footsteps reverberating off the corridor's marble walls. 'Whatever debt of gratitude I might owe you all as a family, I cannot influence Narcissus on this matter.' He stopped suddenly and turned to face Vespasian, Sabinus and Gaius, halting them too, and continued in a whisper: 'Believe me, gentlemen, if there was any argument that I could put forward to keep you out of this, I would have made it this afternoon whilst Narcissus and I were discussing what to do after Messalina persuaded Claudius to order Asiaticus' arrest.'

Gaius was outraged. 'You planned this with Narcissus!'

'Keep your voice down,' Pallas hissed, looking up and down the corridor, 'Narcissus has ears everywhere. Of course I did; our positions with the Emperor are at stake. We're nothing without him and if we lose his trust then Messalina would have us dead within a matter of hours. And what then, senator? Would you place the governance of Rome in the hands of that harpy?'

Sabinus thrust his face close to Pallas. 'But forcing me to accuse an innocent man of a crime that I've committed is—'

'Is what's going to keep you safe, Sabinus; that was my idea and it was the only way that I've been able to help you.'

'Help me?'

'Yes!' Pallas snapped. He paused to gather himself, having raised his voice, albeit in a forced whisper, for only the third time in Vespasian's recollection. He turned and continued down the corridor so that their conversation would again be masked by their footsteps. 'Who do you think is behind all this?'

'Messalina, of course,' Sabinus hissed dismissively.

'Think, Sabinus. Yes, she wants Asiaticus dead because she covets his gardens and was preparing smaller false charges against him; but how did she manage to come up with just the right charge that would not only finish Asiaticus but also compromise Narcissus and me?'

Vespasian suddenly understood. 'Callistus!'

'Exactly. It must have been him who suggested to Messalina that she accuse Asiaticus of being the man behind the mask because he's the only other person who knows who it really was. He's sure that neither Narcissus nor I will try and save Asiaticus by naming Sabinus – for obvious reasons.' He paused as they went by a couple of slaves tending to the oil lamps; the slaves bowed as the group passed. 'Then, once Claudius has been manoeuvred into executing or forcing his old friend to suicide, Callistus will go to the Emperor and tell him that he's found out that Asiaticus was innocent after all and both Narcissus and I knew it was Sabinus but said nothing. Claudius' remorse will then be our downfall.'

Gaius panted as he struggled to keep up with the pace of their walk and the conversation. 'But surely you'll tell Claudius that Callistus was in on the cover-up too.'

'He's gambling, and correctly too in my opinion, that Claudius will just think that we're trying to take Callistus down with us out of spite. After all, why would Callistus endanger himself by admitting such a thing to Claudius if he was a part of it?'

'Then how can Callistus claim to have found this out?'

'Does it matter? He can say anything he likes: that he over-heard us talking about it or one of his agents did; even that he dreamt it. Before things got really bad between them, Narcissus and Messalina got rid of a mutual enemy by going to Claudius at different times saying that they had had a dream that this man was plotting to stab Claudius; the unfortunate man was executed the same day. Claudius sees conspiracies all around him and is always willing to believe whoever comes to him with news of treachery; witness his old friend Asiaticus fighting for his life tomorrow on trumped-up charges.'

'So how will Narcissus forcing me to testify against Asiaticus make me safe?' Sabinus asked as they reached the more populated, grand atrium of the palace.

Vespasian gave a weary sigh. 'Because, brother, if Narcissus brings you forward as a witness to corroborate Messalina's accusation then Callistus can't successfully claim after the fact that you were really the guilty man; if he tries to then he'd be walking into a trap. Narcissus can say to Claudius that if Callistus knew that you were guilty all along then why didn't he expose you at Asiaticus' hearing? He'll then remind Claudius privately that he had nothing to gain by seeing Asiaticus condemned; in fact, quite the reverse as he put himself in danger of Asiaticus exposing Poppaeus' murder, which is something that Callistus knows nothing about. Claudius will believe that reasoning and Callistus will be exposed as a liar even though for once he'll be telling the truth. It's perfect; but Narcissus will only take that course if, during the hearing, he sees that Claudius believes Suillius' accusations and thinks Asiaticus is guilty.

'If, on the other hand, Claudius is sceptical then Narcissus will expose you; but he was lying when he said that would put him in danger, and Pallas was being disingenuous, to say the least, for not refuting that claim.' He cast a sidelong glance at the Greek; a brief flicker in his eye told him that he had hit the mark. 'Narcissus will say that Gaius came to him with the information; when he heard that Asiaticus was being falsely accused he couldn't stand by and let him be found guilty for Sabinus' crime that has brought shame on the family.'

Gaius looked at his nephew in alarm. 'He can't make me say that.'

'Of course he can and you know it; it'll be that or a trumped-up charge that will force your suicide. And you, Sabinus, will have no option but to admit to it.'

'Bollocks I will.'

'You will, brother, because you'll be given the choice between committing suicide and your family keeping your property if you admit to the deed; or, if you deny it, execution and Clementina and the children becoming destitute. You know which one you'll choose; you'll have to admit to it and Messalina will have some explaining to do to her husband for bringing false charges against his old friend. So whatever happens, Narcissus is going to score a victory against one of his enemies. You almost have to admire him.'

Pallas gave a rare half-smile. 'I can see you understand well how things are, Vespasian.'

'I'm afraid that I've seen enough of your lives to know how sordid they really are, old friend.'

'We have no choice now that we've risen so far and attracted so much envy; it's that or death.'

'If it comes to me facing death, Pallas,' Sabinus muttered, 'then I could still tell Claudius about the deal I had with you and your colleagues.'

Pallas shook his head. 'I don't think that you'll want to do that.'

'What would I have to lose?'

'Nothing more than you would already, but Clementina and the children would also be joining you in the afterlife.'

Sabinus rounded on Pallas, grabbing the neck of his tunic. 'You wouldn't do that.'

Pallas gripped Sabinus' fist and pulled it away. '*I* might not, Sabinus, but then again I might. However, you can be sure that Narcissus would without a thought, given the choice between his life and theirs.'

'You scheming little cunts!'

Gaius pulled his nephew back. 'That is not helpful, Sabinus.'

'Helpful? I could be dead this time tomorrow.'

'But you might not be and if you're still breathing then Narcissus will never be able to hold Caligula's assassination over you again; you'll be free of it.'

Sabinus rubbed his temples, breathing deeply. 'This is no way to live.'

'Then leave Rome and go back to the estates.'

'And do what, Uncle, wait and see whether next year's wine is better than this year's? No, I have to be in Rome.'

'Then this is how you live. Come, I'll walk you home to the Aventine. Vespasian, I assume that you'll stay here.'

'I will, Uncle; nothing that Flavia can do or say could be worse than the last half an hour.'

'I think you're right. Goodnight, Pallas; we appreciate your suggestion of the second course of action.'

Pallas inclined his head a fraction. 'I'm truly sorry that it's got so out of hand, Gaius, for old friendship's sake.'

'But has it really? I can't remember a time that wasn't fraught with danger.' Gaius led Sabinus off across the atrium with his hand on his shoulder.

'Could you show me to Flavia's apartment, Pallas?' Vespasian requested, watching them go. 'I've no idea where it is.'

Pallas remained silent for a few moments, lost in his own thoughts, before turning away. 'That will be one of the more pleasant tasks that I've performed today.'

Vespasian was alarmed to see two Praetorian Guardsmen on duty outside the door that Pallas led him to on the first floor of the palace. 'What are they doing here?'

'There's no need to be concerned,' Pallas assured him, switching to Greek; he signalled the guards to move aside. 'They're to keep intruders out, not to imprison people within.' He knocked on the lacquered door, black with rectangular golden inlays.

Vespasian frowned, eying the two men suspiciously as they stared, unblinking, over his shoulders. A viewing slot opened and Pallas gave a quick order; the door opened.

'I'll leave you, my friend.' Pallas held out his arm; Vespasian grasped it. 'I'll do whatever I can to ensure a good outcome for your family tomorrow. If it looks as if I'm doing otherwise just trust me because, as you are well aware, things are seldom as they seem.'

Vespasian released his grip, shaking his head; a rueful half-smile bent his lips as he held Pallas' eye. 'I don't know how you keep up with all these machinations.'

'The day I don't will be my last; until then I enjoy the wealth and luxury that power and position bring whilst trying to ignore the third gift of those two fickle bitches.'

'Fear?'

For the first time in their acquaintance Pallas let his mask slip; his eyes half closed and he sighed. 'Constant.' As quickly as it had disappeared the mask was redeployed; Pallas nodded a good-night and walked away.

Vespasian turned to the open door, paused to compose himself and then walked through to meet the family that he had not seen for six years.

A gasp escaped Vespasian's lips as he entered Flavia's apartment and looked around.

'Master, you are welcome,' a middle-aged, brown-skinned slave in a well-cut tunic of fine, sky-blue linen said, bowing low. 'My mistress heard of your arrival in the palace this evening and awaits you in the *triclinium*. My name is Cleon, I am the steward here; please follow me at your convenience.'

Vespasian barely heard the slave's words as he took in the room around him. He was standing in an atrium, forty paces long by twenty wide, complete with an *impluvium* beneath a rectangular opening to the night sky in the ceiling above it; at its centre stood a bronze fountain depicting Venus holding a jar on her shoulder from which water cascaded into the white-lily-strewn pool below. But it was not the fact that he was standing in an atrium that should have been, by rights, on the ground floor of a villa and not in an apartment on the first floor that had made him gasp; it was the sheer luxuriousness of the décor. Low, marble tables on gilded legs of animal design, around which were neatly placed couches and chairs of polished wood of differing origins, all sumptuously cushioned or upholstered, surrounded the central pool. Ornaments stood on the reflective marble so that there seemed to be twice their number: silver and bronze stat-uettes, bowls of coloured glass containing freshly cut rose blooms, vases worked of stone or glazed earthenware, painted with geometrical designs or depictions of gods and heroes; Vespasian's eyes took them all in and his brain swiftly calculated their approximate worth. Around the walls, busts of great men from times gone by were placed in niches on marble pedestals and in each corner stood a life-size, or larger, statue, painted in flesh tones and with eyes that followed the beholder around the room. But it was not just all this that made Vespasian stare open-mouthed, as the slave waited in the doorway at the far end for him to follow; it was the frescos, and one in particular: Mother Isis, resplendent in her blue robe, looking down on lines of her worshippers, dressed in contrasting vibrant colours, as her priest performed a sacrifice over the fire on her altar, bedecked with chains of holly and surrounded by waterfowl. Each figure, whether human or animal, was of such exquisite craftsmanship that Vespasian knew that it was the work of one of the finest schools of artists in Rome. He also knew that Isis was Flavia's guardian goddess and he shuddered as he realised that this fresco would not have been here when she had first moved in; she had commissioned it – at what cost?

He swallowed, adjusted his toga and, hoping against hope that the fresco was the only luxury in the room that he had paid for, followed Cleon through the door and into the triclinium.

'Husband,' Flavia purred as he entered the room, adjusting her position on the couch so as to flaunt the full, round shapeliness of her body beneath her stola of deep red linen. 'I have prayed to Mother Isis for this moment every day since we parted.' Gracefully she placed her feet onto the mosaic floor and stood up, causing her breasts to sway enticingly and Vespasian's scrotum to tighten. Erect, she sashayed across the room to him, her neck straight and her head held high as if the elaborately tall coiffure crowning it was difficult to balance; dark ringlets fell down either side of her face highlighting the natural milkiness of her skin. Her dusky eyes glistened as they fixed on him, and her lips, painted an intimate shade of pink, parted invitingly. Dangling earrings swung gently from her lobes, a bejewelled necklace at her throat glinted and rings flashed on her fingers as she raised her hands and tenderly cupped Vespasian's face; her perfume, musky and heart-quickening, enshrouded him as she pulled him towards her and into a fiery kiss that completed his full-blooded arousal onto which she pressed her belly.

'I knew that you'd come to me first this time,' Flavia murmured as their lips parted.

Surprised by the heat and coquettishness of her welcome, all thoughts of her profligacy were pushed to one side and he smiled with genuine feeling for the mother of his children but not the keeper of his heart. 'You are my wife, Flavia; it's only right that I come to you first.'

'It may be right but it's not always the case.'

Vespasian was not about to argue as he knew this to be true and, had circumstances been different, he might well have been holding Caenis right now. But he was here and his body was obviously pleased to see her; as was he. He turned to the steward hovering at a discreet distance beyond the open door. 'Leave us, Cleon.' The door closed; Vespasian led Flavia back to the couch and, without much preliminary fuss, urgently began to make up for six years being apart from his wife.

'They'll both be asleep,' Flavia murmured with her eyes closed in response to his question.

Vespasian sat up on the couch. 'I know; that's why I want to see them now. I want to look at them, see their faces and get to know them a bit before I actually talk to them in the morning.'

Flavia opened her eyes and looked up at him. 'If you insist, husband; who is a wife to keep a father from his children?' She got to her feet and began to bring some semblance of order to her stola, which had had a rough ride during the last half an hour or more; her coiffure was beyond repair and she contented herself with giving it a couple of half-hearted pats before retrieving an errant earring from the couch. 'Come,' she said, taking Vespasian's hand and leading him from the room back out into the lavishly appointed atrium. 'Isn't it lovely? I was so grateful to the Empress when she invited me to move in. She and I have become such firm friends and Titus and Britannicus adore each other; they take it in turns to sleep in one another's rooms. Britannicus is here tonight, which is why the door is guarded. It's a singular honour having the heir to the Empire under my roof; the other women around the palace are so jealous.' She giggled and fluttered her eyelashes up at Vespasian. 'The Emperor must favour you greatly to have allowed this to happen.'

Vespasian forced a smile, but knew it was not very convincing. He did not reply, marvelling instead at how quickly Flavia had returned to form after having won, in her eyes, the first battle between his women that Magnus had predicted. 'Was it furnished when you moved in?'

'Yes, but rather shabbily; the apartment hadn't been used since Tiberius' time and then only occasionally by minor officials and suchlike. It's kept me very busy getting it fit for your return. Do you like it?'

Vespasian gave the most enthusiastic grunt he could in the circumstances as they left the room and passed into a wide corridor with windows down one side and doors down the other.

Flavia stopped at the second one outside which stood another two Praetorians. 'This is Titus' room, you must be very quiet.' She turned the handle and stepped inside; Vespasian followed her into a room lit by a single oil lamp in which two boys were sleeping. Flavia went to the right-hand bed and looked down. 'This is your son, husband; see how he has grown.'

Vespasian's eyes took a few moments to adapt to the gloom. As they did the sleeping face of Titus came into focus and Vespasian drew in a sharp breath: it was as if he was looking at himself thirty years ago. His son had the same physiognomy: full round cheeks either side of a strong if slightly bulbous nose, large ears with pronounced lobes and a well-proportioned mouth with thin lips set over a slightly rounded, jutting jaw; but all this was contained in the immature face of a boy not quite eight. Vespasian gazed at Titus and felt sure that their similarity in feature would extend to closeness in temperament.

He bent to kiss his son's forehead and then put an arm around Flavia's shoulder whilst stroking Titus' soft, light-brown hair. 'He's beautiful, my dear; let's hope that we can make something great of him.'

'We will, Vespasian; he's getting one of the finest starts to life that a child can get. He's the companion of the next Emperor.'

Which was what concerned Vespasian, although he did not voice it. As he turned to leave the room he glanced at the sleeping form of Britannicus and recalled Pallas' prediction, four years before in Britannia, that the boy would be too young at Claudius' death to be considered a viable successor; instead of reaching manhood he would be murdered by the man who stole his rightful inheritance – whoever that might be. Vespasian left the room with a prayer that somehow he would be able to keep his son safe during that tumultuous time in the not so distant future.

Flavia led him down the corridor to the next room; it was unguarded. She opened the door and ushered Vespasian inside; again it was dimly lit by a single lamp. He crossed the floor to a small bed on the far side beneath a shuttered window and with a fluttering within his chest beheld his daughter for the first time. Born soon after he had left Rome, Domitilla was now almost six; she lay on her back sleeping with the serenity that only a young child can. One arm was draped above her head, entangled in her long brown hair, and the other dangled off the side of the bed; her head was tilted to one side so that it faced Vespasian and he saw that she was beautiful. She had inherited her mother's features; Vespasian could not help but wish that she would not also share her mother's taste for the finer things in life but knew that to be a forlorn hope, given the comfort she was already used to. As this thought went through his mind, Domitilla stirred in her sleep and opened her eyes, looking directly into Vespasian's; for a moment she held his gaze and then smiled at him before turning over and resuming her soft, rhythmic breaths. Vespasian could not be sure if she had actually seen him, having been so deeply asleep, but he had seen her eyes and he was smitten. It was with abundant joy that he kissed his daughter for the first time and then followed Flavia from the room.

'And now, Vespasian,' Flavia said as she closed the door, 'it's time for you to remind me again what it's like to have a husband at home.'

Vespasian acquiesced with a grin and took her by the hand. Having seen his children, he was feeling very affectionately disposed towards his wife.

*

The dawn was warm and resounded in birdsong. Vespasian looked down from his bedroom window into a garden at the heart of the palace complex, surrounded by a colonnade crowned by a sloping terracotta-tiled roof, still damp after a light, nocturnal summer rain. Within the garden, slaves were moving around, watering the plants and bushes and preparing the lush oasis for Rome's élite to use.

There was a knock on the door and Vespasian glanced down at Flavia, still asleep in the bed; she did not stir. 'Enter.'

Two female slaves stepped into the room with their heads bowed; the younger one had a robe draped over one arm and held a pair of slippers.

'What is it?'

The elder of the two, a dumpy woman in her thirties with the vague hint of a moustache, raised her eyes. 'We've come to attend to the mistress, master; she asked to be wakened at dawn.'

Flavia opened an eye and let out a contented sigh as she focused on Vespasian. 'Good morning, husband.' She then noticed the two slaves in the doorway and her countenance changed. 'Out! Both of you!'

The two slaves fled as ordered, closing the door behind them.

'Come back to bed, Vespasian,' Flavia offered, raising the blanket and revealing the shadowy outline of her naked body.

'I don't have the time,' Vespasian replied, picking up his tunic from where it had been discarded the night before and slipping it over his head. 'I want to be presented to the children and then I have to go.'

Flavia made a noise that sounded like a cross between disappointment and an enticing purr.

'Do you always treat your dressers like that?'

'Oh, they weren't my dressers, Isis no; they're just the girls who get me out of bed and escort me to my dressing room. My dressers attend me there, along with my make-up girls and hairdressers; those two come back here and clean the bedroom whilst I get ready.'

'You've got slaves to do each of those things?'

'Of course, my dear; what fashionable woman does not?'

Vespasian eased his feet into his red senatorial shoes. 'So, Flavia, how many women help you to make yourself presentable each morning?'

'Oh, very few; not nearly as many as Messalina has.'

'I should hope not; she's the Empress and you're just the wife of an ex-legate – a very poor ex-legate at that.'

'There's no need to worry about the money, Vespasian; I've got plenty of it. How else could I have afforded to furnish this place and purchase nine girls?'

'Nine! Whatever for?'

Flavia sat up and began to count off on her fingers. 'Well, three hairdressers, two make—'

'Did you just say that you had plenty of money?'

'Yes.'

'But I told the Cloelius Brothers' banking house in the forum not to advance you more than five thousand a year.'

'I know, and the horrid little men couldn't be talked out of it; that's why Messalina kindly gave me a very generous loan. She said—'

'She did what!'

'Gave me a loan.'

'A loan!' Vespasian almost spat out the word as if it were the most deadly of poisons. 'You never asked permission from me to take a loan.'

'You had much more important things on your mind and, besides, I didn't need to. It was just a little arrangement between good friends, as a personal favour – from the Empress, no less, the other women were so jealous – to tide me over until you got back and could see that the allowance you'd given me wasn't nearly enough to cover my outgoings and could remedy the situation. She said she'd charge only a nominal interest.'

'How much interest?'

'I can't remember now, but it's written down on the contract somewhere.'

'You signed a contract?'

'Of course.'

Vespasian sat, with a jolt, on a convenient chair and attempted to master his growing rage. 'Just how much have you borrowed?'

'My dear, hardly anything; just half of the value of that money that you brought back from Alexandria eight years ago, and have done nothing with since.'

Vespasian's eyes narrowed as he struggled to prevent himself from slapping his wife. 'You've borrowed one hundred and twenty-five thousand denarii from Messalina?'

Flavia's voice hardened. 'I'm now a lady of consequence, the mother to the heir's companion; I need to appear as such and your allowance was insufficient. How else was I going to make a comfortable home for the children and for you to come back to? We need somewhere to entertain the finest people in Rome without feeling humiliated each time they turn their noses up at our tawdry furnishings.'

'The Alexandrian money has already been spoken for: Gaius used it to secure a house on the Quirinal; your house! The one I bought for you to move into as soon as I can extract you from this labyrinth of intrigue without causing offence.'

'Why should we move out of here? I've made it very comfortable.'

'With borrowed money from Messalina, which puts me in her debt! No one in their right minds would put themselves in that situation! And at the moment I can't afford to pay her off.'

'Nonsense, one hundred and twenty-five thousand is nothing, husband; you must have made a fortune in slaves and plunder. Everyone always does; Messalina told me so.'

Unable to take any more without risking serious damage to either Flavia or her precious furnishings, Vespasian rose to his feet and stormed out of the door.

'What about the children?' Flavia called after him.

'I'll see them later – once I think you'll be safe in my presence again!'

Vespasian had calmed somewhat by the time he saw his uncle arriving on the Palatine. Gaius was surrounded by his retinue of clients and preceded by Magnus and a couple of his crossroads brethren bearing stout staves to beat a way through the crowds. In the hour since leaving Flavia's apartment in a rage greater than he could recall ever being in before, other than in battle, he had stalked up and down outside the palace cursing Flavia and contemplating his options. He had to extract himself from Messalina's debt before she could call it in. Once he had begun to compose himself he thought of a way to do so without mortgaging any of his property; however, he still had no idea how to curb his wife's extravagance and naïvety. That would have to wait, he decided, as Magnus approached and Gaius began to dismiss his clients.

'You don't look too pleased,' Magnus commented.

'That's because I'm not. I need you to do something for me,' Vespasian replied, pulling his friend to one side to explain the situation.

Magnus stared at Vespasian for a few moments in amazement, and then burst into a roar of laughter. 'You've taken a loan? I never thought I'd see the day.'

'Keep your voice down! I've not taken a loan, Flavia has.'

'Well, it's the same thing, ain't it? She's your wife so you're responsible for her actions.'

'I know; and the stupid woman doesn't realise the danger that she's put me in because her vanity can't see past the glory of being on good terms with the Empress and wants to milk the jealousy that it provokes in other women.'

'I did warn you about marrying a woman with expensive tastes.'

'Saying "I told you so" gets me nowhere; and you were wrong, by the way; she didn't get herself two hairdressers.'

'No?'

'No, she got three!'

'I seem to remember saying that she would need *at least* two, so I was right, but I won't rub it in. So what is it you want me to do?'

'I need cash and I need it fast without borrowing against my property so I want you to find that slave-dealer, Theron, and bring him to me with all the money that he owes me. He should either be in Rome or at Capua.'

'Fair enough, sir; that won't be a problem.'

'Thank you, Magnus,' Vespasian said, hastening to finish the conversation as he saw Sabinus approaching.

'I imagine that you'll not want me to mention your loan to your brother?'

Vespasian scowled while Magnus tried but failed to hide a grin, and then turned to greet his brother, who looked as sombre as the situation dictated.

'I've written a new will,' Sabinus said, handing Vespasian a scroll. 'I haven't had time to lodge it with the Vestals so will you keep it and read it if it becomes necessary?'

Vespasian's personal worries disappeared as he was confronted with the reality that Sabinus may well not see the day's dusk. He took the scroll and placed it in the fold of his toga. 'Of course, brother; but it won't come to that.'

Sabinus' look made Vespasian regret his crass remark; only Narcissus could make that decision.

'Dear boys,' Gaius said with less of a boom than was normal, having dismissed the last of his sixty or so clients, 'I trust we have all made the necessary sacrifices to the relevant gods? We'll need their help today.'

As Vespasian followed his uncle and brother he was only too aware that he had been so angry he had completely neglected to appeal for divine protection. It was with a prayer to Mars running through his head and a promise of a sacrifice at the close of the day that he entered the palace and submitted to the body-search that was now compulsory for anyone wishing to come into the presence of the Emperor.

A slave was waiting for them in the atrium, which was alive with imperial functionaries, the products of the bureaucracy that Narcissus, Pallas and Callistus had created since their master had come to power. 'Follow me, masters.'

They were led through the high, wide and labyrinthine corridors of the palace complex, every echoing step becoming heavier as the weight of the power within the building seemed to grow and oppress them. Each felt helpless; their destinies were now out of their hands. They were to be used as pawns in the political manoeuvrings, for his own personal gain, of a man of inferior birth who had become the most powerful person in the Empire.

Vespasian felt the bile rise in his throat, knowing that there was nothing that they could do. They could not run or hide or plead for mercy. For a few moments he envied Corbulo the certainties of the military camp, of which he had spoken so wistfully, and the decent Roman values of discipline and honour. But a career in Rome could not be forged by military achievement alone if a man was to rise; the politics had to be endured. All they could do now was accept their positions in this most hierarchical of societies; to do otherwise would mean exclusion and that would lead to obscurity. And that, for their family's honour, they could not countenance.

Vespasian followed the slave out of a side door of the palace and across a garden, walled off from the outside world with no sign of a gate, and then through a second door and on into another building. After they had turned a couple of corners recognition hit him with a jolt. 'This is the Lady Antonia's house, Uncle,' he said with some surprise.

'It *was* Antonia's house; now, of course, it belongs to Claudius. However, he gave it to Messalina last year because she told him that she wanted somewhere quiet to keep out of his way whilst he dealt with the weighty matters of state.'

'Oh, I see.'

'Exactly.'

The presence of the slave meant they could say no more, but Vespasian understood well enough what the house of his old benefactress was now used for.

They turned another corner and Vespasian recognised the corridor in which Antonia had confronted Sejanus, all those years ago, as Sabinus, Caligula and he had hidden behind an unlocked door; it was to this very door that the slave led them, ushering them in with a bow to a small room, no more than an ante-chamber, sparsely furnished with three stools. Narcissus and Pallas waited within, along with two Praetorian centurions.

'Good morning, senators,' Narcissus said, waving the slave away. 'I'm sure that you remember this room and the view that it has into the house's formal reception room.' He indicated the curtain through which the brothers and Caligula had spied on Sejanus on the evening that they had rescued Caenis from his and his lover Livilla's clutches. Since then the curtain had been replaced with one of a finer material and the room beyond was visible so that the features of those already within could be discerned. 'I want you to be able to see and hear the proceedings so that when I call upon you to speak you will be able to answer the questions asked of you with the benefit of knowing how the arguments have been made.'

'Or what I was supposed to have said, I suppose,' Gaius muttered.

Narcissus looked at him in surprise. 'Exactly. So you've worked out why you're here.'

'Vespasian did.'

Narcissus gave Vespasian an appreciative look. 'You'll make a politician yet.'

'I don't think I have the stomach for it.'

'It has nothing to do with your stomach but, rather, your natural instinct to survive.'

'I have that all right; we all do. That's why we're here and not helping Sabinus into a warm bath and giving him a sharp knife.'

Gaius looked into the brightly lit reception room where Asiaticus sat in profile, guarded by Crispinus, opposite a dais with two chairs upon it, and then turned nervously to Narcissus. 'Won't people see that we're in here?'

'No, this room is much darker; from out there you can see nothing through the curtain so no one will know that you're here except Pallas and me as well as these two gentlemen.' He indicated to the centurions. 'They are here to ensure that, on the off-chance that Claudius or Messalina order the curtain to be drawn back, I can't be accused of putting their lives in danger seeing as you are being guarded by two seasoned killers.' With a

curt nod of his head, Narcissus walked past them to the door.
'You'll be called if and when you're needed.'

As Pallas followed him he whispered, 'Remember that whatever happens I'll try and secure the best outcome for you all.'

Vespasian watched him go and then looked at his brother and
uncle; neither would meet his eye as they struggled with their
own thoughts. Two men entered the reception room; one,
whom Vespasian recognised as Lucius Vitellius, sat next to
Asiaticus and the other, whom he guessed was Suillius, took his
place next to the dais. Claudius' freedmen then made their
appearance and placed themselves on three chairs in a row,
facing Vespasian, between the accused and the imperial seats.
Vespasian slumped down onto a stool, feeling his belly churn –
more violently, even, than before combat, when at least a man
holds his life in his own hands – and, with an increasing sense of
helplessness, waited for the arrival of the Emperor and Empress.

CHAPTER XIIII

CLAUDIUS ARRIVED FIRST, a quarter of an hour later, causing the occupants of the room to spring to their feet and look at one another with barely concealed concern. Wearing a purple toga and a laurel wreath over his sparse grey hair, the Emperor shambled in on weak legs, which only just supported the extra weight that he had put on since Vespasian had last seen him at Camulodunum; he had to be helped up the steps to the dais by an accompanying slave. His expression, made sorrowful by a downturned mouth and eyes with drooping care-lines set in a long, slack-skinned face etched with the ravages of heavy drinking, changed to one of confusion as he noticed Messalina's vacant seat. 'W-where's my w-w-wife? She should have b-b-been here b-b-before me.'

'Indeed she should, Princeps,' Narcissus agreed with a silken voice.

'She arrived some time ago,' Callistus lied, bobbing his bald head and wringing his sinewy hands, 'but then she remembered that she had left an important item behind.'

No one raised an eyebrow at this patent untruth but it satisfied Claudius who chuckled as he sat down. 'She's a f-f-forgetful little thing sometimes; women can be so sc-sc-sc-scatter-brained. But we must get on as it's the climax of my Secular Games and I d-don't want the beast hunt to be delayed this afternoon because I'm late in arriving.' He pulled a scroll from the fold of his toga and, with shaking hands, unrolled it. 'The charges against D-Decimus Valerius Asiat-aticus ...' A spray of saliva erupted from his mouth as he enunciated the last word, splattering the parchment, but everyone in the room affected not to notice. Claudius wiped his lips with his toga and then began to read aloud.

Vespasian observed the two men in the room whom he did not know as Claudius stumbled through the list. Lucius Vitellius he knew by sight but he had never had any dealings with him; a martial-looking man, despite his baldness, with a square jaw and hooked nose, but running to fat in his old age, Vitellius had conducted a war against Parthia whilst Governor of Syria in Tiberius' reign, concluding it on very favourable terms for Rome and had won the favour of successive emperors by his unabashed sycophancy. He had enthusiastically worshipped Caligula as a god and it had been to Vitellius that Claudius had entrusted Rome when he had rushed to Britannia to claim the credit for the fall of Camulodunum. But it was his attitude to his elder son, Aulus Vitellius, for which he was infamous. He had pandered him to Tiberius, who had greatly prized his oral favours and, no doubt, much else.

Publius Suillius Rufus, a nondescript man of medium height and unremarkable features – unless it was to comment on their blandness – Vespasian knew only by reputation. What he lacked in physical charisma he made up for with his vicious oratory; he was as skilled at reasoning with false, honeyed arguments as he was at cajoling with slanderous fabrications to ensure the condemnation of his victims whose only crime had been to cross him or his imperial patroness.

Claudius had finished reading the charges and was drawing to the close of a long, rambling speech about how saddened he was that his great friend Asiaticus should be appearing before him in such dismal circumstances, although he was sure that Vitellius' eloquence would clear him, when a commotion at the door, two Praetorian Guards snapping to attention, heralded the arrival of Messalina.

'My dearest!' Claudius exclaimed, turning in his seat and almost falling from it. 'You've arrived just in time.'

Messalina made her entrance with all the hauteur of one who revels in power: slow, self-assured and with no recognition of anyone else in the room; even Claudius got to his feet. Slight of build but made taller by the pile of intricately woven, jet-black hair that rose from the crown of her head, part-covered by a crimson palla and studded with jewels, she processed into the room attended by four slave girls so richly attired that they could have been mistaken for great ladies in their own right. She mounted the dais and held out a languid hand, weighed down by rings, for her husband to slobber over before turning her dark, kohl-rimmed eyes to Asiaticus; her full lips creased with a faint smile, which could have been interpreted as one of regret had it not been for the hardness in her eyes. She sat, adjusting her palla so that it flowed with studied elegance from her head to her shoulders and then, covering her left arm but baring her right, perfectly down either side of her body to the floor. Her poise was exquisite; beautiful and delicate, with fair skin, fine cheekbones and a slender straight nose, she exuded a sexual aura that was mesmerising and animal. Every man in the room was drawn to her whether they were for her or against. She had grown in presence since Vespasian had seen her last, six years ago, when Claudius had just become emperor; he now understood what Corbulo had meant when he had talked of her allure. Her delicacy made her seem almost fragile and brought out the urge to protect and cherish her, and yet all knew what ruthless power lurked behind that innocent façade. Vespasian drew a breath and wondered if he would have the strength to resist her if she tried to bend him to her will, but in his heart he knew the answer.

All eyes rested on the Empress and nobody in the room made a sound until she was comfortable.

'D-d-did you find whatever it was you'd forgotten, my dearest?' Claudius ventured as everybody sat back down.

Messalina frowned at her husband and then caught Callistus' look and slight nod. 'A trifling thing that I thought to give to you, my darling; but then I decided to wait until later – when we are alone.' She brushed the back of her hand along the outside of Claudius' thigh making his head twitch and his eyes blink rapidly. 'Shall we read the charges that have been brought against this unfortunate man?'

'I-I-I've already read them, d-d-dearest.'

'Then read them again; I wish to hear them because I'm sure that they can't be true.' She cocked her head and looked at Claudius girlishly with wide eyes and parted lips. 'After all, that's why we decided to hear them informally, in private, so this calumny wouldn't become public and ruin poor Asiaticus' reputation.'

Claudius tore his eyes away from his wife's inviting mouth and hastily stemmed a flow of drool with his toga. 'Of course, anything for you, my darling; you are so considerate of others.'

Messalina composed her face into an ideal of feminine modesty and looked down at her hands folded in her lap as Claudius once more laboured through the list of charges. As he drew to a close with Sosibius' accusation of Asiaticus being a party to Caligula's assassination, she wiped a tear from her eye and let out a soft sob. 'That we could have chosen such a disreputable man to tutor our darling Britannicus. Oh husband, once you've thrown these charges out we shall dismiss him and banish him to the most unwelcoming of provincial towns to rot in his own maliciousness.'

'Then let's just d-d-dismiss them now.'

With a sad sigh, Messalina shook her head. 'Would that be wise, my darling? We must hear the arguments for and against, in case there be the slightest truth in one or two of the allegations. I'm sure that even dear Asiaticus would agree that he should be punished if he has any guilt; as a two-times consul he better than anybody else other than you understands that the rule of law must hold firm, and to ensure that, justice must be seen to triumph.'

Despite himself, Vespasian found himself sympathising with the argument although he knew it to be specious.

Claudius looked at Messalina with wonder in his eyes as if he were beholding the wisest, most beautiful and compassionate being ever to have been given life. 'You are so right, little bird, we must hear the arguments if only for my good friend Asiaticus' sake.' He jerked his head away from Messalina and looked at Suillius. 'You may b-b-begin.'

Asiaticus slammed his fist down onto the arm of his chair and leapt to his feet interrupting Suillius mid-flow. 'What proof do you have of any of these allegations, Suillius? You have accused me at some length of passive homosexuality with rank and file soldiers and then adultery; it's not enough just to say these things, however eloquently – you must back them up.'

'I haven't finished making my case, I still have—'

'This is not a court of law! Nor is it a hearing before the Senate, both of which have protocols to follow; this is an informal hearing before *our* Emperor.' Asiaticus rubbed his smooth pate to calm himself and then addressed Claudius. 'Princeps, as there is no precedent to follow, may I be allowed to deal with the accusations one by one, as they arise, so that the weight of each of the falsehoods levelled at me don't combine to make the case against me seem overwhelming before I even begin my defence?'

Claudius contemplated the request for a few moments, remaining surprisingly still, his expression hinting at the great pleasure he had in deliberating on such a matter. 'The differences between precedents and protocol in legal hearings, both formal and informal, must be weighed against the ways of our ancestors.'

Claudius launched into a legal argument of such pedantry that it could only have been of interest to the most petty-minded minor official of a ghastly provincial backwater who had nothing better to do all day than exercise his own self-importance. For Vespasian and everyone else suffering it, however, it was eye-wateringly tedious. It was to vacant, pallid faces that Claudius eventually concluded: 'So to sum up with the briefest of answers: in this case, but only in this one instance, my judgement, Asiaticus, is yes.'

Evidently having lost track of the argument and therefore whether the judgement was for him or against, Asiaticus stood bewildered for a moment before gathering himself. 'So I may defend each allegation in turn, Princeps?'

'Th-th-that was my j-j-j-judgement,' Claudius replied testily, his stammer, absent during his fluent legal ramble, returning full force.

'I'm grateful, Princeps.' Asiaticus faced Suillius. 'Firstly, the most disgusting allegation: that I allowed, no, actively sought to be penetrated by other men – common legionaries – in return for favours. As if, had I wanted such base entertainment, I couldn't just get one, or even half a dozen, of my slaves to defile me any time I liked – as many men in Rome do, I believe.' He raised his eyebrows at Suillius. 'How did you come up with that idea? What were you doing when it occurred to you that you should level false allegations of buggery with lowlife against me?'

Suillius sneered. 'Inferences like that won't hide the truth. I have a witness.'

'Have you? Then he should be able to recognise me seeing as we've been so intimate, or is he going to claim that he only saw the back of my head? Princeps, can I suggest that this witness comes into the room and, without any prompting from this creature here, tries to identify the man whom he alleges was accommodating enough to part his buttocks for him?'

Claudius nodded with enthusiasm. 'That w-would be an ad-admirable way to settle this.' He turned to the guards on the door. 'One of you, fetch this man in.'

Asiaticus took his place back next to Vitellius and then pointed at Suillius. 'Sit down.'

Suillius did so reluctantly as a squat man of powerful build, in his fifties, wearing a plain citizen's toga was led in, looking as if he already regretted agreeing to appear in front of such august company. He swallowed as he stood before the Emperor and Empress.

'W-w-what's your name, citizen?'

'Sextus Niger, Princeps.'

'So, Niger, you allege that you buggered Decimus Valerius Asiaticus in return for favours.'

'He forced me to, Princeps; I would never do—'

'Never mind your p-p-personal habits, man; is that what you allege?'

Niger closed his eyes. 'Yes, Princeps.'

'Then describe him.'

'He's bald, Princeps.'

'B-b-b-bald? Is that all?'

Niger looked in panic at Suillius.

'Look at me, N-N-Niger; is that all that you can remember about the man you buggered: he was bald?'

'It was dark, Princeps.'

Crispinus stifled a guffaw and Claudius shot him a warning look. 'But he was your commanding officer; you must know what he looks like.'

Niger was momentarily flummoxed. 'I had just transferred in, Princeps.'

'If you're lying, N-N-Niger, I'll have you stripped of your citizenship and given a starring role in the games this afternoon. Now identify h-h-him.'

Terrified, the man turned and looked around the room to see three men who could be described as bald: two sitting together opposite the Emperor, and a third sitting with two other men. Without a pause he made his choice, knowing that hesitation would be an admission of dishonesty. 'It's him.'

Claudius roared with laughter as he looked at Callistus gazing back at the false witness's finger. Vespasian was sure he detected both Narcissus and Pallas trying to cover amusement under their neutral masks.

Asiaticus joined in with his Emperor's mirth, looking across at a deflated Suillius. 'The irony is, Suillius, that at the time this buggery was alleged to have taken place, I wasn't bald.'

'Take him away,' Claudius ordered through his laughter. 'I look forward to seeing more of you later, Niger; a lot more.' He took Messalina's hand. 'You were so right, dearest one; none of these charges will prove to be true. I think that your friend Suillius has been misled; but nevertheless we should press on so that Asiaticus can prove his innocence.'

As the hapless Niger was dragged off, screaming, Asiaticus got to his feet. 'I am no taker, Suillius. Just ask your sons, they will confirm that I'm a man. We'll take up the issue of how and why you got someone to lie about me to the Emperor later, once he's thrown the rest of your charges out.'

'He came to me,' Suillius protested. 'I don't trawl the gutter for false witnesses.'

'Don't you? Let's see what your next witness is like; I hope that he's better coached. What's he going to accuse me of? Ah yes, adultery with Poppaea Sabina, daughter of the late Gaius

Poppaeus Sabinus. So tell me, Suillius, does her husband, Publius Cornelius Lentulus Scipio, a distinguished man in his own right and descended from so many great men, also accuse his wife of adultery? And, if so, does he accuse me of being her lover?'

Suillius spread his arms. 'Does a husband always know of his wife's …' He trailed off as he felt Messalina's cold stare pierce him; everyone in the room shifted uneasily, including Claudius, and Vespasian wondered just how aware of Messalina's extra-marital activities he really was.

Asiaticus seized on the moment and spoke directly to Claudius. 'What husband cannot be aware of being cuckolded, Princeps, even if he refuses to acknowledge the signs?'

Claudius answered with a series of uncontrolled head twitches spraying saliva in an arc about him. Messalina stared at Asiaticus, her face rigid.

'I'll ask you again, Suillius: does Scipio accuse his wife of adultery?'

'No.'

'Then who does?'

'One of his freedmen.'

'A freedman? And did he take this accusation first to his patron, the man to whom he owes complete loyalty?'

'He came to me first.'

Asiaticus met Messalina's eyes and held them for a couple of heartbeats before addressing Claudius. 'Princeps, what would you make of a freedman casting such aspersions on the character of his patron's wife to strangers?'

'I-i-in-int-t-t-tolerab-b-ble.'

'And yet here we have it: a freedman going about saying such things. Imagine, Princeps, the gods forbid, should your freedmen go making such accusations in public instead of coming to you? Would that be acceptable?'

Claudius made a sound akin to a man being slowly garrotted as he tried to form his answer and Vespasian realised that Asiaticus had hit the mark: Claudius must give some credence to certain of the rumours about his wife.

Messalina sat rigid whilst Narcissus observed Asiaticus through half-closed eyes, revolving a ruby ring on his little finger; Pallas and Callistus both looked as if they had not taken a breath for a long while. A droplet of sweat dripped down Suillius' forehead whilst Vitellius and Crispinus both gaped at Asiaticus in unconcealed horror as he stood patiently awaiting the Emperor's protracted efforts to give his reply.

'No!' Claudius finally exploded, his face puce and his chin slimed with drool. 'No one will accuse my Messalina of such a thing in public; in public she is beyond reproach.' He jerked his shaking head towards his freedmen and continued his tirade. 'But if one of my freedmen thought that there was the slightest stain on her character it would be his duty to bring his proof to me, the h-h-husband, and no one else; a man's wife's conduct is for him alone to deal with and not for public consumption! It's the way of the ancestors!'

There was complete silence in the room apart from Claudius' panting and snuffling as he fought to regain his composure. Messalina's eyes, black as beads and cold as the Styx, fixed on Asiaticus as he waited patiently, seemingly unruffled by the outburst that he had goaded his Emperor into, staring at Narcissus who gazed back with the faintest of cold smiles.

'He's just forced Narcissus' hand,' Gaius whispered to the brothers. 'If Claudius were to get proof of Messalina's infidelity from any source other than his freedmen he would never trust them again. Asiaticus knows Messalina will ensure that he's found guilty today and has just guaranteed his quick vengeance.'

A loud sob broke over Claudius' laboured breathing and Vespasian looked up to see Messalina with tears running free down her cheeks.

'My d-dearest!' Claudius cried. 'I wasn't suggesting for one moment that you are anything other than a model wife.'

'I know, my darling,' Messalina croaked, dabbing at her face with her palla and looking at Claudius with wet, pleading eyes. 'But it's the injustice of a woman's lot in society that grieves me; aspersions are cast upon our characters by jealous people, and despite our innocence some of the slander sticks. Poor Poppaea's reputation is being sullied by a freedman and she can't even defend herself. Promise me, my darling, that should such lies about me ever reach your ears that you will give me the chance to put your mind at rest, and once I've done that you will punish the scandal-monger as you will this freedman who has behaved so dishonourably.'

'Of course I will, sweet girl; I would never b-b-believe anything b-bad of you until I have seen your eyes.' He leant over and kissed her cheek, adding to its moistness, before turning to Suillius. 'I have no wish to see this freedman witness of yours, other than in the arena with N-N-Niger this afternoon. That charge is thrown out. Now, what of the next, Suillius, have you been misled on this one too?'

'No, Princeps, on my honour; and you know the witness to be of the highest integrity having entrusted the education of your son to him. This is the most serious charge: that Asiaticus was heard boasting that he was the unidentified man who took part in Caligula's murder.'

'T-time is running on so b-b-bring Sosibius in.'

Pallas stood. 'Before we hear from Sosibius, Princeps, I feel obliged to make one admission.'

'Well?'

'It's just that this morning I heard my dear colleague, Callistus, saying that he thinks that he has proof as to exactly who this man was and that Narcissus and I have covered up the evidence. I thought that I'd mention it so that he could have the chance to enlighten us all and stop this charade.'

Vespasian's heart leapt and he glanced at Sabinus; the colour had drained from his face.

Callistus swallowed and then got to his feet, casting a quick sidelong glance at Pallas that Vespasian assumed was one of hatred, despite his expressionless face. 'Princeps, I'm afraid that Pallas is mistaken; I said no such thing.'

Pallas insisted. 'But I heard you say, my dear Callistus, that you had evidence that Asiaticus was not the man and that we knew all along.'

'I said nothing of the sort, I assure you, Princeps.'

Claudius twitched impatiently. 'Well? D-d-did he or didn't he, Pallas?'

Pallas bowed in apology. 'I must insist that he did and I'm bringing it to your attention, in an open hearing, because I wouldn't want him to come to you in private, should you find Asiaticus guilty, and cloud the issue and, at the same time, cause you to question Narcissus' and my loyalty to you. I believe that it's best to get this out into the open, Princeps, for all our sakes.'

'Yes, yes; to whom did he say this?'

Pallas cleared his throat as Callistus wrung his hands aware of Messalina's distrusting gaze. 'To Titus Flavius Vespasianus.'

Vespasian swallowed a bile retch.

'Vespasian? Is he back in Rome?'

'He arrived yesterday and I have him here ready to confirm the conversation.'

'Bring him in.'

Vespasian stood before the Emperor and Empress knowing that he had to answer Claudius' question quickly and fluently. 'Yes, Princeps; I spoke to Callistus this morning in the palace. I was on my way down from my family's apartment. The Praetorians guarding Britannicus, who had spent the night there with Titus, will confirm that.'

'Ahh, they are such good friends those two,' Claudius said, his concentration shifting, 'aren't they, my dear? It was such a fine idea of your brother's to move young T-T-Titus into the palace.'

'Yes, dearest,' Messalina replied without the same enthusiasm. 'But we should listen to what Vespasian has to say. Please continue.'

'I met him in one of the corridors ...'

'W-where were you going?'

Where had he been going? For an instant he felt panic well up and then came the moment of clarity in which he saw exactly what Pallas had done: he had defied Narcissus whilst at the same time compromising Callistus with both the Emperor and Empress and he, Vespasian, was expected to lie to condemn an innocent man, a man who had showed him hospitality only the evening before. 'I was coming here, Princeps.'

'What for?'

'Because Narcissus asked me to be present to corroborate my brother's evidence.'

'What evidence?'

'That Asiaticus had also boasted to him, whilst they had been in Britannia together, that he took part in Caligula's assassination.' He was acutely aware of Asiaticus' eyes boring into his back as he blatantly bore false witness against a guiltless man, but he knew that he had been dragged in so deep and so quickly that there was no way of extracting himself without condemning his brother and putting his own life in danger. There was nothing he could do; it was just how Rome worked. 'Sabinus told me of it later. Naturally I was shocked and told him that he should speak to Narcissus about it as soon as he got back to Rome; which he did and that's why he's here today to back up Sosibius' evidence.'

'So why did Callistus talk to you in the corridor?'

Vespasian did his best nervous glance in Callistus' direction – although no acting was required as he felt the genuine emotion. 'Callistus said that he had evidence that Asiaticus was innocent and he accused me of being in collusion with Narcissus and Pallas; he said that they knew that Asiaticus was being framed and that the culprit was actually my brother and he was testifying against Asiaticus to keep himself in the clear. It's nonsense of course because everybody knows that at the time of the assassination Sabinus was a thousand miles away serving as legate of the Ninth Hispana; it's a matter of record.'

'So why did Callistus say this?'

Vespasian lowered his head. 'I don't know, Princeps; you'll have to ask him.'

'It's all lies!' Callistus shouted. 'I haven't seen this man since he was in Narcissus' office, with his brother, helping him beg for his life two days after Caligula's murder.'

Claudius frowned and held onto the arms of his chair to prevent his body twitching in his excitement. 'Is this true, V-Vespasian?'

'Yes and no, Princeps; before this morning that was the last time I saw Callistus. But it was a month after the assassination and no one was begging for their lives; your freedmen had recalled my brother from Pannonia in order that he and I should retrieve the Eagle of the Seventeenth for you, which, I'm ashamed to admit, we failed to do.'

'Yes, Gabinius got that for me but you loyal Flavians found the Nineteenth's Capricorn and I will always be grateful to you for that. Narcissus, what do you have to say?'

Narcissus got to his feet looking as if the whole thing was a matter of such little significance that he could not quite believe that anyone was taking the trouble to discuss it. 'It is all exactly as Vespasian says, Princeps; I'm afraid that Callistus has just been mistaken and it would seem that Asiaticus' guilt is beyond doubt. I also have reason to believe that Asiaticus has transferred a great deal of his wealth back to his home province in Narbonese Gaul; it would seem that he is planning on leaving Rome, although for what purpose I couldn't say. However, I would remark that a man who evidently has so little respect for the imperial family could well be a threat back in his homeland surrounded by members of his tribe whose loyalty to Rome is, to say the least, unenthusiastic.'

Vespasian did not turn around to look at Asiaticus but he could well imagine his face and that image added to the sickness that he felt at his own actions; but then, he reflected, he had been forced into lying, although that was no balm for his conscience.

'D-d-do you have any defence to this charge, Asiaticus?'

Asiaticus did not bother getting to his feet. 'What can I say, Princeps, apart from denying everything and calling Vespasian a liar?'

'But it all fits. Lucius, will you speak for him?'

As Vitellius got to his feet, Messalina let forth another stream of tears. 'I'm sorry, beloved husband, but the proof of this dear man's guilt has unsettled me, I must leave before I swoon.' She rose from her chair. 'I hope that Lucius' eloquence in defence will persuade you to mercy, but whatever you decide I know it will be just.' Descending from the dais she paused in front of Vitellius as he took the floor, and on the pretext of kissing him on the cheek she whispered in his ear before leaving the room with her retinue.

Vitellius cleared his throat, evidently aroused by close proximity to Messalina's tempting mouth, and took an orator's pose with his chin in the air. 'Princeps, it grieves me more than I can say that you believe Asiaticus to be guilty as we all know him to be a loyal man. When he spoke to me this morning to ask if he might be allowed to choose the manner of his death I said—'

'He d-d-did what?'

'He asked to choose the manner of his death, Princeps.'

'Well, that proves it beyond question! Any man asking to be able to choose the manner of his own death before he is found guilty *must* be guilty. I'll waste no more time on this, I have the beast hunt to open.' Claudius rose unsteadily to his feet. 'Asiaticus, I will show mercy owing to our long friendship and the service you have done Rome in Britannia and elsewhere; you may take your own life and your family may inherit your property. I expect you to be dead by morning.'

Without waiting for a reaction, the Emperor lurched down the steps and then paused in front of Vespasian. 'You and your family shall join us in the imperial box, V-V-Vespasian. N-n-naturally I shall be taking Britannicus to the games and I'm sure that he'd love to have Titus for company and my Messalina always enjoys Flavia's conversation. We shall see you later.'

Unable to refuse the invitation, Vespasian bowed his head. As Claudius turned and lurched out of the room, he glanced at Pallas who acknowledged him with an inclination of the head as if to say that he had played his dishonourable part well. As he made to leave he felt a hand on his shoulder; he turned to see Asiaticus looking at him with a wry smile. 'I would have done exactly the same in your place, Vespasian; I bear you no malice. I shall spend my last evening dining with friends in the Gardens of Lucullus. I would be grateful if you would join me at my table.'

CHAPTER XV

'OF COURSE I would love to go, Father,' Titus affirmed, earnestly looking Vespasian directly in the eyes, 'especially if it's with you. I've seen gladiators fight but I've never been to a wild-beast hunt.'

Vespasian smiled at his son and ruffled his hair. 'This will be very different from watching two armed men fight one another honourably according to rules.'

'I know, Father; criminals get ripped apart by wild animals and then *bestiarii* fight the animals afterwards. Britannicus told me, he's been to quite a few and he says that they're good fun to watch.'

'I wouldn't describe them as good fun, Titus; I'd describe them as a very bloody way of re-enacting man's struggle against beasts.'

Titus' earnest expression changed to that of a child in deep thought, processing a new piece of information gathered from an unimpeachable source. 'But the games are always bloody; especially when the bad people get their heads or limbs chopped off between the fights.'

Vespasian sighed and accepted that there was little he could do to shield his son from the things that he had not witnessed until he had been in his early teens. It was not that he disapproved of the blood-sports of the arena; on the contrary, he enjoyed the spectacle and the skill of gladiatorial competition, the heated excitement of a close finish in a chariot race – even though he still could not bring himself to bet on the outcome – and the sheer nerve it took for a bestiarius to face down a rampant bear or charging lion. However, he considered these to be pleasures for adults and youths, not prepubescent children. The average citizen did not take his seven-year-old boy to the gruesome spectacles in the arena but Claudius did, anxious to keep his son and heir in the public eye. And as the son and heir's companion, Titus was therefore subject to the rather questionable parenting of his friend's imperial father, who, it was well known, enjoyed the spilling of blood with an intensity that many considered vulgar.

He knew that he could not talk Titus out of wanting to go as the conversation would certainly be repeated to Britannicus. This would doubtless mean Claudius hearing of it and perhaps taking it as implied criticism, so Vespasian had to accept his son's desire to attend the games. 'Very well, you shall come.'

'Oh, thank you, Father.'

'And we shall be in the imperial box,' Flavia purred. 'The other women will be so jealous.'

Vespasian refrained from comment, unwilling to stoke his lingering anger at his wife in front of the children, and smiled instead at his daughter. 'And you'll stay here with your nurse, Domitilla.'

Domitilla twisted a rag doll in her hands and smiled back. 'Yes, Tata.'

'Oh, but she must come, Vespasian,' Flavia insisted, 'we should be seen as a family.'

'She will stay here and I won't discuss the matter any further.'

'But it would—'

'You will start doing as you are told without questioning me, Flavia; then we may have a small chance of harmony in the house and you might find me better disposed towards you than I'm currently feeling. Domitilla will stay.'

Flavia caught the steel in her husband's voice and stilled her tongue.

Vespasian pulled his daughter close and kissed her. 'I'll see you tomorrow.'

'Won't you be back after the games, Tata?'

'No.'

'Where are you going?'

'I've got to go and say goodbye to a man who has to leave Rome because of me.'

*

A white handkerchief fluttered in the light wind; a quarter of a million pairs of eyes fixed on it and a quarter of a million voices echoed around the Circus Maximus calling for its release. With a shaking hand, Claudius held the handkerchief aloft, displaying it to the masses crammed on the stepped-stone seating along both sides of the circus's six hundred-pace length. Messalina stood next to him at the front of the imperial box, her head held high and her arms around her two children, Britannicus and Claudia Octavia, bathing in the reflected glory of the husband who had been an object of ridicule and the butt of countless jokes when she had married him. But now the people of Rome loved their Emperor for his gift of the Secular Games, which, for the last ten days, had been celebrated in lavish style. Today would be the climax of the festival and they cheered Claudius with savage ferocity as he dropped the handkerchief and the first of the hundred pitch-soaked prisoners chained to stakes around the track burst into flames.

A team of men wielding torches jogged around the circus igniting the howling victims, one by one, to the roars of approval of all who watched. Black smoke rose in columns from the flames and then, wafted by the breeze, circulated around the crowd, bringing the acrid tang of blazing pitch and burning flesh to the nostrils of delirious spectators as they savoured every writhe and scream of the agonised human torches. Once the last had been fired, and his skin had begun to shrivel and blister, the torch-bearers left the circus through the great gates at the northern end, passing a herd of filthy, condemned prisoners. Whipped onto the sand-covered track, soon to be soaked in their blood, the hapless men – and a few women, there to add spice to the proceedings – looked around with eyes wide with terror at the scene that greeted them. On either side of the *spina*, the low barrier running down the centre of the track around which chariots sped on race days, the flaming carcasses of the human torches sagged against their chains, life still just evident in a few of them, whilst the onlookers jeered at their suffering. Forced even further out onto the track by the lashes of their drivers the prisoners cried, unheard above the din, to their disparate gods to save them from a fate worse than burning: to be ripped asunder and their flesh consumed before their very eyes by beasts starved to the point of madness, for the delectation of the people of Rome.

With vicious farewell cracks of their whips, the drivers retreated to the gates and the noise began to dull. Bored of the opening act of the spectacle, which was now doing nothing more exciting than spasm occasionally, the crowd eyed the huddled prisoners with interest. There were a lot of them, at least a hundred, and the knowledgeable in the audience – which was most of them – knew what that meant: many beasts. Anticipation settled on the Circus Maximus.

'I b-b-believe the crowd are pleased, my d-dearest,' Claudius observed, seating himself on his well-padded chair.

Messalina took her seat next to him. 'It was an original idea of yours to surprise them by setting fire to those prisoners. I'm sure everyone thought that they were going to be mauled to death. You're so clever, dear Claudius.'

Claudius twitched and took his wife's hand. 'We must keep them entertained if we're to keep their love.'

Vespasian sat behind the imperial couple, between Lucius Vitellius and Flavia, who could not help but scan the crowd nearest the imperial box to see who was looking at her. Behind them sat a sallow-faced little man with a crooked back, whom Vespasian knew by sight to be a drinking companion and toady of Claudius.

'The Emperor has a real talent for pleasing spectacles,' Vitellius commented to Vespasian loud enough for Claudius to overhear.

'He has a talent for many things, consul,' Vespasian replied, playing Vitellius' sycophantic game, 'justice being one of them, as we saw this morning.'

'Indeed; allowing Asiaticus the mercy of suicide and keeping his property was the act of a wise and just ruler.'

Vespasian detected a stiffening in Messalina's posture but then the roar of the crowd turned his attention to the gates through which a dozen carts were being wheeled, each supporting a large wooden box. There was a stirring amongst the prisoners as the guttural roar of bears emanated from the boxes and the huddle began to disperse as the natural human instinct to put as many other people as possible between oneself and the threat took over. Prisoners ran to either side of the spina, sheltering close to the still burning torches in the hope that the flames would protect them.

Ropes, pulled from behind the boxes, opened the doors and the muzzles of twelve snarling bears poked out.

'That's split them all up,' Claudius exclaimed, rubbing his hands together.

The crook-back smacked his lips in anticipation. 'I do admire the strength of a bear.'

'Th-th-that, Julius Paelignus, is because you have so little yourself; hunchback.'

Paelignus flinched and Vespasian was amused that the crippled emperor had someone more unfortunate than him to be the butt of his jokes. He wondered idly what unsightly creatures Paelignus consorted with to help him feel better about his deformity.

The bears' keepers rapped rods on their boxes to encourage the beasts out in the face of the mighty roar of the crowd. One by one they emerged, shaking their huge frames and prowling up and down as a small gate, at the rounded far end of the circus, opened and at least twenty scraggily thin lions swooped onto the sand. The crowd's din rose to even greater heights as the delicious prospect of the possibility of beast versus human and beast versus beast in the same combat became apparent.

Britannicus clapped his hands in excitement and Titus ran to join his friend to get a better look; together they leant on the box's wall craning their heads left and right as the beasts fanned out and their victims ran about screaming, knowing there was no place to hide other than in death. Claudius smiled benevolently at the two boys, enjoying their enjoyment, before turning round. 'What do you say to a wager, Lucius?'

'With pleasure, Princeps; what's it to be?'

'A thousand denarii says that the bears will do for the prisoners and the lions before the bestiarii come in to finish them off.'

'Caesar, my money is on the lions.'

'What about you, Vespasian?'

'Well, Princeps, I'm certainly not going to bet on the prisoners.'

Claudius chortled, spraying spit in abundance. 'Oh, very good, not going to bet on the prisoners indeed. No, my friend, that would be foolish, you may sit this bet out. I won't b-b-bother to ask you, Paelignus, you p-p-pauper.'

Paelignus flinched again. 'If you make me procurator of Cappadocia as you promised then I'll be able to afford to wager with you again.'

Claudius seemed unconcerned by such an importune demand. 'We'll see; until then you can make a note of the bets.'

Relieved at having got out of such a large wager, Vespasian turned his attention back to the track just as the massive jaws of a bear clamped onto a prisoner. Britannicus whooped and jumped in the air as the spilling of the first blood sparked a killing frenzy. Fleet and agile, the lions hunted their slower two-legged prey, twisting and turning in sprays of sand as they ran down and then pounced upon their victims, shredding flesh with their razor claws and blood-dripping teeth. Bears lumbered with rolling shoulders then, suddenly accelerating, bounded on screaming targets, punching them to the ground to dismember them with gore-spattered ferocity as the people of Rome cried out for yet more blood.

Claudius leant forward in his chair, his head jerking this way and that, taking in every gruesome detail of the carnage that now raged along the length of the track on both sides of the spina, shouting with glee at each limb ripped from its socket and laughing uncontrollably at the sight of Niger stumbling with a wild cat on his back and a length of his colon, spilling from a hideous gash in his belly, cradled in his hands. 'That'll teach him not to lie about poor Asiaticus,' he managed to say between bouts of laughter.

'About poor Asiaticus,' Messalina said, keeping her eyes fixed on the spectacle. 'Do you think it was wise to let his family inherit all of his wealth, my dearest?'

'He was consul twice, sweet girl, which was a feat of some note for a man whose grandfather fought against Caesar. Were I to ruin his family because of a crime that he committed I would lose their loyalty as well as the loyalty of all their clients, which is the entire Allobroges tribe in the northern Narbonensis near Lugdunum. Seeing as the imperial mint is in Lugdunum that might not be considered good politics.'

'You see, there I go again, questioning your wise judgements without knowing all the facts or taking into consideration the wider political implications; you must think me such a silly girl.'

Claudius squeezed his wife's thigh and then brushed his hand against her breast as he withdrew it. 'N-n-never. There's no reason why you should bother your beautiful head with large matters such as this; it was enough just to be there by my side this morning, supporting me through a very regrettable hearing.'

Messalina licked her lips as a couple of lions started fighting with a bear over the rights to a badly mauled corpse. 'It was the least that I could do. It's so sad when an old friend turns out to be treacherous; it must make you wonder whom you can really trust.'

'I trust *you*, my dearest girl.'

'Of course; and you know that I only have your best interests at heart?'

Claudius turned and smiled at his wife with a look of genuine affection as beyond him a screaming woman was eviscerated. 'I would never doubt that.'

'Then you won't mind me giving you some advice?'

'I t-t-treasure your advice, little bird.'

'Well, it's just this, my dearest: I think that you let Asiaticus off too lightly. I completely understand your reasoning about keeping the loyalty of the Allobroges, and you're so clever to have thought of that, but I think that if his family get to keep *all* of his property then it doesn't act as much of a deterrent to other wicked men who might be contemplating treason. They must be deterred if we're going to keep you safe.'

'Yes, they must; but I've already given my judgement.'

Messalina took her husband's hand, brought it up to her mouth and let her tongue flick across the tips of his fingers. 'You're the Emperor, you can do anything; you can change your mind any time you want to.'

Claudius watched Messalina's tongue working on his fingers and dabbed away a trail of errant saliva from his chin with the other hand. 'I can, can't I?'

'You can, dearest.'

'Then I will. What would you suggest?'

'Take his most prized possession; his family get to keep his fortune but they lose the one thing that he valued above all else.' Messalina began to suck Claudius' trembling fingers, one by one.

'That's a wonderful idea, little mouse; I'll take his entire library.'

'No, husband, there's something that he prizes more than that.'

'What?'

'His gardens.'

'His gardens; what use are they to me?'

'Not for you, dearest, nor for me but for our children; it would do them good to have a place just outside the city walls.' She turned to Flavia. 'Flavia, I value your opinion above all other than my husband's; do you think that the Gardens of Lucullus would be a perfect place for children?'

'I've never seen them but if the stories of their beauty are true then they would be a perfect place for young people to learn to appreciate the finer things in life.' She smiled beneficently at Britannicus and Titus enjoying the sight of a bear being ripped apart by three bloodied lions.

'You are so right, my dear; children must learn to appreciate beauty.' She turned her attention back to Claudius' fingers.

'Th-th-that settles it,' Claudius decided, unable to take his eyes from his wife's mouth, 'I shall confiscate Asiaticus' gardens for Britannicus and Octavia.'

'That is a wonderful idea, dear husband; I know they'll appreciate them so much and their friends will have the use of them too, of course. Vespasian, you will allow Titus to go there, won't you?'

Vespasian hid his grudging admiration for the way that Messalina had got just what she wanted from her husband. 'Of course, domina; it will be an honour for him to go.'

Messalina smiled but her eyes remained cold as they fixed Vespasian with an intensity that could only be described as predatory. 'And you will accompany him from time to time, I hope; you too should be allowed to sample the pleasures of such a garden and savour the nectar of its fruit.' She sucked on Claudius' thumb whilst keeping her attention on Vespasian.

Vespasian decided against mentioning his invitation to Asiaticus' last supper later that day and shifted uncomfortably in his seat. 'It would give me great pleasure to do so, domina.'

'I am very partial to nectar and appreciate the subtle differences between the tastes of the juice from similar fruit.'

Messalina took the thumb from her mouth and licked between Claudius' forefinger and middle finger; her eyes warmed as they turned to Flavia and her predatory look melted into one of genuine affection. 'I think no two ever taste exactly the same and that means that every fruit should be sampled. Don't you agree, Flavia, dear?'

Flavia's eyes widened with delight as she smiled at the Empress. 'Oh, I do; you know it too well.'

Messalina dropped her husband's hand and reached back to squeeze Flavia's knee. 'Then it shall give me great pleasure to enjoy the children's gardens together with you, Flavia – regularly.'

Vespasian tried to clear his mind as he once again passed through the gates of the Gardens of Lucullus with the westering sun on his back. His ears still rang with the relentless cacophony of the day's spectacle, and bloody images, gathered over five hours of butchery, still played in his head. Once the first group of prisoners had been slaughtered and partially consumed, the bestiarii had entered and, displaying prodigious skill and courage, which Vespasian had greatly admired, despatched the surviving lions and bears with the loss of only three of their number. Claudius had claimed the bet on the grounds that more lions had been killed by bears than the other way around and Vitellius had happily and fawningly conceded to his Emperor.

Enthused by his win, Claudius had then proceeded to bet on every display: how many bestiarii would the bulls gore; whether the giraffes would manage to kill a single wolf; whether the camels would put up a fight or just make people laugh; and how long would a dozen Nubians, armed only with daggers, last against a couple of maddened rhinoceroses – the stars of the show. Vespasian had been left very badly off, having lost every bet he had been forced into by his gambling-minded Emperor; his shows of losing with good grace had become weaker as his purse became lighter. Paelignus' fawning congratulations each time he announced Claudius' winnings had irritated Vespasian considerably and he hoped fervently that the nasty little syco- phant would not be given the province that would restore his finances.

The games of dice that Claudius insisted upon between the acts had further eaten into Vespasian's finances: he had no interest in dicing so he was no expert. Claudius had promised him a copy of his new book on the subject to help him before they played together again. Vespasian had thanked him, brimming with conjured enthusiasm at the prospect of reading such a scholarly work on so deserving a pastime. Paelignus had praised Claudius' expertise at the game, regretfully adding that such expertise had been the cause of his present reduced circumstances.

Eventually, after the demise of three or four hundred wild beasts of many different varieties and almost twice that number of humans, the people of Rome had cheered their Emperor as he left the circus until they were hoarse. No one could dispute that it had been a fitting climax to the games of a lifetime and Claudius' popularity had soared; no one bothered to question the fraudu- lent calculation that had enabled him to pull such a massive propaganda coup. The Secular Games, with their long cycle, served as a reminder to the people that Rome would last far longer than anyone's lifetime, except, perhaps, the deified Julius Caesar and his adopted son the deified Augustus whose blood flowed in Claudius' veins.

But it was the memory of Messalina's dark eyes staring at him with such cold desire and then warming as they beheld Flavia that Vespasian found hard to forget as he walked up the fragrant path, curving through each beautifully designed and manicured section of the gardens. He knew that he had to avoid being drawn into her entourage, as Flavia had quite evidently already been; but how intimate the relationship was he did not know, nor did he want to guess. Instead, he allowed the tranquillity of this hillside retreat to soothe away the cares and troubles of his first two days back in Rome.

Putting Flavia's profligacy and suspect morality to the back of his mind, as well as Messalina's lasciviousness, Claudius' gambling, Titus' friendship with Britannicus and the fact that he still had not properly seen Caenis, Vespasian walked through the apricot orchard enjoying the soft cooing of doves and the dappled sun playing on his cheeks.

'It needs to be moved at least ten paces further back,' a voice ordered from beyond the trees.

Vespasian turned a final corner and came out in front of the villa to see Asiaticus standing in front of his funeral pyre with a well-dressed slave whom Vespasian presumed was his steward. Beyond them guests mingled on the terrace.

'Yes, rebuild it in front of the steps up to the terrace; if it burns here it'll damage the apricots.'

'Yes, master,' the steward replied. There were tears clearly visible in his eyes.

'And stop crying, Philologos, you'll make all my guests feel gloomy; this is going to be a happy occasion.'

'Yes, master.'

'You of all people should be celebrating as I've freed you in my will.'

'I'm deeply grateful, master,' Philologos said, bowing and backing away.

'Good evening, Asiaticus,' Vespasian ventured. He was slightly nervous as to how he would be received.

'Ah! My false-accuser, welcome!' Asiaticus clasped Vespasian's arm with surprising affability. 'There is someone here that I want you to talk to.'

'Of course, Asiaticus. But first I want to assure you that when I enjoyed your hospitality last night I had no idea of what I was going to be pushed into this morning.'

'I believe you, my friend; and I do not blame Pallas for doing what he did. My fate was sealed the moment that I refused to sell these gardens to Messalina; as she left the room she primed Vitellius to lie about me asking if I could choose the manner of my death as if I had recognised my guilt. Pallas knew she would get me and was just trying to make something positive out of it. I assume that your brother was the real culprit?'

'He was.'

'Some honesty at last. So my death will clear him.'

'You can accept being condemned for a crime that you didn't commit without rancour?' Vespasian took a cup of wine from a passing slave and put it to his lips.

'Yes, because my revenge is assured.'

Vespasian paused, mid-sip.

Asiaticus' face creased in amusement; he took the cup, downed half its contents and then handed it back. 'It's not poisoned; I would consider it the height of bad manners to poison a guest at a dinner party. And anyway, you have nothing to fear from me because you will be an instrument of my revenge.'

Vespasian drained the rest of the wine and looked at his host uneasily as Philologos arrived with half a dozen slaves to begin dismantling the pyre. 'I suppose that would be the least that I could do after this morning.'

'This morning has nothing to do with why I've chosen you.' Asiaticus put an arm around Vespasian's shoulders and led him off towards a man leaning against an apricot tree with his back towards them, looking out over the Campus Martius to the Seven Hills of Rome awash with soft, evening light. 'These gardens are about everything that is good in Rome,' Asiaticus said, gesticulating with his free hand. 'Here there is peace, cultivation – both literal and metaphorical – beauty and a remarkably fine view of the world. However, because they represent all that, they are also a mighty lure to the other forces that prevail in Rome: greed, ambition and a lust for power. Claudius told me this morning that I may keep them to hand on to my heirs; but I'm not stupid, I know that Messalina will persuade him to confiscate them and give them to her, because someone who possesses those last three qualities in such abundance will never be able to resist such beauty.'

'She already has, Asiaticus, this afternoon at the games.'

'She was quick,' Asiaticus commented dryly as they drew close to the figure next to the tree.

'She has always been good at getting what she wants,' the man said, keeping his back to them. 'But this time her greed will be her downfall.'

The man turned and Vespasian failed to hide his surprise as he saw the hated, familiar face with its haughty patrician sneer. 'Corvinus!'

'Hello, bumpkin; it seems that we're to be friends – for a while.'

The guests applauded as the main dish was brought out on six silver platters held high by slaves. Six roast fowl, each with their small heads still attached and propped up so as to give the impression that the birds were roosting; three of them had their magnificent tail plumage reinstated behind them in a resplendent fan, whilst the other three, the duller females, looked less magnificent but equally delicious.

'The only way that I can take my peacocks with me is to have them in my stomach when I'm cremated,' Asiaticus announced to the good-humoured reaction of the two dozen senators reclining around three separate tables. 'Because I'm certainly not leaving them here to be enjoyed by the next owner; whoever *she* may be.' This raised a nervous laugh and Vespasian was aware of more than a few eyes glancing at Corvinus, next to him, as a pair of peacocks was placed on each table.

The presence of Marcus Valerius Messalla Corvinus had been a source of confusion all evening, which neither Corvinus nor Asiaticus had done anything to alleviate. Vespasian had had to assume that only he and his host were party to Corvinus' treachery towards his sister. However, why his old enemy had had a change of heart remained unclear.

Vespasian reached over and carved a slice off the breast of the male bird; it was perfectly roasted, remaining moist and with a texture that did not strain the jaw. 'My uncle said that they would taste far better than they sounded,' he observed to Corvinus, who surprised him with a smile that could not quite be classified as a sneer.

'That is hardly difficult.' Corvinus leant closer to Vespasian as the conversation around the tables grew louder with the guests commenting on the rare delicacy. 'I'll answer your unspoken question, bumpkin: it's because I don't wish to go down with her. She has become so arrogant that she's getting careless. She believes that Claudius will always swallow her version of events. Even you will have the gumption to realise that in that state of mind she's about to make a major mistake.'

'Insulting me is not going to help enlist my aid; I assume that's what you want.'

'Force of habit, sorry; and yes, that is what I want although it makes me sick to the core that Fate has chosen you, bumpkin.'

'My name is Vespasian.'

'Indeed. Well, Vespasian, despite you leaving me to the slavers out in Cyrenaica—'

'From whom I rescued you; an act for which I still haven't received any gratitude.'

Corvinus waved the comment away and placed another morsel of the succulent flesh into his mouth. 'And despite your and the cuckold's insolent—'

'My brother's name is Sabinus.'

'Indeed.' Corvinus chewed as if the taste of the meat was not at all to his liking. 'Well, despite your and your brother's insolent interruption of my attempt to steal Claudius' glory in the invasion of Britannia—'

'Oh, so you admit that, do you?'

'Vespasian, it would serve no purpose to deny it to you; I'm trying to be candid.'

'Candid? If you want to be candid then explain to me why you seized Sabinus' wife and gave her to Caligula for him to fuck repeatedly!'

The conversation around the table died; Corvinus raised an apologetic hand to his fellow diners. 'Excuse us, gentlemen, I made a jest in bad taste.'

'A jest?' Vespasian hissed as the chatter resumed, fuelled by four slaves bringing a bronze bath out onto the terrace. 'That was far from being a jest, that was—'

'Business! As I told you at the time. Although, I do remember it being tinged with a hint of pleasure that she was your sister-in-law; as far as I was concerned that made up for the slavers and we were all square. But giving Clementina to Caligula was a smart move on my part.'

Vespasian grudgingly accepted this statement with a slow nod of his head as he carved another portion of peacock. 'It forced her brother, Clemens, to assassinate him and paved the way for your sister to become empress. And now you regret that?'

'It's not been as advantageous to me as I'd hoped. In a few days' time Geta and your brother become consuls and yet here I am, overlooked and with no prospect of a lucrative province to govern. One word from her to Claudius would have got me the consulship at any time she liked but no, nothing. In fact, quite the opposite: she's purposely holding my career back, out of jealousy, I would assume. Claudius has always favoured me so she must have persuaded him not to grant me a consulship.'

'That's more likely to be Narcissus' doing.'

'No, it's Messalina's without a doubt; Narcissus doesn't have that much influence over Claudius when it comes to family matters. And now she seems determined to pursue her lifestyle to the point of self-destruction; well, her demise won't herald mine.' He paused as a group of slaves came out with pitchers and poured their steaming contents into the bath. 'It would seem that our host is planning to say goodnight soon.'

'I suppose that it's the appropriate time seeing that he's served the most delicious course of the evening.'

Corvinus smothered a smile by gnawing on a thigh bone. 'So to carry on in this candid spirit; I have not repaid you for what you did in Britannia even though I've had ample opportunity to do so with your wife and children living in the palace. That, of course, was what I originally intended when I persuaded Claudius to insist that they move in.'

'So what made you change your mind?'

'The pointlessness of it. What would it have got me? A small amount of pleasure but nothing tangible. However, your wife's growing friendship with Messalina – I wonder, does fawning constitute friendship? Well, that was of far more use to me over the last couple of years as my relationship with my sister cooled. She's told me some very interesting things about a few of Messalina's new little habits.'

'You talk to her?'

'Occasionally; you know what Flavia's like: being anxious to impress people of higher status can make a person very garrulous.'

'What else does she do?'

'With me? Nothing.'

'With other people?'

'Gentlemen,' Asiaticus called, rising from his couch, 'I hope that you are enjoying the meal as much as I am.' A chorus of approval greeted this remark. 'There will be another three courses, which, although not as exotic as peacock, will nevertheless be delicious. I will watch you enjoy them from the comfort of my bath as my life slips away.' He raised his arms in the air and his steward pulled his tunic over his head. Removing his loincloth, Asiaticus stepped into the bathtub and lay back with his head on the raised end. He took a cup of wine from a waiting slave and raised it to the assembled company. 'My one regret is that my death would have been more honourable had it resulted from Tiberius' cunning or Caligula's fury rather than from a woman's treachery and Vitellius' poison tongue. However, at least I've been allowed to choose the manner of my passing. I drink to Rome and better times for you all.'

Everyone present echoed the first part of the toast but ignored the second sentiment, much to Asiaticus' obvious amusement as he drained his cup. He handed the cup to Philologos who gave him a short dagger in return. Without any pause Asiaticus put the blade to his left wrist and slowly slit it lengthways.

With a gush of blood the artery opened and Asiaticus looked up at his guests and smiled. 'So my life comes towards its end, my friends. Come and greet me one by one and we'll say our farewells. Philologos, order the next course to be brought to the tables.'

The steward gave the order with tears streaming down his cheeks as the first of the guests moved forward in the now sombre atmosphere. Vespasian and Corvinus joined the queue and waited in respectful silence as plates of poached perch in a cumin sauce were brought out from the villa.

With his time now at a premium, Asiaticus did not waste it on long goodbyes and as Vespasian bent to kiss him the fading ex-Consul looked at him in earnest and clasped his arm. 'Do as Corvinus asks, Vespasian; with Messalina's death mine will be avenged and you will have repaid your debt to me.'

'I will, Asiaticus, you have my word.' Vespasian placed a kiss on Asiaticus' cheek as his arm fell back into the blood-red water. With a final nod to the dying man he joined Corvinus waiting for him to walk back to the table together. 'I gave him my word, so tell me what you want of me.'

'I need you to speak to Narcissus for me and organise a meeting. I can't go directly to him because Messalina's bound to find out. She has spies everywhere – even here, I expect – so the meeting has to be as if by accident, in a crowd. I would suggest that it take place at Plautius' Ovation in six days' time; tell him to look out for me on the steps of the Temple of Jupiter.'

'Why would my asking him make a difference?'

'He knows how much we hate each other. That's why, distasteful as it may be to me, Asiaticus advised me to choose you as my messenger; Narcissus will believe it if it's you who tells him that I won't stand in his way nor demand revenge if he gets rid of my sister. In fact, I will help him in any way that I can.' Corvinus grabbed Vespasian's shoulder and lowered his voice, looking at him intently. 'Tell him that I know her future plans for the Empire over the next year and they don't involve Claudius.'

'And they involve you?'

'They do but not in the way that I would have wanted them to and certainly not in a way that makes me feel secure. Therefore I'm prepared to divulge them to Narcissus in return for my life when she falls. But in order to ensure her fall you have to do another thing.'

Vespasian removed Corvinus' hand as the grip became more intense. 'Go on.'

'You must talk to Flavia and get her to confide in you everything that she sees and hears whilst she is with Messalina. With a spy that close to my sister we'll be able to monitor her plans.'

'Surely you could do that.'

'I'm not that close to Messalina any more; she only confides in me when she wants me to do something for her. Flavia, however, is very close to her; closer than is natural, and shares more than I ever did or could.'

Vespasian's eyes narrowed. 'What are you implying, Corvinus?'

Corvinus shook his head and wrinkled his nose in distaste. 'Let's just say that a good time to probe a person's secrets is whilst lying face to face on the same pillow.'

Vespasian's fist lashed towards Corvinus' face, crashing into his jaw with a hollow thump. 'I don't believe you!'

Taking a step back to soak up the impact, Corvinus shook his head and exhaled with a couple of long puffs before resuming his haughty sneer and looking down his nose at Vespasian. 'You really do have rustic manners: upsetting a dying man's last dinner, bumpkin, is vulgar.' He raised his hands to indicate to the company that the altercation was at an end and then nodded at Asiaticus who managed to give a thin smile. 'Believe what you like but the fact is that your wife is in the best position in all of Rome to know Messalina's mind because, as opposed to the rest of her lovers, who are transient whims, Flavia is a regular in her bed. The only other person who shares that honour is Gaius Silius, but I doubt that he'd be a party to Messalina's plans – he's merely an insignificant nobody who just happens to be extremely good-looking and well built. So you have to tell your wife to carry on being unfaithful to you; you never know, you might find the thought of it rather titillating once you get used to it. Now, you gave your word to the man whose death you're partly responsible for – are you going to keep it?'

'And if I don't?'

'Then you have even less honour than the little I credited you with before and I'll have to resort to threatening the wellbeing of your wife and children.'

Vespasian glanced over to the dying Asiaticus and felt himself deflate; he could not go back on his word and Corvinus knew it. He could tell by the expression on his old enemy's face that

Corvinus was enjoying using him to save himself but there was nothing he could do to resist him. 'I'll speak to Narcissus and he'll see you at the Temple of Jupiter.'

'And you'll have spoken to Flavia by then?'

Vespasian took a deep breath. 'Yes.'

Corvinus nodded with grim satisfaction. 'You've made a wise decision, bumpkin; once Messalina's gone, Flavia and your children will be free to leave the palace and we'll be square once and for all.'

'No, Corvinus, we won't.'

'You'd be a foolish man not to accept those terms.'

'And you'd be a foolish man to think that I would.'

'Have it your own way. Now, out of politeness to Asiaticus, we should recline and finish the meal.'

But eating was the last thing on Vespasian's mind.

CHAPTER XVI

VESPASIAN OPENED HIS eyes to see the familiar whitewashed ceiling of Caenis' bedroom. Rolling over he found himself to be alone but that did not surprise him as it was well past dawn; the sun shone through the opaque glass window above him with a soft, diffused light that he found calming after the events of the previous day.

He had picked at the remainder of the meal in silence, unable and unwilling to converse further with Corvinus and uninterested in the forced conversation of the other guests as they waited for their host to meet the ferryman. The blood finally drained from Asiaticus' wrist and he began his last journey across the Styx. With a coin under his tongue as payment for Charon he was borne to his pyre and his body was consumed without damage to his beloved apricot trees.

Vespasian had left as soon as the fire had taken hold and had made his way to the open arms of Caenis. Enfolded in them, he had lost himself in the one thing that he knew that he could trust: her love. They had barely spoken as they re-explored each other's bodies for the first time since saying goodbye on the northern coast of Gaul, four years ago, on the eve of the invasion of Britannia. Finally satiated, they had fallen asleep and Vespasian had found peace: a peace that, as the door opened and Caenis appeared fully dressed with a cup of warmed wine, he knew would soon be broken.

'Don't you have slaves to bring wine?' he asked, enjoying the sight of her sapphire-blue eyes shining in the soft light.

'I used to be a slave and I haven't forgotten how to please.'

'And you did that very well last night.'

She handed him the cup and sat on the bed. 'So did you.'

He put his hand around the back of her head, feeling the soft-ness of her raven-black hair and drew her into a kiss, bathing in the musk of her scent.

'I let you sleep, my love,' Caenis said, breaking off after a few tender moments, 'because I can tell that you are troubled. Narcissus dictated his account of Asiaticus' hearing to me yesterday; I assume it's about what Pallas forced you to do?'

'It's much more than that, my love; much, much more.' He raised his head with his eyes closed, breathed deeply and then looked into Caenis' eyes. 'Since I was given the Second Augusta, six years ago, I've been used to command; I've made decisions for me and the men below me. For the four years that I was in Britannia my legion worked as an independent unit. Yes, I had orders from Aulus Plautius as to what objective I was to achieve in the campaign season, but it was I who decided how best to effect them and everybody obeyed me. That's what I've become used to. But now, after just a couple of days back in Rome, I have no control any more; I've been forced into situations that I don't want to be in by people who I don't want to be involved with, just like when I was younger. Back then I accepted it because I had no choice if I wanted to rise in this city.

'Now, however, I've risen. By rights I'll be consul when I'm forty-two in four years' time, the highest honour a man from my station can aspire to; and yet look at me, I'm being used as if I was a mere boy on his first trip to Rome rather than a man who commanded one of Rome's legions in the biggest military opera-tion since Germanicus crossed the Rhenus to avenge Varus' lost legions. I'm being blown this way and that by forces fighting each other to gain as much personal advantage as they can in the shadow of a weak emperor. I'm sick of it already. I want to get out, but if I want that consulship, which, for my honour and that of my family's, I do with all my being, then I have to stay here and let myself be subjected to the will of others because that's how it works in the Rome we live in.'

Caenis stroked his cheek. 'We all have to accept that our society works because it is a strict hierarchy, my love, just as the men under your command accepted their positions; the legion is just a smaller version of Rome.'

'No it's not; no one plays politics in the legion. In the legion every man knows exactly where he stands, be he me, the newest recruit or the lowliest slave. Here, one's standing changes by the hour.'

'Tell me what's happened, my love.'

And then it all tumbled out: Corvinus, Messalina, Flavia, Pallas and Narcissus, all of whom Caenis knew and understood thanks, mainly, to her position as secretary to Narcissus, the imperial secretary.

'Corvinus would carry out his threat against Flavia and the children, I'm sure of it,' Caenis said once Vespasian had finished. 'He knows that Narcissus has never forgiven him for trying to hijack the invasion for his own personal gain so he's fighting for his life. He has nothing to lose.'

'So what do I do?'

'You have to do what he's asked and tell Flavia to carry on sleeping with Messalina.'

'Does she really do that?'

Caenis' full lips pursed and she gave a little shrug. 'What can I say, my love? I don't know; she certainly wouldn't confide that sort of information to me – or anybody for that matter. But why would Corvinus tell you such a thing unless it was true?'

Vespasian was not surprised by this confirmation but resolutely pushed the information aside. There was no point delving deeper until he could confront Flavia. 'And will Narcissus consent to meet with Corvinus?'

'Narcissus never refuses any opportunity to strengthen his position. You'll have to see him today as he's leaving with Claudius tomorrow morning to inspect the construction work in the new port and won't be back until the day before Plautius' Ovation.' She cocked her head and added innocently, 'And I won't charge you for the access.'

Vespasian was astonished. 'You charge people for appointments to see Narcissus?'

Caenis raised her eyebrows conspiratorially. 'Of course. He's the most powerful man in the Empire and people can only get official access to him through me; they pay handsomely for a quick appointment and I'd be a fool not to take their money.'

Vespasian chewed this over for a moment. 'Yes, I suppose you would be; after all, no one gets paid for serving Rome.'

'And I've got one of the most important commodities in the city to sell and I'm doing very nicely from it.'

Vespasian smiled and kissed Caenis again. 'Even the most beautiful woman in Rome sells her favour.'

'It's just business, my love; there is nothing wrong with the accumulation of wealth.'

'I agree, but I was brought up to believe that a man should make a profit by working his estates hard.'

'You do it your way and I'll do it mine. But remember that every denarius that you pass up will belong to somebody else and seeing as wealth is power the best way to defend yourself from the powerful is to gain as much wealth as they have – as quickly as possible.'

'And in the process make others less wealthy.'

'Exactly.'

Vespasian thought for a few moments, toying with Caenis' hand. 'So I should use this situation that's been forced on me to do precisely that. If I take the offensive and gain some advantage from this I'll feel a lot better.'

Caenis leant forward and nuzzled his neck. 'Much better.'

Vespasian responded, feeling the arousal of the previous night returning. 'I think that if Corvinus really wants me to set up a meeting with Narcissus to bargain for his life then he should pay for the privilege.'

'Just like everyone else does. But you've already agreed to do it free of charge.'

'So I'll have to find another way of extracting the money from him.'

'And you will, my love.' Caenis began working on his earlobe, flicking it gently with her tongue. 'And because I'd rather have power over you than let Messalina have that pleasure, I'll lend you the money to pay off Flavia's debt, seeing as I can well afford it. Are you starting to feel better now?'

'Far more in control,' Vespasian said, sliding her stola from one shoulder and kissing the exposed flesh. 'In fact, I'm feeling really quite manly again.'

'That's quite a boast; I'd be interested to see if it stands up under close scrutiny.'

He rolled her onto her side. 'I shan't dignify that with an answer.'

'I wasn't expecting an oral response from you.' She smiled with a mischievous twinkle and then eased herself down and kissed his chest. 'I was planning on doing the talking.'

'I'll be very attentive.'

Caenis began to kiss her way lower and Vespasian looked back up at the ceiling, smiling, and then closed his eyes.

A soft knock at the door made him open them a few moments later.

'Mistress?' a voice from outside called.

'What is it?'

'The master's friend, Magnus, is here; he says that it's very important.'

'Are you sure that it was him?' Vespasian asked Magnus as they hurried along the busy Alta Semita, the main street running the length of the Quirinal Hill.

'I didn't see him. I've had my lads watching all the gladiator schools in the city; Marius and Sextus sent me a message saying that a man answering Theron's description arrived at the school on the Campus Martius soon after dawn. Whether he's still there now I don't know; but the lads will follow him. If you hadn't taken such a long time "getting dressed", we'd be there by now.'

Vespasian mumbled an apology.

'I've never known someone take almost half an hour to put on a loincloth, tunic, belt, sandals and toga; and you must have had help because Caenis came out of the bedroom with you.' Magnus looked at Vespasian, his expression a study of innocence. 'I just don't understand it.'

'What's happened to your eye?' Vespasian asked, keen to change the subject.

Magnus put his hand to his left eye, which stared sightlessly and unmoving directly ahead in a very unnatural manner. 'I bought a glass one. Not bad, eh?'

'You'd never know the difference,' Vespasian lied as they passed the roofless Temple of Sancus, the god of trust, honesty and oaths.

'That's what all the lads say. They tell me that you have to look really carefully to spot that it's a fake.'

Vespasian smothered a smile and refrained from giving his honest opinion as they passed through the Porta Sancus and out onto the Campus Martius.

Magnus' crossroads brethren, Marius and Sextus, a couple of bull-like men in their fifties, were waiting for them leaning against the arched façade of the Circus Flaminius sharing a loaf of bread and an onion.

'He's still in there, sir,' Marius said, pointing the leather-bound stump at the end of his left arm to a substantial, high-walled complex built of brick, with a single well-guarded gate, across a wide thoroughfare, next to the Theatre of Balbus. 'That's the only way in or out.'

'Thank you, Marius,' Vespasian said, handing each of the brethren a couple of sesterces. 'Did he have anyone with him when he went in?'

'It was Sextus that saw him; I was in Agrippa's Baths taking a shit.'

Vespasian's confidence in the sighting plummeted as he looked at Marius' companion. 'Well?'

Sextus scratched his shaven head and squeezed his eyes tight shut as if he were attempting a piece of complex mental arithmetic. 'More than four, sir,' he announced eventually with a look of relief.

'How many more than four, Sextus?'

'One or two.'

Hiding his annoyance, Vespasian decided not to pursue the finer details of Theron's entourage – if, indeed, it was Theron.

'Well, we'll soon find out. Stay here, lads; there's a tavern next to the baths and we'll be in there having breakfast – one of you come and find us when they emerge.'

'Theron!' Vespasian called, walking fast to catch up with his quarry, with Magnus and his brethren following.

The Macedonian did not turn around even though he must have heard the shout. Surrounded by eight ex-gladiator body-guards and a boy holding a parasol over his head, he walked on towards the Carmenta Gate in the shadow of the Temple of Jupiter, towering above on the Capitoline Hill to the right.

The deliberate slight annoyed Vespasian but he did not break into a run: it would have been beneath his dignitas as a senator to chase after a slave-trader in the streets.

As the Macedonian slowed to get through the crowds filing in and out of the gate, Vespasian drew level. 'If you ignore me again, Theron, it'll be more than just money that you owe me.'

Theron turned. He cranked his face into his most ingratiating smile and stepped towards Vespasian, holding out his arms as if greeting a long-lost friend. 'Excellency, I did not know that you were back in Rome. I thank the gods for your safe return; news of your valiant exploits have travelled before you and I am honoured by your attention.'

'I'm sure that you are, Theron, and I'm sure that you'll be equally as honoured to pay the money that you owe me immediately.'

'Noble senator, nothing would give me greater pleasure but, alas, you find me between transactions and—'

'I don't care for excuses, Theron, you've sold the stock that I allowed you to choose and therefore you have the money to pay me. I want it delivered to my uncle Gaius Vespasius Pollo's house on the Quirinal this afternoon along with the bills of sale, which I shall verify with each of the parties involved to make sure that you haven't cheated me. If it doesn't arrive I'll have no choice but to make use of the contract that you signed.'

Theron opened his mouth and eyes in mock horror. 'Take me to court! The humiliation of it when our sordid little deal is exposed to the public; and you a senator, what disgrace!'

Vespasian took a pace forward and thrust his face close to Theron's. 'I've no intention of taking that contract anywhere near a court for the reasons that you've just outlined.'

Theron scoffed; all pretence at subservient friendship had now disappeared. 'And what will you do with it then that'll make me pay you?'

'I strongly advise you to bring the money this afternoon because I don't think that you'll want to find out what I intend to do; and I certainly don't think that you'll want to see just how much I'll enjoy doing it. Don't forget, Theron, I really don't like you.'

Theron hawked and then spat at Vespasian's feet before turning to go.

Vespasian did not demean himself by responding to the insult. 'I think I've had my final answer. Have one of your lads follow him and find out where he lives, Magnus.'

'Do you want me to arrange for his house to be heated up a touch, if you take my meaning?'

'No; but thank you for the offer. He will be my price for Flavia's co-operation.' Enjoying the confused look on his friend's face, Vespasian set off to confront his wife, determined to regain some control over his affairs.

Flavia stood before Vespasian with defiance in her eyes, her arms tense by her side and her shoulders shaking. 'Who told you such a wicked lie?'

'It's not a lie; I saw how you and Messalina looked at each other at the circus yesterday. I suspected then what was going on – though I didn't really believe it. But when it was confirmed to me last night, I knew it had to be true because I didn't feel surprised.'

'It's not true!'

'Flavia, keep your voice down.' Vespasian rose from his seat and paced quickly to the door of the triclinium and opened it abruptly; it crunched into the heads of two of Flavia's slave girls. 'Get away! And draw lots between you, because one of you will be sold; and tell the rest of the household I'll get rid of anyone else I ever find listening in on our private conversation.'

The women fled, too terrified to plead for forgiveness.

Vespasian slammed the door and rounded on Flavia. 'Let's stop this accusing and denying. Admit the charge and then we can discuss how best to take advantage of the situation.'

Flavia wrenched an ivory comb from her hair and hurled it at her husband. 'What did you expect me to do for six years? Lie in my bed every night as unfulfilled as a Vestal? I played the faithful wife for you; I kept my virtue for four years.'

'And then you cuckolded me!'

'With another woman!' Flavia screamed. 'Yes! But that is not the same.' She pointed to the couch upon which they had made love. 'Since the day you left no man has touched me until you took me there on your return. And don't tell me that you didn't have another woman in all that time; Caenis was with you for a few months and then there would have been all those captives.'

'My actions are irrelevant in this, woman. We are talking about your chastity, or lack of it, whilst I was away serving Rome.'

'I was chaste! No one impregnated me. I didn't feel an erect penis for six years. Do you know how hard it was to deny myself that? Can you understand the longing, the images burning in my head night and day, the trembling desire each time I caught the scent of a man? I had to do something before I broke and straddled the nearest slave, as many of the women do. But I didn't, out of respect for you, husband, even though I was well aware that you wouldn't be showing me the same consideration – not that I expect it of you. Messalina offered comfort of a different sort, not as satisfying but at least it was physical; now you're back I don't need that any more so I won't be going to her bed again.'

Vespasian stared at his wife, his mouth gaping in astonishment. 'Do you have any idea what would happen if you broke off your affair with her?'

'She would understand now that you're back.'

'Understand? What do you know of this woman?'

'She's the Empress and she has been my friend ever since Claudius invited me to move into the palace. We weave together and talk about the children and—'

'And do whatever it is that women do together; you don't have to go into the details, I can imagine.'

'I'm sure you can.'

'Does she not involve you in her other affairs, try to tempt you into bed with her other partners?'

'She has suggested it but I said no.'

'You refused Messalina?'

'Yes, husband; I know what she does, she confides in me. I know about all the men, I know about her going out into the city and whoring herself in rough brothels. I have no wish to do that; at least, I wouldn't let myself do that. I just enjoy her when she wants me.'

'And have you noticed what happens to people who refuse her?'

'They end up either dead or banished.'

'And you still think you will be able to say: "That's it, no more, Messalina; I shan't open my legs for you again"?'

'She loves Britannicus and values the friendship that he has with Titus; she won't harm me if I refuse to "open my legs" for her.'

'Well, you won't refuse; you will carry on as before.'

'What, in Mother Isis' name, do you mean?'

Vespasian found himself cooling in the face of her obvious confusion. 'Flavia, you weren't asked to move into the palace as a favour or an honour to me or you; quite the reverse: Claudius was manoeuvred into extending the invitation to you by someone who wanted vengeance on me, someone who wanted to scare me by showing how much power he could have over my family.'

'Who would do a thing like that?'

'Messalina's brother.'

'Corvinus? But he's so polite to me; he's even taken Titus on his knee on the few times that he's visited.'

Vespasian shivered at the image. 'He fully intended to harm you and still might. We are not safe. Somehow he knows of your relationship with Messalina and he wants to use it to his advantage; and to be frank, we'd be stupid if we didn't take advantage of it ourselves.'

'What do you mean?'

'I mean that the tide has turned against Messalina and she is not long for this world. Corvinus is conspiring against her and if he adds his weight to Narcissus and Pallas they will soon persuade Claudius how worthless she is; but to do that they need someone close to her to report her activities and, if possible, her plans.'

Flavia put her hands to her chest. 'Me?'

'Yes, my dear, you. You are to act as if nothing is wrong; you'll tell her that just because I'm back doesn't mean that you should deprive each other of – what was the word she used? – ah yes, each other's nectar. You'll kiss her sweetly and moan at her touch and listen to all her stories. If Narcissus agrees to Corvinus' proposal then he will reveal what she's planning and it will be down to you to keep us informed of the progress. If we're part of bringing her down we'll gain tremendously from it.'

'You're asking me to whore myself for our political gain.'

'No, Flavia, it's not whoring, any more than sleeping with another woman is cuckolding your husband. You just said so. This is business. It may be business that I would rather not be involved in, but seeing as your affair with this harpy has dragged us into imperial politics it seems to me that the best thing that we can do is try to survive and come out with credit.'

Flavia slumped down onto a couch. 'How am I supposed to act naturally with her when I'm part of a plot to bring her down?'

'I'm sure you'll manage; you were quite prepared to lie to me just now and pretend you had been faithful. If it helps, try to remember that this woman has already caused the deaths of over a hundred senators and equestrians, the latest one being Asiaticus. There will be many more if she stays in power and I may well be one of them if I refuse the advances that she made to me yesterday.'

'She wouldn't harm you, you're under my protection.'

'Under your protection! Flavia, just who are you trying to delude?' Vespasian scoffed. 'However, whilst we're in a position to take advantage of your relationship with Messalina, we should try and make some money out of it.'

'But we're already in her debt.'

'I'm now in a position to pay that off and retrieve the debt marker, which will release us from any obligation to her for the moment. However, it would be a shame if she was to cross the Styx and we didn't owe her money; so when the time draws near you will ask her for another loan, twice the amount. Tell her that it's without my knowledge so you'd appreciate it if it was just a private agreement between the two of you.'

'So that there's no record of it when she dies?'

'Exactly; without the debt marker we get to keep the money and you'll see some reward for all your hard work.'

'Vespasian, don't put it like that, that's not fair.'

'How else can I put it? You're going to get money out of her because you have sex with her.'

'What if she refuses?'

'Do whatever you must to make sure that she doesn't and you'll find me a little better disposed towards you. If not you'll find me extremely well disposed towards Caenis, who's offered to lend me the full amount to pay off *your* original debt.'

'Don't start playing me off against her after I've been so understanding about the situation, Vespasian, I beg you.'

Vespasian paused and drew breath, contemplating his wife's pained expression. With a conciliatory nod of the head and a half-smile he held out a hand. 'You're right, my dear, that was unbecoming of me. Just do your best.'

Flavia took the peace gesture and held it to her cheek. 'I will, husband; and I'm sorry, I was weak and I didn't think about the consequences of what I was doing.'

Vespasian cupped her face in his hand. 'It'll all be fine if you play your part over the next few months or however long it takes. Now I wish to see the children.'

'Of course, husband, and whilst you do that I'll make the arrangements to dispose of whichever of my girls drew the long straw; we can't afford to have the slaves snooping—'

A knock at the door interrupted her.

'Enter.'

The door opened to reveal Cleon the steward.

'What is it?'

'Caenis has sent a message for the master. The imperial secretary will see him at the fourth hour.'

'I don't suppose you had to pay for the privilege of such a quick appointment,' Narcissus observed as Vespasian was shown into his office, 'at least not financially.' A rare trace of a humorous smile graced his lips and he indicated the chair on the opposite side of his desk.

'We all use what we have to gain advantage, imperial secretary.' Vespasian sat and adjusted his toga, conscious of Narcissus' penetrating gaze.

'And what advantage are you trying to gain? Be quick because I'm leaving for Ostia with the Emperor to inspect progress on the new port.'

'I'm here to offer you a way into Messalina's plans and thoughts.'

'I already have access to them.'

'Access through kin and lovers or just through the titbits picked up by spies?'

'Only the latter, I'll admit.'

'Well, I can give you the former.'

Narcissus steepled his hands and tapped his forefingers against his pursed lips, studying Vespasian intently. 'At what price?' he asked eventually.

'At no cost to you personally.'

'What do you want?'

'I've got three requests. The person who offers their services has come to me to broker a meeting between you both as they are naturally wary of contacting you directly for fear of Messalina's agents. This person is prepared to give you information that'll help you bring down Messalina in return for their life. I want you to charge them for access to you and give me half the fee of two hundred and fifty thousand denarii.'

'That's a lot of money.'

'Which they will be willing to pay if it buys them their life.'

'Granted. And if you set up the meeting and I don't pass on my share to you?'

'I will get the money off them in advance and give you your share before the meeting.'

'And if I take the money but don't bother with the meeting?'

'Then you won't have access to Messalina's private pillow talk.'

'None of her lovers is going to be foolish enough to admit sleeping with her to me, even though I have a list of some of them already. There'll be a lot of executions when she falls.'

'I imagine that once Claudius finally believes in his wife's infidelity then he'll want any man who slept with her punished.'

'Impossible, we'd lose most of the Senate, the command structure of the Praetorian Guard and a goodly amount of the normal citizenry who frequent the brothel that she whores in when she fancies it rougher than usual. But certainly her more regular lovers will die; he won't pardon them.'

'But if I were Claudius I think that I might be able to pardon a woman – if she was even to come to my attention in the first place.'

Narcissus leant forward, genuinely interested. 'A woman, you say? I know she has sessions with men and women together but I'm not aware of a female lover.'

'A lover of two years' standing; a regular lover to whom Messalina talks intimately.'

'Information from that source would be priceless. Are you sure that you can deliver it and that it would be trustworthy?'

'Yes, Narcissus, because that lover is also my wife.'

For the first time in their relationship Vespasian was aware that he had actually surprised Narcissus. He watched the freedman's eyes widen a fraction and his steepled hands fall to the desk.

'Now that was something that I confess I was not aware of.'

'Well, it's true; Flavia has just admitted it to me.'

'And you are willing that this, er, arrangement carries on?'

'As a favour to you, yes.'

'And what favour would you ask in return?'

'My second request is just as simple.' Vespasian took a scroll from the fold of his toga. 'Do you know the slave-trader, Theron?'

Narcissus thought for a few moments, trawling through the vast amounts of information stored in his head. 'He has a licence to purchase captives in Britannia, doesn't he?'

'That's right.' Vespasian unrolled the scroll and placed it on the desk between them. 'This is a contract that I had with him that gave him exclusive rights to the pick of prisoners in return for a percentage of their end sale price. He's refusing to honour it.'

Narcissus picked up the document and perused it. 'Because he thinks that you won't take him to court as it shows you being, shall we say, a bit too Republican in these days of the Emperor?'

'That's what he's gambling on but I didn't get him to sign a contract so that I could take him to court; I did it for precisely a time like this. Everything was done legally; the Emperor got his purchase tax in Britannia and I would assume that Theron was not stupid enough to avoid paying the sales tax here in Italia.'

'Very commendable. So what do you want me to do?'

'Revoke his licence for Britannia, ban him from conducting business in Italia and make it clear to him that unless he honours his debt to me and pays a premium of another hundred per cent of the amount, he will never have the chance of favour from you again.'

Narcissus raised his eyebrows. 'You set a high price on your wife's virtue.'

'I just intend to benefit from a situation that is not to my liking.'

'Very well; I'll have Caenis summon this Theron for a little chat as soon as I get back from Ostia.'

'I have men following him to find out where he's staying; I'll give the address to her.'

'Very good. To show my good faith in this matter, that business will be concluded by the time I meet with Messalina's mystery relation. How will we manage that?'

'We'll be on the steps of the Temple of Jupiter at Plautius' Ovation. Look out for us; the meeting will be as if by accident as he doesn't want to risk the—'

'"He"?'

'What?'

'You've been careful with the sex of your kinsperson, I was assuming that it was because it was a woman; perhaps one of her cousins, like Vipstania, the sister of the Vipstanus Messalla brothers.'

'Knowing the way that imperial politics works, I was just keeping as much information to myself as possible.'

Narcissus inclined his head and spread his hands. 'You've learnt well.'

'I've learnt from the masters.'

'I'll take that as a compliment.' Narcissus got to his feet, indicating that the interview was at an end. 'I will look out for you at the Ovation. My guess is that you will be accompanied by Lucius Vipstanus Messalla; I've heard that he's disaffected because I blocked his consulship next year and Messalina couldn't persuade Claudius to overrule me. Perhaps he wants me to unblock it in return for his cousin's life.'

Vespasian kept his face neutral as he rose. 'Perhaps, Narcissus.'

'I would like to think it was Corvinus, but that would be too good to be true: you and him working together; I don't think that you've come that far yet. But nothing should surprise one in imperial politics.'

Vespasian shrugged non-committally. 'Before I go there is the matter of my third request, which I believe is the hardest of the three.'

'Go on.'

'When all this is over I want you to persuade Claudius to allow me to remove my family from the palace. If he wishes that Titus is still educated with Britannicus then he can come on a daily basis, but I have to get Flavia out before she spends all my money or compromises me again.'

Narcissus picked up Theron's contract. 'You are asking a lot of me.'

'I'm giving a lot to you.'

'If I get everything that you've promised then I'll see to it.'

'Thank you, imperial secretary,' Vespasian said, turning to go. For the first time in his political career he did not feel out of his depth. He walked to the door with an accelerating heart and allowed himself a satisfied smile only after he closed it behind him.

CHAPTER XVII

THE PEOPLE OF Rome had begun to congregate along the route of the Ovation well before dawn; now, at the commencement of the third hour, the centre of the city swelled with the populace bent on watching the spectacle and benefiting from the largesse that would accompany it. Every street was crammed and every vantage point had been taken along the circular route from the Porta Triumphalis – the gate at the foot of the Quirinal Hill only opened for a Triumph or an Ovation – along the Via Triumphalis, then around the base of the Palatine, in the shadow of the Temple of Apollo, along to the Circus Maximus, back up to the Via Sacra and then into the Forum Romanum.

Vespasian walked with Gaius and Sabinus, amongst the senators as they processed, in the growing heat, from the Curia to assemble in the shadow of the Servian Walls. Here they would greet Aulus Plautius as he returned to Rome to give up his command officially and celebrate a lesser Triumph through the graciousness of his Emperor.

'Where's Claudius?' Vespasian asked Gaius, looking towards the head of the procession, led by the two outgoing Consuls each preceded by their twelve lictors.

'I've no idea, dear boy, but I presume that he's going to make the day his own. There's no precedent in these modern times for the conduct of an Ovation for a man not of the imperial family; Claudius can do just what he wants.'

Sabinus wiped the sweat from his cheeks with a handkerchief. 'Don't you mean he can do just what his freedmen want?'

'It comes to the same thing, dear boy.'

The Senate arrived at the Triumphal Gate and lined the street on either side; the crowd quietened and a sense of expectation hung in the air filled with the aromas of roasting meats and baking bread from the kitchens set up to feed the spectators throughout the day and on into the night. A booming series of knocks on the gates prompted the Consuls to step forward and unbolt them as the first fanfare of massed bucinae, cornua and tubae rang out from the head of the parade, waiting on the Campus Martius beyond the walls. Slowly the gates swung open to the thunderous cheering of the populace and the lead horn players processed through with unhurried dignity.

Rank upon rank of musicians slow-marched into the city, their horns blaring out a repetitive, ponderous tune, and their feet moving in time to the measured beat of resounding drums that was taken up by the chanting and clapping of the crowd.

Following them came wagons laden with booty drawn by lumbering oxen that had no trouble keeping up with the pace. Files of shackled, matted-haired prisoners punctuated the inanimate plunder, their overseers cracking their whips in unison over their filthy backs in bizarre accompaniment to the music. Cart upon cart, file upon file of the spoils of war were driven into Rome and her citizens cheered every one.

'The odd thing is,' Gaius commented, 'I seem to remember most of these bigger pieces of booty from Claudius' Triumph.'

'It's very kind of the Emperor to share his spoils with the man who won them for him,' Vespasian observed as the first of the floats carrying tableaus depicting scenes from the invasion came trundling in; each had a figure representing Plautius in a heroic pose amongst cowering Britons but each also had a depiction of Claudius, much idealised, placed higher and more prominently and vanquishing more foes. Interestingly, for Vespasian, none of the tableaus specifically depicted Caratacus. He had heard no news of the rebel Britannic King since leaving the infant province; it was as if he had just disappeared. Nevertheless, Vespasian suspected that his resistance was still as bloody and resolute as ever but Rome's masters had decided not to trouble Rome's citizens with the details – especially on this day. The sight of druids, however, even though they were represented as almost comedic caricatures, gore-splattered, wreathed in mistletoe and brandishing bloody, golden sickles, brought a chill to his heart as if it had again been squeezed by the hand of the Lost Dead. As they passed, Vespasian muttered a prayer of thanks that he would never have to face such horrors again.

Following the floats were the four white bulls destined as gifts for Rome's guardian god in thanks for yet another victory. Beribboned and unblemished they plodded along, led by tethers, slowly tossing their heads and lowing as they went. Then came the weapons and the standards of the defeated chieftains followed by the men themselves and their bedraggled families. Some Vespasian recognised as men he had conquered in his push west; amongst them he spied Judoc, looking very much the worse for wear after his spell in his own tin mines. Unable to resist gloating he jeered at the treacherous chieftain of the Cornovii sub-tribe but as he did the cry was strangled in his throat. He pulled at his brother's sleeve. 'Look, Sabinus,' he said pointing to a man just behind Judoc.

Sabinus' eyes followed his finger and he whistled softly. 'Well, well, Jupiter's tight sack; am I pleased to see him. I wonder if Plautius knows that he's got Alienus amongst his dignitaries. I pray that he does and he's brought him all the way back here to give him to me; it would be such a shame if he's just strangled along with the rest.'

'What are you boys talking about?' Gaius shouted as the figure of Aulus Plautius appeared in the gateway and the noise escalated beyond what seemed possible.

'That, Uncle, is the man responsible for Sabinus being kept in a cage for three months.'

'Then I should like to take him by the arm!' Gaius roared.

Sabinus grinned. 'You'll have plenty of opportunity; I intend to display him in a cage of his very own.'

At an unheard order the procession came to a halt and Aulus Plautius – on foot rather than riding in a chariot and wearing a purple-bordered toga praetexta as it was only an Ovation, and crowned with a wreath of myrtle rather than laurel, for the same reason – stepped into the City of Rome to be greeted by the two Consuls and to lay down his command and once again become a private citizen.

As the ancient formulae were spoken by the three men, unheard above the hubbub, there was a stirring in the crowd and fingers were pointed up to the Arx, above the gate, on the Capitoline Hill. There, before the Temple of Juno, resplendent in purple and crowned in laurel stood Claudius. He raised his arms and gestured for silence.

'B-b-brave Plautius,' the Emperor declaimed, once the crowd was quiet, in a high-pitched voice that carried remarkably well. 'Welcome back to Rome!' He threw both arms in the air to raise a cheer that was forthcoming and mighty. With an expansive swipe of his arm he cut it off and continued: 'Stay there, b-b-brave P-Plautius, so that I may come and embrace you.'

Claudius turned and disappeared to the cheering of the crowd and the obvious fury of Plautius. He stood and waited as the crowd's enthusiasm dwindled and restlessness set in until eventually Claudius lurched into sight. The senators parted for their Emperor as he approached Plautius and, with melodramatic pleasure, enfolded him in the imperial bosom whilst liberally spreading saliva over each of his cheeks.

Once Plautius was released, a white horse was led through the crowd; Claudius was helped into the saddle and gave the signal for the parade to recommence. With a slave leading his mount, Claudius moved off, towering above Plautius, who, with as much dignity as he could muster, walked in his Emperor's shadow as an accessory in his own Ovation.

'Well, that was well managed,' Gaius said as the senators turned to follow the Consuls up to the Temple of Jupiter for the climax of the spectacle – again, it being only an Ovation, they did not lead the procession around its route. 'Narcissus, Pallas and Callistus hijacked that brilliantly and Plautius can't complain: the Emperor has shown him honour by accompanying him, yet because of his physical deformities he has to ride a horse. Very clever; even Plautius would have to admire it.'

Vespasian was forced to agree. 'It was; the one surprise was that Messalina didn't manage to inveigle her way into the proceedings.'

'Oh, I'm sure that she has business of her own to attend to whilst Claudius is busy.'

Vespasian smiled and clapped his uncle and brother on their shoulders. 'I'm sure she has, as have I. Don't be surprised if you see me in strange company in the next couple of hours; and please, whatever you do, don't remark upon it to anybody.'

'This is a very expensive way of doing Narcissus a favour,' Corvinus complained, joining Vespasian on the steps to the Temple of Jupiter and standing just behind his left shoulder. Around them the Senate waited, sweating in the noon sun, watching the Ovation process into the Forum Romanum below.

Vespasian did not turn to greet him. 'You wouldn't have paid it if you didn't think that it was a fair price for the chance of saving your life.'

'Narcissus wouldn't have asked for it if you hadn't put him up to it.'

'Narcissus is a businessman as well as a politician; he always charges for his time.'

'And he just upped his price tenfold when he heard that it was me?'

'He doesn't know who it is that he's meeting today; so don't feel discriminated against.'

'You didn't tell him that it was me?'

'No. If you have information to sell it holds its value best if you keep its contents secret.'

'So you are benefiting from this, aren't you, bumpkin?'

'Narcissus received the full quarter of a million, Corvinus.' He handed him a small scroll. 'Here's the receipt with his seal. What my arrangement is with him is none of your business. Just be thankful that I persuaded him to come to this meeting.'

Corvinus glanced at the receipt and then hissed a stream of obscenities into his ear, which just added to Vespasian's enjoyment of the situation. He was careful to conceal it, however, with a solemn expression as he watched Plautius begin his ascent of the Gemonian Stairs on his knees.

Corvinus had flown into a fit of rage when Vespasian had presented Narcissus' demand for payment. He had threatened all kinds of torment for Flavia and the children, to which

Vespasian had shrugged his shoulders and pointed out that Narcissus' business practices had nothing to do with him, and Corvinus could threaten as much as he liked but that would not get him any closer to a meeting with Narcissus in a manner that would not rouse Messalina's suspicions. Corvinus had handed over the money in ten small chests, each containing a thousand gold aurei, with ill-concealed bad grace, which Vespasian had stoked by hinting that Narcissus was sometimes apt to change his mind even after payment had been received. Magnus and a couple of his brethren had helped Vespasian to take five of the chests directly to the Cloelius Brothers' banking business in the forum and the other five, along with a note as to the whereabouts of Theron, to Narcissus' secretary. Caenis had thanked him kindly for both and had issued a receipt for the full amount in Narcissus' name and had promised that Theron would be first on Narcissus' appointment list on his return from Ostia. She had again neglected to charge for this favour on the understanding that Vespasian would be especially attentive over the next few days.

Now in possession of the wherewithal to pay off Messalina's loan to Flavia without having to borrow from Caenis, Vespasian ignored Corvinus' insults, contemplating instead the delicious irony that he would pay off the sister with the brother's money.

The four white bulls appeared in front of the temple having been led up the winding path along the summit of the Tarpeian Rock as Plautius completed his ritual mounting of the Gemonian Stairs and was helped to his feet by his Emperor to another roar from the crowd. The senators applauded him formally as he approached the Temple of Rome's guardian god with his toga covering his head. The bulls had been lined up under the portico of the temple and priests with the instruments of sacrifice attended them.

Claudius did Plautius the honour of taking the mallet and prepared to stun the bulls in turn in readiness for the sacrificial blade.

Corvinus had now quietened and Vespasian watched Plautius turn his palms to the sky; he addressed Jupiter with a prayer so ancient that it could be barely understood but reminded everyone present of how venerable this ceremony was, and had been down the long years of Roman history.

'This is the second time that you've surprised me, Vespasian,' Narcissus muttered, sliding into the gap to the left of him. 'I saw your slave-dealer yesterday; I think that the conclusion will be satisfactory for you.' He turned to Corvinus. 'How nice to bump into you at this ceremony.'

'Did you get my money?' Corvinus demanded.

'Naturally, otherwise I wouldn't be here.'

'How much?'

'A quarter of a million, as it said on the receipt.'

Vespasian felt Corvinus' eyes bore into the back of his head as Claudius crashed the mallet onto the forehead of the first beast to die. The sacrificial blade flashed in the sun and a moment later was dulled by gore.

'Well, Corvinus,' Narcissus asked with a silken tone, 'what do you have for me that will make my sparing your life on your sister's demise worthwhile?'

'My sister is planning to get married again.'

Vespasian had seen Narcissus at a loss for words once before in Britannia but this was the first time he had seen him not only struggling for the right response but also reeling from shock. In front of the temple the first bull collapsed to its knees as the blood flowed from its gaping throat.

'She has to be mad!' Narcissus eventually managed to whisper. 'She can't unilaterally divorce Claudius.'

'You know perfectly well that in law she is entitled to do just that and she doesn't even have to inform her husband that she's left the marriage.'

'What is she planning then? Giving up being the Empress, losing the right to see her children, retiring to private life and allowing somebody else to take her place?'

'No, she's planning a change of emperor not empress.'

Narcissus' mouth gaped open. 'How?'

'By having her new husband adopt Britannicus.'

'But Claudius will just have him executed.'

'Not if he's a consul.'

Narcissus looked vacantly into space as he digested the idea. In front of the temple another bull crumpled into a pool of its own blood. 'Of course,' he muttered. 'Although in law a consul's person is not sacrosanct like the tribune of the Plebs used to be in the old Republic, technically no one has the power to order a consul's execution. Claudius, with his knowledge and respect for the law and the way of our ancestors, wouldn't dare breach that convention, nor would he be able to force the man to renounce his position and thereby condemn himself to death. Nor could he have him murdered because that would be seen as an affront to Jupiter Optimus Maximus to whom the Consul will have made an oath to serve Rome. Messalina is a genius: she'd be married to two men, one of whom is all but inviolate and the other, although emperor, is not because technically he has no official position in the state. Therefore he can be removed or killed at any time – as was proven with Caligula.'

Corvinus nodded. 'And a promise of a large donative to the Praetorian Guard will be enough to get rid of the vulnerable one.'

'How do you know this?'

'Because this was how we'd planned to make me regent to Britannicus; she would've persuaded Claudius to award me the consulship for my conquest of Camulodunum and I would have adopted my sister's children and Claudius would have been isolated. However, you managed to sabotage that so now she's going to try again.'

'Which consul is she planning to marry? I assume it must be Geta.'

'It's not one of this year's Consuls; she's not ready to make her move until she has more confidence in the Guard; she's ... er ... bolstering her relationship with the senior officers, one at a time.'

'I'm well aware of that. So she'll choose one of next year's Consuls then?'

'Yes. I don't know whom; but that should be obvious once the nominations are announced. Then it's a question of how, when and where they'll marry; that's what Flavia will have to find out.'

'The Emperor hasn't finalised who they will be yet; so I've still a good chance of getting all my people on the list, which will buy me another year.'

'I don't think that you'll be involved in the decision. Messalina's given her list to the Emperor and has told him that unless he accepts each one there'll be no brother for Britannicus.'

'Who told you that?'

'My cousin, Gaius Vipstanus Messalla Gallus, who couldn't resist gloating about it to me: he's one of her choices. He wouldn't tell me the rest except to say that I wasn't one of them. That's what made me finally decide to turn against her.'

'But I've blocked him and his brother with Claudius.'

'Messalina's unblocked them.'

'She's planning to marry her cousin?'

'Well, it's not illegal like marrying her uncle or nephew would be.'

Narcissus sighed and then considered the situation for a few moments. 'How do you suggest I stop this?'

'You can't, Narcissus, however powerful you are you do not bear the Emperor's children. Messalina is now taking advantage of that fact. All you can do is wait for it to happen then somehow persuade Claudius that in order to survive he has to do what has never been done before.'

'Order the execution of a sitting consul? Impossible. It'll turn the whole Senate against him!'

'Then he will be a dead man, as will you.'

Narcissus' normally unreadable face betrayed the fact that he knew Corvinus to be right.

Gaius dipped a piece of bread, smeared with garlic, into a bowl of olive oil and then chewed on it, deep in thought, whilst Vespasian sat contemplating the steaming cup of wine in his hands. Behind him, Hormus stood with a toga folded over his arm in readiness to drape it over his master once breakfast had been eaten.

Picking up the loaf, Gaius tore another hunk from it and began to rub a crushed clove of garlic over it. 'Claudius won't believe that she'll do such a thing until she's done it, so there's no way that Narcissus can pre-empt her and have Claudius order the execution of whoever she's chosen before he's sworn in as consul.'

'But Narcissus will know in advance who it is as soon as Claudius announces his nominations for next year's consulships and then it's down to Flavia keeping him informed as to the timing of Messalina's plans.'

'So you can't move her out of the palace then?'

'Not yet, but Narcissus has promised to organise that once this is over.'

'If he's still alive, that is.'

Vespasian frowned and shook his head. 'I never thought that I'd hear myself say this but let's hope he is. Anyway, until then I'm not going to move into the new house. With Mother away at Aquae Cutillae, I'll stay here, if that's all right with you, Uncle?'

'Of course, dear boy,' Gaius replied as a loud knock on the front door echoed around the atrium. 'Who could that be trying to get in before I've even opened my door to my clients?'

Vespasian took a sip of his wine as the very attractive door-boy padded over and addressed his master. 'There's a man to see Senator Vespasian; he says his name is Theron.'

'Excellent!' Vespasian exclaimed, standing. 'I've been looking forward to this. Let him in as soon as I'm ready; but just him, none of his bodyguards. Hormus, my toga.'

'Most noble senator!' Theron oozed with his old obsequiousness as he was shown into the atrium. 'And your honoured uncle, Senator Pollo, I believe; I am at your service.' He bowed to them both as they sat regarding him in frozen-faced silence. His eyes flicked nervously between them as it became obvious that he was not going to get a response; he licked his lips and then pressed on: 'I've come about the terrible misunderstanding that we had the other day.'

'I didn't notice any misunderstanding, Theron,' Vespasian said in a cold, quiet voice. 'I asked for the money that you owed me and you refused to pay it; it was all very clear, especially you spitting at my feet.'

Theron wrung his hands, trying his best to smile but managing no more than a grimace. 'Such a terrible lapse of memory as to whom I was dealing with; I mistook you, noble Vespasian, for another person with whom I have dealings.'

'No you didn't, Theron; you knew exactly whom you were insulting. What you didn't know was that I have a deal of influence with Narcissus. That, I imagine, has come as rather a shock to you. I expect, too, that with his cancelling your contract in Britannia and forbidding you to trade in Italia you're now regretting the way you treated me.'

Theron cringed his apologies and begged forgiveness as Vespasian looked on in disgust before turning to Hormus. 'Can you believe that you were afraid of this,' he waved his hand dismissively at the slave-dealer, 'this snivelling piece of eastern dishonesty? Look at him, Hormus; take away his living and he's more wretched than a slave like you and yet the other day he was confident enough to spit at the feet of a senator. I think that today I shall have my slave return the compliment with interest; piss on his feet.'

Hormus stood, paralysed, looking with fearful eyes between his current and previous owners.

'Do it, Hormus! Do it for me because I command you to humiliate him; but also do it for yourself. I'm giving you the chance, for once, to do something that will make you feel some self-worth. Vengeance is the sweetest of sensations and every man should taste it at least once; even a slave.'

Drawing a series of deep, gasping breaths, Hormus fixed his stare on Theron; his face hardened and for the first time Vespasian saw an expression on his slave that was neither meek subservience nor timidity: it was hatred. Hormus walked steadily towards the slave-dealer, hitching up his tunic. Theron made no attempt to move but stood, clasping his hands, with his head bowed, staring dumbly at the slave's penis as it emitted a short squirt of urine that spattered on the floor between his feet. Hormus strained his body and the flow increased, drenching the ground and splattering up Theron's ankles and calves. Hormus looked directly at his former owner as he swayed left then right, spraying Theron's feet until the pressure died off and with a few flicks of his wrist the last drops were teased out.

'Thank you, Hormus,' Vespasian said as his slave adjusted his dress, 'I think that everyone has benefited from that. So Theron, now that you've apologised for the gross insult you showed me perhaps we can talk business. How much do you owe me?'

Theron looked miserably at the pool of urine surrounding him. 'All the stock survived the journey, senator; being fine specimens, they fetched between one and two thousand denarii each. I cleared just over six hundred thousand; I will bring you the bills of sale.'

'So twelve and a half per cent is seventy-five thousand, which, as I'm sure Narcissus has explained, you've consented to double, making a total of one hundred and fifty thousand denarii. That is correct, isn't it?'

'Yes, noble sen—'

'Let's drop the pretence that you consider me to be noble! Where is my money?'

'I can give you a promissory note.'

'I want cash.'

'I don't have it; I took it all back to Britannia and reinvested it in more stock.'

'All of it?'

'Yes, senator.'

'Then you had better sell it quickly; where is it?'

'Here in Rome; but Narcissus has forbidden me to trade in Italia.'

'In which case I shall arrange a quick sale; I'll do a job lot to one of your competitors for, say, one hundred and fifty – no, make it sixty – thousand denarii; I think that sounds fair. That gives you ten thousand to start again with once you're given permission to trade once more.'

'But they're worth much more than that,' Theron pleaded.

'Not to me they're not.'

'But there're thousands of them; you saw them all yesterday.'

'The prisoners in the Ovation?'

'Yes.'

'Even the chieftains and lesser dignitaries?'

'Yes, except for the two who were ritually strangled.'

'Was either one of them a young man?'

'No, they were both older.'

'Theron, this could be your lucky day.'

'This had better be important, Vespasian,' Sabinus said as he arrived with Magnus and Sextus at the huge slave compound on the Vatican Hill on the west bank of the Tiber. 'My inauguration begins at the sixth hour.'

'If vengeance isn't important then I've brought you here for nothing.'

Sabinus raised an eyebrow. 'Alienus? But I asked Plautius about him yesterday and he told me that there was nothing that he could do as the stock had all been sold.'

'It has, but to a man who owes me money and favours – you remember Theron, from Britannia, don't you? Come with me.' Vespasian led his brother and Magnus and Sextus to the compound's main gate where the slave-dealer waited, reunited with his bodyguards.

Without any pleasantries, they followed Theron through the gate into a large corral divided into scores of square pens; each one was crammed with manacled slaves, squatting or sitting in their own filth. Despite their numbers they made barely a sound and the eerie silence of unmitigated misery hung over the whole complex.

Theron issued an order to a couple of his guards who nodded and then strolled off. 'If I give you this man, will you speak to Narcissus about restoring everything that he took?'

'Once you give me my hundred and fifty thousand denarii, yes.'

'And he will let me sell my stock at a fair price to raise that?'

'I'm sure Narcissus will let you do so for a percentage of the proceeds. I'll speak to him.'

'You are generous, noble se … sir.'

'And you are lucky, Theron.'

Theron acknowledged the fact with a cheerful – if sycophantic – bow that surprised Vespasian, considering he had just been urinated upon by an ex-possession of his.

'There he is,' Sabinus growled as the two bodyguards appeared from between a line of pens dragging the weakly struggling figure of Alienus between them.

They pushed him forward so that the weight of his chains dragged him down onto the dirt. He got to his knees with sand adhering to the broken scabs of numerous whiplashes across his back and shoulders and looked at the brothers. He smiled wryly. 'So it's your turn now, is it?'

Sabinus returned the smile. 'Yes, Alienus; although I don't look upon it as taking turns. But tell me, how did I have the good fortune of possessing you?'

'With both Rome and Myrddin after me I decided the safest place to lose myself was here in the largest city in the Empire. Since I had no silver I thought that the best way to get here was to offer my services to one of the many slave-traders travelling back to Rome. Unfortunately I chose Theron.'

Theron shrugged. 'One of his own, whom I had just purchased, betrayed him.'

'Judoc!' Alienus spat.

'Perfect!' Vespasian laughed. 'I might even forgive the bastard.'

'The gods have seen to him; he was strangled.'

Sabinus grabbed Alienus' hair and hauled him to his feet. 'And the gods have seen fit to bring you to me. You're going to learn what it is like to spend three months dangling in a cage five times over; and then, if I'm feeling merciful, I'll just strangle you.' He thrust him at Magnus and Sextus. 'Take him to my house, Magnus, and stay with him until I get back from my inauguration.'

Magnus grinned. 'It'll be our pleasure, sir; you take your time, we'll enjoy hanging about with him, if you take my meaning?'

As he was hauled off, Alienus shouted over his shoulder, 'You'd do best to strangle me now, Sabinus, before it's my turn again!'

*

The Father of the House examined the ram's liver on the altar, a fold of his toga pulled over his head out of respect for the divine presence of Jupiter Optimus Maximus.

Similarly attired and seated on folding stools in straight rows down either of the long sides of the rectangular Senate House, the five hundred senators present watched with interest the deliberations of the most senior of their number.

Standing to either side of the altar at the far end of the building were the causes for the divine invocation and consultation: Titus Flavius Sabinus and Gnaeus Hosidius Geta, the Suffect-Consuls.

Vespasian sat next to his uncle watching the ceremony with a mixture of jealousy and pride. Pride that for the first time a member of his family had been raised to the consulship, thus ennobling it; and jealousy in that it was not him but his older brother.

The Father of the House turned his palms to the sky and gave a prayer of thanks to Rome's best and greatest god for consenting to favour them with a good omen and ensuring that the day was auspicious for the business of the city. With that done he went on to administer the consular oath to the two new incumbents and they solemnly swore loyalty to the Republic and the Emperor, who sat, twitching, on a curule chair before the altar.

'They used to have to swear their readiness to prevent a return of the King,' Gaius whispered. 'For some reason the line was removed from the oath.'

Vespasian smiled. 'I imagine someone felt it was redundant.'

Gaius chuckled. 'Yes, but it's rumoured that Claudius, with his legal pedantry and fastidiousness in preserving the ways of the ancestors, is going to reinsert it.'

'Without seeing the irony of it?'

'He'll do it with as straight a face as the gods allow him.'

The oath administered, the assembly removed their head coverings and the newly inducted Consuls took their seats either side of the Emperor.

'C-C-Conscript Fathers,' Claudius declaimed, 'it pleases me to have two of the legates who commanded legions in my great and historic invasion and subjugation of Britannia as consuls at the time when Aulus Plautius has come back to Rome and celebrated the Ovation that you granted him as a favour to me.'

There was a general muttering of agreement at that novel restructuring of the facts.

'I am now in a position to nominate the Consuls and Suffect-Consuls for next year.'

This announcement caused genuine interest as the possibility of patronage was dangled in front of every man present.

'For the first six months, the Senior Consul will be Aulus Vitellius followed in the last six months by his brother, Lucius Vitellius the younger.'

There was a communal intake of breath as well as a few expressions of surprise from senators less adept at concealing their feelings than was wise as they looked at the two portly young men, both far too young to receive the honour, seated either side of their beaming father, the elder Lucius Vitellius.

'So that was the price that Vitellius extracted from Messalina to help her get hold of Asiaticus' gardens,' Gaius muttered 'To persuade Claudius to nominate both his sons to the consulship ten years too early.'

'But would Vitellius be foolish enough to allow one of them to marry the Empress?'

'I've heard it said that Aulus had a horoscope cast at his birth that was, shall we say, imperial in its outlook. Perhaps old Lucius has decided that Fortuna is on the Vitellii's side. He's always used his sons to his own advantage; like pandering Aulus to Tiberius when he was fourteen, for example.'

'I remember; Sabinus and I met him on Capreae. He offered Sabinus an interesting form of relaxation.'

'I suppose it is a good choice from Messalina's point of view: a patrician family that can trace itself back to the time of the Kings; even longer than her own. They would certainly be in line for the Purple if the Julio-Claudian blood failed.'

Claudius signalled for quiet and continued: 'And as the Junior Consul for the first six months I nominate Lucius Vipstanus Messalla Poplicola to be followed by his brother, Gaius Vipstanus Messalla Gallus.'

At this announcement only the very self-controlled managed to contain their astonishment and many eyes turned to Corvinus who sat, rigid-faced, opposite Vespasian and Gaius.

'Both Messalina and Corvinus' cousins!' Gaius hissed under the commotion.

But Claudius was not finished. 'However, Conscript Fathers, there will in addition be one further suffect-consul for the last three months of next year. Gallus will stand down and in his place I nominate Gaius Silius.'

This time there was stunned silence. Vespasian caught Corvinus' eye; to his amazement his old enemy's look told him that he thought Silius was Messalina's choice to replace her husband.

All eyes turned to a very good-looking young man, seated in the front row, who had only recently been made a senator by Claudius at the behest, as everyone present knew, of Messalina. Furthermore, everyone present, with the exception of Claudius, was well aware that Gaius Silius was the Empress's lover and no one was under any illusion as to how and why this Adonis had risen so fast.

What they did not know was just how much further Messalina intended him to rise.

PART IIII

❧ ❧

ROME, AUTUMN AD 48

CHAPTER XVIII

CLUTCHING AT HER mother's waist the girl struggled against strong arms trying to rip her away. Her flame-coloured veil matched the colour of her shoes and covered her hair, which was dressed ritually in six locks fixed in a cone atop her head, but did not totally obscure her face; Vespasian enjoyed the expression of grim determination on it as Paetus tried to wrench his bride from her mother's grip. With a small shriek that turned into a giggle, Vespasian's niece, Flavia Tertulla, fell into the arms of her new husband.

'Hymen, Hymenaeee!' Vespasian shouted along with the other guests as Paetus released Flavia Tertulla; blushing, she stood next to her husband outside the open front door of Sabinus' house on the Aventine Hill. Slender-faced with pale skin, auburn hair and young-leaf-green eyes, Flavia Tertulla was the image of her mother, Clementina, when Vespasian had first set eyes on her, seventeen years before. Paetus smiled jovially whilst exchanging crude banter with the more rakish of the guests, putting Vespasian in mind of his father, his long dead friend, whom he resembled so closely.

Spotting nine-year-old Titus, standing proudly in his boy's toga praetexta in his capacity as one of the three boys with parents still living who escorted the bride, Vespasian ran a hand through his thinning hair and then clapped his brother on the shoulder. 'Where does the time go?'

'I know what you mean, brother, I've been feeling like that all day. It seems just a few days ago that Flavia Tertulla used to keep me awake with her mewling; now look at her, she'll be producing mewling infants of her own very soon. In fact, with all the best appointments going to Messalina's cronies, by the time I get a governorship she'll probably have a whole pack of them.'

Sabinus threw a handful of walnuts, symbolising fertility, up into the air so that they rained down on the newlyweds as his fifteen-year-old son and namesake came out of the house with a flaming torch lit from the hearth with which he ignited a bundle of torches held by Paetus. With the torches, burning with the bride's hearth-fire, distributed amongst the guests the procession from the bride's parents' house to that of her new husband on the Esquiline Hill was ready to begin. Flavia Tertulla took the spindle and distaff that Clementina offered her, representing her role as a weaving wife, and then, together with Paetus, set off down the hill, proceeded by the young Sabinus, Titus and a relation of Paetus' whose name Vespasian was vague about.

Vespasian walked next to his mother, Vespasia Polla, on the bride's side of the procession, smiling with a sense of wellbeing at the sight of so many of his family around him. His mood had been further improved by an excellent wedding breakfast and the sight of an emaciated Alienus hanging in the foul-smelling cage that had been his home for over a year now. Despite his condition he had still displayed defiance and had thrown a turd at the brothers as they gloated; it had fallen short. However, Vespasian had had a grudging respect for Alienus' refusal to admit defeat; it had been Rome's same stubbornness during the long struggle with Carthage, centuries before, that had eventually seen her through to victory. He foresaw a long struggle in Britannia if even half Alienus' compatriots showed the same resilience; which, with the encouragement of the druids who were fighting for their very existence, he thought highly likely. His humour was even more enhanced by the knowledge that folly raging on in Britannia was no longer his fight.

With shouts of 'Talasio!' from passers-by – the ritual good-luck greeting for a bride, so old that its origin and meaning were now lost to time – the wedding party processed in a carnival atmosphere with much good-natured walnut lobbing.

'I'm starting to feel my age, Mother,' Vespasian commented. 'Children grow so quickly.'

Vespasia snorted in derision. 'Wait until you reach seventy and have outlived your spouse; that's when you feel your age.' She grabbed Domitilla by the shoulder as she went skipping past.

'Child, show some decorum; you're a member of a consular family and should behave as such.'

Domitilla looked up at her grandmother, evidently having no real understanding of what had been said.

Vespasia turned to Flavia walking behind her with Gaius. 'You should keep the girl under control.'

Flavia's lips tightened. 'She was just enjoying herself on a happy day, Vespasia; leave her alone and don't try to discipline my children again.'

'I'll discipline them as much as I like if I see them behaving in a way unbecoming for this family.'

'What do you mean, "this family"? Do you mean the equestrian family that you produced or the senatorial family that my husband and his brother turned it into? There's nothing worse than the snobbery of a person who has been raised up beyond their birth rank.'

'My husband may have been only an equestrian but Gaius, my brother, was a praetor and has been in the Senate for over thirty years. I have always been of senatorial stock. At least I don't have the taint of slavery in my blood, daughter of Titus Flavius *Liberalis*! Your grandfather was undoubtedly a slave and your lax way of rearing children bears out that fact.'

'Mother!' Vespasian exclaimed, his good mood fast disappearing. 'You will not talk to my wife like that.'

'No? I'll talk to her however I see fit. A woman with morals like hers does not have my respect – or the respect of anyone in good society.'

'Just what do you mean, Vespasia?' Flavia asked coldly.

'I mean that a woman who whores herself to the Empress is not fit to be treated as anything other than what she really is: a disgrace to her family name.'

'You wicked old bitch! I'll—'

'Flavia!' Vespasian snapped, stepping between the two women and grabbing his wife's outstretched hand before the nails made contact with his mother's cheek. 'Control yourself.'

'Control myself! After what she just said?'

'Mother, you will apologise.'

'I won't apologise for telling the truth. What interests me, Vespasian, is that you don't seem very surprised by the revelation.'

Vespasian kept hold of Flavia's hand and forced it back down by her side as they walked on. 'What interests me, Mother, is what would make you want to make such an accusation in the first place?'

'Dear boy, keep your voice down,' Gaius urged, 'you're spoiling the wedding procession.'

Flavia shook her hand free. 'Defend me from such slander, Vespasian. I demand you to.'

Vespasia's face contorted in spiteful triumph. 'He's not defending you because he knows it to be true.'

'Mother, of course it's not true and you will never say that again. Who told you such a thing?'

'I got it from a very good source: Agrippina.'

Gaius looked doubtful. 'Claudius's niece has hardly been seen since the Emperor recalled her from exile at the beginning of his reign and married her to Passienus. She won't go near the palace as she's convinced that Messalina will try and murder her son, Lucius. The rumour is that the Empress has already made a couple of attempts on his life.'

'Well, I see her,' Vespasia said as the procession passed between the Appian Aqueduct and the southern end of the Circus Maximus. 'After Passienus died last year he left all his property to young Lucius, including the neighbouring estate to ours at Aquae Cutillae. If you'd bothered to come up, Vespasian, you would know about it.'

'I have better things to do with my time than to pry into my neighbours' affairs; besides, I've been obliged to stay in Rome.'

Vespasia sniffed. 'So you say. Anyway, Agrippina took up residence there a couple of months ago; she has invited me on numerous occasions since and is very well informed about Messalina.'

'That's no reason to repeat her malicious gossip.'

'It's not gossip, it's true.'

Vespasian restrained Flavia again as her hand reached out, claw-like, towards Vespasia's eyes.

Gaius steered his sister out of range. 'I'd be very careful about becoming friendly with Agrippina; she's not known for her kindness. In fact, the rumour is that she murdered Passienus. And don't forget what her first husband, Gaius Domitius Ahenobarbus, said about their child – what was it? "I don't think anything produced by me and Agrippina could possibly be good for the state or the people."'

'Nonsense, Gaius, she's perfectly charming to me; it's a great honour to be an intimate of the Emperor's niece, the daughter of the great Germanicus, and it could be very useful for our family.'

'How? She's hardly ever in Rome.'

'She's going to be in Rome far more in the future, Gaius; she has her eyes on Messalina and in revenge for her trying to murder Lucius, she is going to take everything that she has away from her.'

'Hush your mouth, woman; that's treasonous talk.'

'Is it? It's also the truth, Gaius.' She looked at Vespasian and Flavia. 'If I were you, Vespasian, I'd remove that whore of yours from Messalina's bed before she's dragged from it clinging to her lover's corpse.'

Vespasian pointed a finger in his mother's face. 'And if I were you, Mother, I would keep my mouth shut and my nose out of things that you obviously don't understand. Don't talk about this to anyone, do not hint that you know of it, don't even think about it. Do I make myself clear?'

'But Flavia—'

'Flavia is my wife and I know perfectly well what is going on and why. You, on the other hand, are just another lonely old woman who enjoys her opinions far too much and talks carelessly about politics and intrigue without knowing just how dangerous her words are.'

Gaius agreed with a wobbly-jowl nod. 'Vespasia, I forbid you to see Agrippina again.'

'Why, brother, are you jealous of my well-connected friend? Are you feeling a little inferior?'

'Don't be stupid, woman; I'm just trying to protect our family.'

'How does forbidding me to cultivate the Emperor's niece do that?'

Vespasian looked at his mother in exasperation. 'Because if what you say is true then Agrippina doesn't just want to take everything away from Messalina, she wants to possess everything Messalina's got; she has her eye on becoming the mother of the next emperor.'

'She can't; it's illegal to marry one's niece.'

'Of course, but she doesn't need to marry Claudius; all she need do is dispose of Britannicus. With him dead then her son, Lucius, would be the obvious choice to be Claudius' heir; and actually he'd be a better choice: he's three years older and he's the grandson of Germanicus. The people would feel that at last the succession had got back to how it should have been.'

'She would kill Britannicus?'

'That's the whole point, Mother; for her plan to work Britannicus would have to be dead. Agrippina is cultivating you because she knows that your grandson is Britannicus' companion. Does she ask about him?'

Vespasia looked concerned, putting her hand to her mouth. 'We always discuss my latest visits with my grandchildren.'

'And if Britannicus had been there?'

'Then she's very interested; she likes to know what they do together, where they go, who supervises them.'

'You see, Mother, you're being used; and the information that you inadvertently give her is putting my son in danger. An accidental death will look much more convincing if two young boys suffered it instead of just the Emperor's heir. You will not speak to Agrippina any more and you will not leave Rome. Am I clear?'

'Yes,' Vespasia whispered, looking suitably chastened.

'And you will apologise to Flavia.'

But this was evidently a step too far for Vespasia and she turned away with her nose in the air as the wedding procession split in two and Paetus' party began to ascend the Esquiline Hill so that they would arrive at his house before the bride, whose party would take a more circuitous route.

*

Flavia Tertulla rubbed oil and fat into the doorframe of Paetus' house and then wreathed spun wool around it. Once she was satisfied that her role as the domestic wife in the house had been announced to the household gods she stepped over the threshold, taking great care not to trip. 'Where you are Gaius, I am Gaia,' she said, taking Paetus' hand as she entered the vestibule.

'Where you are Gaia, I am Gaius,' Paetus replied before leading her on into the atrium with the guests following.

Vespasian threw his torch aside as he entered the house with his uncle.

'Vespasia does have a point,' Gaius remarked in a hushed tone as they walked into the atrium. 'Perhaps it is time to think about protecting Flavia. Gaius Silius will be sworn in as suffect-consul in four days; Messalina will make her move very soon after that and you don't want Flavia caught up in it, do you?'

'That's just it, Uncle; Flavia has to stay close to Messalina now of all times. Narcissus needs to have the wedding witnessed so he must know in advance where and when it's going to be.'

'Surely he could get that information from other sources; Corvinus, for example?'

'Perhaps; but if Flavia doesn't provide him with that information, there'll be no reason for him to persuade Claudius to let me take my family away from the palace. If what Mother says is true and we're going to replace one poisonous bitch with another possessing even more venom, then that has to be my highest priority – for Titus' sake. And besides,' Vespasian added, with a conspiratorial grin, 'Flavia hasn't yet received the quarter of a million denarii that Messalina has promised to loan her.'

Gaius chuckled and clapped Vespasian on the shoulder. 'You seem to be making a lot of money recently.'

'I've made up my mind to profit whenever I can from the unpleasant situations that the politics of this city push me into, Uncle.'

'Very wise, dear boy; no one is going to give you a handout for getting your hands dirty.'

They watched in silence as Flavia Tertulla passed her hand through the flame burning in the atrium hearth and then dipped it in a bowl of water placed next to it. Having touched the two elements essential to life through cooking and washing, Flavia Tertulla placed her hand in that of her father. Sabinus then formally handed his daughter over to Paetus, who was standing next to a miniature marital bed decorated with flowers and fruit and set next to the impluvium for the newlyweds' spirits to consummate the marriage in. The guests broke into a song encouraging the couple to imitate their spirits and then Flavia, as the matron of honour, led Flavia Tertulla away to the bridal chamber to pray and sacrifice with her and then to help her undress in readiness for Paetus' arrival.

'The hypocrisy of it!' Vespasia snorted. 'She may be married just once to a husband who is still living but she can't be accused of being the incarnation of a faithful wife.'

'Mother, if you carry on about my wife any more then I shall see to it that you no longer visit the children; which judging by the unfair way you reprimanded Domitilla just now will probably come as a relief for them.'

Vespasia turned to Vespasian, outrage in her eyes. 'You support your wife against the woman who gave you birth?'

'I support the mother of my children against the uninformed opinions of an ageing woman who does not understand what is going on and why; the fact that you gave birth to me is irrelevant. Now let that be an end to it, Mother.'

Vespasia snorted again and walked off to join a group of similarly aged females.

'She's been getting worse every year since your father died,' Gaius informed him as slaves came round with trays of wine and bowls of fruit.

'She's becoming dangerous, Uncle,' Vespasian said, watching his mother break into the conversation of the women she had just joined. 'If she starts to gossip about Flavia then her affair will become public knowledge.'

'I wouldn't worry about that, dear boy; if it suits her purposes, Agrippina will have seen to that.'

Vespasian knew that his uncle was, in all likelihood, right and cursed the situation that had kept him in limbo for the past year.

Messalina had made no move to marry either of the first four Consuls of the year and it was now beyond doubt that it was Silius, the final nomination, that she had chosen for her husband. However, as she could not marry him until he had the protection of the consulship, which was not due until October, the few people in Rome who knew of the plot had settled down to a period of uneasy watchfulness. Narcissus and Pallas had eyed the antics of Messalina's court with growing incredulity that their master's ears were deaf to all rumour and report of their actions.

Messalina had grown even more reckless: she was now whoring herself out to the people of Rome almost every night as well as sleeping with her many lovers amongst the aristocracy. Despite her hectic sexual schedule, however, she still found time to enjoy her more constant lovers, Silius and Flavia, although Flavia was becoming less keen on Messalina's favours as she spread them around so many of the insalubrious city folk.

But Vespasian had insisted that Flavia act as if nothing was wrong and she had borne the ordeal with reluctance and fortitude. The information that she had got from her pillow talk with Messalina had been of great value to Narcissus and Pallas: the names of new lovers, clandestine supporters in the Senate and, eventually, the final confirmation of her plan to marry Silius as a sitting consul; however, the date was never discussed.

Vespasian took a deep breath as he consoled himself that soon the wait would be over now that October was fast approaching.

He was pulled out of his reverie by the sound of Sabinus leading the cheering of his new son-in-law as he left the atrium to perform his marital duties whilst the guests drank and feasted, waiting for news of the coupling.

Vespasian raised his cup to Paetus and then took a long sip of wine, letting his eyes wander over the happy crowd. He was surprised to see Marius, looking rather out of place, walking towards him. 'Are you looking for me?'

'Yes, sir, you and your brother,' Marius replied. 'Magnus has asked if you can both come to the tavern at the sixth hour. He says to be as discreet as possible as there's going to be someone there who wants to talk to you in private.'

*

Vespasian and Sabinus struggled through the crowds, up the Vicus Longus to its acute junction with the Alta Semita on the southern slope of the Quirinal Hill. Wearing tunics and cloaks rather than senatorial togas, there was nothing to signify their status so their progress towards the tavern at the apex of that junction was impeded by the citizens of Rome, male and female, free, freed and slave, all going about their business, which was, naturally, far more important and urgent than the next person's.

Traders shouted their wares, either edible or functional, from open-fronted shops on the ground floors of the three- or four-storey brick-built tenements lining the street, and haggled with customers. Goods were inspected and then chosen or rejected, arguments flared and were quickly settled, either by violence or reason, bargains were made, coinage changed hands and deals were concluded. Acquaintances met with exaggerated geniality and discussed business over cups of wine, standing at the bars of open taverns emitting wafts of pungent smoke from charcoal grills upon which sizzled cuts of pork and chicken. The aroma helped to sweeten the sour odour of human sweat and stale urine that hung in the air warmed by the midday sun and was stirred only by the passage of the multitude.

Keeping to the crowded pavements, so as not to soil their sandals in the squelching refuse that befouled the street, Vespasian and Sabinus wended their way uphill, through the heaving knots of humanity that made Rome the busiest city in the Empire.

'I was afraid that you might have been too occupied,' Magnus said as they finally reached the tavern that acted as the head-quarters of the South Quirinal Crossroads Brotherhood; a few of the brethren sat outside at wooden tables, playing dice.

'I hope this is worth it on my daughter's wedding day, Magnus,' Sabinus growled. He had not been keen to come even though the marriage had been consummated and the ceremony was now over, but curiosity had got the better of him.

'You can judge that for yourself, sir.' Magnus rattled a dice-shaker and rolled its contents onto the table; with a look of disgust he slammed the shaker down. 'That's your fourth win in a row, Tigran; I ain't playing with your dice again.' He pushed his stake across the table to his eastern-looking opponent and got to his feet. 'Were you followed?'

Vespasian shrugged. 'I don't think so, but we told Marius to trail behind us and keep an eye on our backs.' He turned to see Marius making his way up the hill. 'Here he is. Well, Marius?'

Marius wiped the sweat from his brow, looking puzzled. 'No one followed you from Paetus' house back to Sabinus', but then when you left that to come here I kept on getting glimpses of two men in deep-hooded cloaks taking it in turns to keep about thirty paces behind you.'

'Did you see their faces?'

'No, all that was visible under the hoods were beards.'

'Eastern?'

'No, more like German beards.'

'What else were they wearing?'

'Normal stuff, tunics and sandals.'

'What happened to them?'

'That was strange as well. Having followed you half the way here they suddenly veered off and disappeared.'

Vespasian looked at Sabinus. 'What do you make of that?'

'Someone knows where I live but wasn't so interested in knowing where I was going?'

'Or they were scared off by someone,' Magnus suggested. 'Did you notice anyone else, Marius?'

'No, brother; they was clean the rest of the way here.'

'All right, then; you hang about out here and keep an eye out for anyone you might recognise.'

'Right you are, Magnus.'

Magnus indicated with a jerk of the head to the brothers. 'He's inside.'

They followed Magnus past the altar to the Crossroads' lares set into the wall of the building and on into the fuggy, raucous interior of the tavern. It was crowded with drinkers and a few whores who all made way for Magnus as he steered a straight course for a door at the far end of the room, next to the amphora-lined bar. The noise dipped as Vespasian and Sabinus passed and then resumed as they followed Magnus through the door and then right, along a short corridor and on into another room, dimly lit by shuttered windows and with the cloying blend of lamp fumes, damp wood and stale wine in the air.

'Thank you for coming, gentlemen,' a voice said as they stepped inside.

'Pallas!' Vespasian exclaimed. 'Why so mysterious? Why go to all these lengths to have a conversation that we could have anywhere?'

Pallas rose from his seat and grasped their forearms in turn. 'Because I can no longer trust anywhere in the palace: there are too many spies about; so I came here taking care not to be followed as I wouldn't want to be seen going to either of your houses. My people have reported that Sabinus' house is being watched and we must assume that yours is too, Vespasian.'

'By Messalina?'

'I would think so but I don't know for sure; what I do know is that my people have reported undue interest in Sabinus in the last couple of days.'

'That would explain the two bearded men, brother,' Sabinus said as they each took a seat.

Magnus poured cups of wine from a pitcher on a table in the corner. 'I'll have my lads take a look at them, see if we can invite them here for a quiet drink and a hearth-side chat, if you take my meaning?'

Vespasian shook his head as he accepted his cup. 'I think we'll find out more by following them and seeing whom they report to.'

'Fair point; I'll go and get that organised.'

As Magnus left, Pallas turned his attention to Sabinus. 'I need to call in the favour that you owe me for getting you cleared of all involvement in Caligula's death.'

Sabinus inclined his head a fraction. 'I acknowledge that I am in your debt for that, Pallas.'

Pallas' semi-shadowed face betrayed no emotion. 'I'm pleased that you accept the fact.' He paused and collected his thoughts. 'I have it within my grasp to supplant Narcissus, get rid of Callistus and become the most powerful man in the Empire, which, I think you'll both agree, considering our past relationship, will benefit your family considerably. The key to it all is to set in train a series of events that move rapidly, so my opponents have no time to think how they are going to react. Firstly, I need to force Messalina's hand by providing an impetus for her to bring her wedding plans forward to the first day of Silius' consulship, rather than wait and react to her move. Vespasian, Flavia can do that for me and in return I'll make good Narcissus' undertaking to persuade Claudius to allow you to move her out of the palace. He won't be able to, seeing as he will not be in a position of favour.'

Vespasian attempted to match Pallas in the neutrality of his expression. 'What do you want her to do?'

'Tell Messalina that she overheard you and Sabinus talking about plans for Claudius to marry again. She must tell Messalina that, according to you, Callistus supports the idea of Claudius marrying Caligula's third wife, Lollia Paulina, while Narcissus and I want him to remarry his second wife, Aelia Paetina. You know, the one with whom he had a daughter before his mother forced him to divorce her because she was the half-sister of Sejanus.'

'Thereby convincing her that a plot to remove her is far advanced?'

'Precisely, and she'll believe it because when she thinks about it she will see that those positions make perfect sense for us in protecting our own interests: Callistus trying to get the wife of his former patron into power and Narcissus and I trying to ensure that power stays in the hands of a woman already known to us. And those *are* our positions at the moment – outwardly at least.

'To panic Messalina into action, Flavia is to tell her that she heard you saying that the whole matter will be decided very quickly, as the most auspicious day for the wedding has been given as the Ides of October at the festival of the October Horse.'

'That will concentrate her mind.'

'That will indeed. It'll force her to declare her intentions publicly; she'll marry Silius as soon as he becomes consul.'

'But then how do you remove him?'

'I've a way to deal with that. I'll need to keep Claudius out of the city by delaying his return from the visit he's making to the building project at Ostia – he's leaving tomorrow. That'll mean he misses Silius' inauguration ... but let me worry about those things. I need you to bring a couple of the wedding guests, using force if necessary, down to Ostia as quickly as possible after the ceremony so that they can confirm the marriage to Narcissus. But on no account must you keep your promise to Narcissus and warn him in advance of this.'

'But Flavia—'

'Flavia will be fine, I'll see to that. I must have Narcissus taken by surprise; it's my only chance to outmanoeuvre him. Once he hears the marriage has taken place without his knowledge the consequences will be inevitable and it will be just a matter of time and timing for me to achieve my aim. And this, Sabinus, is how you can repay your debt to me: I need to have a decree ratified in the House the morning following the wedding and then a law changed the moment Messalina crosses the Styx. With your consular status, your right to wear Triumphal Regalia won in Britannia and the fact that you go to Moesia as governor next year should give you the authority that you need to muster enough support to do that for me in the Senate.'

'Which law?'

'The law against incest between an uncle and his niece.'

The brothers simultaneously sucked their breath through their teeth.

Vespasian recovered first. 'That's one of the oldest and most sacred laws there is, Pallas.'

'Which makes it perfect for my purpose because no one will foresee the move.'

'You intend for Claudius to marry Agrippina.'

Pallas twitched an eyebrow in appreciation of the insight. 'It's the only thing that makes sense. Consider this: we rid ourselves of

Claudius' wife but his son must be allowed to live – for the time being, at least. Now, should he reach manhood and inherit the Purple one of his first duties *should* be to avenge his mother and I will be a dead man, as, indeed, will be Narcissus and you, Vespasian, despite your son's friendship with Britannicus, because your part in this cannot be kept secret. Narcissus believes that by promoting a marriage between Claudius and Aelia Paetina and then supporting Britannicus as Claudius' heir he can avert this, for he will have put the boy deep in his debt. Perhaps that would work, who knows? However, for once he has missed something. If I get Agrippina into Claudius' bed, she will never forgive Narcissus and Callistus for supporting different candidates even though she technically wasn't eligible at the time.' For once Pallas allowed himself a self-satisfied smile. 'After the Asiaticus affair that would spell at least banishment for Callistus – but hopefully worse – and a massive loss of influence for Narcissus. It will also guarantee my safety from future vengeance by Britannicus – and yours incidentally, Vespasian – by providing a more suitable heir in Lucius Domitius Ahenobarbus, whom Claudius will adopt without too much persuasion because Agrippina will insist on it. And there we have it.'

Sabinus scratched the back of his head and cleared his throat. 'But how am I meant to get that legislation through the Senate?'

'The normal way: bribery with the money that I shall give you and appealing to everybody's common sense. This will finally unite the Julian and Claudian families in marriage and will provide an heir who, if he marries Claudius' daughter—'

'But she'll be his adoptive sister!'

'Yes, but that can be easily dealt with when the time comes. When Lucius marries Claudia Octavia and disposes of Britannicus he becomes irrefutably the heir to Julius Caesar and Germanicus and the people will love him. The other consideration is that Agrippina is already forty-two and unlikely to conceive again and cloud the succession issue even more. If the Senate wants stability then that's what they should have in their minds when they vote to make it legal for an uncle to marry his niece.'

Although Vespasian knew that Pallas had always thought Britannicus' chances of survival to be slim – they had discussed the matter five years previously when Pallas had accompanied Claudius to Britannia – it was the clinical way that the freedman made the assessment that gave him a chill. He now saw the boy's death as inevitable; it was what he dreaded for personal reasons. 'What about my Titus? What happens to him as Britannicus is culled in this scheme of yours?'

'He will be kept safe, you have my word; after all, what threat is he to Agrippina and Lucius? No one could dream of him becoming emperor.' Pallas cocked his head and widened his eyes. 'Unless perhaps there's no issue from Lucius and Claudia Octavia's union and the blood of the Caesars runs dry?'

'It would be treasonous to explore that thought.'

'I'm sure that most of the Senate have committed treason in that way. However, for the present, if you both want to advance your family's position then I suggest you do as I ask; do I have your support, gentlemen?'

The brothers looked at each other and quickly came to a silent mutual agreement.

'Yes, Pallas,' Vespasian confirmed, 'out of loyalty to you and the obvious gain to us, we'll do it.'

'Good. Flavia must go to Messalina tonight.'

'She will. But I have a favour to ask.'

Pallas inclined his head.

'If your scheme works—'

'Which it will.'

'Which it will. Then Narcissus will not be in any position to save people close to Messalina.'

'Indeed.'

'So Corvinus will die?'

'Undoubtedly.'

'Will you save him if I ask you to?'

'As a favour to you, yes, I would; but why would you want such a thing?'

'Because I took money off him indirectly in return for his life; I should honour that and in doing so I have the chance to finish our feud once and for all.'

'Then consider his life as being in your hands.'

'I've one question,' Sabinus interjected. 'What is the decree that you want me to have ratified by the Senate?'

Pallas got to his feet. 'A small whim of the Emperor's that mistakenly got overlooked.'

Vespasian rolled up the scroll and laid it down on the table, smiling at his wife sitting opposite him on the terrace of their suite. 'A bankers' draft from Messalina, redeemable at the Cloelius Brothers in the forum for a quarter of a million denarii payable to the bearer – well done, my dear; I'll get Magnus to exchange it for another draft issued by the Cloelius Brothers themselves, again payable to the bearer, which I'll cash in and there'll be nothing to link the money to Messalina.' He patted the scroll as if it were a treasured possession of rare beauty and then inhaled a satisfied breath of cool morning air. 'How did she take the worrying news from a concerned lover who accidentally overheard her husband's private conversation?'

Flavia took her husband's hand over the table. 'Vespasian, I shall be so glad when this is over and I think that it'll be soon; she believed me and flew into a rage, cursing everyone from the Emperor and his freedmen to her four personal attendants, one of whom she had whipped in front of her to make herself feel better.'

Vespasian thought back to the slave girls who had accompanied Messalina to Asiaticus' hearing and wondered which had been the unfortunate one. 'Did she give any indication of what she plans to do?'

'She swore that she'd see everyone plotting against her dead before the Ides of October and then left to go to the Gardens of Lucullus to calm down and meet with Silius.'

Vespasian contemplated this for a while, gazing over the rooftops of Rome in the direction of Messalina's ill-gotten gardens. 'Of course,' he murmured, 'that's where she'll do it to keep it secret; there'll be no procession from one house to the other, no veneration of household gods in the street or re-enactment of the abduction of the Sabine women, it'll just be a private party in the most private gardens in Rome. No one outside her circle will know until the new Suffect-Consul announces in the Senate the following morning that he is now married to the Empress who has divorced the Emperor and he is going to adopt Britannicus. If she really has managed to seduce enough officers in the Guard then the plan has a very good chance of succeeding. All he has to say is: choose between Claudius and Messalina because one of them is going to die; and, by the way, if it's Messalina who perishes here's a list of all her lovers, which will make interesting reading for the Emperor. Perfect.'

Flavia tightened her grip on her husband's hand. 'What will you do?'

Vespasian got to his feet. 'First of all I'm getting you and the children out of Rome. Cleon!'

'Yes, master,' the steward replied, stepping out onto the terrace.

'Have the mistress and children's things packed up, enough to last for a month, and organise transport for them to my estate at Cosa. They'll leave tonight under cover of darkness.'

'Yes, master.' Cleon bowed and backed away.

'Are you sure that's wise?' Flavia asked. 'I thought you said that you couldn't move us out of the palace without permission from the Emperor.'

'He's at Ostia and by the time he comes back to Rome I'll have that permission.'

'How can you be sure?'

'Because in the struggle between all the would-be masters of Rome I'm backing the winner.'

CHAPTER XVIIII

GAIUS SILIUS STOOD before the Father of the House, his toga draped over his head and the most solemn expression etched on his well-carved features. 'Before you, Jupiter Optimus Maximus, or whatever name by which you wish to be called, I swear, as a consul of Rome, to uphold the laws of the Republic and to give my loyalty to, and protect the life of, the Princeps of Rome, Tiberius Claudius Caesar Augustus Germanicus.'

'That is the first lie of his consulship,' Gaius muttered, looking at the Emperor's empty chair in front of the altar. 'It's a shame that he didn't tell it to Claudius' face.'

'He won't get the chance,' Vespasian asserted, 'he'll be dead in two days.'

'I hope you're right, dear boy, it'll be very awkward for us if he's not.'

Silius finished off the oath and, as the Father of the House performed the purification rites, Vespasian sent up a silent prayer to his guardian god for success in his endeavours over the next night and day and a further appeal to the gods of his household to hold their hands over his family.

As Silius seated himself in the curule chair next to his senior colleague, the younger Lucius Vitellius, the Father of the House removed the fold of his toga from his head and addressed the Senate. 'Conscript Fathers, the Emperor has been unfortunately delayed in Ostia by matters that only he has the wisdom to deal with. He has therefore asked that we conclude business for today now that the new Suffect-Consul is sworn in. He will endeavour to return by the seventh hour tomorrow and asks that you reassemble in this House then to hear his report on the progress of the new port – provided, of course, that the day is deemed auspicious for the business of Rome. This House shall rise.'

Vespasian picked up his folding stool and he and Gaius joined Sabinus in the crush to get out. 'I detect the hand of Pallas behind the House sitting at midday rather than dawn.'

'I hope that I'll have had a message from Pallas by then.'

'You will have and I expect that it'll be me bringing it. How are you doing with gathering support?'

'It's difficult without being able to tell people what they'll be supporting, but I've been spreading Pallas' money about with vague promises of preferment from the Emperor in return for supporting an upcoming motion and then an amendment to a law. Paetus has been very helpful with some of the younger ones and Uncle has done as much as he's dared with his contemporaries.'

'Without exposing my position or giving any views, obviously,' Gaius put in.

'Obviously, Uncle; we wouldn't want it said that you ever had an opinion, would we?'

'I've known people executed for just considering the possibility of having an opinion.'

'I'm sure.'

'However, I am working on Servius Sulpicius Galba to support the motion in order to repay the debt that he owes Pallas for getting him the governorship of Africa so soon after coming back from Germania Superior.'

Sabinus looked suitably impressed. 'A man like that from such an old family and with well-known conservative views would be a great asset. Anyway, brother, I have enough people to be able to speak in favour of whatever it is I'll be proposing.'

'Good. I'll see you later this afternoon at Magnus' place,' Vespasian said as they burst out into the warm morning sun.

'I'll be there.' Sabinus clapped his brother on his shoulder and moved off into the crowd.

'What are you going there for?' Gaius asked.

'We're meeting there before we arrive unannounced at a party.' Vespasian sighed as he saw Corvinus standing waiting for him at the top of the Senate House steps.

'Try not to goad him, dear boy,' Gaius said, watching Corvinus walk towards them.

'Don't worry, Uncle, I don't need to; when this is over he'll be irrelevant to me.'

Corvinus looked down his nose at Vespasian. 'Well, bumpkin?'

'Well what, Corvinus?'

'Silius is now sworn in, so what news of my sister marrying him and what is Narcissus planning to do?'

'No news is the answer to the first question and I don't know is the answer to the second.'

Corvinus' sneer was made even haughtier by an incredulous frown. 'Narcissus is doing nothing?'

'I didn't say that; he just hasn't told me what he is doing. If you want news of when your sister is getting married then I suggest that you ask her. But there is one thing I do know and that is that the way things are playing out your life won't be in Narcissus' hands.'

'What do you mean?'

'I mean that Narcissus won't be able to save you.'

'Who will be able to?' Corvinus asked.

'Me, if I should choose to.'

'You owe me, Vespasian.'

'I could just ignore that fact, Corvinus, and leave you for dead; which after the way you threatened my family I'd be entitled to do. But I won't. Now, as far as I'm concerned you are going to be dead in the next few days, so from now on you are dead to me. If I allow you to keep your life, which I will, then do me the courtesy of behaving in my presence as if you are a dead man. Then we'll be even.'

A thin blue-grey cloud floating far out over the Tyrrhenian Sea bisected, almost perfectly, the sun, blazing deep orange as it fell into the west. With his shadow lost somewhere in the crowds before him, Vespasian made his way along the Alta Semita assailed by the aromas of thousands of evening meals.

Fortified by the knowledge that a successful conclusion to the coming events would see his family safe and considerably wealthier, he walked with a firm step and a straight back. The money he had made from Corvinus, Theron and now Messalina made him wealthy beyond the wine-fuelled imaginings of ninety-nine per cent of the inhabitants of the Empire; it was, however, as nothing compared to many in Rome's élite. But it was a start and as he passed, dressed in an old travelling cloak and rough tunic, unnoticed through the throngs of citizens whose collective wealth was probably a fragment of his own, he felt an aggressive pleasure in what he had achieved for himself by reacting to the will of others. He thanked Caenis, her face burning bright on his inner eye, for her insight into the accumulation of wealth and the sense of power and enjoyment it gave to be active in its pursuit. So much for the high ideals of selfless service to Rome that he had espoused when he had first entered the city with his father almost twenty-three years before.

'Are you deep in thought or just trying to pass a reluctant turd?' a voice asked.

'What?' Vespasian saw Magnus standing in front of him.

'Thinking hard or having a hard shit? Which was it, because it was taking all your concentration and you nearly walked straight past the tavern.'

'Thinking, obviously!' Vespasian replied with a little more terseness than he had intended. 'Where's Sabinus?'

'He's with the rest of the lads just outside the Porta Collina checking the cart and the horses. I was just waiting for you.'

'Well, I'm here so let's go.'

'Perhaps you should have a shit first; it might improve your mood.'

'I'm sorry, Magnus.'

'Well, what's on your mind? It must be pretty weighty.'

Vespasian took a deep breath as they headed towards the Porta Collina, just two hundred paces distant. 'I've finally realised that after all this time of thinking that I'm serving Rome, I'm not; I've just been serving one or other of Rome's masters or mistresses. No one ever does anything out of altruism in order to benefit the public good. On the contrary, everything that I've ever been involved in since arriving in the city has been solely for an individual's personal gain. I very rarely profit from it directly and Rome certainly never does – or at least the idealistic view that I had of Rome because that Rome doesn't exist, it never really did. All Rome is really is the pole over which the powerful fight to place their own personal Eagle upon, in order to rally support for themselves in the name of the people. So in the end what difference does it make who holds the power? Claudius, Caligula, Tiberius, Narcissus, Pallas, Sejanus, Antonia, Macro, Messalina, whoever, they're all the same; some just smell nicer than others. But none of them do anything for Rome other than make sure the people are fed and entertained so that they don't notice the misery in which most of them live whilst the powerful fill their coffers with what should be public money.'

'There you go, sir; how many times have I tried to point that out to you? You with your high ideals, playing at politics, as if it really mattered, when you know that you can never rise to the top because you come from the wrong family. I remember you saying that your grandmother warned you about it.'

'Yes, and I thought that meant there was a straight choice between staying on my estates for the rest of my life or accepting Rome how it is and understanding that although I could never hope to rise to the very top I could bring honour to my family by my service. I was so wrong.'

Magnus barged an importunate urchin off the pavement, ignoring his shrill protests. 'You shouldn't do anything that doesn't benefit yourself; however small it may be you should always make a profit or pay off a favour in everything you do.'

'Exactly. I've just come to realise the absolute truth in that and it's made me feel a lot better. I used to think Rome was great and glorious; well, that was just the naïve idealism of youth. It's no more than an arena in which wild animals tear each other apart for the right to chew on the bone. I've had my first few gnaws on that bone and they tasted good. From now on I'll be supporting whoever can help me get my teeth back into it again. It makes no difference who they are or what they profess to believe in because all they want is what I want.'

'More bone?'

Vespasian grinned. 'A lot more bone. And you? Do you get your bone?'

'Regularly. But then I've never done anything that hasn't involved the prospect of bone.'

'Then why are you helping me tonight?'

'Only a beast can't wait for its bone, if you take my meaning?'

Vespasian slapped Magnus on the back. 'I do and I can see that I'm going to be very busy doing you favours when I'm consul.'

'Sabinus spent much of his term making sure that I had adequate bone; I don't see why you should be any different.'

'I'm sure I won't be; I'll never be free from obligation.'

'Talking of which, my lads who've been keeping an eye on those bearded bastards watching your and Sabinus' houses say that they never report to anyone; no one comes near them and they don't go anywhere other than back to a filthy room to eat and sleep.'

'So if they're not working for anyone, why are they taking an interest in Sabinus and me?'

'I've got no idea, but they stopped watching your house yesterday and are now just concentrating on Sabinus; perhaps he's got a bone of theirs.'

'Then I think that it's time to bring one in for that little hearth-side chat that you so kindly offered to have with them.'

'My thoughts exactly.' Magnus gave a cheery wave to the two Urban Cohort guards on the gate as they passed through. 'Evening, lads.'

''Right, Magnus.'

Vespasian walked through the gate to see Sabinus with Marius, Sextus and three more of Magnus' brethren waiting with a covered cart, with Marius at the reins, pulled by two mules and with four saddled horses attached to it by traces.

'Ready, brother,' Sabinus asked.

'Readier than I've ever been.'

'Good; up and at them.'

*

Points of flickering light from torches and blazing sconces delin-
eated and filled in the shape of the Gardens of Lucullus as if it
were a rectangular constellation consisting of countless stars in
an otherwise sparsely populated firmament. The noise of revelry
drifted down on the light breeze as Vespasian and his party made
their way in the dim light of a newly risen quarter moon along a
tomb-lined narrow lane, around the base of the Pincian Hill,
approaching the gardens from the east. Slow-beating drums
supported by lyres and flutes accompanied singing, both tuneful
and discordant, which was regularly drowned by bursts of
raucous, alcohol-fuelled laughter, squeals of pleasure, jovial yelps
of mock indignation, rising and falling wails and shrieks of
ecstasy. A soundscape of carnal gratification.

Passing the occasional building, Vespasian led the group to
within shouting distance of the open gates at the centre of the
two hundred-pace-long whitewashed wall, grey with the night,
ranging along the foot of the hill; a couple of guards leant against
the gateposts in pools of light cast from the torches burning to
either side. He nodded to Marius who pulled the cart out of the
lane and into the precinct of the Temple of Flora so it was hidden
from view from the gate.

'I don't know how long we'll be, Marius,' Vespasian said. 'Just
keep your eyes and ears open; you and Sextus must come at the
speed of Mercury as we appear through the gates.'

'Right you are, sir. Do you want us to do anything about the
guards?'

'No, they're there to stop unwanted people getting in, not out;
we'll manage them all right.'

'Come at the speed of Mercury,' Sextus ruminated aloud, as
ever slowly digesting his orders, 'as they appear through the gates.'

Magnus took a sack from the back of the wagon and hefted it
at one of the brothers, who sported a ragged scar along the left
side of his jaw that cut through his Greek-style beard. 'You keep
the ropes, Cassandros; Caeso and Tigran, get the two ladders out
of the wagon.'

Once the brothers, a young lad and a bearded, trouser-
wearing easterner, had done as they had been told, Vespasian

and Sabinus pulled up their hoods, flitted across the lane and began to make their way, over rough ground, up the hill at an angle heading for the three hundred and fifty-pace-long ascending wall. Magnus and his brethren followed.

Coming to the approximate middle of it he halted. 'Up you go, Tigran, and keep low.'

The ladder fell a couple of feet short of the wall's full height, but Tigran managed to get astride of its terracotta-tiled summit, lying along its length, and within a few moments had placed the second ladder on the other side and disappeared from view. Vespasian went next and quickly found himself in an aquatic area of the gardens scattered with ponds. Gravel paths wound between them upon which slept scores of wildfowl with their heads tucked under their wings to shield their eyes from the torchlight. Fewer people within the gardens were singing now; the music played on but could barely be heard over the growing cacophony of pleasure.

Within a hundred heartbeats they were all over the wall with Magnus bringing up the rear and pulling up the outside ladder after him.

'Have the lads bring the ladders with us,' Vespasian whispered in reply to Magnus' questioning look, 'just in case the gate is not an option after all.' With that he turned and began to make his way up towards the villa, keeping as far as possible to the shadows, and following the intensifying sound of hedonists at play.

Passing through a bed planted with shrubs trained together into the shape of the sphinx, Vespasian came to a ten-foot-high miniature pyramid and halted suddenly at the sound of a loud, grating exhalation of breath. Raising his hand to stop his companions he crept forward along the pyramid as the breath was drawn in with a long rumbling snore. Vespasian eased his head around the far corner of the pyramid to see a small figure lying on his back, dressed in a Thracian cap and a very short tunic from under which protruded, vertically, an artificial phallus almost as tall as the wearer; a spilled cup lay by his side.

Magnus moved up next to him. 'What is it?'

'Judging by the size of the false penis it's a dwarf dressed as Priapus.'

'He seems to have overindulged somewhat in the juice of Bacchus as any self-respecting Priapus ought to.' Magnus pulled a knife from his belt. 'Let's find out if it's affected his memory.' He eased around the corner of the pyramid and, bending over, clamped his hand over the sleeping dwarf's mouth whilst holding the blade in front of his eyes, which snapped open in alarm; very quickly they registered terror.

Vespasian knelt down, grasping the over-sized phallus and leaning on it so that its base pushed into the flesh and blood original. 'Yes or no: has there been a wedding here this evening?'

The dwarf's eyes now registered pain as he looked from Magnus' blade to Vespasian and back; he nodded.

'Messalina and Silius?'

The dwarf looked confused.

Vespasian eased the pressure on the phallus and then jammed it back into the dwarf's genitals. 'Do you know who was married?'

The dwarf exhaled in pain through his nose, shooting a globule of mucus over Magnus' hand, and shook his head with his eyes squeezed shut.

'Nice!' Magnus hissed.

'Send him back to sleep, Magnus; he's no good to us. He's just a slave who's got no idea what's going on.'

Magnus pulled the dwarf's head up and cracked it back down onto the pyramid, knocking him out cold, and then wiped the mucus from his hand on the miniature Priapus' hair.

Vespasian moved on across another pathway to an area of lawn bordering the apricot orchard, strewn with statues of Gauls in defeat. Creeping by a wounded warrior, naked save for a neck torc, pierced in the chest and sitting on the ground clutching his bleeding thigh, Vespasian darted across the lawn and took cover behind a substantial pedestal. He looked up to see a statue of a Gaul standing proud, and looking over his shoulder whilst supporting the slumped body of his dying wife and plunging his sword vertically down past his collarbone and on into his heart. Vespasian could not help but contrast the honour of the Celtic warrior with the debauchery of the power that had defeated him. What would Caratacus make of Messalina's behaviour? The answer was obvious.

The orgiastic uproar was close now; he edged his head around the pedestal and peered through the apricots towards the villa at the heart of the gardens.

Vespasian drew breath.

He had witnessed some of the worst of Caligula's sexual excesses as the libidinous young Emperor had publicly displayed his sister, Drusilla, in obscene acts with multiple partners, but what he beheld now took wild abandonment a stage further. Knot after knot of entwined bodies in various states of undress, some in couples but most in groups, heaved and rubbed against each other; on couches and tables, balanced on or over the balustrade surrounding the terrace and spread up and down the steps to it as well as in large tubs filled with freshly harvested grapes that turned skin red. Men on women, boys or other men; women, draped in animal skins, with phalluses strapped to them using other women, men or youths; all both gave and took as fancy would have it as the sexual free-for-all raged. In amongst the writhing mass, drinkers tottered, raising their cups with wine sloshing over the rims, toasting Bacchus, Priapus, Venus or just the act of copulation itself as musicians strummed, blew and beat their instruments in an improvisation that pulsed with the rhythm of sex. A couple of dwarves dressed as satyrs sporting goat-like phalluses cavorted and danced to the sound, adding to it with shrill sequences from pan pipes.

Silent around the edge of the terrace, naked slaves, both male and female, stood holding torches to illuminate the carnality. With blank expressions they watched their masters, the élite of Rome, pay homage to the gods of excess; uncomplaining if bent over and taken against their will or forced to kneel and languish before one of their betters, they endured the decadence of the race that had conquered their peoples.

Naked at the centre of it all, astride a seated man, with her back towards him as she rode his lap as if galloping a stallion, Messalina howled with a pleasure so intense as to be just a fraction away from agony. Her hair had fallen loose and swung in great sweeps as she tossed her head back and forth, back and forth; then it arced back, spraying droplets of sweat glowing golden in the torchlight. Her spine arched and her face turned to the sky and she released a cry to the heavens so piercing that those around her paused in their exertions and turned to see Messalina juddering, her whole body in spasm; and then the cry broke and the muscles in her back released, sending her falling forward to slump exhausted on her partner's knees and revealing Silius' exultant face and the ivy crown set on his head.

'Well, that would seem to make their intentions clear,' Sabinus observed, as he and Magnus joined Vespasian behind the pedestal.

Magnus stared at the scene, his eye agog. 'They certainly know how to enjoy themselves.'

The revellers burst into cheering as Silius rose to his feet with Messalina still hanging off him, her chest heaving as she sucked in huge gulps of air. Wearing only his ivy garland and a pair of high boots, he capered with one arm waving free whilst the other held Messalina in place, her fingers trailing the ground, as she swayed to and fro with his movements, like a rag doll.

Vespasian studied the faces that he could see and recognised many of them: senators, equestrians, actors and Praetorian Guardsmen along with rich matrons – mostly unaccompanied by their husbands – courtesans and, most scandalously, unmarried daughters of the élite. 'Somehow we've got to get a couple of them away from here without anyone noticing.'

'I don't think that'll be a problem,' Magnus said, shaking his head in awe. 'If I was in the middle of all that I reckon that you could slit my partner's throat and I'd carry on tupping her without a care until she was cold, and probably after that too.'

'Thank you for that image.' Vespasian pressed closer to the pedestal as a young man staggered down the steps supported by a couple of equally tipsy women, all singing a paean to Bacchus and covered in the juice of red grapes. Behind them, Messalina eased herself off Silius and picked up a *thyrsus*, a staff of giant fennel, wound in ivy and topped with a bulbous pine cone.

Brandishing this symbol of fertility in one hand and grasping Silius' still erect penis with the other she looked about in triumph. 'I am Gaia to his Gaius; with the gods' help, tonight I have conceived and will bear the child of my new husband.'

Silius rolled his head, bellowing incoherently, and her guests roared their approval of this piece of news as the young man reached the first of the apricot trees and began to climb it, leaving his companions leaning against its trunk, giggling and rubbing the sticky juice of Bacchus' fruit into each other's bodies.

'What do you see, Vettius?' one of the women called, glancing up in the direction of the man's buttocks.

'I see all things, Cleopatra; but most clearly, to the southwest, I see a great storm coming to hit Ostia. The Emperor is in its path.'

'Pray that it doesn't pass over Ostia and come to strike us.'

'We'll have plenty of warning if—' With a loud crack followed by the rustle of leaves accompanied by a brief yell, Vettius plummeted to the ground, landing on his shoulders and cracking his head on a tree root; he made a weak effort to rise before slumping back to lie motionless.

Cleopatra giggled at the sight before turning her attention back to her companion and, with feline intensity, began licking the sticky juice from her skin.

'Come on.' Vespasian moved forward. 'These two will be perfect. Walk towards them as if we've an absolute right to be here.' He ambled into the orchard, with a roll to his gait, as if he had been in lengthy commune with Bacchus; Magnus and Sabinus followed, imitating his manner.

Beyond the orchard on the terrace the revellers had returned their concentration to the pursuit of blind ecstasy, as Messalina took to a tub of pounded grapes accompanied by two youths whilst Silius strutted back and forth penetrating, briefly, any orifice pointing in his direction.

Passing the unconscious body of Vettius, Vespasian paused, swaying slightly, and focused on Cleopatra and her very good friend just ten paces away; both were entirely in the thrall of one another's juice-stained breasts. Looking back at Magnus and

Sabinus, he nodded and walked forward at a slow pace so as not to attract undue attention. With just three paces to his quarry he pounced forward and, throwing his arms around both of the women, hauled them to the ground as they squealed with a mixture of fright and delight.

'Shut them up and drag them away,' Vespasian hissed.

Magnus showed the women his knife; they went limp, sealed their lips and allowed themselves to be manhandled back to the lawn where Magnus' brethren waited. It took just a few moments for Cassandros and Tigran to secure their wrists behind their backs whilst Caeso gagged them.

'Don't struggle, don't slow us down and you won't be hurt,' Vespasian promised, trying to ignore the well-shaped female forms sheened with a glaze of drying nectar.

'Cleopatra! Calpurnia!' a voice called from behind them.

Vespasian turned to see the silhouetted figure of Vettius stumbling to his feet. 'Quick! Go, Magnus. Sabinus, take that one.' He grabbed Cleopatra by the arm and led her off at a jog following Magnus and his lads.

'Cleopatra! Calpurnia!'

Keeping low and moving as fast as he dared with the bound women, Vespasian passed behind the pedestal of the warrior committing suicide and then on to the dying Gaul.

'Cleopatra! Calpurnia? Calpurnia? Hey!'

Vespasian glanced back to see Vettius at the edge of the apricot grove waving his arms; for a moment their eyes met and then the dying Gaul temporarily obscured him from view.

'Hey! Come back!'

Vespasian sped on with Cleopatra by his side, struggling to keep her feet; in front of him Sabinus was having the same trouble with Calpurnia. With a second quick glance back, as they reached the pyramid, he saw Vettius emerge from the orchard and shout before turning and racing away back towards the festivities. 'Shit! He'll raise the alarm. Magnus, we need to carry them.'

'My pleasure. Tigran, take the other one,' Magnus said as he turned, lowered his shoulder and levered Cleopatra onto it. He took a firm grip of a buttock and then sped off past the sphinx-like shrubbery.

Vespasian raced ahead, using his memory from the previous visits to navigate the quickest route down to the gates without using the serpentine path. Leaping over low, ornamental hedges, skirting pools and fountains, scattering deer and fowl, crunching across gravel paths and crashing through carefully laid out flowerbeds, they hurtled downhill through the different themed sections with a complete disregard for the beauty of the gardens. Behind them, the revelry had broken up and the sounds of pleasure and music had been replaced by the clamour of pursuit; calls and shouts rang through the night adding urgency to their flight.

Bursting through a wall of rhododendron bushes, Vespasian finally saw the exit, just thirty paces away, at the same time as the guards saw the cause of the commotion up the hill; with a quick glance to one another they heaved the grille-gates closed and turned the key in the lock as Vespasian came to a skidding halt on the gravel path. 'Caeso! Get a ladder up the wall.'

Caeso ran on to a section of wall a little distance to the left of the gates; leaning the ladder against it, he climbed swiftly, peered over the top and then hastily ducked back down as a fist-sized stone flew over his head.

Looking through the gate, Vespasian could see only one of the guards, now armed with a sword. 'Cassandros, take the other ladder to the right.'

As Cassandros moved off, the guard tracked him, leaving the gate unattended but locked firm. Sabinus crashed a foot against it but it barely shook.

'They could keep us pinned here for a while,' Magnus puffed, laying down his burden without any ceremony, 'and I don't reckon that we've got anywhere near that amount of time.' He pointed up the hill; the fluorescence of massed torches moved through the gardens at speed but at an angle.

'They're using the path; that gives us a bit of time,' Vespasian said as Cassandros ascended his ladder. With a cry the Greek fell back, clutching the left side of his face as a stone cracked off him.

A shout of triumph came from the other side of the wall. Sabinus gave the ironwork another resounding blow with the sole of his sandal with Tigran adding his weight to it.

'This won't move,' Sabinus shouted, retreating as the first guard returned and grinned mirthlessly whilst pointing up the hill.

'Now, Caeso!' Vespasian called, looking back to see the torch-light less than a hundred paces away.

The crossroads brother leapt up the ladder and with a fluid rolling motion hitched his legs over the summit of the wall and jumped down the other side. The guard reacted to the sound and raced back. Hollow impacts – fists on flesh – and then iron striking brick accompanied by the strained grunts and snorts of combat ensued as Cassandros picked himself up and Sabinus, Vespasian, Magnus and Tigran all lent every ounce of their strength to the gate; still it did not move. A cry of pain followed by the rattle of breath escaping a dying body added urgency to their endeavours; behind, the cries of pursuit were growing with every corner of the snaking path rounded.

Cassandros attempted a second ascent and again was forced back by another well-aimed stone as the first guard reappeared, blood smearing his sword arm, vicious pleasure on his face and menace in his eyes; he thrust his gore-slick blade through the gate forcing Vespasian and his companions to back off. 'Reckon you're trapped,' he gloated, withdrawing his sword. 'Should be interesting.' His eyes opened wide, his back arched and his body shuddered as he exhaled violently; his left hand reached out for the gate but never made it as his hair was pulled back and a knife exploded out of his mouth like a pointed iron tongue spitting blood. Sextus looked over the dying guard's shoulder; beyond, Marius drew up in the wagon with the horses attached.

'The key's on his belt; unlock the gate, fast, Sextus,' Vespasian urged as Magnus and Cassandros ran back to retrieve the two women. Sextus grinned and then with surprising speed spun his huge frame, side-stepping a thrusting blade, and lashed out with a massive fist, planting it squarely in the second guard's face; the nose disintegrated into a pulped mush as the man arced back, his legs flying up, and he dropped to the earth as if felled by a ballista shot.

Sextus retrieved the key hanging from the first guard's belt and inserted it in the lock; it held fast.

'Turn it the other way,' Vespasian bellowed in exasperation, looking over his shoulder. Up the hill a posse of naked men came around the last corner of the path, less than fifty paces away. With a roar they burst into a sprint as Magnus and Cassandros made it back to the gate.

The lock clicked and the gates swung open. Vespasian and his companions piled through, the women rocking like sacks on Magnus' and Cassandros' shoulders; the wagon was open and they were thrown inside as Vespasian, Sabinus and Tigran unhitched the horses and swung themselves up, urging them forward. Magnus and Cassandros followed their erstwhile burdens into the wagon and Sextus jumped up next to Marius.

The wagon accelerated away leaving a score of naked men standing in the torchlight under the gates of the Gardens of Lucullus.

CHAPTER XX

'WHY WAS I not warned of this in advance?' Narcissus' voice was hushed and it rasped in his throat giving it the sibilant quality of a snake about to strike. 'Why am I woken in the middle of the night to be told that the Empress has married the new Suffect-Consul and there are two whores covered in coagulated grape juice who can testify to the Emperor that he is divorced and that his ex-wife is going to replace him with a man who wasn't even a senator this time two years ago?' His eyes ranged over Vespasian and Pallas, both seated opposite him. 'Why – didn't – Flavia – warn me?' His fists crashed down onto the desk and the hollow thump echoed around the sparsely furnished, newly built room; scrolls and wax tablets jumped and an inkpot slopped a portion of its contents, rocking precariously before returning to the upright position.

Vespasian held Narcissus' malignant glare, staying still and straight-backed in his chair. Upon arrival at the new port soon after midnight he had been warned by Pallas of Narcissus' likely reaction, and knew how to counter it. In fact, he was going to enjoy doing so now that he saw the normally unruffled imperial secretary in such a state of agitation. 'She didn't have time to because she didn't know; no one in Messalina's circle knew apart from her and Silius. You only know now because of Flavia; she heard about the wedding this afternoon and came to me. There wasn't any time to come down here and ask for instructions so I just did what I thought best and seized two people who could bear witness to the fact. If it wasn't for Flavia, Narcissus, you wouldn't have heard about this until the Emperor walked into the Senate at midday tomorrow to find himself without a wife and with a serious rival. Because of Flavia, you've got a little time to take action.'

This time Narcissus' palms slammed down. 'I don't want a *little* time; I want fair warning!'

Pallas leant forward, his face betraying a rare emotion: urgent worry, which Vespasian knew to be false. 'Dear colleague, this is getting us nowhere. We must react to the situation we have rather than regret what we don't have.'

Narcissus took in a great gulp of air and shook his head; his weighty earrings rocked on his lobes catching the lamplight and his be-ringed hands combed through his hair, pulling back his head.

'Vespasian has done the best that he could do in the circumstances,' Pallas continued once he had regained Narcissus' attention. 'He's left his brother, who's loyal to us, in Rome to forestall any attempt to convene the Senate earlier than planned tomorrow and he's brought two witnesses, both of whom, by chance, the Emperor knows, having made use of their services himself on a regular basis. We can use them to persuade Claudius, finally, of Messalina's debauchery and get him to order her execution.'

'But what if the Senate and the Guard take her side? She's married to a consul!'

'So it would seem; but is she really?'

Claudius gibbered to himself, wringing his hands and drooling copious amounts of saliva down his chin and onto his night-robe as he sat on the edge of his bed looking at the two naked whores kneeling before him; each grasped a shaking, imperial leg in supplication.

'We did not know, Princeps,' Calpurnia pleaded, 'she told us that you had divorced her.'

Claudius looked up at Narcissus. 'D-d-d-did I d-divorce her?'

'Of course not, Princeps; although I have hinted many times that you should.'

'Hinted?' Claudius' legs jerked, kicking away the supplicants. 'Why should you hint such a thing when my Messalina is a perfect wife?'

Narcissus cleared his throat. 'As you know, there have been rumours—'

'Rumours? But none of them were true; M-M-Messalina told me so herself.'

Vespasian felt Pallas' hand touch his elbow; he stepped forward. 'But this is not a rumour, Princeps; I saw the nuptial feast and these women witnessed the marriage as they have already sworn to you. Look at them, naked and sticky with the juice of Bacchus; they have told you what the feast was like. I saw Messalina copulate with Silius and then declare that she was Gaia to his Gaius.'

Claudius shook his head, trailing mucus from his nose. 'I must see her face before I believe this; I promised that to my little bird.'

'No, Princeps,' Narcissus urged, 'she would gull you again as she has all of us for so many years. It is your duty to act and it is ours to keep you safe.' He brandished a scroll at the Emperor. 'You must order her execution.'

Claudius' hands twisted around each other, entangling the fingers. 'But I can't order the death of the mother of my children.'

'You must, Claudius! Don't you understand? Is it so difficult to comprehend the danger that you're in? That all of us are in. Messalina is going to attempt to set herself and her new husband up as regents for Britannicus and that leaves no place for you; you are a dead man in her plans. Whatever happens now your children will lose one parent.' Narcissus walked up close to the Emperor, closer than deference to his position should allow. 'Tell me, Claudius, do you want to deprive them of a mother or a father? Because if it's the latter you might just as well fall on your sword now and we'll all follow your example. Or you can start acting like an emperor and order the execution of someone who threatens your position. Which is it to be?'

Claudius seemed not to notice the lack of respect his freedman was showing him but, instead, took his hand and, looking up into Narcissus' face, burst into fits of ragged, choking sobs; tears now ran from his eyes as freely as the mucus from his nostrils and the saliva from his mouth. Narcissus released the Emperor's hand and stepped back, his face working hard to conceal the disgust that Vespasian knew he must feel at such a pathetic sight.

'I, I, I ...' Claudius began and then trailed off. 'I just want to be emperor.' His voice was barely audible. He looked with pleading eyes at his chief freedman. 'Am I still emperor, Narcissus?'

'You are, Princeps; and you will remain so if you act like one.'

'Are you sure?'

'Yes! Now sign that bitch's death warrant.' He thrust the scroll in Claudius' face.

Vespasian sensed that it was as much as Narcissus could do to restrain himself from striking the quivering wreck of a man.

Claudius eased the scroll away. 'All right, I will.'

Narcissus heaved a sigh of relief.

'But not here,' Claudius continued, pushing himself up from the bed. 'I shall do it in Rome.'

'But why wait, Princeps?'

'I want to be taken to the Praetorian camp; I want them to watch me sign it so that they know the sorrow that it causes me but realise that I have no choice.'

'But, Princeps—'

Claudius raised his hand. 'No, Narcissus; you have already overstepped the mark, we'll have no more. I will sign it there.' He looked down at the two whores, suddenly distracted. 'We'll leave as soon as I've ... er ... got over the shock of the situation.'

'Yes, Princeps.'

Pallas stepped forward, unrolling a parchment upon which was written out an Imperial Decree. 'Princeps, as you are aware there are two problems in this issue: the first one you have just dealt with in a forthright manner; may I suggest you deal with the second in the same vein? The problem of Silius being consul can, I believe, be solved by you signing this Imperial Decree, now. Vespasian will deliver it to his brother, who, as an ex-consul, has the right to speak first in a session; and with a decree from you in his hand, no one will gainsay him.'

Claudius took the scroll and read it, his mouth moving silently with the words. After a short while his slimed face broke into a smile. 'Yes, yes; it's what I wanted anyway.' He took it to his desk, signed it and put his seal to the signature before handing it back to Pallas. 'Thank you, Pallas.'

Pallas added a handwritten note before rolling up the decree and passing it to Vespasian. 'Get this to Sabinus, watch the session and then come and report to us, on the road between here and Rome, as soon as the second vote has been taken.'

'The second vote? What'll that be?'

'Immensely satisfying.'

Vespasian found Sabinus waiting on the steps of the Senate House with Gaius. Sweat ran freely down Vespasian's face, for he had walked as fast as dignity would allow, with Magnus, Cassandros and Tigran clearing the way for him, from the Porta Ostiensis where they had left Sextus and Marius in charge of their horses. 'Wait for me here, Magnus.'

'Well?' Sabinus asked as Vespasian mounted the steps.

Vespasian handed him the Imperial Decree. 'Here it is; read it out before any other business is discussed. There's also a note in there for you.'

Sabinus unrolled the scroll, perused it quickly and then looked at Pallas' note; a broad smile of satisfaction crept over his face. 'It would seem that I'm not only paying off my debt but I am also to do Pallas a favour for which he will reward me handsomely.'

'What with, dear boy?' Gaius asked, interested, as always, in any patronage offered the family.

'Moesia.'

'A province with two legions! That shows great favour.'

'With the added financial incentive of Macedonia and Thracia.'

Gaius rubbed his hands together. 'That's enough to secure your finances for a long time.'

'As well as further my military ambitions.' Still beaming, Sabinus turned and made his way up the steps.

'What has he to do?' Gaius asked Vespasian as they followed.

'I don't know, Uncle; but if Pallas has offered him so much it must involve being conspicuous.'

'I hope that's not the case, dear boy.' Gaius grimaced. 'Nothing but the animosity and jealousy of others ever came from being conspicuous.'

Gaius Silius turned from the altar and presented the assembled Senate with the unblemished livers of two geese; gifts to Rome's guardian god. 'Jupiter Optimus Maximus favours us; the day is auspicious for the business of the city.'

The senators sat down on their folding stools, murmuring gratitude to the Junior Consul for conducting the sacrifice as he threw the livers into the altar's fire and wiped his hands.

'He's got no idea just how auspicious it really is,' Sabinus whispered, the broad grin still on his face.

Silius walked forward to his curule chair and sat with exaggerated dignity.

The Senior Consul, Lucius Vitellius the younger, waited for him to finally settle. 'Gaius Silius wishes to address the house.'

'My thanks, colleague. Conscript Fathers, I appear before you for the first time as consul since being inaugurated yesterday to that most prestigious position. However, since my induction—'

'Senior Consul,' Sabinus interrupted, standing and brandishing the scroll, 'I have here an Imperial Decree that I've been charged by the Emperor to read to you in his regrettable absence.'

The Senior Consul did not hide his puzzlement. 'Why has it been given to you to read out and not sent to the Consuls or the Father of the House?'

'It's not my place to question the Emperor's motives. All I know is that he has entrusted this task to me as a man of consular rank.'

'Then the ex-Consul should read it to us.'

Sabinus stepped out into the middle of the floor, holding the decree in both hands. '"I, Tiberius Claudius Caesar Augustus Germanicus, out of respect for the ways of our ancestors do decree that from this day on, the day before the calends of October in the year beginning with the Consuls Aulus Vitellius Veteris and Lucius Vipstanus Messalla Poplicola, that all consuls at their inauguration should swear the ancient oath that they shall always strive to prevent the return of the King." Would the Senate now vote to ratify this law?'

The Senior Consul hastily called for a vote on this latest, seemingly innocuous, piece of legal pedantry; it was passed unanimously.

Sabinus looked at Silius once the vote had passed; he remained unmoved by the development. 'It would seem, Conscript Fathers, that this was made law by our learned Emperor the day before Gaius Silius took his oath, therefore the oath he took was not complete.' Sabinus walked forward and handed the decree to the Senior Consul.

Lucius Vitellius glanced at the seal and date and then at his junior colleague next to him. 'I agree; it looks as if you have not completed your oath, Silius.'

'A formality,' Silius replied, waving a dismissive hand, smiling imperiously and getting to his feet. 'I shall swear the line immediately.'

'Would that it were so simple,' Sabinus said as Silius headed for the altar, 'but as we all know if there is a fault in any ceremony then it is void and the whole process has to start again from the beginning. The fact that you were willing to swear the extra line just now means that you acknowledge that your oath isn't complete, does it not, Silius?'

Silius turned, his face betraying the first vestiges of concern. 'What of it? We shall just start the inauguration again now.'

'Of course we will; but first of all the correct sacrifices have to be made so that we know whether the day is auspicious.'

'I've just pronounced it auspicious.'

'You did, but only a consul can do that and you are not yet a consul.'

The full implication of this hit Gaius Silius and his handsome face froze as Sabinus tilted his head and looked at him with raised eyebrows and an innocent expression.

'It would seem that the party that you co-hosted last night in the Gardens of Lucullus to celebrate your inauguration was a bit previous, was it not? It was to celebrate your inauguration, was it not?'

'I ... er ... yes, of course it was.'

Sabinus looked around the house for senators he had seen the previous evening. 'Juncus Vergilianus, you were there, I know; was it a party to celebrate Silius' consulship, or non-consulship as it plainly is now?'

'As far as I was aware,' Virgilianus replied hesitantly.

'As far as you were aware? Hmm. What about you, Plautius Lateranus? Was it anything more than what Silius says it was? Perhaps your enthusiastic participation was mainly because you were still celebrating your uncle's Ovation fifteen months later?'

Lateranus squirmed in his seat but said nothing.

Sabinus rounded on an effete young man. 'And you, Suillius Caesoninus? What were you aware of whilst you spent the evening on your knees either facing – as it were – your partners or backing onto them? No, there is no need to answer as I'm sure that you had absolutely no idea what was going on.' Sabinus raised his arm and pointed at a young senator. 'But you, Vettius Valens, you knew exactly what the party was because I heard you when you climbed that apricot tree; I heard you say that there was a storm coming that would strike the Emperor. I heard you say that as we snatched the two whores that you were with; yes, Vettius, we took Cleopatra and Calpurnia to the Emperor. They told him what the celebration was really for, Vettius, what do you think they said?'

Vettius looked in panic at Silius who slumped in his chair, not meeting his eyes.

'Admitting the truth now, Vettius, might help you later. What did the whores say?'

Vettius hung his head and then drew a breath. 'They told the Emperor that the party was to celebrate the marriage of Silius to Messalina.'

Silence was complete as if the senators hearing this for the first time were straining their ears in an effort to perceive a different answer: one that they could believe. But it never came and gradually it dawned on the senators that what Vettius had said was, indeed, the truth.

A chill ran through their ranks.

The Senior Consul had visibly paled as he addressed his ex-colleague. 'You've married the Empress! To what purpose? To live privately with her or … ?' The last question was left unspoken but all knew its content.

Silius drew himself up to answer but Sabinus interjected. 'There is no question of Messalina living privately, is there, Silius? No, Conscript Fathers, this is a direct challenge to the Emperor's position; in her arrogance she thought that she could force you to choose between the rightful successor to Augustus and her. Yes, her; not this well-sculpted, prize figure of Roman manhood that we see before us. He was just to be her route to ultimate power. You see, Silius, the gods bless very few with both beauty and brains and unfortunately for you, you're not one of them; you would have been dead the moment that you stepped down from the consulship having got Messalina what she wanted.'

Vespasian enjoyed the look on Silius' face as the truth of Sabinus' words sank in.

Sabinus, too, was evidently enjoying himself. 'This puppet, Conscript Fathers, was about to give a speech before I took the floor. Would you like to summarise for the House what you were going to say, Silius, or would you prefer that I do it?'

Silius jumped to his feet. 'You have no idea what I planned to say.'

'Try me.'

'I was going to say that I propose that in future all senatorial documents should be written incorporating the three new letters that the Emperor wishes to add to the alphabet.'

Sabinus smiled with exaggerated patience. 'No, Silius, that's a lie.' He looked at Pallas' handwritten note. 'You were going to inform the Senate that you were now the husband of the Empress and as consul you would call for a vote to depose the Emperor and appoint Messalina as regent to his son Britannicus in his place. You were going to reassure the Conscript Fathers that they need fear nothing from the Guard as the most senior officers had been bought and then you were going to produce a list; where is that list, Silius?'

Silius' right hand moved involuntarily a fraction towards the fold in his toga. 'What list?'

'The list of every man here who has, in the past, slept with your new wife. But no matter.' Sabinus turned to address the whole Senate. 'Conscript Fathers, with this list he was going to blackmail you. Not to be too indelicate, I believe that the majority of you would not enjoy the prospect of that list ending up in the Emperor's hands if he were to be finally persuaded of Messalina's infidelity.' Again he glanced at Pallas' note. 'However, I am instructed to offer you this: there will be an amnesty for everyone who has defiled the Emperor's bed now that Messalina has seen fit to officially leave it. A small fee will be charged for this, negotiable through me on a case by case basis.'

At that, Vettius Valens leapt to his feet and sprinted from the chamber.

'Let him go; Messalina will hear the news soon enough anyway. Conscript Fathers, I move that rather than restart Silius' inauguration we should take advantage of his non-consular status and vote on whether or not he should be escorted by me to the Praetorian camp to await the Emperor's judgement. Who would prefer to debate that motion? Or perhaps you would all prefer to carry on with the ceremony, vote to depose Claudius – trusting that the Guard have no objections – and then have Messalina, whose character is no secret, rule Rome as regent to a child who won't achieve manhood for seven years, by which time her claws will be in all of us?' Sabinus looked up and down the lines of Rome's élite, before adding, 'Those of us still left alive, that is.'

Sabinus walked back to his seat as the Senate erupted in competitive indignation at the treatment of their beloved Emperor by his harpy of a wife and a nonentity, a man who had only just been raised to the Senate and had never even served as a quaestor, let alone consul. Silius stood, watching them in silence as a condemned man would watch the approach of his executioner.

'That's got them going,' Gaius observed as Sabinus sat back down. 'It's also made you very conspicuous, dear boy, especially if you're going to be naming the amount that each man has to pay for an amnesty.'

Sabinus smiled as Lucius Vitellius finally managed to get himself heard and seconded the motion. 'They'll have forgotten about it by the time I'm back in Rome.'

'I wouldn't count on it, brother,' Vespasian warned, 'three years is not such a long time.'

Sabinus waved Pallas' note. 'Which is why I've been guaranteed at least seven in Moesia.'

Without waiting for anyone to be rash enough to oppose the motion, the Senior Consul called upon the House to divide. But there was no division; unanimously, the Senate voted to send Gaius Silius to Claudius so that the Emperor, whom he, along with most of the men who had condemned him, had cuckolded, could decide his fate.

Rumour of Messalina's marriage had spread throughout the city as senators passed on the news to clients awaiting them outside the Curia and they in turn informed their hangers-on. Before Vespasian and Magnus had returned to the Porta Ostiensis it was already being discussed in the Fora and the baths; in markets and over the counters of shops and taverns; and by just about every person that they passed in the streets as they pressed through the crush of a city ripe with salacious gossip. Outrage grew as the perceived wrong done to their Emperor – the conqueror of Britannia, the man who had added Mauritania and Thracia to the Empire, the holder of the Secular Games, the builder of the new port that would solve all Rome's supply problems, the brother of Germanicus and the rightful heir of the Caesars, the dynasty that had kept the common people of Rome fed, entertained and free from civil war for three generations now – the wrong done to him by a notorious nymphomaniac well known in the brothels frequented by the masses.

'It makes you wonder how she ever thought she would succeed,' Magnus observed as they mounted their horses surrounded by crowds of common people gathering at the Porta Ostiensis to welcome their wronged Emperor back to Rome.

'It's not so hard to imagine how she saw it,' Vespasian replied, tugging on his mount's reins as it shied at the crowd. 'Claudius gone, Silius, Agrippina and Lucius murdered, the Guard paid off and the populace showered with money and games; in three months she could have been safe as the mother to the last true heir of the Caesars. The trouble was that she failed to take into account the loathing that most people have for her.' From within the city came the ever-swelling sound of mass disapproval moving closer. 'It sounds as if Messalina also has it in mind to come and greet Claudius.' Vespasian urged his horse forward, down the Via Ostiensis. 'Let's hope Narcissus manages to keep her away from the fool.'

'Sabinus has taken Silius to the Praetorian camp,' Vespasian informed Claudius as he rode next to the imperial carriage; two turmae of Praetorian cavalry rode in escort.

'And my w-w-wife?'

'She is no longer your wife,' Narcissus reminded Claudius.

'We do not know that for sure,' the elder Lucius Vitellius pointed out, earning a vicious sidelong look from Narcissus. 'We only have the word of two whores.'

'And the word of Vettius Valens in the Senate,' Vespasian countered, 'plus the fact that Silius did not deny the fact.'

Claudius squeezed out a couple of tears to add to the sheen on his face. 'Oh, my little bird, where is she?'

'I would surmise that your wi ... Messalina has heard that Silius' consular oath was void and therefore realises the serious-ness of her predicament as I believe that she was on her way to the Porta Ostiensis to greet you as I left.'

'I won't see the treacherous b-b-bitch until she's dead!' Claudius began to twitch as his cheeks reddened and his breathing became irregular.

'Indeed not,' Narcissus crooned.

Vitellius shook his head. 'Ah, such a crime.'

Narcissus fixed Vitellius with another vicious stare. 'What do you mean, Vitellius? Is what Messalina has done a crime or is what's about to be done to her a crime?'

Vitellius smiled vaguely. 'Such villainy, such villainy.'

Narcissus wrinkled his nose in disgust at Vitellius' careful avoidance of declaring his position.

Claudius quickly calmed, sinking back into self-pitying reverie. 'Alas, my little bird, for the sake of the children I'll forgive you.'

'You must not talk like that, Princeps.'

'Oh, how happy we were for so long; the children playing as we sat together in our garden, always together, never apart, every night a first. Oh, little bird, fly back to me.'

'She'll see you dead, Princeps, unless you kill her first.'

'Ah, such villainy.'

Narcissus rounded on Vitellius. 'If you are determined to say nothing that could be construed as support for either side then I suggest you stay silent.'

Vitellius looked to the sky. 'Such a crime.'

Vespasian watched Narcissus struggle to control himself, surprised by just how rattled this normally neutral-faced politician had become; he glanced at Pallas, riding up front, next to the carriage driver, and saw the placid face of a man in control.

'The filthy whore! I'll snap her neck!' Claudius exploded, before sinking his head onto his chest and mumbling about the milky smoothness of the little neck that he planned to snap.

Beyond the lead turma of cavalry the city walls were no more than a mile away; but closer, less than three hundred paces distant, stood a cart and kneeling in it was the figure of a woman with her hands outstretched in supplication.

Pallas signalled to the tribune, a dour-faced man in his forties, commanding the escort to come closer. 'Burrus, ride that cart off the road, but be careful as he hasn't yet signed her death warrant. And tell your men to start singing.'

Burrus nodded as if ordering his men to sing was the most natural thing in the world and rode to the head of his column. As repeated, high-pitched, female screams rose over the clatter of hoofbeats the escort broke out into a raucous military march.

Claudius looked up, his eyes wide with hope. 'Was that my little bird I heard? Oh, t-t-tell them to stop singing, I'm sure I heard her.'

'Nonsense, Princeps,' Narcissus reassured him, whilst rummaging in the satchel by his side. He pulled out three writing tablets and handed them to his patron; again Claudius cocked his ear at the sound of another brief shriek between verses of the song. 'Please take a look at these, Princeps; one is a report on how the new letters that you wish to have inserted into the alphabet have been received.'

Claudius was immediately all interest. 'Ah! I've been waiting for this.' He snatched the tablet and began reading; he was instantly immersed and failed to notice another series of screeches piercing the boisterous singing of his escort. The carriage slowed a fraction as the lead turma, too, reduced its speed; another shrieked call broke over the song and then the column picked up speed and Vespasian saw the cart carrying Messalina driving away over the rough, freshly ploughed farmland on the other side of the road.

'Claudius!' she cried as the out-of-control horses carried her off. 'Claudius!' She held out her arms towards him, her hair awry and her robe in tatters.

'That was my little bird!' Claudius exclaimed, tearing his eyes away from his report.

An instant before he turned his head in Messalina's direction Narcissus thrust another tablet at him. 'This is about your safety, Princeps.'

'My safety?' Once again Claudius was all attention.

'Yes, Princeps. We're sure of Burrus and his cavalry's loyalty but we feel that as we don't know just how far this plot has spread through the other senior officers of the Guard it would be best to transfer their command to someone neutral just for the day.'

'Yes, y-y-yes, that will make me feel much safer. Who do you suggest?'

'Whom would you trust, Princeps?'

Vespasian knew the answer before it was spoken as he watched the cart bearing Messalina speed off into the distance out of earshot.

'I trust you, Narcissus.'

Narcissus' face smoothed into a mask of modest gratitude. 'I am honoured that you should entrust me with such responsibility, Princeps.' He opened the tablet. 'Would you put your ring to the wax to make it official?'

As Claudius signed over the command of the Praetorian Guard to an ex-slave, Vitellius carried on gazing at the sky. 'Such villainy!'

Narcissus and Lucius Vitellius assisted Claudius up the steps to the main entrance of the palace as he railed at his wife and blubbered for his lost love in turn. Since seeing the size of the crowds waiting for him at the City Gates and lining the streets to the Palatine and feeling the warmth of their affection towards him, Claudius had become increasingly unstable, swinging from pathetic melancholy to murderous rage and then back again, in heartbeats. The people of Rome had watched in sympathy as their wronged Emperor had gibbered and seethed and snivelled his way through the streets; they had called out words of consolation and had urged him to avenge himself on his errant spouse, beseeching the gods that her death would bring him happiness.

Leaving Magnus with his horse, Vespasian followed the Emperor into the palace at Pallas' side.

'The next couple of hours are the most crucial,' the Greek whispered as they passed through the vestibule into the atrium. 'Narcissus needs to be driven to distraction by Claudius' behaviour.'

Before Vespasian could ask him what he meant a wail of grief echoed around the atrium.

'Uncle! Oh, Uncle! How are you, dearest Uncle?' A female came running barefoot across the chamber, her hair loose and streaming behind her and her cheeks lined with kohl-stained tear-tracks. 'Oh, how could she?' She launched herself at Claudius and flung her arms around his neck, kissing him all over his face and leaving black smudges in her wake. 'Are you all right, Uncle?'

'I don't know, Agrippina, I don't know; it's all such a shock.'

'Yes, Uncle, who'd have thought it of such a model wife?'

'That's just it, my child; there were no warning signs.'

Pallas gave the slightest of nods as if pleased with the entrance and Vespasian understood exactly what was happening and silently admired the audacity of it as Claudius disentangled himself from his niece and sat on the nearest couch. Before Narcissus could interpose, Agrippina had planted herself firmly on her uncle's lap and with her left hand gently around the back of his neck, stroked his hair with her other whilst cooing soothingly in his ear and moving her rump slightly more than necessary. The effect on Claudius was immediate; he drew her close, rested his head on her full breast and let fly finally with abundant sobs dredged from the very core of his being.

'There, Uncle, there,' Agrippina purred, kissing the crown of his head as if he were a small boy woken in the middle of the night from a bad dream. 'It'll soon be over; I'll look after you until you find another wife. You can trust me, you can trust family. Never forget that, Uncle: you can trust me because I'm family.'

'Yes, yes, my child, I know that I can trust you; but I still can't believe that I misplaced my trust in my little bird.'

Agrippina softly pulled Claudius' face away from her breast, its imprint marked by a moist patch on her stola, and held it in both hands; she looked deep into her uncle's eyes. 'I shall take you to see all the proof you need to believe her to be false, once and for all. Would you like that, dearest Uncle?'

Claudius nodded and twitched, gazing back at his niece who, although now in her early forties, still retained a beauty and sensuality purchased by a lifetime's use of the finest cosmetics. 'I should like that very much.'

Agrippina slipped from Claudius' lap, working her buttocks gently against him as she did so, leaving him obviously aroused but too transfixed by her spell to notice his public embarrassment. 'Follow me,' she purred, turning from him and swinging her hips as she walked away.

Claudius followed as if in a trance.

'Where are you taking him?' Narcissus demanded.

'Not far, Narcissus; you should come too.'

Having no choice other than to follow his patron, Narcissus complied.

'Shall we go and see what she's found?' Pallas asked Vespasian.

'By all means; although something tells me that you already know.'

'How could I? I've been in Ostia for the last few days.'

Vespasian smiled as he and Pallas followed Agrippina out of the atrium.

Lucius Vitellius trailed in their wake, shaking his head slowly. 'Such villainy.'

Agrippina took the route that Vespasian and Sabinus had been taken along on the day of Asiaticus' hearing and soon they were in the familiar corridors of the house that had once belonged to Antonia.

Taking Claudius by the arm as he lurched beside her, Agrippina led him past the formal reception room – the scene of Asiaticus' hearing – and on into the atrium that Vespasian had first entered twenty-two years before when his uncle had brought him and his brother to dine at Antonia's request. The high-ceilinged room had changed beyond recognition: it was now stuffed with statuary, furniture and ornaments, some modest, some brash, but all together gave the gaudy impression that the décor had been fashioned by Caligula after a three-day drinking session.

But it was not with Messalina's lack of taste that Agrippina hoped to demonstrate beyond all doubt her untrustworthiness; it was with the furnishings and ornaments themselves. She said nothing as she held out her arm and swept it around the room, encompassing each and every item on display.

And Claudius' mouth dropped open in disbelief.

Every item was an heirloom of his house.

Vespasian recognised Antonia's writing desk and polished walnut dining table with the three sumptuously upholstered matching couches that had once graced her private rooms. The much-copied original bronze statue of a young Augustus painted in breathtakingly life-like detail: in military attire, his right arm raised and pointing the way and with a cupid at his feet; it had been, Vespasian knew, the prized possession of Claudius' grandmother, Livia. Statues of Claudius' kin and ancestors going back to Julius Caesar littered the room as if they were just being stored there amongst the elegant furniture, bowls and vases, each with a story to tell about the family that had ruled Rome for almost a century.

'Where d-d-d-did she g-get all this?' Claudius spluttered, going up to a statue of his father, Drusus. 'I'm sure I saw this in the palace on the day I left for Ostia.'

'Grief and shock can play tricks on the memory, Uncle,' Agrippina said, taking his hand and kissing it. 'She's had this for months. And then look at that.' She pointed to two statues side by side taking pride of place in the collection as if overseeing the stationary horde. 'On the left is Silius' father. Well, his image has been banned by the Senate ever since he was executed for treason by Tiberius, hasn't it? Her just possessing it is enough to send her into exile. But look, dearest Uncle, look at the one next to it.'

As Claudius examined it, Vespasian drew in a sharp breath; he was shocked not so much that there was a statue of Silius himself in the room but because of what was draped around it: hanging from a baldric over the figure's right shoulder was a sword in a plain scabbard; a scabbard that Vespasian recognised as belonging to Marcus Antonius' sword, the sword that his daughter, Antonia, had gifted to Vespasian on the day of her suicide. She had told him that she had always meant to give it to the grandson whom she thought would make the best emperor. Claudius had seen Vespasian with it during his short stay in Britannia and, jealous, had taken it for himself, knowing full well the story behind it.

'My sword!' Claudius exclaimed, spraying the scabbard with spit. 'The bitch has even stolen my sword!'

'Hush now, Uncle.' Agrippina laid a soothing hand on his cheek. 'Now do you believe?'

'The wanton, the harpy, the goat-fucker, I'll have her dead within the hour.'

'You're so wise, Princeps,' Narcissus crooned, stepping forward with a scroll. 'I've her death warrant drafted; here it is. You can sign it now.'

Agrippina turned Claudius away from his chief freedman. 'Come, Uncle, decisions like that should not be made on an empty stomach.'

Vespasian looked at Pallas, puzzled as to why Agrippina should delay Claudius doing the very thing the freedmen wanted, but the Greek was looking down a corridor on the right as if he expected to see something imminently; and he did.

Two silhouetted figures, a boy and a girl, came running down the corridor. 'Father! Father!' they shouted in unison.

'What's that?' Claudius asked, turning in the direction of the noise.

'Oh Uncle, I'll deal with them,' Agrippina said. 'You shouldn't see your children whilst you're in such a rage.'

Claudius looked at Britannicus and Octavia as they appeared in the atrium, tears running down their cheeks, and took a step forward as Agrippina spread her arms and stopped them in their tracks. 'Come on, little chicks.' She pinched their cheeks and turned them around. 'Your father is very tired and emotional; you don't want to upset him further, do you? Let him eat and rest and then you can see him after that.' With an arm around each of them she led them back down the way they had come. 'Oh, look at you both, so adorable, I could eat you.'

'I think that your niece is right,' Pallas said, walking towards the Emperor. 'You should eat, Princeps.' He gestured Claudius towards the corridor that led back to the palace. 'But first you need to go to the Praetorian camp to pass judgement on Silius and then with a full stomach you should decide Messalina's fate.'

With red, vacant eyes, Claudius moved off as if spellbound, assisted by Pallas. Narcissus stared at his colleague, unable to read his face and guess his motivation.

Looking forward immensely to witnessing the next choreographed moves in the unfolding drama, Vespasian followed them out, passing Lucius Vitellius staring at all the items crammed into the room.

'Ahh, such villainy.'

CHAPTER XXI

T HE ENTIRE PRAETORIAN Guard crashed a salute for their
Emperor as he was borne, on a litter, into the parade ground
at the heart of their camp. Birds, perched on the roofs of the long
lines of two-storey barrack buildings, were startled into flight as
thousands of arms slammed across chests and as many deep
voices roared a greeting for the man who gave reason for their
existence as a unit.

Yet it was not with unanimous joy that Claudius was greeted;
kneeling before a dais in front of the massed ranks of Rome's élite
soldiery were two dozen forlorn figures, dressed only in tunics,
humiliatingly unbelted, like a woman's.

The sound of the Guard's roar echoed around the camp,
bouncing off the brick walls of the barracks, and eventually faded
into no more than the fluttering of scores of standards and the
complaints of the birds circling overhead.

The litter was placed on the ground and Claudius, resplendent in imperial purple and wreathed in laurel, was helped to his
feet by the man who now commanded, for this single day, the
true power in Rome. Narcissus escorted his patron up the steps
to the dais and saw him seated with as much dignity as an
emotionally broken man in his mid-fifties could muster.

Vespasian stood to one side, next to Pallas and Sabinus,
enjoying the sight of the two Praetorian prefects, Rufrius
Crispinus and Lucius Lusius Geta, approach the Emperor with
Gaius Silius grasped firmly between them. 'They must be feeling
particularly guilty if they're demeaning themselves by acting as
prisoner escort,' he observed to Pallas under his breath.

'Your brother negotiated with them on my behalf this afternoon when he brought Silius to the camp.'

Sabinus obviously enjoyed the memory. 'Once they both understood that Silius wasn't consul they realised that Messalina's plot against Claudius had almost no chance of succeeding and were only too pleased to accept the terms.'

'Which were?'

'Lenient, considering that almost every man in the Guard over the rank of centurion has sampled Messalina's wares.'

Pallas watched with satisfaction as Lucius Vitellius mounted the dais and placed himself next to Narcissus behind the Emperor. 'That won't help soothe Narcissus' growing agitation. As to the prefects, all I asked is that they provide two dozen of their number for Claudius to punish however he pleases. How they chose them was up to them. The two prefects keep their posts—'

'And are well and truly in your debt,' Vespasian butted in, understanding completely.

'Precisely; I deemed it safer to hold something over the present incumbents rather than replace them with new ones who might not be as loyal to me as I would wish.'

The two prefects stamped to a halt in front of the dais and thrust their charge down onto his knees. Claudius began shaking visibly at the sight of the man who now claimed Messalina as his wife. Vitellius laid a firm hand on his shoulder and his body calmed.

'W-w-w-well, wh-what have you to say for yourself, S-S-Silius?'

Silius held his head high and stared Claudius in the eyes. 'I am guilty of everything that I've been accused of; I took your wife and planned to take your place with her. However, although I am guilty of these charges I am not guilty of conceiving the plan that, in my weakness, I consented to go along with. That was Messalina's idea alone and if she is to be granted the mercy of a quick death then I ask for myself the same favour.'

Vitellius bent to whisper in Claudius' ear, keeping his hand tightly gripped on his shoulder. Narcissus immediately began to speak in the other ear. A brief unheard argument seemed to ensue before Claudius eventually nodded at Vitellius and again addressed Silius: 'Very well, a clean death it shall be. Crispinus!'

The Praetorian prefect swept out his sword with a metallic ring and, standing next to Silius, showed him the blade. Silius contemplated it for a few moments and then bowed his head, stretching his neck forward. Iron flashed, slicing through flesh and bone, releasing heart-pumps of spurting blood that propelled the severed head forward to roll almost to the foot of the dais and stop, staring open-mouthed at the Emperor. Claudius ejaculated a growl of deep satisfaction and smacked his lips as he watched the life flee from Silius' eyes. The body twitched, and the flow of blood lessened as the heart gave out and silence covered the parade ground.

After a few moments more relishing the sight, Claudius looked at the men kneeling in front of the parade before turning to the two prefects. 'What crime are they accused of?'

Crispinus wiped his sword on Silius' tunic. 'To the shame of the Guard, these men are all guilty by their own account of sleeping with Messalina.'

Claudius looked at the accused again and then threw his head back in laughter. 'If only a q-q-q-quarter of what I've been told in the last few hours is true then that pathetic little group would be less than three days' work for my ex-wife.'

Vespasian felt Pallas tense.

Claudius snapped out of his mirth as quickly as he had entered into it. 'Very well, bring them forward.'

Pallas relaxed.

The prisoners, each escorted by a ranker, walked to the dais.

'On your knees! Escorts, draw your swords.'

Again, Vitellius bent the Emperor's ear and again Narcissus spoke into the other one and again an argument followed in which again Claudius eventually ruled in Vitellius' favour. 'I will not ask for these men's lives; I will not even ask for one of them as an example to the rest. Instead, I dismiss them from my service and forbid them fire and water within three hundred miles from Rome for the rest of their lives.'

As this news was relayed through the ranks and files of the Praetorian Cohorts a cheer rippled through the formation causing Claudius to incline his head and wave a shaking hand towards his audience.

'I do this because I'm well aware that there were far more people guilty of adultery with my ex-wife than have admitted it. I now wish to let the matter drop. Let her punishment and that of a few of her closer associates be an end to the matter. I shall decide her fate after consultation with the gods of my household.

'I've been made a fool of by that woman and now rejoice in the fact that I am divorced. Men of the Praetorian Guard, there will be a donative of ten aurei per man to celebrate my new freedom and I charge you to kill me if I ever get married again.'

To the massed cheers of thousands of men now richer by four times the annual salary of an ordinary legionary Claudius turned and hobbled back down the steps, this time helped by Vitellius, whilst Narcissus watched, clenching and re-clenching his right fist as the other hand played with his beard.

Pallas moved to join the imperial party. 'Without him knowing it, Vitellius' attempt to steer a neutral course is proving very useful to my cause.'

'But it looks as if you'll have trouble persuading Claudius to marry again, Pallas,' Vespasian observed as Vitellius helped the Emperor into his litter.

'Not when he finds out just who he can marry.'

Agrippina sighed with exaggerated sympathy and reached along the dining couch to place an understanding hand on her uncle's arm. 'I know it must have been hard to show Silius such mercy, dearest Uncle, but Vitellius was right: if you'd not granted him the clean death of a citizen and had acted like an animal instead then you would have reminded people of my poor brother, Gaius Caligula.'

Vitellius, placed on the other side of Claudius, beamed his gratitude at Agrippina for supporting his point of view to the Emperor; he then helped himself to a stuffed cabbage leaf.

'I agree, Princeps,' Pallas said, nibbling on an olive and reclining on the couch to Claudius' left. 'The best way to come out of this with credit is to act with dignity as if the antics of an unfaithful wife are too small a matter to unduly upset a man of your standing and nothing more than rightful retribution need be taken.'

Vespasian caught a brief flash of anger in Narcissus' eyes as he glanced sidelong at his colleague next to him before his face returned to studied neutrality.

'I-I-I suppose so,' Claudius said, spilling semi-masticated brown morsels from his mouth and adding to the mess on his napkin. 'But I would've loved to have seen more suffering from him; he seduced my little bird.' His mouth fell open, disgorging more of its contents as he lapsed back into melancholy.

Narcissus was quick to support his patron. 'I agree, Princeps; I believe that you were wrong to take Vitellius' advice; we need to fully secure your position. You would have been better off following what I suggested. To show mercy makes you look weak; you should never have spared those Praetorian officers.'

Claudius mumbled something about the joys of Messalina's bedchamber, a subject that no one felt any desire to enlarge upon.

Vespasian toyed with his half-full golden wine beaker. 'But surely, Narcissus, the Emperor's magnanimous gesture has earned him the gratitude of the entire Guard?'

'And, of course, their renewed loyalty strengthened by a deep sense of shame,' Sabinus, next to him, added, earning a brief look of appreciation from Pallas.

Vespasian picked up his brother's argument. 'The Emperor has won their love forever by forgiving so many of them who have acted despicably.'

'And now, Princeps,' Vitellius said, 'you can make yourself even more popular with them by choosing a new wife whom they, and the whole city, will respect.'

Claudius was still immersed in his maudlin reverie. 'What? A new wife? No, I couldn't.'

Agrippina leant over and kissed him on the cheek. 'Don't worry, Uncle; I'll look after you until we find someone who can see to all your needs. I'm sure we'll get you just the right person.'

'There are some very suitable women in my family,' Vitellius suggested helpfully.

Agrippina gave him the sweetest of smiles. 'You're so kind, Lucius, but I think my uncle should look a little closer to home, shouldn't you, dearest Claudius? And seeing as I'm your niece I'll be the perfect person to help you judge.'

Narcissus leant forward. 'Pallas and I both think that you should remarry your second wife, Princeps; don't we, Pallas?'

Pallas picked up and examined another olive. 'Should we be discussing this now when the Emperor hasn't yet decided what to do about Messalina?'

'Yes, Uncle, what do you intend to do?' Agrippina shot Pallas a quick look and Vespasian caught a glimpse of something more than mere mutual interest. He realised that they were working much more closely together than he had imagined … She turned back to Claudius. 'I said that you should decide after a good dinner.'

Claudius' reply was delayed by a Praetorian cavalry decurion striding into the room. 'Princeps, Tribune Burrus has sent me to tell you that the chief Vestal, Vibidia, is here on Messalina's behalf.'

Claudius looked at the tribune, his long face a study in sorrow. 'I don't wish to see her now. Tell Burrus to say to Vibidia that I'll send for that poor woman in the morning and she can plead her case to me then in person.'

'Yes, Princeps.'

As the decurion turned to go, Narcissus got to his feet and picked up his satchel. 'I shall go and tell her your words myself, Princeps.'

'As you wish,' Claudius said with little interest.

As Narcissus left the room he signalled Vespasian, with his eyes, to follow him.

Vespasian looked over to Pallas who twitched the corner of his mouth into a satisfied half-smile and nodded almost imperceptibly.

After a few moments, Vespasian rose from his couch making his excuses and followed Narcissus out.

'The Emperor assures you that he will allow Messalina a fair hearing tomorrow,' Narcissus informed a tall woman in white as Vespasian came out into the atrium. 'In the meantime he requests that you do not allow this matter to interfere with your sacred duties.'

Vibidia put her hands to her chest and dipped her head. 'I shall go and inform the Empress of that good news.'

'The Emperor asks that you return to the house of the Vestals immediately with his thanks and has requested me to send Tribune Burrus to Messalina with the news.'

'It is good of him to spare me the journey.'

'Your wellbeing is always at the forefront of his thoughts. Where would Burrus find Messalina?'

'She's at the Gardens of Lucullus; her estranged mother, Lepida, has joined her there to bring her comfort. Tell the Emperor that he has the prayers of our house at this delicate time.'

'I shall, Lady.'

Vibidia turned and walked away with gliding grace.

'Burrus!' Narcissus called to the waiting tribune. He pulled a writing tablet from his satchel as Burrus approached. 'This afternoon, Claudius gave me charge of the Guard to deal with this crisis; you can understand why, can't you?'

'Yes, imperial secretary.'

'Take eight men to the Gardens of Lucullus and execute Messalina on the Emperor's orders.'

Burrus held Narcissus' gaze for a few moments and then acquiesced. 'It shall be done.'

As the tribune marched away Narcissus turned to Vespasian. 'I don't know what you were playing at in there, Vespasian, but you can make up for it by going with him and making sure that he does as I've ordered.'

'It'll be my pleasure, imperial secretary.' As he turned to follow Burrus, Vespasian marvelled at the panic he had seen in Narcissus' eyes; panic that Pallas and Agrippina had sown by delaying the Emperor signing the death warrant. Panic that Claudius would calm down and forgive Messalina had just forced

Narcissus into making his first, and quite possibly his last, political mistake.

The contrast in the appearance of the Gardens of Lucullus between that evening and the one before could not have been more acute: gone were the multifarious points of light outlining a solid rectangular shape on the southwestern slope of the Pincian Hill and in their stead was a solitary glow from what Vespasian knew to be the villa at the heart of the gardens.

He walked in silence next to Burrus as they approached Messalina's retreat from the Quirinal Gate. The sound of the measured footsteps of the contuburnium of Praetorian Guardsmen following them, echoing off the buildings to either side, was sufficient to clear their way; carts and pedestrians moved aside as they passed, not wishing to interfere with what was obviously an imperial matter, and it was not long before they reached the locked gates in the whitewashed wall, guarded by two new sentries.

The glint of Burrus' blade leaving its scabbard and a growled order were hint enough for the two guards to place the keys in Vespasian's outstretched hand and make off into the night.

With a metallic clunk the lock turned, the gates swung open with a high-pitched creak, the execution party crunched onto the gravel beyond and then began to snake its way along the stone path up the hill. Even with no torchlight and the moon yet to rise, the gardens' beauty and variety could still not be disguised; the sweet scent of rosemary shrubs gave way first to the sea-air aroma of autumn-blooming crocuses and then the musk of deer resting by freshwater pools. As they climbed, the different scents blended into one another, and Vespasian remembered Asiaticus' words about how the gardens represented everything that was good in Rome but that their beauty would attract what was bad, and he understood finally what the condemned man had meant. He was aware of, but unable to see, the beauty all around him that harboured the cause of so much of Rome's present troubles. He was now to witness the canker being cut out, but what would grow in its stead? Who would desire these gardens once Messalina had gone? And for what reason?

Instinctively he knew the answers to those questions. With the memory of the look that Agrippina had given Pallas earlier that evening in his mind, Vespasian prayed that his old acquaintance would use the evident influence he had with the Empress-in-waiting to ensure his and his family's safety and prosperity during the coming changes.

They passed into the gloom of the orchard, hobnailed sandals striking the mosaic path in unison with a sharp clatter and the occasional flash of sparks. Up ahead, silhouetting the dark forms of Asiaticus' beloved apricot trees, Vespasian could see the glow of two torches on the terrace in front of the villa. Gone were the couches, tables, silent slaves, strident musicians, tubs of grapes and mounds of naked flesh; instead, in the dim light, sat two women, one feverishly writing as if her life depended on it – which it would have done had Narcissus' fear of her being forgiven and returned to power not pushed him into going behind his patron's back.

The sound of the arriving footsteps reached Messalina's ears and she stood and stared down the path, one hand reaching instinctively for the woman next to her; her mother, Lepida, Vespasian surmised.

As he cleared the final apricot tree, with Burrus at his side, Messalina screamed. It was the cry of one whose worst imaginings have suddenly materialised before them and who is forced to accept that what had been deemed impossible has come true. The shriek pierced the night, filling it with the sound of terror; Messalina turned to run but her mother caught her arm, clutching it tightly, and pulled her back into an embrace as her executioners mounted the steps, two by two, their hands grasping the hilts of their swords.

Messalina stared at them from her mother's arms. 'Tell them to go away, Mother! Tell them I command it!'

'You command nothing now, my child; your life is over.'

'It can't be; my husband would never order that.'

'Your husband is dead,' Burrus informed her. 'It's the Emperor that has ordered this.'

'My husband is the Emperor!'

Lepida stroked a hand through her daughter's wild hair and kissed her brow. 'That ceased to be so when you divorced Claudius and married another man.'

'But he was consul, I was safe and then they cheated me!' Messalina spat and hissed like a goaded serpent. 'How dare they change things; it wasn't fair.' Now tears streamed down her cheeks. 'Can't they give me another chance, Mother? Can't they forget a little wrong? I've so much life left to enjoy, so much pleasure yet to feel, so much want to be satisfied; I need to be allowed that. Who would dare deny me?'

'Child, no one would have denied you that had you not tried to have everything all at once. You have brought yourself here and the manner of your doing so means that you will not be allowed away from this place alive.'

Messalina looked her mother in the eyes, screamed at her and pulled away, before landing a ringing slap across her face. 'You bitch! How dare you say things like that? Now I remember why I banned you from my sight for so long; you always blame me and poison everyone against me. It's not my fault! I would have been safe if they hadn't changed things and somehow stopped that idiot being consul. I would have been safe, do you hear? Safe! They must be told to give me another chance. They must, Mother!'

'They'll never do that. Now all that remains to you is to seek death with honour.'

'I – will – not – die!'

'For the first and only time in your life, child, you will do as you are told.'

Vespasian stepped forward and offered Messalina his sword, hilt first. 'If you don't do it, Messalina, it will be done for you.'

'You!' she shrieked, ignoring the proffered sword and seemingly noticing him for the first time. 'Why are you against me? Flavia is my friend.'

'And lover; I know. But for the last year and more she's been Narcissus' spy in your bed.'

'Liar! No one would dare betray me.'

'Why? Because you alone have the right to live life as you wish and everyone else in Rome should serve your every need?'

'I am the Empress.'

'You were the Empress but, like Caligula's, your behaviour could not be tolerated; you took everything and gave nothing back. Narcissus and Pallas may guard their power jealously and use it for personal advantage but at least they spread patronage; people can gain by them. The two of them ensure that Claudius gives back also: the new port, the draining of the Fucine Lake for more agricultural land, new aqueducts and much more. But who profits from you being in power? How does Rome benefit from you, who would not even help your own brother?'

'He was of no use to me any more!'

'Which was why he betrayed you; it was he who told Narcissus what you planned to do. Flavia spied on you because I told her to; because I knew it would strengthen my standing with Narcissus and Pallas who were determined to get rid of you – rightly. Now they have you, and Claudius, in his folly, can't protect you any more.'

'But he promised to look into my eyes.'

'So you could lie to him?' Vespasian pushed his sword hilt into Messalina's midriff. 'Well, that won't happen now. Take the sword. There will be no reprieve for you, Messalina. You will die here in the gardens that you killed to possess and Asiaticus gets the vengeance that he foresaw.'

'What do you mean?'

'You sealed your fate when you drove him to suicide. He set this all in motion: he put Corvinus in touch with Narcissus even though they hate each other; he knew about you and Flavia and how useful she would be; and he judged me, correctly, to be ruthless and unscrupulous enough to use my wife to gain favour. Yes, Messalina, your death was ordained the moment you grabbed the most beautiful place in Rome. So embrace it now with the dignity befitting your status.'

Messalina stared in horror at the sword and then looked to her mother, who just shook her head slowly and then gently lifted the weapon with the palm of her hand. Tears welled in

Messalina's eyes as she slowly grasped the hilt. 'Must I, Mother? Can't I be granted exile on an island somewhere? Then Claudius will have time to change his mind!'

Lepida eased her daughter to her knees. 'That's the whole point, child, Rome has seen you deceiving Claudius openly, relying on the fool's love that he has for you; no one is going to let you take advantage of that again. No, be strong and do this; I shall help you.' Lepida turned the sword so that the point was just beneath her daughter's heart and then, placing herself behind Messalina, wrapped her hands over hers. 'Ready, Messalina?' Mother and daughter tensed, tears flowing down both their faces, and then Lepida jerked her arms towards her. With a squeal, Messalina twisted and buckled; blood coloured the blade and Lepida cried out as she looked down at the cut on the outside of her left thigh.

'I won't die, Mother!' Messalina shrieked. 'No one has the right to—' She stopped abruptly and looked around, shocked, and then focused on Burrus' forearm, just in front of her. She followed it with her eyes, down to the wrist and then on to the hand that grasped the hilt of a sword. Along the blade her eyes went and they widened with horror; only half was visible. She tried to scream but succeeded only in spewing blood on Burrus' hand as it thrust forward and twisted left then right. Messalina looked at her executioner with fury raging on her face before falling back into her mother's arms.

'Enough talk,' Burrus said, pulling his blade free with a wet sucking sound and then wiping it clean on Messalina's palla before turning to his men. 'Let's go.'

Vespasian looked down at the dead Messalina, blood seeping from her breast and soaking her clothes, and felt nothing: no joy, relief, pity, triumph, regret … nothing. 'Take the body and deal with it privately, Lepida,' he said and turned to follow Burrus and his men, leaving Lepida, weeping softly, clutching her daughter's corpse.

As he walked down the steps Vespasian looked up at the newly risen moon shining through the branches of the apricot trees that had witnessed so much, and swore to himself that he would never again set foot in the Gardens of Lucullus.

CHAPTER XXII

ALMOST TWO HOURS after he had left it, Vespasian walked back into the triclinium at the palace; apart from the addition of a group of musicians the scene was exactly the same. Narcissus looked at him questioningly and he replied with a tired nod as he slumped back down onto his couch, next to Sabinus.

'Such villainy,' Lucius Vitellius pronounced, just loud enough to be heard over the music, whilst peeling a pear.

Vespasian ignored the remark as he caught a brief, silent exchange between Pallas and Agrippina before she returned her attention to her uncle who was now well into his cups and adding to them.

Signalling a slave to fill his, Vespasian turned to his brother, keeping his voice low, so as not to be heard over the music. 'What's happened? Why is everyone still here?'

'None of them wants to leave the others alone with Claudius.'

'They'll be here all night then. Why are you still here?'

'I was waiting for you, to remind you to be at the Senate at dawn and make sure that Uncle Gaius comes too.'

'Of course, the incest law; I'll speak directly after you.'

'I'd appreciate that. Gaius has managed to persuade Servius Sulpicius Galba to speak for the motion. I'll have him follow you.'

Vespasian grimaced as he took a full pull on his cup, remembering his dealings with Galba when he was first assigned to the II Augusta. 'He'll shout them into submission.'

'He can do whatever he likes as long as he helps get the motion passed and I can get off to Moesia, Macedonia and Thracia; and if you want my advice, brother, you should get out of Rome for a while too, because after witnessing Agrippina's behaviour this evening I can tell you that life with her in power is going to be just as precarious as it was with Messalina.'

'I will. I'll go back to the estates until my consulship and after that hopefully Pallas will get me a province.'

'Don't rely on him too much. He's sleeping with Agrippina, I'm sure of it; there's a hint of it in her eyes when she looks at him.'

'I noticed that too and thought that it would be a good thing for us.'

'That would depend on which one of them has the stronger will.'

Vespasian looked over at Agrippina, wiping her uncle's mouth and talking soothingly in his ear.

'But I want her,' Claudius suddenly cried out. 'I miss my little bird already.'

'Then summon her now to account for herself. If she is indeed innocent, why wait till morning to find out? And if she's guilty then have done with her and choose another.'

'I could do that, couldn't I?' Claudius' face lit up at the prospect.

'Of course you could, Uncle,' Agrippina purred, looking directly at Narcissus, who paled visibly, even in the soft lamplight.

Claudius indicated to his freedman with his cup, slopping much of its contents onto his couch. 'Narcissus, have Messalina brought to the palace.'

Narcissus regained his composure. 'Surely you're joking with me, Princeps? You ordered me to have her executed just two hours ago.'

Claudius opened and closed his mouth and then his features froze, staring blankly into vacant space.

'Uncle!' Agrippina cried. 'How brave of you to do so. But why didn't you tell me? In fact, why didn't I hear you give the order? I've been reclining next to you all evening.'

Claudius did not answer or even register that he had heard the question. Nor did he seem to hear loud wailing from out in the atrium.

'It was what you wanted, Princeps, after all,' Narcissus insisted, 'otherwise I would have questioned it when you gave me the command.'

'Did you give the command, Uncle, really?'

Claudius lifted his cup to his mouth as if by an automatic impulse, took a swig and then placed it back on the table. An instant later he repeated the movement as the wailing closed in.

'I think that it's time for us to leave,' Vespasian suggested to Sabinus. 'I doubt that our departure will be noticed.'

The brothers got to their feet as Claudius and Messalina's two children burst into the room. Obviously in an advanced state of grief they set about their father with slaps and scratches whilst he did nothing to defend himself or even show that he knew that he was under attack.

As Vespasian left the room he caught Pallas smiling at Agrippina, who returned it with interest whilst Lucius Vitellius mouthed two words, inaudible over the commotion.

'The vote to remove Messalina's statues and name from all public places has been passed unanimously,' the Father of the House announced in the absence of any consuls. 'The order will be given to the Urban prefect to proceed without delay so that our beloved Emperor can begin the process of choosing a new wife without always being reminded of the old.'

Claudius sat in his chair, his eyes still vacant and his skin pallid as a rumbled chorus of agreement greeted this thought. He nodded absently and fluttered a shaky hand in acknowledgement of the Senate's gesture but failed to make a verbal reply. In its absence Sabinus stood and caught the attention of the Father of the House.

'Titus Flavius Sabinus has the floor.'

Sabinus walked to the centre of the House, stood still for a couple of moments and then began: 'Conscript Fathers, who here does not have the Emperor's welfare at the forefront of his mind? Who here does not consider the Emperor's happiness to be of paramount importance to the wellbeing of the Empire? Who here would therefore deny the Emperor the right to marry the woman most suitable to him?'

*

The House sat in stunned silence as if each man had just been struck a blow on the forehead by the priest wielding the mallet before the sacrificial knife is applied. No one moved as Sabinus sat down after his short speech proposing the law of incest should be changed so that the Emperor could marry his niece. Claudius, too, was speechless but not as before: his eyes had lost their vacant stare and had become focused.

Vespasian got to his feet and was immediately called to speak since no one else had recovered from the shock at the idea of changing a tenet so old and enshrined in the ways of the ancestors.

'Conscript Fathers,' he began, feigning a look of awed surprise, 'I did not know what my brother was going to propose when he stood to address you. But I, like you, have heard his words and have weighed them in my mind and have come to the conclusion that my brother has had an idea inspired by the gods; an idea so simple and obvious that no one here could see it until Titus Flavius Sabinus stood up and pointed us in its direction.

'I have heard rumours of Lollia Paulina and Aelia Paetina being put about by various factions in the palace for their own personal gain; their own personal gain! How dare they play with our beloved Emperor's wellbeing for their own personal gain!' Another rumble, this time of outrage, was emitted from the lines of seated senators. 'But it took an intellect like my brother's to see exactly where to look for a bride for our Emperor: as close to home as possible – closer even – so that finally the Julian and the Claudian lines in the imperial family are united by a doting uncle and his loving niece. Think, Conscript Fathers, think of the consequences of such a union.'

Vespasian sat, watching the faces of his colleagues as they contemplated the security that the final union of both sides of the Julio-Claudians would bring. Only Claudius seemed to be envisioning a different aspect to that union and he twitched with visible excitement.

'I believe that we should beg Caesar to make this match!' Galba roared in his harsh, parade-ground voice, startling his neighbours. 'For the good of Rome. Although marrying a niece is not the way of our ancestors and consequently there is no precedent for a woman to be escorted to the house of her uncle, we should not consider it as incest, which surely can only be committed by siblings or parents with their children.' He jutted out his jaw as if defying anyone to gainsay him. 'And if it is not incest then the gods will view the union with pleasure.'

At the intervention of such a renowned conservative, the idea began to gain traction as Sabinus had predicted and one by one the senators began to implore Claudius to consent to the match if they changed the law to allow it.

'That's got them going,' Gaius observed, as the senators vied with one another to be the most vociferous in support for Agrippina. 'Even Vitellius looks as if he feels it safe to have an opinion.'

'Which is one more than you've ever admitted to, Uncle,' Vespasian quipped as the elder Vitellius got to his feet and dramatically held out his arms towards Claudius. 'Still, his support will make the vote a formality.'

Vitellius waited dramatically for silence. 'Princeps, will you answer us? Will you take Agrippina as your wife if the law allows you?'

Claudius made an attempt to look solemn but failed to conceal his eagerness for the proposal. 'I am a citizen of R-R-Rome; I must accept the orders of the people and the authority of the Senate and cannot resist their united voice.'

'Conscript Fathers, there we have the words of a true servant of the State. Our Emperor, upon whom such crushing labours are placed in the governance of the world, needs to be able to attend to the public good free from domestic worries. We, Conscript Fathers, can ensure that he is. I move that we vote to make it legal for an uncle to marry his niece.'

Vespasian felt a hand touch his shoulder as the House erupted in agreement. He turned to see one of the public slaves used as messengers from people waiting outside. 'What is it?'

'Master, there is a man by the name of Magnus waiting for you and your brother; he says that you must come at once.'

'Did he say why?'

'Only that it's a matter of the utmost urgency.'

Vespasian leant close to Sabinus. 'We've got to go, brother; Magnus needs us urgently.'

'But the vote hasn't happened yet.'

'Look around, it's a foregone conclusion now.' Vespasian got to his feet.

'In my experience,' Gaius shouted over the uproar, 'when Magnus says it's urgent, it always is.'

'But Pallas wants me to propose an auspicious day for the wedding.'

'I thought that it was to be on the festival of the October Horse.'

'No, that was just to goad Messalina into swift action.'

'I'll propose it for you, dear boy,' Gaius offered. 'What's the date?'

'The first of January.'

'Why wait for two months?'

Sabinus handed Gaius a list. 'Because Pallas wants time to have all these men prosecuted properly in the courts and condemned to death for conspiring with Messalina, so that they can be executed on or before the wedding day. Read out the list after you've proposed the date, and have the Senate order their arrest; they'll do anything for Claudius at the moment.'

Gaius' jowls wobbled. 'But that'll make me very ...'

' ... conspicuous? Yes, but it will also gain you the favour of the man who has just become the most powerful person in Rome.' Sabinus followed Vespasian from the chamber, leaving Gaius staring unhappily at the death-list.

'We've got to hurry,' Magnus told the brothers as they came through the Senate House door, 'I've sent Marius and Sextus on to tell Clementina to get out of the house but I don't suppose that she'll listen to them.'

'What do you mean: tell Clementina to get out?' Sabinus asked, hurrying down the Senate House steps after Magnus.

'I mean that I think she's in danger.'

Vespasian was surprised to see Magnus so agitated. 'From what?'

'I'm not sure exactly. A couple of hours ago we finally managed to get hold of one of the slippery bastards who've been watching Sabinus' house and we took him back to the tavern for that chat we talked about.'

'Did he talk?'

'No, not a word, no matter what we did to him; I was really impressed.'

'So we don't even know where they come from?'

'No, we don't; but we do know one thing: he must have been a fanatic to endure what he did in silence.'

'Either that or he's more scared of whatever it is he's protecting than of your knives and hot irons.'

'Yeah, well, either way, they're not just some hired thugs who've been paid to keep an eye on you; they evidently want something that's in the house, so we need to get Clementina out.'

Sabinus increased his pace, forcing passers-by to dart out of his way. 'What makes you think that it's her they're after?'

'Nothing for sure; but the fact is that they've been watching just your house for a few days now, which would mean that whatever interests them is in there. I would guess that once they notice the disappearance of their mate this morning they'll be prompted into some immediate action.'

A steady, thin drizzle from a heavy sky moistened the raised pavement as Vespasian, Magnus and Sabinus hurried up the Aventine Hill. A hundred paces to their left the massive hulk of the Circus Maximus towered above them, grey in the damp morning light. To their right the Appian Aqueduct carved its way across the hill to its final destination at its foot; turning towards it and passing under one of its diminishing arches, they skirted around the Temple of Diana and entered Sabinus' street, which ran the last couple of hundred paces gently to the summit.

Having been destroyed by fire a dozen years before, most of the residences on the Aventine had been rebuilt and, on a normal day, the area had an elegant feel about it, unusual in the residential quarters of Rome, most of which had grown shabby through age. But this did not seem like a normal day as they drew in sight of Sabinus' house. It was not the oppressive greyness of the weather or the dampness of the paving underfoot and the plastered brick to each side; nor was it the continual dripping from overhanging vegetation splashing into puddles below or down the necks of passers-by. It was not even the cold that had suddenly descended with unseasonal harshness as they approached their destination.

It was the emptiness and consequent quiet.

No other person moved in the street; no stray dog or darting cat crossed their path, nor were there any signs of birds flitting across the dull sky or sheltering from the rain in trees or on windowsills or in other nooks. It was as if a plague had carried off every living creature and the fear of its return had dissuaded others from taking their place.

Neither Vespasian nor his companions spoke as they approached the substantial façade of Sabinus' house, painted ochre with dull, deep red outlines to the door and the few windows. They stopped at the foot of the steps and looked up at the door; it was intact and there was no sign of a forced entry, nor was there any sound of violence coming from within.

Vespasian glanced up and down the street. 'Well, either they've stopped watching your house or they've got what they came for and have disappeared.'

'Either way, Marius or Sextus, or both of them, should be around,' Magnus said, clenching his thumb in his fingers and then spitting. 'This ain't natural, this quiet at the second hour of the day. Where is everyone?'

Sabinus took some tentative steps towards the door. 'There's only one way to find out.' He knocked quietly on the wood and received no response; a slightly louder attempt also passed without notice from within. With a shrug he turned the handle and the door swung open, unbarred on the inside.

Vespasian's innards turned and he and Magnus shared an uneasy look as Sabinus stepped into his house before following him in.

And then he felt it: it was the same cold sensation as the touch of the Lost Dead and yet he knew that they could not possibly be so far from the damp island that they infested; those spirits could not cross water. And then he remembered the cold malice of their masters and his stomach lurched.

Sabinus sensed it too. 'There's something in here,' he whispered, stepping carefully through the vestibule. 'There's a dread reminiscent of the Vale of Sullis.'

Magnus sniffed the air as they entered the atrium. 'Something's burning and it don't smell like it's just the hearth—' He stopped mid-sentence as they all three simultaneously drew breath and swallowed fast-rising bile. 'Now that ain't natural.'

To the left of the impluvium lay a bloodied mess, steaming faintly in the cold atmosphere of the chamber. Even at a distance of twenty paces it was only just recognisable as human. Its surface glistened with fluids; here and there a twitch or a muscle contraction showed faint evidence of life. Reacting to the sound of the three men entering the room, the ghastly vision lifted its head, its lidless eyes making unfocused contact.

'Magnus,' it croaked in an undertone, 'finish it.' It lifted its left arm; there was no hand attached and the stump was old.

'Marius?' Magnus ran over to the bloodied wreck. 'What happened?'

Vespasian and Sabinus joined Magnus staring down in horror at Marius in his agony; the skin had been stripped from his head and limbs as if a Titan had sucked each in turn, scraping them with razor-teeth to remove the hide. His torso had received less damage but flayed strips of flesh hung from it in a surprisingly regular pattern as if it had been slashed by a mighty claw.

Marius' eyes rolled in their sockets and blood and mucus seeped from the hole where his nose had been. 'Don't ... know. Torn apart.'

Magnus knelt down. 'Who by?'

'I saw ... nothing.'

'Where's Sextus?'

'Gone. Finish me.'

Magnus pulled his knife from its sheath, placed the point under Marius' ribcage and placed a hand around his raw shoulders. 'You'll be remembered, brother.' The two men tensed and then with a brutal thrust the iron sliced through the exposed flesh and on up into his racing heart.

An agonised grimace set across Marius' peeled lips. 'Brother,' he whispered with the last breath that left his lungs. His lidless eyes fixed and his body slumped; Magnus removed his arm and laid his crossroads brother down as a scream that curdled blood rang out and reverberated around the marble walls.

'Clementina!' Sabinus cried, spinning round and looking in the direction of the noise.

'The garden!' Vespasian shouted. 'Have you any weapons handy?'

Sabinus nodded and ran to a closed door; a few moments later he emerged with a sword and a long knife that he threw to Vespasian. 'That's the best I can do.'

Vespasian caught the hilt in the air and, along with Magnus, rushed after his brother into the *tablinum* at the far end of the atrium and then on into the courtyard garden. They stopped, aghast at the sight that awaited them at the far end of the garden, forty paces away.

Their long hair and beards were matted and their ankle-length robes were smeared with filth; their dark eyes fixed on Vespasian and his companions. All five druids stretched out an arm towards them.

'Juno's fat arse!' Magnus exclaimed. 'What the fuck are they doing here?'

Vespasian stared in fearful disbelief at the Britannic priests, his heart chilling by the moment. Two held Clementina by the wrists, rigid with terror, and another two had Alienus, who shook and sobbed; his body was filthy and his hair and beard more disgusting than those of his captors. The lead druid stepped forward and Vespasian felt a jolt of recognition, and yet it could not be for the man was patently younger than when he had last seen him.

'Myrddin?'

The druid stopped and smiled without mirth. 'No, not yet. I have been Myrddin in a previous life and I will be him again when my time comes; until then I serve the living Myrddin and he demands the life of the treacherous Alienus and the sacrifice of two brothers. Myrddin always gets what he demands. Heylel himself, the Son of the Morning, is present to witness this triumph over the fiends who unchained his captive Sullis and the death of the man who was destined to let the canker that will destroy the old, true ways grow in Rome's belly. And here you are, Vespasian, come of your own free will.'

Vespasian felt the same chill grasp at his feet as when he had faced druids before; the malevolent aura enshrouding them began to slip over him, his terror mounted and he could not move. To either side of him Sabinus and Magnus were also rooted to the spot.

Alienus was brought forward and the chanting began; he looked around in dread, struggling feebly, his body weak and emaciated from his long captivity. 'It was Theron,' he shouted at the brothers. 'They said it was Theron who told them where I was and where you lived; kill him for me.'

The yet-to-be-Myrddin interrupted his chanting to laugh. 'Yes, it was Theron who told us your whereabouts when he returned to Britannia in the summer; we had been watching out for him for a long time. He told us what we wanted to know with very little persuasion and then Heylel feasted on his skin; so it's too late to claim vengeance on him – even if you could.'

Alienus was brought to the fish pond at the centre of the garden; the chant rose and Vespasian watched appalled, unable to move as if a force, unseen, willed him to stay still. He tried to lift a foot but it felt as if it were made from freezing lead. Alienus' head was pulled back and, as before with the young girl in the Vale of Sullis, something was stuffed into his mouth, which was then clamped shut whilst his nostrils were squeezed.

Alienus' body shook in weak defiance but he had not the strength to resist; soon he swallowed and, an instant later, convulsed. His mouth and nose were freed and immediately shot forth torrents of blood; blood oozed from his eyes and trickled from his ears. Blood flowed like urine from his penis and exploded from his anus in great bursts, splattering the lower areas of the druids' robes. His head rolled back and he called in terror to the heavens, his cry dulled by the crimson mist that sprayed from his mouth as the blood drowned his gorge. His legs buckled and his captors released him to fall into the pond, jerking and twitching.

With a massive effort of will, Vespasian fought against the cold fear gripping his heart and rendering his body immobile as Clementina was brought forward to the pond.

'Pray to your god!' he managed to say. 'Cogidubnus and Yosef both defeated the druids using the power of their gods; we must do the same.'

Vespasian heard Sabinus intone a prayer to Mithras whilst he invoked his guardian god, Mars, praying that he spare him for the destiny foretold at his birth; Magnus clenched his thumb and spat repeatedly. Clementina shrieked as the pond water churned and the body was sucked under briefly before it shot back up and stood, with its feet just below the surface, bellowing guttural malevolence.

With each prayer he offered, Vespasian felt the cold power gripping him lessen and became aware again of the knife in his hand.

The druids' chant continued and the name of 'Heylel' could now be distinguished.

Alienus' head turned to face Clementina, rotating well past his shoulder before his body moved to catch it up. The druids released Clementina but she did not run; she could not run. She stared wide-eyed at the bloodless corpse before her that was now the vessel for a god of unspeakable malice and wrath.

And its wrath was fuelled by its hunger.

With preternatural speed, the god grabbed Clementina's right wrist. Her mouth opened in a soundless scream. Sabinus cried out, imploring Mithras to hold his hands over his wife. Vespasian managed a step forward, raising his knife. The god outstretched its hands and pulled them down Clementina's right arm; although there was no sign of claws at the end of the fingers, they shredded her flesh, flaying her as easily as skinning a ripe fig. Now she found her voice and it conveyed the full horror of helplessly watching her skin being torn away.

The druids continued their chant, their voices growing more powerful as the god's strength grew.

Sabinus wept, still rooted to the floor; Vespasian, praying with all his will to Mars, managed another couple of steps forward. Magnus continued spitting and clenching his thumb.

Another shriek as the god stuffed the gore-dripping feast into its mouth with a bass rumble of pleasure and then seized Clementina's other arm with one pale hand whilst slashing the other across her face with hideous effect.

Vespasian forced his foot onward another pace; Clementina's screams and the horror being inflicted on her filled his senses so that he hardly registered the flashing iron that spun in from the right-hand side of the garden. So fast did it fly that it seemed a knife simply materialised in the yet-to-be-Myrddin's temple; his eyes widened with shock and his chant abruptly ceased. His four colleagues continued, unaware of the reason for their leader's swaying. A massive roar followed the knife and drew the druids' attention as the yet-to-be-Myrddin fell forward onto his knees; Sextus catapulted himself off the sloping roof of the colonnade to land with a body-roll in the garden. The chant faltered, the god thundered its filth, Clementina wailed in agony but the spell was broken. The chant ceased. Forward dashed Vespasian, Sabinus and Magnus as Sextus came barrelling in from the right. The druids did not run; they did not even raise their arms to defend themselves; they picked up the chant but too late. Sextus piled into two of them, sending them sprawling with a splash to the blood-puddled ground with him on top, stabbing with his knife at a speed that belied his lumbering ways, and adding to the gore already spattered about. With a straight arm, Vespasian powered his blade through the left eye of his adversary as Magnus ripped the throat from his with a shower of blood, severing his long beard.

Sabinus thrust his sword into the small of the god's back; it roared, its mouth full of flayed skin; it turned to face its attacker, pulling the embedded sword from his grasp. Freed from her tormentor, Clementina slumped to the ground bleeding from hideous wounds. Vespasian glanced down at her before launching himself at the husk of Alienus as it struck out at Sabinus, knocking him far back as if suddenly dragged by an invisible rope. Vespasian's blade sliced through pallid flesh into the ribcage; no blood flowed or even seeped; the body was devoid of it. The god turned to him and spewed obscenities, loose skin falling from its mouth; Vespasian thrust again with his knife, piercing the shoulder but doing no harm to the lifeless body as Magnus and Sextus joined him facing the terror. They all three attacked at once and with a wild swipe of its pale arm the husk of Alienus smashed them aside, breaking both its forearm bones so that the hand hung at an impossible angle.

Its head turned, surveying each of them on the ground in turn; the dead eyes had vision and staring at their lifeless gaze Vespasian realised how to put an end to such a monstrosity. 'The head! We must get the head!' he shouted. 'I need to grab that sword.'

Magnus understood immediately and picked himself up as the god stepped out of the pond, its eyes rolling and the ground shaking beneath it. 'Sextus, take the left!'

Sextus nodded, his breathing laboured; he sprang forward at the same time as his leader, each in a different direction as Vespasian circled around the dead druids and the crumpled body of Clementina to get behind the god.

Using its shattered forearm as a club, the god pounded Sextus' chin, sending him into the air, back arching and arms flailing. Vespasian leapt forward as Magnus landed a knife wound to the unfeeling thigh of what had been Alienus. Vespasian grabbed the sword and, raising his foot to brace himself against the god's buttock, wrenched it free as Sabinus charged back in and the god rumbled out its hatred.

Vespasian felt the weight and balance of the weapon, his eyes fixed on the neck just three paces in front of him; the image of Sejanus' freedman, Hasdro's, head, spiralling through the air flickered across his inner eye. He recalled the sensation of decapitation that he had first felt as a sixteen-year-old and the finality of it made his heart sing with joy as the blade hissed through the air; the impact of iron on flesh and bone juddered up his arm but the honed edge was true. It carved through the neck's flesh, muscle, sinew and bone, sending the head up and forward, spinning on an axis through the ears but spraying very little fluid to mark its passing. The body remained upright, its limbs in spasm; the guttural roaring had ceased and in its place came the rush of expelled air. The head bounced on the ground and then rolled to where Sextus lay unconscious, coming to rest in the crook of his arm as the noise of rushing wind increased, seemingly from nowhere. The loose flesh around the gaping neck wound vibrated as if being blown upon and then the noise stopped with an abruptness that was almost a sound in itself and a faint scream could be heard; but no one could ascertain whence it came.

The headless corpse of Alienus collapsed to the floor and Vespasian stared at it with his chest heaving. Sabinus jumped over it and rushed to his wife's side. Vespasian joined him but one glance at her skinned arms and slashed face was enough to assure him that there was no hope. He left his brother to his grief to help Magnus rouse Sextus.

'I thought I'd seen the last of them when we left Britannia,' Magnus muttered as he pulled his crossroads brother up into a sitting position. 'How did they get here?'

'Myrddin said that they would find Alienus to punish him and they did once Narcissus restored Theron's licence to trade in Britannia. He also told me that he still demanded my death but I never, in my darkest dreams, thought they would leave their island to pursue it.'

Magnus hawked and spat at the corpses. 'They should have stayed there and we should leave them well alone.'

'I agree; it's a worthless island and I don't know anyone who's been there, other than the Emperor and his freedmen, who think the effort spent subduing it is worthwhile; especially with that canker at the heart of it.'

'What was that about letting cankers grow?'

'Magnus, I have no idea; but at Messalina's death I did realise she was a canker growing in the very heart of Rome's beauty and wondered what would take her place. Perhaps the next canker that grows here will threaten the old ways. The druids needn't worry; they'll all be dead before it will have had the chance to mature. If we really are going to stay in Britannia then such abominations cannot be allowed to survive.'

Magnus did not look so sure. 'The trouble is that abominations can be very difficult to kill.'

Vespasian looked down at the five druids. Blood further matted their beards and hair and befouled their filthy robes, but in death their malevolence had disappeared. Their faces were serene, as if merely asleep, and showed no hint of the pain that had ripped their lives from them. Vespasian still felt fear as he beheld them. 'I'm afraid that you're right, Magnus; and even if you do manage to get rid of one, another will always come along to replace it.'

EPILOGUE

�⚘

1 JANUARY AD 49

AGRIPPINA GAZED UP at the slobbering fool that she took for husband; her eyes filled with a love that Vespasian knew did not exist. 'Where you are Gaius, I am Gaia.'

Claudius recited the formulaic words with excruciating difficulty as the guests all hid their feelings behind their happiest faces. Vespasian knew that the only people truly happy at the ceremony were the bride herself, her son, Lucius, and their surreptitious supporter, Pallas. But it had been Agrippina's triumph and it had shown on her face as she revelled in the executions that morning of the men condemned for associating too closely with Messalina and Silius. Juncus Vergilianus, Vettius Valens and a dozen others had all been executed, although Suillius Caesoninus was spared because he only ever took the passive role in Messalina's extravagances; Plautius Lateranus had also been spared as a mark of respect for the conduct of his uncle, Aulus Plautius, in the invasion of Britannia.

And now as Claudius eventually concluded the ceremony Agrippina's triumph was complete; she was the Empress. She took Claudius' hands and smiled with such innocence that all who beheld her would be tempted into thinking that here was the most honest and unselfish person in Rome. 'Come, dear husband, we should consummate our love.'

Claudius gibbered something to the affirmative.

'But before we do you should complete our family; I will not be able to relax and be truly comfortable with you until we do.'

Claudius' head jerked to the left a couple of times in alarm. 'W-w-what w-w-would you have me do, little bird?'

'I am your wife, so my son should be your son.'

'B-b-b-but of course he is.'

'Then give him your name.' The steel in her voice was palpable; no one present moved.

Claudius had a blinking fit that was rounded off by a couple more jerks of his head. 'Of course, little bird, I shall do that; he shall have my name, your father's name and your elder brother's name. He shall b-b-be, he s-s-shall be: Nero Claudius Caesar Drusus Germanicus.'

'And when will you adopt him?'

Narcissus stepped forward. 'Princeps, is that a wise course—'

Claudius did not turn to face him. 'Silence! You've over-stepped your limit once in my family's business, Narcissus, do not do it again. I may have given you the rank of quaestor with the right to sit in the Senate but I can no longer trust you completely, especially as you wanted me to marry someone whom I've already d-d-divorced once. In future when I want your advice, I sh-sh-shall ask for it.'

Vespasian could guess what the once all-powerful imperial secretary would think about being given the rank of a mere quaestor. Narcissus retreated with haste, back to where Callistus stood looking forlorn having never returned to favour after the disaster for him of Asiaticus' hearing.

Agrippina stared at her husband's out-of-favour freedman with cold contempt before turning to Pallas. 'What do you think, Pallas? Is the Emperor embarking on a wise course by adopting my son?'

Pallas inclined his head a fraction. 'Indeed, domina, all the Emperor's decisions are wise; like his decision to marry you, for example.'

Agrippina raised her carefully plucked eyebrows. 'But that was your idea.'

Claudius started. 'I thought that it was Sabinus' idea.'

'No, my sweetest husband, Sabinus was acting under Pallas' instructions; we have him to thank for our happiness.'

Claudius put an imperial hand on his freedman's shoulder. 'I am grateful indeed, Pallas, that you should have understood what would make me happy. You shall escort me to the bridal chamber once my little bird has prepared herself.'

'An unimagined honour, Princeps.'

'Before I do that, husband, I have one more favour to ask.'

'Anything on your wedding day, little bird.'

'Seeing as Lucius is to be the Emperor's son, should he not have the best tutor that money can buy?'

'Of course he should.'

'Then recall Lucius Annaeus Seneca whom that bitch, Messalina, in her spite, persuaded you to banish to Corsica; only he has the intellect to educate the son of an emperor.'

'As s-s-soon as we are man and wife in body as well as in spirit, it shall be done.'

Agrippina went up onto her toes and, leaning forward, gave her drooling new husband a passionate kiss.

Vespasian looked around the gathering of Rome's élite; from his family only Sabinus was missing, having left for Moesia two months previously to drown his grief in work.

'Come, Lucius, my baby darling, or Nero as I shall now call you,' Agrippina purred to a ginger-haired boy of ten escorted by a dark-haired youth in his early teens. 'You and Otho should escort me to the marriage chamber; I would rather a pair of lovers such as you do that for me.'

'Mother my love, we would be delighted,' Nero almost squealed with pleasure. 'Will we help you undress?'

'But of course; and then you shall both help me prepare my body.'

'She's breaking taboos before she's even been married an hour,' Gaius whispered to Vespasian. 'I wonder if she'll know where to stop?'

Vespasian looked over to Pallas now standing well in front of a broken-looking Narcissus and a cringing Callistus. 'I wonder if he'll be able to stop her.'

Gaius shook his head sadly. 'I don't think so; and her husband certainly won't be able to.'

Vespasian looked around the guests again and wondered if there would be anyone who would be able to curb Agrippina. Claudius shuffled at her side giving her sidelong lecherous glances; he would do anything she told him to. Nero preceded her holding Otho's hand; when he grew up would he exert influence over her or would he always be in her thrall? Vespasian caught sight of Corvinus, who studiously ignored him, keeping up his promise to conduct himself as a dead man in his presence. Next to him stood Galba and Lucius Vitellius with his sons, young Lucius and Aulus Vitellius; would the ancient families of Rome stand for such a woman? Of course they would, she was the daughter of Germanicus, the man who should have succeeded Augustus.

Vespasian's face tensed as he thought of the future; he put his arms on his son, Titus', shoulders and gave them a comforting squeeze. At Titus' side stood Britannicus, watching his father remarry with tears in his eyes. As Agrippina came close, Vespasian saw behind the smile she offered her new stepson a cold hatred that would not be satisfied by anything less than the child's death. Britannicus felt it too for he grabbed Titus' hand and tried to pull his friend close.

Vespasian held onto his son, drawing him away. To allow Titus to continue being intimate with Britannicus would mean that he too would die at the hands of Agrippina.

And that, Vespasian would not allow to happen.

AUTHOR'S NOTE

THIS HISTORICAL FICTION is based upon the writings of Tacitus, Suetonius and Cassius Dio.

We do not know any details of the latter part of Vespasian's four years in Britannia other than he subdued two tribes, fought thirty battles, captured twenty hill-forts as well as the Island of Vectis, as Suetonius tells us. Tacitus' account is lost and Cassius Dio has a reference to Vespasian being hemmed in by barbarians and being saved by his son, Titus, which is obviously a mistake seeing as Titus was only six or seven at the time! However, we can assume from Suetonius that he was very busy and the excavations of various hill-forts in the southwest of England attest to the long and methodical advance west that the II Augusta must have made. The battles, therefore, are fictitious as is Caratacus and the druids' attempt to lure Vespasian into a trap using his brother as bait.

As to the druids, we just do not know as they left no record of themselves. The best book on the subject that I have found is *The Druids* by Stuart Piggott; his conclusion is that you can have druids as imagined or druids as wished for, but never druids as really were. My druids are totally imaginary but backed up by five references. Tacitus gives us an interesting insight when he describes them as lifting their arms to the heavens and showering imprecations that struck the Roman soldiers invading Anglesey with such awe at first that their limbs were paralysed and they left their bodies open to wounds without attempting to move. I have taken this quite literally. Pliny tells us that they wore white robes and Cicero in his *On Divination* implies that they practised human sacrifice as they were keen on reading the intestines of humans; Diodorus Siculus confirms this by saying that they sacrificed their victims with a dagger in the chest. Caesar tells us that victims were also sacrificed by burning in a wicker man; he also tells us of the druids' belief in the transmigration of the soul, which is what gave me the idea of an immortal Myrddin. Their keeping alive the rites of the old gods of Britannia that were worshipped before the coming of the Celts is, of course, fiction; but I've often wondered what gods inspired the building of so great a monument as Stonehenge, which was already ancient by Vespasian's time.

Having Tintagel as a smaller version of the druids' main stronghold of Anglesey is my fiction.

The Cornovii were a tribe in the northwest of Britannia, but there must have been a sub-tribe in the area of Tintagel as implied by the name of the settlement, Durocornavis or 'fortress of the Cornovii'.

Legend has it that Yosef of Arimathea came to Britain and founded a church on Glastonbury Tor, bringing with him either the Spear of Destiny or the Holy Grail or both. Legend also has it that Jesus' children – or at least his son of the same name – accompanied him; this may have given rise to the belief that Jesus himself walked on our green and pleasant land and caused William Blake to write *Jerusalem*. Having already been, rather sadly, accused of 'heresy' for similar offences I have felt free to incorporate the legend into this fiction.

I am indebted again to John Peddie who suggests, in his *Roman Invasion of Britain*, that the portage way between the Axe and the Parrett would have been important to the invaders because it would have been a lot safer and quicker than sailing around the peninsula with its contrary tides and winds. Given the manpower at their disposal the Romans would not have blanched at the prospect of dragging ships overland.

Tacitus mentions Hormus as being Vespasian's freedman in *The Histories* so I thought it appropriate that he should be the first slave that Vespasian purchases.

Messalina did covet Asiaticus' Gardens of Lucullus and forced his suicide in order to get hold of them. Asiaticus' private hearing before Claudius and Messalina is recounted by Tacitus and happened pretty much as described apart from Vespasian's intervention. Asiaticus did have his pyre moved so that it would not damage his gardens before eating with friends and then bleeding to death in his bath. The gardens were on the Pincian Hill; however, the hill was not known as that until the fifth century when it took its name from a family that lived there. I have used the name to avoid confusion.

The *Dying Gaul* and the *Gaul Killing Himself and His Wife* were both rediscovered at the Gardens of Sallust just close by in the early seventeenth century; it's not beyond the realms of possibility that they may have been in the Gardens of Lucullus in Vespasian's time.

Messalina's excesses are a matter of record in all three of the primary sources; the question is why did she go so far and marry Silius? Even the normally unshockable Tacitus feels that his readers would find it hard to comprehend. Silius was consul-designate in AD 48 according to Tacitus – but not Wikipedia! At the time of writing, that is – maybe that could explain it and perhaps I'm not that far from the truth; perhaps, though, it was just madness. The details of their wedding, the orgiastic behaviour, the tubs of grapes, Messalina's thyrsus, Silius' boots, wreath and head-tossing and Vettius Valens climbing the tree and seeing a storm over Ostia, all come from Tacitus. He also tells us that it was two prostitutes, Cleopatra and Calpurnia, who brought the news to Claudius in Ostia.

Narcissus did keep Claudius distracted with documents to prevent him noticing Messalina's attempt to see him as he returned to Rome and Vitellius did remain ambiguous in his criticism of the villainy.

Vibidia, the chief Vestal, did intercede on Messalina's behalf causing Claudius to say that he would call for his wife in the morning and allow her to plead her case. It was Narcissus who ordered her execution having been given command of the Guard for one day because the prefects' loyalties were suspect.

Vespasian's part in Messalina's death is my fiction as is Burrus being the tribune who finished her – but more of him in later volumes. She did die, with her mother in attendance, in the

Gardens of Lucullus, the seeming justice of which both Tacitus and Cassius Dio make much of.

Lucius Vipstanus Messalla Poplicola and his brother Gaius Vipstanus Messalla Gallus did become consuls with the Vitellius brothers that year; they being cousins of Messalina is my fiction but I enjoyed the coincidence of their name.

Corvinus betraying his sister is fiction but I felt justified in doing it as he not only survived her downfall but also went on to become consul a few years later. I am indebted to Ridley Scott's fine film *The Duellists* for the idea of Corvinus conducting himself as a dead man.

Sabinus, Vespasian and Galba's part in changing the law to enable Claudius to marry his niece is fiction; however, the law was changed and the Senate, at Lucius Vitellius' instigation, begged Claudius to accept the match – a match that Pallas had proposed.

Tacitus tells us that Agrippina used the niece's privilege of sitting on her uncle's lap and kissing him – isn't it strange how the definition of privilege has changed?

Agrippina's second husband, Passienus, did die in AD 47 – perhaps poisoned by his wife – and left everything to her son Lucius. That the inheritance included an estate next to the Flavians at Aquae Cutillae is fictitious. Claudius did introduce three new letters into the alphabet but they fell out of use after his death; he also wrote a book on dice and was an inveterate gambler. He also did some constructive arithmetic that allowed him to hold the Secular Games.

Finally, Claudius did adopt Lucius Domitius Ahenobarbus – who became known as Nero – which was as good as signing his own son's death warrant. Sometimes you just can't make it up!

Once again my thanks go to all the people who support me through the writing process: my agent, Ian Drury, at Shiel Land Associates and Gaia Banks and Marika Lysandrou in the foreign rights department – although sometimes I think it should be renamed the foreign writs department. Those publishers know who they are and shame on them for their dishonesty.

Thanks to Sara O'Keeffe, Toby Mundy, Anna Hogarty and everyone at Corvus/Atlantic for their constant enthusiasm for the Vespasian series; I'm very grateful. Farewell and good luck to Corinna Zifko in her new job.

As always, much gratitude and respect goes to my editor, Richenda Todd, for such a thorough structural edit, which improved the manuscript considerably, and also for correcting my O-level grade D Latin. Thanks also to Tamsin Shelton for the copy-edit, picking up so well on all the minute mistakes that I could stare at all day and never notice.

Finally, my love and thanks to my wife, Anja Müller, for listening to me read my work aloud and supplying so many great ideas.

Vespasian's story will continue in *Rome's Lost Son.*

Read on to enjoy the first gripping chapter of Vespasian's next mission

ROME'S LOST SON

ROME, DECEMBER AD 51

CHAPTER I

PERSISTENT AND SHRILL, the cry echoed around the walls and marble columns of the atrium; a torment to all who endured it.

Titus Flavius Vespasianus gritted his teeth, determined not to be moved by the pitiful wail as it rose and fell, occasionally pausing for a ragged breath before bellowing out again with renewed, lung-filled vigour. The suffering that it conveyed had to be borne and Vespasian knew that should he not have the stomach for it he would lose the ongoing battle of wills; and that was something that he could not afford to do.

A new cacophony of anguish emitted from the writhing bundle in his wife's arms, its movements caught in the flickering glow of the log fire spitting and crackling in the atrium hearth. Vespasian winced and then held his head high and crooked his left arm before him as his body slave draped his toga over and around his well-muscled, compact frame, watched by Titus, Vespasian's eleven-year-old son.

With the heavy woollen garment eventually hanging to his satisfaction and the howls showing no sign of abating, Vespasian eased into the pair of red leather, senatorial slippers that his slave held out for him. 'The heels, Hormus.' Hormus ran a finger around the back of each shoe so that his master's feet fitted snugly and then stood and backed away with deference, leaving Titus facing his father.

Doing his best to remain calm as the din reached a new level, Vespasian contemplated Titus for a few moments. 'Does the Emperor still come every day to check on his son's progress?'

'Most days, Father; and he also asks me and the other boys questions, as well as Britannicus.'

Vespasian flinched at a particularly shrill bawl and strove to ignore it. 'What happens if you get them wrong?'

'Sosibius beats us after Claudius has gone.'

Vespasian hid his less than favourable opinion of the *grammaticus* from his son. It had been Sosibius' fallacious allegations at the Empress Messalina's behest, three years earlier, that had set in train a series of events that had ended up in Vespasian bearing false witness against the former Consul, Asiaticus, in order to protect his brother, Sabinus. Using Vespasian as a willing tool, however, Asiaticus had had his revenge from beyond the grave and Messalina had been executed; Vespasian had been present as she shrieked and cursed her last. But Sosibius was still in place, his fabricated charges corroborated by Vespasian's false testimony. 'Does he often beat you?'

Titus' face hardened into a strained expression, startling Vespasian by its similarity to his own, older version. The thick nose not so pronounced, the earlobes not so long, the jaw not so heavy and with a full head of hair rather than his semi-wreath about the crown; but there was no mistaking it: Titus was his son. 'Yes, Father, but Britannicus says that it's because his step-mother, the Empress, has ordered him to.'

'Then deny Agrippina that pleasure and make sure that Sosibius has no cause to beat you today.'

'If he does it'll be the last time. Britannicus has thought of a way to have him dismissed and at the same time insult his step-brother.'

Vespasian ruffled Titus' hair. 'Don't you get involved in any feud between Britannicus and Nero.'

'I'll always support my friend, Father.'

'Just be sure that you don't make it too public.' Vespasian took the boy's chin in his hand and examined his face. 'It's dangerous; do you understand me?'

Titus nodded slowly. 'Yes, Father, I believe I do.'

'Good, now be off with you. Hormus, see Titus out to his escort. Are Magnus' lads waiting?'

'Yes, master.'

As Hormus led Titus away the bawling continued. Vespasian turned to face Flavia Domitilla, his wife of twelve years; she sat staring into the fire doing nothing to try to soothe the babe in her arms. 'If you really want my clients to mistake you for the wet nurse when I let them in for the morning *salutio*, my dear, then I suggest that you plug little Domitian onto one of your breasts and sing Gallic lullabies to him.'

Flavia snorted and carried on staring at the flames. 'At least then they'll think that we can afford a Gallic wet nurse.'

Vespasian pushed his head forward, frowning, unable to credit what he had just heard. 'What are you talking about, woman? We've got a Gallic wet nurse; it's just that this morning you've chosen not to call for her and instead you seem to be intent on starving the child.' To emphasise the point he picked up a piece of bread from his recently abandoned breakfast, dipped it in the bowl of olive oil and then chewed on it with relish.

'She's not Gallic! She's Hispanic.'

Vespasian suppressed a sigh of exasperation. 'Yes, she is from Hispania but she is a Celt, a Celtiberian. She's from the same race of huge tribesmen that all the *finest* women in Rome choose to have breastfeed their sons; it's just that when her ancestors crossed the Rhenus they didn't stop in Gaul, they carried on over the mountains into Hispania.'

'And therefore she produces milk so thin that a kitten wouldn't survive on it.'

'Her milk is no different from any other Celt's.'

'Your niece swears by her Allobroges woman.'

'How Lucius Junius Paetus chooses to indulge his wife is his own affair. However, to my mind, allowing a baby to go hungry because its wet nurse isn't from one of the more fashionable Celtic tribes is the act of an irresponsible mother.'

'And to my mind dragging a wife to live in the squalor of the Quirinal Hill and then not allowing her to purchase the staff that she needs to look after the family is the act of an uncaring and heartless husband and father.'

Vespasian smiled to himself but kept his face neutral now they had got to the nub of the matter. Two and a half years previously Vespasian had used his good standing with Pallas, as the freedman had manoeuvred himself to the most powerful position in Claudius' court, to remove Flavia and their children from the apartment in the imperial palace where they had lived for most of Vespasian's four years as legate of the II Augusta in Britannia. The accommodation had been offered by Claudius ostensibly so that their two sons could be educated together and also so that Messalina, Claudius' then wife, would have a companion in the palace. However, Vespasian knew that the Emperor had been manipulated into making the offer by Messalina's brother, Corvinus, so that his old enemy could have the power of life and death over Flavia and their children. After Messalina's violent end, Pallas had kept his word to persuade Claudius to allow Vespasian to move his family to a house in Pomegranate Street, on the Quirinal Hill, near to that of his uncle, the senator Gaius Vespasius Pollo.

Flavia had resented this.

'If you call protecting my family from the ravages of imperial politics uncaring; and if you call being prudent with money so as not to be subject to the fripperies of the ladies of fashion heartless, then you've understood my character perfectly, my dear. It is bad enough that Titus goes to the palace each day to share Britannicus' education but that was Claudius' price for allowing me to move you out; having executed the boy's mother he didn't want his son to be deprived of his little playmate as well. Surely our son being educated alongside the Emperor's is enough to satisfy your vanity, despite the danger that puts him in; surely that makes up for all this *squalor*?' He indicated with a lazy hand the good-sized atrium around them. Although he would freely concede its decoration was not up to the standards of the palace – it having been built 150 years before, during the time of Gaius Marius – what it lacked in splendour with the mosaic floor's geometric black and white motif or the faded pastoral frescoes, designed to fool the beholder into thinking that they were looking through windows, it made up for with his wife's extravagance. It was filled with furniture and ornaments that Flavia had acquired during her lavish spending sprees while under Messalina's profligate influence.

Vespasian still shuddered every time he surveyed the room's décor surrounding the *impluvium*, the pond with a fountain of Venus at its centre: low, polished-marble tables on gilded legs covered with glass or silver ornaments, statuettes of fine bronze or worked crystal, couches and chairs, carved, painted and upholstered. It was not because of its vulgarity – he could cope with that even though it offended his country-born taste for the simple things in life – it was because of the amount of wasted money that it represented. 'Surely having all the other women jealously arguing amongst themselves as to whether Agrippina will kill Titus along with Britannicus as she clears the way for her son Nero to succeed his stepfather is enough to make you feel special and the centre of attention; like any self-respecting woman would wish for?'

Flavia clutched the bundle of their two-month-old son so tightly that for a moment Vespasian was worried that she would do him some damage. Then she relaxed and stood, holding the child to her breast with tears in her eyes. 'After all that I've done for you, for us, you should accord me a little respect, Vespasian. You are one of the sitting Consuls; I should be able to deport myself as the wife of a consul and not some lowly equestrian upstart ...'

'Which, when you consider the matter, is what we both are.'

Flavia's mouth dropped open but no sound emerged.

'Now, my dear, I'm going to open the door to all this squalor for my clients; they will greet me not only as the master of this squalor but also as the Consul of Rome who can do great favours for them and they will ignore the fact that I come from a Sabine family that can only boast one member of the Senate before me and my brother, just as they will ignore my rough Sabine accent. And then, having dealt out private patronage, I shall, as Consul of Rome, publicly deliver one of Rome's greatest enemies to the Emperor for punishment. If you like, you and our daughter may come to watch, along with all the other women, and you can enjoy the false compliments that they give you. Or perhaps you're too afraid to show your face because your husband bought you a wet nurse who belongs to a tribe that is so out of fashion that she cannot even produce decent milk.'

Vespasian turned and signalled to his doorkeeper to open up; it was with some relief that he heard the brisk clatter of Flavia's retreating footsteps over the mewling of his youngest son.

Vespasian sat on his curule chair in front of the impluvium at the centre of the atrium; the gentle spatter of the fountain, issuing from a vase on Venus' shoulder, remained constant as the dawn light grew, adding a steely tinge to the lifelike, painted skin tones of her naked torso basking in the oil lamps' glow. Hormus stood behind him making notes on a wax tablet. To either side of him were posted the twelve lictors who would accompany him, as consul, everywhere in Rome, carrying the fasces, the axes bound with rods, as a symbol of his power to command and execute. However, it was not civic power that Vespasian was exercising now but, rather, personal power as the last and least important of his two hundred or so clients greeted him.

Vespasian nodded his acknowledgement to the man. 'I have no use for you today, Balbus, you may return to your business once you have escorted me to the Forum.'

'An honour, Consul.' Balbus adjusted his plain white citizen's toga and withdrew to one side.

'How many waiting for a private interview, Hormus?' Vespasian asked, looking around the room filled with respectful men talking in murmurs as they waited for their patron to leave the house.

Hormus had no need to consult his tablet. 'Three that you asked to stay and then a further seven who requested an audience.'

Vespasian sighed; it would be a long morning. However, as the Senate was not due to sit that day it was one of the few occasions that he had the time to deal with personal business before his public duties would call him away; and it was with great interest that he was looking forward to his public duties.

'And then there's a man who is not your client asking for an interview as well.'

'Really? What's his name?'

'Agarpetus.'

Vespasian was none the wiser.

'He's a client of the imperial freedman Narcissus.'

Vespasian raised his eyebrows. 'A client of Narcissus' here to see me? Is it a message or is he trying to ingratiate himself with me?'

'He didn't say, master.'

Vespasian digested this for a few moments before rising to his feet; formality dictated that he would have to see this man last, after his own clients, so it would be a while before his curiosity would be satisfied.

But first, business.

Followed by his slave, he walked with the slow dignity of the leading magistrate in Rome, past the men awaiting his favour, to the *tablinum*, the room curtained off at the far end of the atrium, and seated himself behind the desk. 'I'll deal with the three that I need favours from, first, Hormus; in order of precedence.'

'What the Emperor did while he held the office of censor, four years ago, cannot be undone, Laelius,' Vespasian said, having heard the final plea for favour from a balding citizen wearing a very finely woven crimson tunic under his plain white toga. A heavy gold chain glinted around his neck.

'I understand that, *patronus*; however, the situation has changed.' Laelius produced a scroll from the fold of his toga and stepped up to the desk to hand it to Vespasian. 'This is a receipt from the Cloelius Brothers' banking business in the Forum Romanum. It is for exactly one hundred thousand denarii, the financial threshold for admittance to the equestrian order. When Claudius stripped me of equestrian rank four years ago he was perfectly right to do so as, owing to a series of unwise investments, my combined wealth in property and cash had fallen well below the limit. But now, thanks to your brother, at your behest, securing me the contract to supply chickpeas to the Danuvius Fleet, I've reversed my fortunes and am now financially eligible for readmittance.'

Vespasian glanced at the receipt; it was genuine. 'The Emperor may not revise the rolls for a few years yet.'

Laelius wrung his hands; there was a hint of desperation in his voice. 'My son is now seventeen; only as an eques can I hope to secure him a post as a military tribune and start him on the Cursus Honorum. In two or three years it'll be too late.'

For all his client's outward appearance of confidence Vespasian could perceive that Laelius was just another middle-aged man dogged by the spectre of impending old age with nothing to show for his life. But, if he could get his son started upon the succession of honours, the military and political career that could lead to a seat in the Senate, then he could justifiably claim to have done honour for his family by bettering it. Vespasian could understand his position well; it had been his parents' ambition for their family that had driven Vespasian and his brother Sabinus to the highest office that a citizen could achieve – barring, of course, becoming emperor; that was the prerogative of one family alone. 'Do I take it that there are two favours that you are asking me: firstly to use my influence with the imperial household to have Claudius enrol you in the equestrian order, and then to ask my brother to get your son a post as a military tribune in one of his two Moesian legions? Having already got him to award you the chickpea contract.'

Laelius winced and produced another scroll from his toga. 'I know I ask a lot, patronus, but I give a lot in return. I know that senators are forbidden to conduct trade; however, I know of no reason why a senator should not benefit from trade that is conducted by someone else. This is a legal document that would make you a sleeping-partner in my business with an interest of ten per cent of the profits.'

Vespasian took the scroll, perused it and then handed it over his shoulder to Hormus standing behind him. 'Very well, Laelius, if you make it twelve per cent I'll see what I can do.'

'Have Hormus make the alteration in the contract, patronus.'

'It will be his pleasure.'

Laelius bowed his head repeatedly in thanks and gratitude while rubbing his hands and calling down the blessings of all the gods onto his patron as Hormus escorted him out through the curtains.

Vespasian took a few sips of watered wine while he waited for his final supplicant of the morning, contemplating, as he did, just what a client of Narcissus' could want from him.

'Tiberius Claudius Agarpetus,' Hormus announced, showing in a clean-shaven, wiry man of evident wealth, judging by the heavily jewelled rings on each of his fingers and thumbs. He had the olive skin of the northern Greeks, which was stretched tight over his high-cheekboned, sharp-nosed face. Regardless of having two Roman names he disdained the toga, despite the formality of the occasion.

Vespasian did not offer him a seat. 'What can I do for you, Agarpetus?'

'It's more about what I can do for you, Consul.' The Greek spoke with a measured tone, his dark eyes never leaving Vespasian's nor showing a hint of feeling.

'What can a freedman do for me? I assume that you are Narcissus' freedman since you bear his names that he took from Claudius when he freed him in turn.'

'That is correct, Consul. Narcissus freed me two years ago and since then I have worked for him on a variety of delicate tasks involving the gathering of information.'

'I see. So you spy for him?'

'Not as such; I gather information from his agents in the eastern provinces and make assessments as to its veracity and importance so my patron only sees what he needs to see.'

'Ah, so you're a saver of time?'

'Indeed.'

'And a possessor of knowledge.'

'Yes, Consul; I am a saver of time and a possessor of knowledge.'

Vespasian could see where this was leading. 'Knowledge that could be of value to me?'

'Very much so.'

'At what price?'

'A meeting: you and your uncle with my patron.'

Vespasian frowned and ran a hand over his almost-bald crown. 'Why didn't Narcissus just ask us himself? He may be out of favour with Claudius but he's still the imperial secretary and retains the power to summon a consul and a senator.'

'That is so, but he wants the meeting to be secret; so therefore it has to be away from the palace, away from the eyes and ears of the Empress and her lover.'

'Pallas?'

'As you know, my patron and Pallas are not on the best of terms ...'

'And as *you* know, my loyalty is to Pallas and I won't be a part of Narcissus' schemes against him.'

'Not even if Pallas would knowingly allow the Empress to block your career?'

Vespasian scoffed. 'Block my career? Does it look like it's blocked? I'm Consul.'

'But you will go no further; there'll be no province to govern, no military command, nothing, just political oblivion. My patron asks you to consider this: why were you made consul for only the last two months of this year?'

'Because my forty-second birthday was in November and so it wasn't until then that I was eligible. It was a great honour to be the Emperor's colleague in the office.'

'No doubt that non-entity Calventius Vetus Carminius thought exactly the same thing when he was Claudius' colleague for September and October; in fact I would suspect that he thought it even more of an honour than you did, seeing as he'd done nothing to merit the position.'

Vespasian opened his mouth to refute the claim and then closed it immediately, his mind racing.

Agarpetus pressed his argument. 'But surely it would have been a greater honour for the victorious legate of the Second

Augusta to have been made consul in January next year? In only a few days' time you could have been the Junior Consul for a full six months, perhaps even with the Emperor as your colleague, and the year would have been named after you both. But no, you were given a crumb after all your loyal service in Britannia, just a crumb, a two-month consulship, just like the man you succeeded whom nobody had ever heard of; and do you know why?'

Vespasian did not answer; his mind was too busy.

'The Empress hates you because of your son's friendship with Britannicus; and Pallas is powerless to help you against such an enemy. It was she who persuaded her gullible husband that it would be a singular honour for you to be made consul in the very month that you were first eligible and it will be her who'll block any appointment that may be mooted for you when you step down on the first day of January, three days hence. Your only hope for advancement is her demise, and loyalty to Pallas won't bring that about. Narcissus, on the other hand ...' Agarpetus trailed off leaving the last thought dangling.

Vespasian still said nothing as his mind worked and the truth of what he was being told became apparent. He did not argue with it because he realised that deep down he had always known; deep down he had been insulted by being given the consulship for the final two months of a year; deep down, he had known it to be a snub; deep down, the honour that he felt at being consul had been gnawed at by resentment. But he had kept all that buried – deep down. 'How will she block me?'

'Your brother has just failed Rome in quite a spectacular way ...'

'What do you mean?'

'This is the knowledge that we thought would be of interest to you; Narcissus will explain if you meet him. Suffice it to say that Sabinus' mistake is excuse enough to halt all ambitions that any member of your family may have. Pallas cannot help you, so that leaves you with one option.'

Trust Narcissus to reach straight for the truth of the matter; trust him to know how to manipulate. Vespasian looked at Agarpetus, his decision made; it had not been hard to choose between obscurity and disloyalty. 'Very well; I'll meet Narcissus.'

Agarpetus gave the wry smile of a man who has had a prediction confirmed – his first change of expression. 'He suggests that the safest place to meet would be at the tavern of the South Quirinal Crossroads Brotherhood; he believes that your friend, your uncle's client, Marcus Salvius Magnus, is still the patronus there.'

'He is.'

'Very good, his discretion is assured; Narcissus and I will be there tonight at the seventh hour as the city celebrates today's executions.'

'Good morning, dear boy!' Gaius Vespasius Pollo boomed as he waddled fast to fall into step next to his nephew, his expansive belly and buttocks and his sagging breasts and chins all swaying furiously to seemingly different beats. 'Thank you for inviting me to share the honour of conducting the prisoners to the Emperor.' Behind him his clients fell in with those of Vespasian to make an entourage of well over five hundred escorting them down the Quirinal Hill.

Vespasian inclined his head. 'Thank you, Uncle, for lending me your clients to add impact to my arrival in the Forum.'

'My pleasure; it makes a nice change to be preceded by lictors again.'

'"Change pleases",' a voice quoted from just behind Gaius, 'and it makes a nice change for me and the lads not to have to beat you a path through the crowds, seeing as you have them do it professionally today; and don't they do it so well?'

'Indeed, and with more satisfaction too, I'll hazard, Magnus,' Gaius suggested, starting to sweat despite the dignified pace and the chill winter wind. 'After all, a lictor gets paid and therefore mixes business with pleasure.'

Magnus' battered ex-boxer's face screwed into an indignant frown and he looked slantendicular at his patron with his one good eye – the painted glass ball in his left eye socket stared futilely ahead. 'Are you saying that my lads don't enjoy beating a path for you, senator? Because you certainly pay us to do so, although, granted, not in the same way as the College of Lictors remunerates its members. However, you reward us in subtle and much more lucrative ways, which means that our business is far more satisfying, if you take my meaning?'

Vespasian laughed and squeezed his friend's shoulder; despite Magnus being nineteen years his senior and considerably below him socially, they had been friends since Vespasian had first come to Rome as a youth of sixteen. He and his uncle knew far better than most just how satisfying Magnus found his business in the criminal underbelly of Rome as the leader of the South Quirinal Crossroads Brotherhood. 'I do, my friend; and it pleases me that even at your age you still derive satisfaction from your work.'

Magnus ran a hand through his hair, grey with age but still thick. 'Now you're mocking me, sir; I may be sixty but there's still some fight and fuck in me left – although I don't see as well as I used to since losing the eye and that is becoming a bit of a problem, I'll admit. I ain't as sharp as I was and some of the surrounding brotherhoods are getting a whiff of that.'

'Perhaps it's time to think about retiring and taking life easy; take your patron's example: he hasn't made a speech in the Senate for three years now.'

Gaius brushed away a carefully tonged and dyed curl from his face and looked at Vespasian in alarm. 'Dear boy, you wonder why, when the last speech I was forced to make was reading out a list of all the senators and equites accused of crimes with Messalina and condemned to death. That sort of exposure makes one very conspicuous and that's how I still feel three years later, having not even countenanced the possibility of holding an opinion, let alone considered expressing one, during all that time.'

'Well, I'm afraid that you may be dragged out of your self-imposed retirement, Uncle.'

The alarm on Gaius' face intensified. 'Whatever for?'

'Not what but whom, Uncle.'

'Pallas?'

'I wish it were but I'm afraid it's not.'

'Is that wise?' Gaius asked after Vespasian had finished recounting his meeting with Agarpetus. 'If you refuse to meet him, there is still a chance that Pallas may be able to exert some pressure over Agrippina; he might get her to change her mind or at least not oppose you so vehemently just because your boy happens to be her stepson's best friend. But once you go behind Pallas' back to Narcissus then all trust and expectation of loyalty is broken and we lose the best ally that this family has in the palace.'

'But that ally is the lover of my enemy.'

'And so therefore Pallas has become your enemy whilst Narcissus is Agrippina's enemy thus making him your friend? Dear boy, think: Pallas has done nothing more than protect his own position by allying himself with Agrippina; he has made the sensible choice seeing as Nero is a far more suitable candidate to succeed Claudius than Britannicus, purely because he's three years older. Claudius won't last more than two, perhaps three, more years; do you really think that a boy could rule?'

Vespasian considered the question as the party passed under a colonnade and entered the Forum of Augustus dominated by the vividly painted Temple of Mars Victorious resplendent in deep red and strong, golden yellow. Statues, togate or in military uniform, equally as brightly painted, stood on plinths around the edge of the Forum, their eyes – which exposed Magnus' false one for the cheap imitation it was – followed the public about their business as if the great men commemorated still guided the city. 'No, Uncle, not without a regent,' he admitted eventually.

'And who would that be in Britannicus' case? His mother, thank the gods, is dead so that leaves his uncle, Corvinus, or Burrus, the prefect of the Praetorian Guard. No one can countenance either option so the weight of opinion is favouring Nero because, since his fourteenth birthday fifteen days ago, he has taken his toga virilis. If Claudius dies tomorrow we have a man to put in his place.'

'If Nero becomes emperor, Agrippina will see to it that I'll never hold office again.'

'Then pull Titus away from Britannicus and the problem is solved.'

'Is it? Claudius would be offended; what happens if he surprises us all and lives for another ten years?'

It was Gaius' turn to contemplate the question as they passed through into Caesar's Forum where the Urban prefect and lesser civic magistrates could be petitioned in the shadow of a great equestrian statue of the one-time dictator himself. 'That would be unfortunate,' Gaius conceded, 'but highly unlikely.'

'But not impossible. If I've earned Agrippina's enmity, would you deem it wise to try to buy her friendship by earning Claudius' as well?'

'If you put it like that, then no.'

'So what choice do we have other than going to meet with Narcissus tonight?'

Massed cheering broke out as Vespasian's twelve lictors came out into the Forum Romanum, their appearance announcing the arrival of one of the Consuls at the Senate House to the thousands of citizenry come to witness the greatest day in Rome since the Ovation of Aulus Plautius four years previously. This would be the day when Rome's great enemy, the chieftain who had led the resistance to her latest conquest, would pay for his temerity and die before the Emperor.

But first, in the absence of his imperial senior colleague who waited at the Praetorian camp, outside the Viminal Gate, it was Vespasian's task to make the sacrifice and read the auspices; it was important that the gods declare the day auspicious for the business of the city to be carried out. Vespasian had no doubt that it would be so.

Blood spurted in heartbeat bursts into the copper basin beneath the white bullock's gaping neck. The beast's eyes barely focused, stunned as it was by the Father of the House's mallet blow to its forehead made an instant before Vespasian, a fold of his toga covering his head, wielded the knife. Its forelegs and shoulders began to shudder, blood flowing down them. Its tongue lolled from its mouth and it voided its bowels with a steaming splatter as the juddering limbs collapsed, bringing the victim to its knees in front of the Senate House. Standing arrayed on the steps in order of precedence, the five hundred senators currently residing in the city looked on with a solemn dignity as this ancient ceremony was enacted, as of time immemorial, in the very heart of Rome.

Vespasian had stepped back, keeping well away from the various discharges emitting from the bullock – it would be considered a bad omen for the presiding Consul to have his toga sullied and the whole ritual would have to be repeated. The Father of the House supervised the removal of the filled basin by two public slaves just before the animal slumped to the ground, its heartbeat fast diminishing as it made the transition from living flesh to inanimate carcass.

Vespasian repeated the formulaic words over the dead beast, entreating Jupiter Opitmus Maximus' blessing on his city, just as they had been intoned by incumbents of his office since the founding of the Republic. Four more public slaves rolled the body onto its back and stretched its four limbs in preparation for the belly incision.

The stench of steaming, fresh viscera assaulted Vespasian's nostrils as his honed blade slit open the gift to Rome's guardian god; the crowd, packing the Forum and beyond, held its collective breath. After a series of careful, expert incisions Vespasian lifted out the still warm heart and, having presented it to his fellow senators and then to the equites at the front of the huge throng, placed it to sizzle and hiss in the fire burning on Jupiter's altar before the open wood and iron doors of the Curia.

Two public slaves on either side pulled back the rib cage and Vespasian began the tricky task of removing the liver without staining his toga. Having presided over many sacrifices he knew that the key to this was steady work; with methodical patience, the organ was soon removed intact and placed on the table next to the altar. Using a cloth put there for the purpose, Vespasian wiped the liver clean of blood and ran his hand over the surface. In an instant he froze and felt his heart attempt to leap into his mouth; his chest heaved with a couple of laboured breaths and his eyes stared fixedly at a blemish, almost purple on the red-brown flesh. But a blemish has no regular or specific shape and that was not true of the mark on the liver's surface caused, it seemed, by two veins coming almost to the surface together; it had a well-defined form, almost as if it had been branded on, in much the same way as a slave-owner would brand his possession: with a single letter. And it was the letter that had startled him; small but prominent, it was the letter with which his cognomen began. What he saw before him was the letter 'V'. But more than that, the mark was in almost the exact centre of the liver just to the left of the thin central lobe; in the area that the ancient Etruscan diviners considered sacred to Mars, his guardian god.

Knowing that an omen, found on a liver gifted to Jupiter in Rome's name, so blatantly referring to him, as the master of the sacrifice, could be open to many interpretations – most of them incurring the jealousy of those in power – Vespasian turned the liver over and examined a reassuringly unblemished underside. Then, taking care to place his thumb over the potentially treasonous mark, he lifted the organ and showed it to the Father of the House and declared the day propitious for the business of Rome. But the image of the mark played before his eyes.

'So be it,' the Father cried in an aged, reedy voice as Vespasian placed the liver on the altar fire. 'Bring out the prisoners!'

There was movement around the Tullianum, the prison at the foot of the Capitoline Hill, next to the Germonian Stairs, in the shadow of the Temple of Juno on the Arx above it. Soldiers of the Urban Cohorts cleared an area in front of the single door before a centurion, with the transverse white horsehair crest on his helmet fluttering in the light breeze, rapped on the door with his vine cane.

The crowd hushed in anticipation.

A few moments later the door opened and a line of manacled prisoners shuffled out and still the crowd stayed silent, waiting for the one man they had all come to see.

And then a bulky figure filled the open doorway to Rome's only public prison, his head bowed as he passed through into the open. There was a massed intake of breath; he was not miserably clad and beaten down like the wretches before him. Quite the contrary; he wore the clothes and held the demeanour of a king.

'Very clever,' Gaius murmured, 'the grander you dress him the higher you elevate him, and the greater Claudius looks when he tears him down and humbles him.'

Vespasian gazed at the prisoner standing there, his bronze winged helmet reflecting the weak sun, his hands manacled but his chest blown out and proud beneath a weighty chainmail tunic as the crowd's reaction grew into a cacophony of booing and hissing. There stood the man whom he had not seen since that night, five years before, when he had led his army out of the shadowed north and come within moments of catching the II Augusta manoeuvring into position. There stood the man who had almost destroyed a legion, Vespasian's legion.

There stood Caratacus.